THE BIGGEST ADVENTURE
IS FINDING YOURSELF.

When Jack's seven-year-old sister Jenny disappears during a game of *Hide and Seek,* he and his parents are overwhelmed with grief. When fifteen-year-old Jack and his best friend Finn get the chance to follow into the strange world that swallowed her, they hope to find Jenny and bring her home. But the blood of children is a commodity in the fantastical land of Frey. The children there can't return. In addition to escaping the creatures around them, Jack and Finn wrestle with their own secrets which could change their lives forever.

Back home, their friend Millie is the dealing with murderous changelings who don't want their originals to return.

* * * * *

"If Alice or Dorothy had a gay big brother who was desperate to get his little sister home, and if Wonderland or Oz were much more dangerous places... that's the core of this fantasy-adventure queer tale of coming-out."

"Beneath the love of absurdity, the satirical observations, swashbuckling adventure, strange creatures, and moments of horror, there is a pervasive sense of kindness in this book."

"An epic of great imagination and ridiculous delights."

Wil Whimsey
Publishing
Company

OLLY, OLLY OXEN FREY

Paul Manchester

Dedicated to my fifteen-year-old self.
This is the book that I wanted to read.

Text, cover & illustrations
copyright 2019 © Paul Manchester

Characters in this book are fictitious
and are not based on anyone alive or dead.

Fonts:
Title/Author/Chapter headings: P22 Arts & Crafts Hunter
Body Text: Adobe Caslon Pro

ISBN Ebook: 978-0-9848489-2-8
ISBN Paperback: 978-0-9848489-3-5

The Purple Fantastic Steam Rating is 2 out of 5
There is some non-sexual nakedness,
and some characters may discuss or think about sex.
If any sexual activity occurs, it happens vaguely off the page.
(Rating system is spelled out on page 523)

Coming in late August 2023
ThePurpleFantastic.com
A website dedicated to fantasy and adventure stories
that I've enjoyed which feature gay romance.

Etymologists aren't absolutely sure of the origin of the phrase *Olly, Olly Oxen Free!* from the game, Hide & Go Seek.

Some think that it's a childish corruption of the German: *Alle, alle auch sind frei!* (Literally, *Everyone, everyone also is free!)*

It is also possible that the phrase has been passed down by children nearly unchanged from the Anglo-Saxon: *ealla, ealla oxan freo,* or Middle English: *olle, olle oxen fri* (*all, all oxen free!)* At the end of the game, it signals that children no longer need to hide and will be granted freedom – like oxen freed from their pen.

Children have been shouting out variations of *Olly, Olly Oxen Free!* for a long time. Most kids don't care about etymology. Whatever the phrase's origins are, it appears to be a cry of freedom for those destined to be eaten.

When you spend an idle afternoon lying in the grass pondering cloud castles far above you, those musings do not vanish when you are called inside for dinner.

While you sniff at your mother's culinary experiments, your lazy thoughts drift away on unseen winds.

And much in the same way that islands of trash collect in the Pacific, these notions float and collect with other dreamy bits over time and gather mass.

In that far away mass of this and that, wind blown seeds of whimsy fall. They take root, and they sprout.

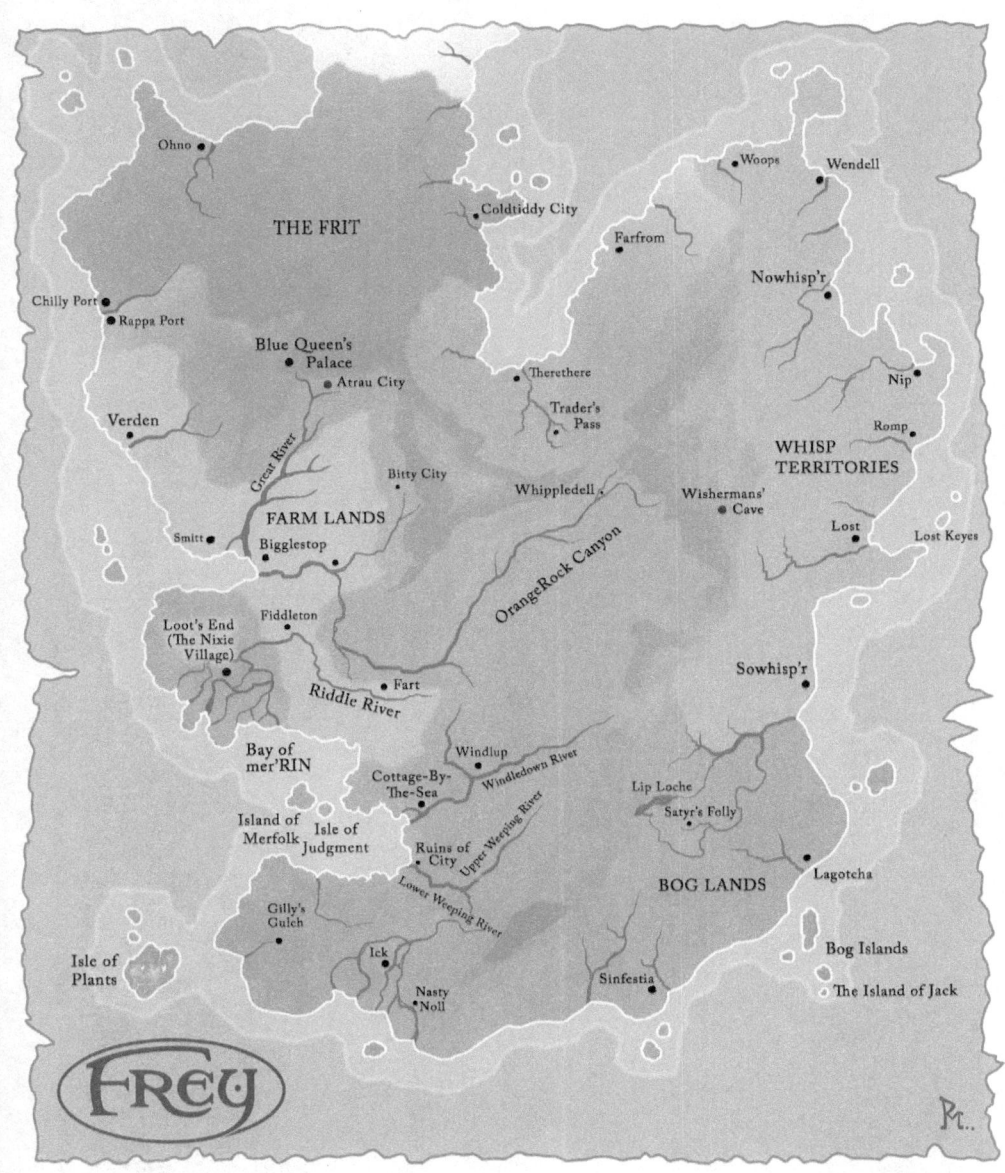

Chapter 1

The Perfect Hiding Place

"… Ten! Nine! Eight! Seven! Six! Five-Four-Three-Two-One! HERE I COME!"

The best part of playing *Hide & Seek* is pretending that you are in the midst of a big adventure and that *anything* might happen.

The little girl in the pirate hat hoped that her big brother wouldn't find her. The floorboards above groaned with his footsteps. Jenny pressed deeper into the darkness. She could see Jack's shadow cross the gaps above her.

A shaft of light peeked down through a crack in the barn floor. *"We see you, Jenny!"* whispered the tiny swarm of dust motes floating within it.

Jenny held her breath and pressed closer to the wooden slats of the mushroom cellar wall. The rough boards poked uncomfortably into her back, but she smiled. He'd never find her! She was small and the barn was enormous.

It was the last afternoon of summer vacation and the barn was rich with black dirt smells. Heavy boy-steps thudded above. She scooted deeper behind the crate, then relaxed a little when the ladder to the loft (far, far above) complained of her big brother's ugly smelly feet.

The bumpy earth beneath her butt complained, "Move!" She considered it.

A squeal of giggles exploded in the loft and pounding footsteps shouted out a desperate race. That would be Millie. Jenny couldn't see what was going on – but she could hear Millie scrambling down the ladder to reach base before Jack.

"Gotcha!" yelled Jack.

Across the barn, more feet started running – thundering rapid beats like a crazed drum machine. That would be Bry and Finn. There was shouting. Jenny considered sneaking closer to base.

"Dinner-time!"

Their mom's voice cut through the laughter.

"We're not finished!" complained Jack.

Mom was tired. "It's dinner-time, *now*! Get in here while it's still hot! You'll see your friends at school tomorrow."

A herd of feet ambled out of the barn and into the yard as Jack hollered, "Olly olly oxen free! OLLY OLLY OXEN FREE!"

Grumbling, Jack started for the house. In his most exasperated sing-song voice he sang, "Hey Jenny! Come out! Come out, wherever you are! It's dinner time!"

But Pirate Jenny didn't answer because she was no longer there.

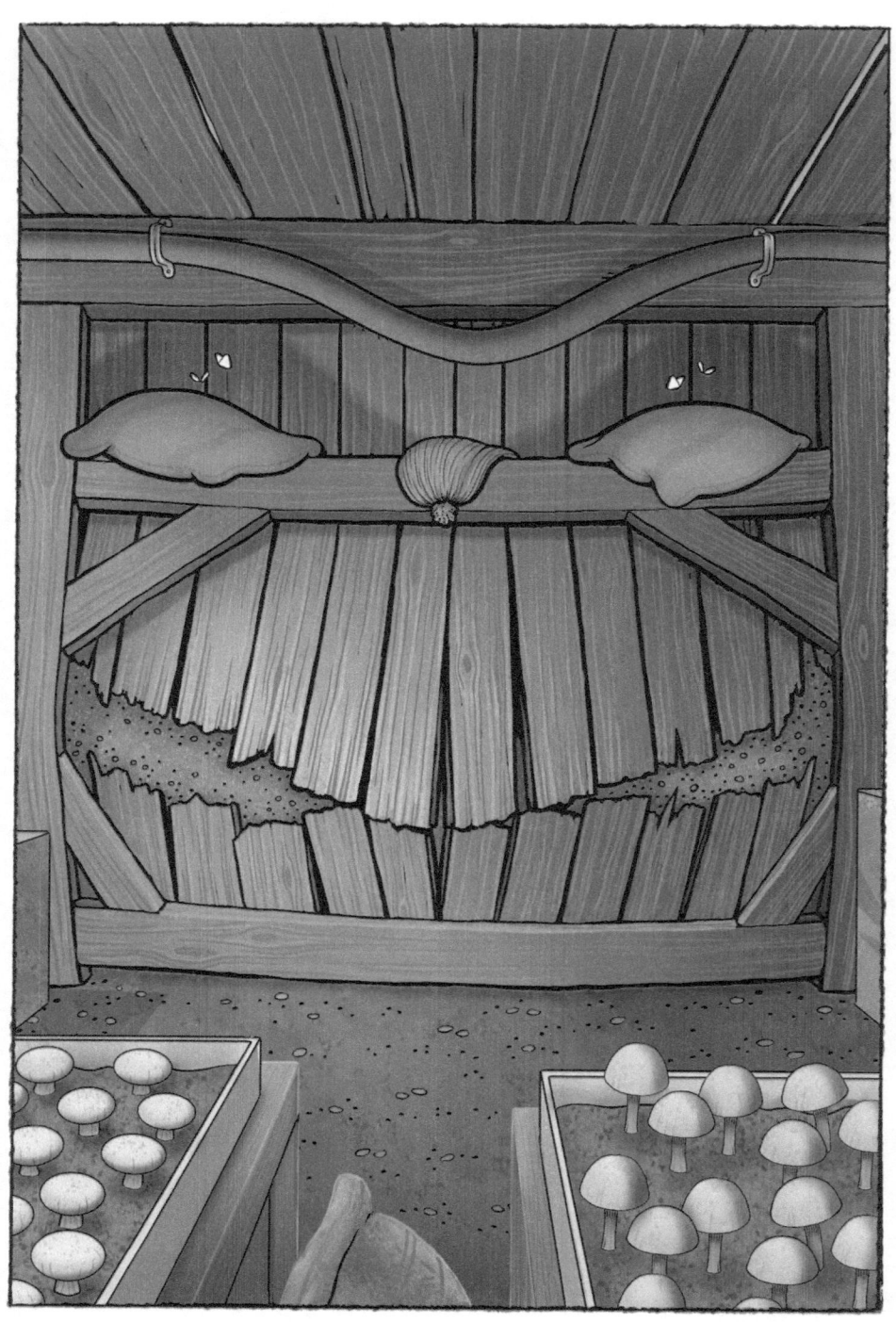

Chapter 2

An Awful Big Brother

Jack

The screen door slammed shut behind Jack. His friends were off to their own versions of home-cooked dinners. He didn't feel like going inside yet. The very aaair was alive with possibility.

Outside was the place to be.

But with the bang of that screen door, the wild smell of late afternoon dandelions and mown grass was replaced by Swedish meatballs and overcooked peas.

Mom was trying to rescue the peas. "Jack, get the silverware on the table! Jenny, get the napkins and glasses!"

"Jenny's still outside," Jack smirked. "She's probably still waiting for me to find her." He started gathering forks, spoons and knives from the drawer.

A fluorescent ring lit the kitchen with a cold buzzing light. His mom laughed when Jack suggested that it should be switched out with something warmer and quieter. Fifteen year olds shouldn't be thinking about lighting fixtures.

"Frank, dinner's ready!"

"The game's still on! Why don't we do TV trays and watch the game?"

"It would be nice if we could have a *real* family dinner once in a while. Where we actually looked at each other? Call me old fashioned."

A low grumble came from the other room, "I should think we all know what we look like by now."

The TV shut off in the other room while Jack set the silverware, the napkins... and the glasses too.

Mom dumped the noodles into a CorningWare bowl. Stray noodles grasped the colander bottom tightly. Mom quietly cursed as she tried to get the noodles to join their soggy siblings.

"Where's Jenny?" Dad stood in the doorway. "I turned off the game 'cause I thought you were all ready!"

"Oh Frank, she'll be here in a minute. She's on her way." Mom set the dish of Swedish Meatballs on the table with a *thunk*.

Jack squirmed at the barely kept truce in the room, but it was nothing new. "I'll see what's keeping Jenny!"

The screen door slammed shut behind him.

Jack loved twilight and warm summer evenings. He found peace in the smells of the open land around the house. The yellow fields of autumn. *School starts tomorrow. Crap.*

"Jenny! Get your butt in here!" He ran his fingers through his messy brown hair out of habit. Mom didn't like the word *butt*... but Jack was a rebel. Not really though.

'The half-light and crickets quieted his mind. The chirping played a counter-point to his parents' patter of petty bickering inside.'

Jack wanted to be a writer someday. Was that too much alliteration? 'Parents', 'patter' and 'petty' sounded good together. But Jack wondered if he should rethink that.

"Jenny! Get your little seven-year-old hiney in here!" There – Mom can't object to *hiney*.

But the yard was silent – except for the crickets of course.

"So, let's go through this again. Where did you last see her?" The Skagit County sheriff's deputy sat across from Jack who huddled on the couch with Finn, Millie, and Bry. Jack thought of ducks in a shooting gallery.

They were all starting tenth grade. Finn and Jack would turn sixteen in November. He was Jack's best friend and the tallest of the four. Finn and Millie lived down the road. She'd just turned fifteen. She had a crush on Finn.

Jack thought Millie was annoying. She moved in when they were eight. He got on great with her until she started crushing on Finn. These days she showed up *every frickin' time that he and Finn hung out together!* She had black frizzy hair that looked like she'd never seen a comb in her life. She was better at sports than all three of the boys. Which of course gave Jack another reason to hate her. *No.* He didn't *hate* her. She was just irritating because she was always there! *That didn't qualify as "hate" did it?* She was like a big sister to Jenny. So, he *had* to like her for that.

Bryton was Millie's cousin who lived down in Tacoma with his Grandma Wilde. He came up sometimes. Bry was an artist. He was okay... but sometimes he also took up too much of Finn's time.

Jack didn't want to think too deeply about why he felt so jealous over Finn. They were buds. It was normal.

But, tonight... Jenny was missing. They were his friends even if he sometimes struggled with a bit of jealousy. He appreciated that they were there with him. Jack was falling apart.

Outside, three officers searched the barn, the yard, and down by the creek.

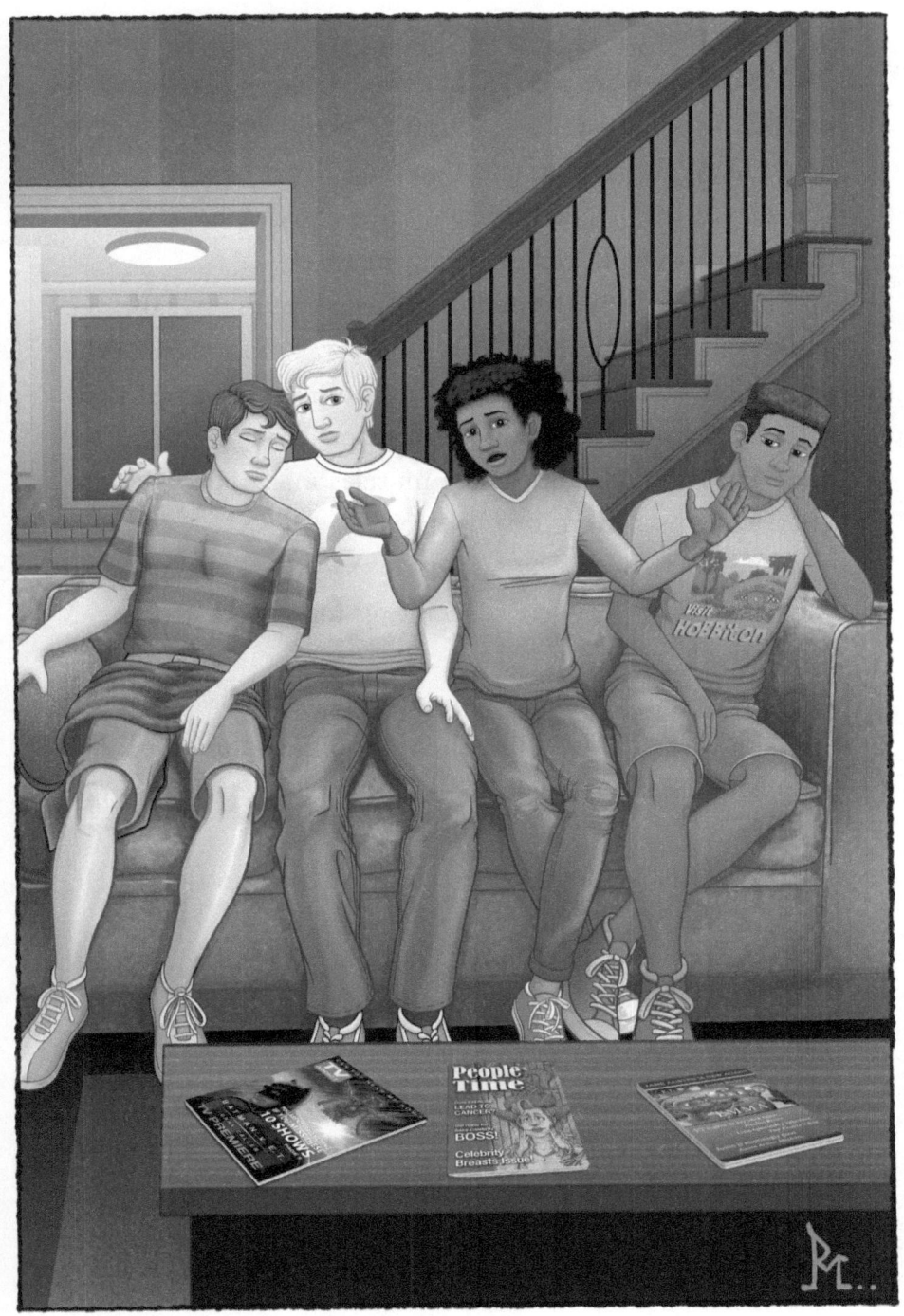

Jack's eyes were red. "I told you, we were playing *Hide and Seek* in the barn. I was counting by the door. I would've heard her if she tried to sneak past me. That door in back is stuck shut. It's practic'ly locked! She couldn't have opened that door. It would've been crazy noisy –"

"Easy now," interrupted the officer – trying to calm the panic spilling out of Jack. This officer was younger than the others. He was dark haired and his uniform stretched tight across gym shoulders. His calm disposition was great for interviewing kids. But the big muscles made Jack nervous. They were distracting in a bad way.

"We weren't paying attention to where Jenny hid." Millie cut in. "We were all looking for a place to hide. I hid in the loft."

"Could Jenny have been up in the loft with you?"

"No," she explained like she was doing an oral report in Science. "There's only one good hiding place up there – and I was in it."

The officer looked at the two other boys on the couch, "So you two boys hid in the tool room?"

Finn fiddled with the key on the chain around his neck.

Bry looked at his purple tennis shoes and muttered awkwardly, "Yeah."

The sheriff raised one eyebrow.

Jack made sure his parents were standing out of earshot. They were outside the screen door. "My Dad keeps his old

Playboys in the tool room – we aren't supposed to be in there."

Bry and Finn were turning a violent shade of red. Millie gave her best look of disapproval.

"I see." The deputy sighed. "Then you weren't paying much attention to where Jenny was?"

The boys shook their heads. "No, sir," they mumbled.

He stood up. "Thank you, kids. I think I've got what I need from you." He looked back at Jack. "We'll do our best to find your sister. She probably just wandered off somewhere."

Jack nodded. He couldn't help leaning into Finn. His buddy put an arm around Jack and gave a gentle squeeze. Jack started crying hard. He didn't care if the others saw.

The beefy deputy folded up his little notebook and walked through the kitchen to the screen door to confer with another officer on the porch. Jack listened.

"Mr. and Mrs. Saunders, Jenny doesn't seem to be on the property," said the other officer. "We've searched the place from one end to the other. She's not here. Officer Peet and I are going to canvas the neighborhood. I've got a couple of officers exploring along the creek." He lowered his voice. "If your little girl tried to find a hiding spot up near the road… kids have disappeared before…"

"Jenny wouldn't do that," interrupted his mom's voice. "She knows she's not supposed to be up near the road by herself."

Dad's voice muttered, "Jack should've kept a better eye on her..."

His mother quickly hushed his dad.

Jack died inside and his gut burned with shame. Finn heard it too and pulled Jack closer.

The officer's voice hesitated a moment, "We'll do everything we can."

Millie's mom had arrived earlier to help where she could. Her tall, dark, elegant figure swept into the living room (she was so different from Millie), "Okay, grab your things, kids. I'm drivin' y'all home."

Jack felt a last hug and Finn's arm disappeared.

Jack was alone.

Jack didn't sleep well that night. Horrible dreams. When he came down for breakfast, his parents were sitting at the kitchen table where he'd left them in a few hours earlier. Jenny was still missing. Their eyes were red. They weren't talking.

He didn't go to school.

Later that day, Jack, his parents, with Finn and his foster-parents, Millie and her mom, the neighbors... everyone canvassed the entire area.

MISSING!
Jenny Saunders, seven years old. Light brown hair, hazel eyes, 47" tall, 45 lbs. Last seen wearing a pirate hat, horizontally striped red and white t-shirt, vertically striped blue and white shorts, and red galoshes.

They stapled and taped up posters with Jenny's face on electric poles and light posts all around the area. She was there among lost dogs, ads for guitar lessons, and tractors for sale. It was crazy to see Jenny smiling in that mish-mash of colored paper. Each flyer was fringed with bent phone number tabs that waited impatiently to be torn off.

The house was oddly silent when Jack and his parents returned from posting notices. No Jenny.

His parents had never been big huggers. His mom once said, "Some people need that sort of thing... but that touchy-touchy thing just isn't *us*."

This evening, Jack really needed a hug because he had screwed up bad. But he was probably being too needy. Real boys didn't need hugs.

Besides, this was all his fault. He should have been watching Jenny better! He didn't deserve a hug.

That evening, there was a long prayer vigil in their living room. Pastor Steve came by to lead it and a bunch of the church folks showed up with him. They all sat in a circle holding hands and prayed for God to bring Jenny home safely. One lady spoke in "tongues" which apparently God understood better than English. Whatever worked. Didn't make much sense to Jack.

Finn and his foster parents were there too. Jack peeked across at Finn every once in a while. Finn looked back and imperceptibly shrugged. Maybe the prayers would work. But it seemed like if God cared all that much, maybe Jenny wouldn't have disappeared in the first place.

He wanted to be out in the darkness looking for her. It drove him bonkers to sit still.

Where was she?

Did some sicko grab her from the barn while they played *Hide and Seek?* Someone really sneaky? Jenny wouldn't wander off like that!

But it happened while Jack was right there! It had to be his fault!

He was an awful big brother.

Chapter 3
The Bodies

Jack

Almost a week had gone by and Jenny was still gone. School had started. Jenny's face was on the nightly news for the first few days, but now her disappearance was yesterday's headline.

Jack wanted to scream at the TV! "SHE'S STILL MISSING! WHY AREN'T YOU TALKING ABOUT IT?" But he bottled up those thoughts after he'd said them too many times out loud. He felt like a ticking time bomb. One of these days he was going to explode and there would be nothing left of him afterwards.

The police had received some calls, but the leads so far were useless.

Jenny was just... GONE.

Although there'd been times when Jack had wished that she'd disappear, he'd never really *meant* it! Did he somehow get his wish? Did everybody know that it was his fault for not watching her?

Jack's parents were a mess. They were stealth fighting. They didn't fight in front of Jack. The house was full of tense words and uncomfortable silences till they got to their room. He didn't need super powers to hear through the walls. They said they weren't *arguing*. They were *discussing*. Jack couldn't tell the difference.

They didn't hug each other either. Not hugging was clearly normal.

The house was silent more often than not. Except for the TV which was on so loud, that no one could talk. Jack suspected it was intentional. Communication consisted of as few words as possible.

His dad took a couple of days off from the office, but on the third day he'd left for work – without breakfast. Dad not eating breakfast freaked Jack out. Dad always ate breakfast. Always. Despite being a church-goer, breakfast was his dad's true religion.

Jack only took one day off from school. Jack's mom thought normalcy would help and she didn't want him to get behind in his classes. *As if he could focus on school.* But for a couple days she imposed strict rules on everything he did. He and Finn couldn't walk to school. Their moms took turns with Millie's mom and drove them all to the nearby high school.

At school, a wave of silence followed Jack in the hallways. Kids stopped talking and stared when he passed. Well meaning kids said sympathetic things, but they acted like Jenny might be gone forever. And Jack couldn't think like that. He just couldn't.

For most of the week Finn's mom wouldn't let Finn come over, as she didn't want Finn to *bother* them in their *time of grief.* Jack hated that. As if Finn could ever bother Jack by his presence.

On Friday afternoon, Finn was allowed to come over for a bit. Jack's mom wouldn't let them go down to their tree fort at the creek... apparently a band of kidnappers might be hiding and would carry them off too. As if. But Jack couldn't help fantasizing that *if* these kidnappers *did* kidnap them, maybe they'd be taken to where Jenny was hidden and Jack could rescue her!

Jack loved to write stories. Stories where he was someone else and more capable. Someone who didn't have bad thoughts. Not that Jack could ever be a hero. He'd be more of a side-kick to someone amazing, like Finn for example. Jack was inherently *not-good-enough.* But his imagination sometimes broke out of its prison. Jack had lots of rescuer fantasies. He could imagine how he'd cleverly discover a clue that the police missed. He'd track the villains to their lair! He'd triumphantly capture the bad guys and bring Jenny home. Maybe he'd get his name in the paper or the nightly news! He'd be famous! Jack would be good enough in his secret thoughts.

But then, he'd feel guilty. He was clearly an awful brother for even thinking about being famous right now. He was cursed with a big imagination and didn't know how to turn it off.

Saturday morning was shorts and t-shirt weather in the Pacific Northwest, and inside was too depressing. The house echoed with his parents' silence and the roar of commercials.

Jack mumbled that he would check on the mushrooms. But he really just needed to get out of the house.

His mom shouted without looking up, "Don't go far!" She was gluing colored rhinestones to baseball caps – making crosses or spelling out spiritual catch phrases. They were for the church bazaar, which was trying to raise funds for a new building to house its growing congregation. It was an activity for his mom to focus on while hoping for news about Jenny.

The half-light of the mushroom cellar was peaceful. The special Reishi mushrooms grew in sawdust and were enclosed in an improvised plastic terrarium. They were supposed to be a medicinal sleep aid. They didn't need all that much attention... at least not like the other mushrooms in the cellar. His dad thought they might sell well to health food nuts.

Jack knew that the cellar was where Jenny would have hidden. She was seven. She always hid in the same places. He quite intentionally didn't go looking in the cellar first. The bigger kids were always faster. He liked to give her a chance.

He felt closer to Jenny down here. Jack wished he could turn the clock backwards and do things different. Do something so Pirate Jenny would still be pestering him. He needed her, even if she was a pain in the tush sometimes. She always hovered when he just wanted to be alone with Finn. But he'd do anything for that now.

He mindlessly shifted his weight on the rickety bench, listening to it squeak... back and forth, back and forth.

Creeeeak. Creak. Creeeeak. Creak.

The percussive sound contrasted with the quiet groaning of the barn's old wood. It sounded like the barn was alive sometimes. It was like he was sitting in the *barn's bowels*. Or maybe not. Not the right metaphor. Bowels? Hmmm. Gross. Maybe not. Sometimes his writer's brain got carried away.

The cellar was cool and moist and kind of smelly. But, not in a bad way. Up in the yard, the sun was still deciding whether it would *Easy-Bake* the world or not. The sun was a welcome reprieve from the frequent rain in Mount Vernon, Washington.

The mushroom cellar was a pet project of his dad's. The barn and its cellar were decades older than the white clapboard, two-story house across the yard. The cellar was big – it mirrored the front half of the barn above. There were tiered tables with square, plastic pallets sprouting baby mushrooms. They each stretched out of their beds with little yawns. Reishi, Oyster, Crimini... many types of mushrooms. Along two walls were longer, deeper trays where his father experimented with different growing mediums. Straw, shredded paper, manure – which Jack found kind of disgusting. Mushrooms were popping up in those bins as well. Spores did travel. One of Jack's chores was to mist them with water each day and check for mushroom flies and mold. But, he hadn't felt like doing it this week. Clearly his dad wasn't thinking about mushrooms either.

Dad had a bit of a heart condition. He wanted to retire. Sell the agency. He always had a side experiment to maybe someday free him from selling insurance. Something less stressful that might allow him to spend more time with his kids. Not that his dad really spent time with them. His dad mostly just watched sports on TV. But every once in a while, they would work on the mushrooms together. Jack liked that. He pretended to moan about it (just for his teenage dignity), but he honestly liked spending time with his dad. It didn't happen very often. He didn't really care what the project was, it was just doing stuff together.

For the last couple of years, the project had been mushrooms, and that was cool. But without Jenny, it didn't matter anymore. His dad blamed Jack that she was gone. Not that his dad actually said that to Jack's face. But it was true. It should have been Jack that disappeared, not Jenny. Without Jenny, who cares about stupid mushrooms?

Jack had always wanted a little sister. When she was born, she was *his* in the same way another kid would have embraced a pet dog. He loved her like crazy. They teased each other mercilessly as she'd gotten older. She followed Jack and Finn like a hornet chases a hamburger at a picnic.

Footsteps entered the barn upstairs.

Jack eased off the noisy bench and slid to the ground behind a bin of newspapers. He couldn't go back into the house. He couldn't breathe around his parents right now. Jack decided that they didn't want him there anyway. Jack knew that he was a disappointment to them. He crouched down between the bin and a crate of loose straw.

Behind him, the wooden slats of the wall lined up vertically like teeth – held in place top and bottom with horizontal boards. Like lips framing a toothy grin waiting to vomit forth all the hard packed dirt behind it. Or perhaps they were waiting to eat him up and make him a part of all that dirt? Where he belonged?

The footsteps thumped to the trap door at the top of the steps. Jack pushed further behind the crates into the dark. He held his breath as the cellar trap opened with a creak and a thud.

Jack squinted as the intrusive light hit the old steps. When he saw Finn's fluorescent green tennis shoes, Jack exhaled.

Finn was like the first star you saw in the evening sky on a warm night. A cuddly puppy. A Hawaiian style pizza. Finn was everything that he loved. With the rest of the world, Jack said *yes* because he was supposed to. With Finn, he said *yes* because he wanted to. Or *no*. It didn't make any difference with Finn. Jack was just himself around Finn. Finn was amazing. Finn was the type of kid who till recently wore board shorts and T-shirts in all weathers. Jack thought he was the coolest guy ever. They'd been practically inseparable since they were six.

Finn was a bit taller than Jack. His hair was so blond it was almost green from too much swimming at the Mount Vernon Y. Finn had been on the school swim team till he quit last year because he said he was getting rashes from public pools. Finn showed him once. Disgusting! Jack would have quit too! Other than swimming, Finn didn't care about sports. Finn mostly loved to draw, and he liked to hang out with Jack. Which was perfect, as Jack loved to write and hang out with Finn.

Finn kept spiral drawing pads in a big, old, leather satchel that was always slung around his shoulder. If Jack had carried that same bag, he'd have been teased without mercy. The other kids would have called it a purse. But they didn't tease Finn. If Finn called it his *bag*, then that's what it was called: *Finn's Bag*. In the schoolyard ecosystem, Finn was considered weird, but interesting weird. In that bag was everything from food and water, to old action figures. It had hidden pockets. You never knew what he was going to pull out of it. It was waterproofed for Washington weather. The outside had a merman design tooled into the leather which Finn had done himself. Jack thought the artwork was really professional looking. Finn loved mermen and mermaids and all things fantastical.

Jack thought it was because of his mysterious origins.

Finn's bag was one of two clues as to who his parents might be.

Almost sixteen years earlier, tourists stumbled across the leather satchel near the otter exhibit inside the Seattle Aquarium. Inside the satchel was a baby, and a pink jade key with the name "Finn" beautifully engraved in the top part of the key. Of course, the department of family services was called. A social worker with a sense of humor gave him the last name of *Otterson*. *Finn Otterson*. He was placed with a foster family. Other kids got adopted. But not Finn. And Finn hung on to that key and that satchel, much like other kids would hang on to their first blankie.

Finn always wore the key on a chain around his neck, and the satchel over his shoulder.

The story triggered Jack's imagination. When they hung out in their tree house, Jack invented stories of royal blood, or aliens... anything but the scandalous stories that Finn's foster parents, Mr. and Mrs. Jones believed. Sometimes Jack was envious – to be an orphan with mysterious beginnings was exciting, even if Finn didn't like to talk about it. *Not that Jack wanted anything to happen to his parents... but being an orphan seemed kind of cool. Disney heroes were nearly always orphans.*

Finn had been an unusually silent toddler, and he was very pale. He didn't start speaking when other kids did. There were whispers that something was wrong with him. His foster parents were not warm people. They were good church folk who did all the right things, but they also loved their monthly checks from the county. Finn got enough to eat, he had clean clothes and his stand-in parents said all the appropriate things. Other foster kids came and went. But not Finn. The Joneses were mildly uncomfortable with this strange mute child. Finn had been a lonely kid till Jack appeared.

When six-year-old Jack moved into the house down the street, everything changed. Finn latched onto him like a life preserver. And Finn started speaking in complete sentences when he met Jack! It dispelled all the rumors about him being *not right in the head.* Over time, Finn

proved that he was pretty clever. This relieved his foster parents, who hoped that he might finally generate some interest from adoptive parents, but still he was never adopted. His pallid complexion made folks suspect that he might have underlying health issues. And now that Jack was around, Finn didn't want to be adopted.

When Jack and Finn were nine years old, they built a tree house in the red branches of an old Madrona down by the creek. The initially wobbly structure became their headquarters for lazy afternoons. They proofed it against rain. Over the years it grew bigger as they got bigger. They'd hole up in their hideout and make up stories.

The boys got into mischief with some frequency. Nothing serious. Mostly exploring places that they shouldn't. Jack and Finn loved to sneak past the *No Trespassing* sign in front of a nearby wood. It seemed enormous when they were younger, but now Jack realized it was just a bunch of trees. They'd discovered a cave in the side of a hill that was clearly the home of monsters. In summer there were cold creeks to swim in and suspicious neighbors to spy on. Despite Finn's height, he was slender enough to squeeze into places he shouldn't be, and Jack appeared innocent enough to get them out of trouble when needed.

Jack was a bookworm and loved reading all types of books. He especially loved writing stories. Stories were a form of magic. Like portals to worlds he'd never get to visit otherwise. Jack would write stories and Finn would draw pictures for the stories. They'd do their homework in the tree house too – once their parents learned to trust that they'd actually do it. They were reasonably good students.

Jack was ordinary in looks. He wasn't tall and he wasn't short. He had forgettable brown hair and brown eyes – which sometimes stared longer than they should and made people uncomfortable. He spent so much time in his head that his words often did somersaults in his brain instead of exiting his mouth in useful manner. Jack definitely had too many freckles. His cheeks were naturally rosy – which made him look permanently embarrassed... which was embarrassing. He didn't have art skills like Finn, and he wasn't great at sports like Millie. He didn't stink at video games but his scores were nothing to brag about. Jack wasn't picked on, but at the same time he wasn't really noticed other than as Finn's sidekick.

Jack envied Jenny for her obliviousness to what other kids thought. If she wanted to march to school in a pirate hat and red galoshes, she did. That's what made Jenny special. Not much made Jack special.

Jack cared a lot about what other kids thought. If Jack had any gift, it was to seem like the person that people wanted him to be. He was a really good chameleon. With elderly people at church, Jack became the perfectly respectful boy whom they could admire. With the kids at school, he knew enough about the latest Xbox games to not be a total doofus. He could fake sports talk with his dad. And the weird thing was that all those people he pretended to be, were actually sides of himself. He didn't have to lie exactly.

There was only one thing that Finn *didn't* know about Jack. But that was just the way it had to be, as Jack didn't want to lose Finn. He couldn't lose Finn.

Especially after losing Jenny.

"Jack? You here?" whispered Finn.

"Yeah. Over here, Greenbean." Jack leaned back against the old wooden wall.

"It's already hot outside. Come outside! We'll go down to the tree house. My mom said not to bother you, but I figgered..." Finn said with a smile.

"Glad you did."

Finn ambled over. He wore a baggy green pullover and old jeans. Finn stood there looking down at Jack where he sat hiding in the dark.

"Hey. It's dark in here." Finn looked at Jack questioningly.

"Nope. No news," mumbled Jack. He closed his eyes. He wasn't crying anymore. Maybe he was cried out. Maybe he was broken and would never cry again. He felt guilty as he probably should still be crying. Jack should be crying. Maybe he didn't love Jenny enough?

"Move over."

Jack grunted and shifted. Finn squeezed through the boxes between them and plopped down next to Jack.

He sat in silence for a bit.

"Kind of figured you'd be here," offered Finn, wriggling back against the toothy wall. The wall had some give to it. He pushed back experimentally.

Jack ran his fingers through his messy hair. "My parents are driving me crazy."

Finn leaned over and nudged Jack's shoulder with his own.

"Jenny's gotta be somewhere..." Finn pressed gently into the wall again. The boards felt spongy.

Jack stared into the cobwebbed ceiling.

"I feel useless. I keep asking myself where-" Jack turned to Finn.

But Finn was gone.

And a moment later, Jack was gone too – even though the old grinning wall looked perfectly solid.

They hadn't noticed a small, quickly-growing, translucent body half-buried in one of the long mushrooms bins at the side of the cellar. It was shaped very much like that of Jenny – with skin as delicate as that of a mushroom.

And within a few moments, there were now two more tiny bodies growing quite rapidly in another tray. Little, white growths, which might soon look like two almost sixteen year old boys.

Chapter 4
A Fork
in the Path

Pirate Jenny

Jenny remembered leaning back against the old wooden wall of the cellar and hearing footsteps overhead – and then she was sitting somewhere quite different.

She was in a dimly lit tunnel. The walls were a hard-packed reddish clay, as was the rocky floor. The arched ceiling above glowed orange from light cast by tall flowered plants growing along the passage walls amid really big mushrooms. She was sitting at the dead end of a path. Ahead of her, it led slightly downhill and disappeared around a bend to the right.

Behind her was only tunnel wall. There were some familiar boards embedded in the dense clay, but there was no opening to the mushroom cellar.

It was certainly curious.

But Jenny had seen lots of movies where young girls fall into strange adventures through looking glasses, wardrobes, and fireplaces. In books and movies kids were transported to fantastic places all the time. Why not a mushroom cellar wall? Now that she was seven, she knew that parents did not always tell kids the truth. She'd figured out that Santa was fake all by herself – despite her parents' crazy insistence that a fat man really squeezed down their chimney on an annual basis. She had looked up that chimney. Not possible. She'd been humoring them for over a year now. Even the stories in Sunday school had started to seem a little dodgy of late.

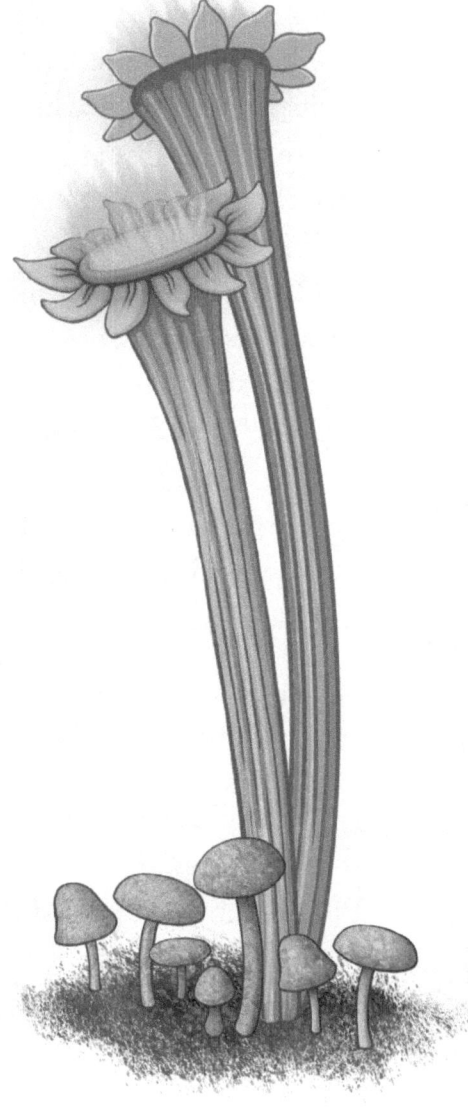

But now, despite mom and dad's laughing to the contrary, it looked like *magical places really did exist!* Maybe this was one of the big secrets of the adult-world! *"Don't tell the kids!"* Maybe her dad really went to a magical land when he said that he was going to the office? How would she know any different? Maybe this is the place that Dad visits all the time when he is *working on his mushrooms.* There was no going back the way she came, so she picked herself up, adjusted her pirate hat, and brushed the dirt off her butt. In her bright red boots, she clomped down to the first bend in the tunnel and looked around the corner. Disappointing. More of the same.

But she was a pirate! *"A BUCCANEER, SHOWS NO FEAR!"* she shouted to an invisible audience.

She thought back to all the stories she'd heard about lost little girls in strange places. She collected a bunch of stray rocks. She carefully spelled out a message in the middle of the path.

PIRATE JENNY WAS HERE!

She didn't see how anyone else was going to get through that wall back there, but if they did, they would know that Pirate Jenny had passed this way.

Jenny pulled her black hat more firmly down on her head. She would see where the path took her.

A FORK IN THE PATH

The red tunnel wove back and forth, and up and down, but no tunnels branched off from the one that she was on. She discovered that the pale pink flowers on the stalks had a yellow flame at their centers, which lit the tunnel. Oddly, they weren't hot at all. Mushrooms of all shapes, sizes, and colors increasingly poked up about the fire-flower stalks.

Really big colorful bugs and three foot long earthworms crawled and wiggled around the mushroom clusters. But they didn't seem scary at all. Large glowing bugs flittered about the ceiling. They flickered like fireflies and were quite pretty. She wasn't exactly sure what they were, but they were bigger than dragonflies. They'd flit close then flutter away before she could get a good look at them.

She stopped at times to pet and talk to fuzzy caterpillars (the size of big cats) which ambled across her path. They had long thick fur and they purred when she ran her fingers through the silky fibers. She wondered if that was why they were called "cat"-erpillars! When she got home, she'd have to pet the tiny caterpillars there and listen very closely. These creatures came in all colors and some were striped. Some had no fur at all but were decorated with amazing patterns.

At one bend in the path, Jenny noticed that a strange bald fleshy caterpillar was curled up by itself and looked lonely. He had red and black furry bits that stuck out oddly here and there. She squatted down and inspected him.

"Hey little guy. Why are you sitting all by your lonesome? You look just as special as all the others."

The caterpillar looked up at her with a little face that had clearly been crying.

"You remind me of my friend, Randy. He's a kid in my class that sometimes gets teased – but he still always wants to play pirates with me at recess!"

Jenny scratched his little chin.

"You'll be alright." She gave 'Randy' a big smile and ruffled the top of his head. Some others had gathered near, so she spent some time petting the other caterpillars, and deciding which of her friends that each one reminded her of. Finally she waved goodbye and left the little smiling creatures behind her.

She was starting to feel a bit thirsty and wondered whether there might be a bathroom nearby, when Jenny reached a fork in the path. An actual giant fork stuck into the path. It was so tall that the top was embedded in the tunnel's ceiling. The glowing moths batted against their reflections in its metal surface.

Jenny looked to the right of the fork. She saw the tunnel bend downwards to the left. Jenny looked to the left of the fork. That tunnel led upwards to the right.

"I think I should go up," pondered Jenny to herself, then muttered, "I wish there was a drinking fountain around here."

She heard a little tinkling sound and suddenly, right beyond the fork, she saw the nicest little drinking fountain you could ever wish for. She took a little sip. Then guzzled down as much as she could. The water was clear and cold – with a touch of lemon – and quite satisfying.

"That was delicious." She sighed.

A muttering noise sounded somewhere near her.

"Thank you?" She looked around. No one was there. "Do you have a bathroom?"

Nothing.

She sighed, started to walk on, and then she stopped.

Jenny reflected. Maybe? She took a deep breath. "I WISH there was a bathroom?"

Again she heard the familiar tinkling sound and a door with a familiar icon appeared in the side of the tunnel. She had to pee so bad that her back teeth were floating.

On opening the door she saw the most beautiful sparkling bathtub she'd ever seen. But *no toilet*. Jenny was downright irritated.

"I *WISH* this bathroom had a TOILET!" She said as politely as she could muster.

Again, a tinkling sound. And there was a toilet!
But...

"Could I get some toilet paper too? I mean..." she took a deep breath. "I WISH there was some toilet paper next to the toilet! GOOD toilet paper! Not that thin stuff!"

Again the tinkling sound.

"Thank you! Whoever you are!"

Jenny stepped in, closed the door, and made her own tinkling sound.

Feeling much relieved, Pirate Jenny stepped back out to the path. She thought for a moment. "I wish–"

"STOP THAT" shouted an angry voice high above her.

She looked in the direction of the voice, and there above her sitting on an outcropping of rock, was a small angry creature holding what looked like a fishing pole with a bag at the end of its line. Beside him was a wicker basket as big as himself.

"This be MY wishing spot. Go find yar own! Ya've already stolen FOUR o' my wishes!" grumbled the voice of the tiny disagreeable being.

The ledge was about seven feet up the side of the tunnel. The light green face glared down at her. He really was small. She reckoned that she might have stuffed animals at home bigger than him. He had big eyes, bald brows, and an extraordinarily large nose. His two bulbous bare feet hung above her head. From what she could see, his body was a ball of lavender fur.

At that moment, one of the little glowing moths flew into his waiting net and he yanked its lid closed. "Whoopee! Got me ANOTHER ONE!" He pulled his line up and quick as anything he slipped the wee glowing light into his basket and slammed the lid down.

"Those little flying moths are wishes?"

"Of course they be! Why else would ah be wasting me time down here!" he snapped. "Flippin' stal'ctites!"

"What do you do with them after you catch them?"

"Ah sells 'em of course! At the Wish Market! What ELSE would ah be doin' wit 'em!"

Jenny shrugged. "I never knew that wishes flew!"

"Of course they fly! That's why wishes be so hard to catch!"

"I've never tried to *catch* a wish before. I thought you just blew out a candle or wished on a star or something."

"But those wishes don't work none do they?" The little man cackled with a knowing look. "Catching wishes that work takes effort! Lots of still-sittin' and good bait! Yup, they do! And ah've got the best bait today!" he cackled.

"What do you use for bait?"

"Aha! Wouldn't ya like ta know, little lady!" He laughed. That's me secret that ah ain't tellin' nobody. Are ya a nobody?"

"I'm Pirate Jenny."

"That sounds like a 'somebody' to me. But, ah'm not sharin' with a somebody neither, as that somebody might then come down here and catch all these wishes that are rightfully MINE! Ah don't want no unfair comp'tition down here. Wishin' be hard enough without somebodies goin' and wishin' fer stupid things like 'bathrooms'."

"Well, I actually meant..." Jenny mumbled.

"Of course ya did! Ah know what ya MEANT! But wishes gotta be purty darn SPECIFIC if ya'r gonna get what ya WANT! How do ya think that darn FORK got there! Sometime back, a stupid git down there done asked for a FORK in the road! Can ya believe it! And now that idiot's wandering 'round down there lost forever! Or till the idiot gets eaten!" The little man touched his finger to the side of his nose. "Ya always gotta remember that WORDS BE MAGIC! Ya gotta know what ya want!"

The idea that something down the trail might eat her changed the adventure considerably. Jenny was not quite sure how to proceed. Should she ask him for help? The little man seemed friendly enough, once you got past his bad manners. But Jenny was not feeling brave any more.

The little man looked down at her lost expression and his heart melted a bit. "Pirate Jenny. So ya'r a pirate?"

She would not cry.

"I've got the hat, ain't I!"

He chuckled. "Well so ya do missy. So ya do."

Jenny had been musing a bit on what he'd said. "I'm thinking I should probably be trying to get back home. Would one of these wishes work for that?"

"Tryin' ta get back ta yar pirate ship, eh?"

"Sort of." Jenny answered with what she hoped was a winning smile.

"These little guppies ain't big enough fer wishin' fer somethin' as big as that! What ya need is one of those wishes that done grow'd up in sunlight. Ya need a whopper of a wish!"

"Then..." choosing her words carefully, "how do I find my way up to the sunlight? Which way do I go?" Jenny asked looking at the two paths the Fork offered.

"Neither of THOSE roads are goin' ta help ya." He sighed and muttered. "Ya'll haf ta come up my way."

He harrumphed.

With a pronounced sigh, the little man unwound the line from his fishing pole and dropped it down to where Jenny stood. She picked up the end of the line.

"What do I do with this?" she asked.

"Hang on!"

She grabbed the line tightly above the little net. And up she went! She was surprised at how strong the little creature was. In a moment she was sitting right beside him, far above the path. Behind her was a small dark tunnel. It was so small that she would have to go on her hands and knees.

"Well, ah've got near 'nuff me quota today. Ah s'pose ah could be gettin' back," rationalized the creature.

"Do you have a name?" asked Jenny feeling suddenly too close to the strange little man.

"Yup! Ah got one." answered the man tartly.

"Uhm. What is it?"

"Ah ain't be tellin' YOU! Ah don't rightly know ya!"

"But I told you my name."

"And ya don't know me no-ways neither!"

"uh, okay..."

He made an exasperated sound.

He looked up at her.

"Ya can call me... hmmm... well... um, uh, Wisherman. That'll do."

At that, Wisherman climbed to his feet and pulled on a purple jacket. He then slung his wicker basket across his round back, and he disappeared down the small dark tunnel.

Jenny took a deep breath and crawled in after him.

OLLY, OLLY, OXEN FREY

Chapter 5

Chaos in
The Palace

Asphixia

Two days later and far away, screams echoed throughout the halls of a twisty castle perched on the edge of a deep abyss. The Redduns screeched and cursed! They coughed and sneezed! The ill-tempered creatures bumped and battered each other as they gathered at the main gate.

But Asphixia the Blue Queen relished that. Chaos made her feel happy as she sat playing with her make-up.

A young page stood at the door to her boudoir.

"Yer majesty, the Water-Witch has landed on the roof." He avoided looking directly at the giant queen. His white

furry body stood tall for a fae, but he only saw her knees if he didn't look up. Looking into the Queen's eyes was dangerous. Everyone suspected that she could read minds.

As a matter of fact, Asphixia could not read minds, but she could happily see that he was terrified. Of course he was. His wife and children were in the dungeon. It was an efficient way to keep staff working at their best.

The Blue Queen smiled, "Of course Floogle, I'll be right down. Have the cook prepare the blue tea for our guest while she waits. I wouldn't want our guest to feel... *slighted*. Put her in... the Sapphire Room."

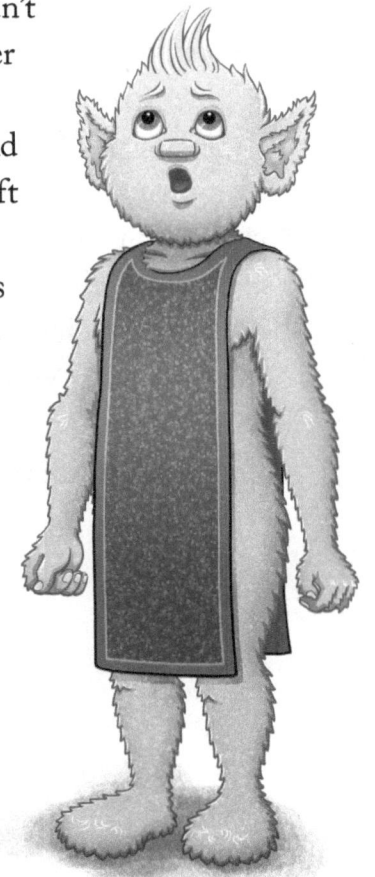

Floogle the page shook at the sound of his name on her lips and speedily left to deliver her message.

So much to do today! There was a rebellion in the eastern Whisp territories, and famine and roving bands of marauders in the Bog Lands to the south. There was something in the jungles causing problems. Disorder. She might need to conscript more soldiers. To keep order.

Everyone likes order.

Asphixia considered herself an artist when it came to sewing chaos, and balancing it with her own flavors of order. Both were necessary tools when ruling a vast kingdom.

She also needed to build up the magical coffers again. A little extra dark magic on hand was always useful. Additionally it was probably time to do something dramatic. Set an example somewhere. A little excitement to keep the populace distracted.

Asphixia inspected her rouge. The tall mirror reflected the perfect right side of her reptilian ice-blue face. She compared it to the perfect left side. She loved to admire herself. If you don't love yourself, who will?

Her makeup was not quite right.

"Hmmm..." She twirled a little lavender powder puff by its arms and legs (which were bound together to make a convenient handle) and dusted more blush along her arched and delicately scaled cheekbones.

"Yes. Much better." She placed the powder puff back in the tray along with its siblings and smiled fondly at their wimperings.

"Yes. I think this will be a marvelous day!"

Rip-One the Reddun

Rip-One groaned.

Doorbell 57 had apparently sounded a few days earlier in the dispatcher's office but nobody had heard it. Rip-One only just noticed the blinking light this morning. He needed to replace the battery in that device. *Barn-snot.* Time to barter with the nixies again.

Rip-One pulled the siren to dispatch the gang. He still needed to do the paperwork, but too much time had elapsed... and *she* wouldn't know if the paperwork was done before or after acquisition. Rip-One was overworked and under-appreciated! Nobody loved him.

The troop of Redduns swirled out the palace gates in a cloud of gooey red dust. They'd snatch up this new child who had slipped into Frey.

Chapter 6

The Nature of Food

Jack

Whoosh! Jack found himself sitting in a rocky red tunnel. He was too stunned to know what to say at first.

"Ah! Pinkcheeks! Nice of you to join me," called Finn arching an eyebrow. He had perfect eyebrows. It was weird how a boy as green-blond as Finn was, still had dark enough eyebrows to punctuate anything he said.

Finn stood a few feet into the tunnel and was surrounded by mushrooms that were two feet tall! Above them were glowing flowers perched atop tall stalks.

Jack twisted to check the dirt wall behind him! He could see vertical wooden planks embedded in hard red clay, but nothing that resembled an opening that he could have fallen through.

"This – where are we... ?"

Jack pounded on the wall! He jumped up and kicked the clay in various places, but it was solid.

"Yup. Not getting through there. I did that earlier." Finn looked at something in the dirt.

Jack scoffed, "Yeah, right. We were sitting together only seconds ago!"

"Dunno. I've been here for a bit." Finn climbed a rock to inspect how the fire-flowers produced light, but something on the trail caught his eye. "Jack!" Finn pointed down the tunnel.

Jack ran over to see:

PIRATE JENNY WAS HERE!

"Jenny! She's here!" Jack shouted, then looking around muttered, "Wherever 'here' is."

Jack looked to Finn who was still balancing on top of a rock and inspecting the fire-flowers. "What are those?"

Finn cocked his head. "No clue. But it'd be dark in here without 'em! What type of mushrooms does your dad grow?"

Jack turned from the tunnel's dead end and considered the enormous fungi around them. "Nothing that looks like these."

Finn just muttered while he looked around.

Jack jogged to the bend in the path and looked back. "Let's find Jenny!"

Finn hopped to the floor and shouldered his bag. "Could we be under the garden out back? Or *maybe* we're sitting exactly where we *were* sitting in the cellar, AND we're dreaming because we inhaled something from your dad's mushrooms?"

Jack shrugged. "Seems real enough to me." He nearly pinched himself but decided it would be more fun to pinch Finn.

Finn jumped away with his hands out. "No pinches!"

"No pinches?!!" Jack said in his monster voice. "PINCHUMS WILL SEE ABOUT THAT!" Jack raised his arms like a hungry troll and chased a giggling Finn down the path. Finn squirmed out of an almost tackle and threw Jack laughing in the dirt.

"NO, PINCHUMS! DOWN BOY!" Finn said sternly, standing over him.

Jack tried to look remorseful.

Finn hauled Jack to his feet, and Jack promptly grabbed Finn around the waist and brought him back down to the ground with him. They wrestled a bit, then they both lay on their backs and laughed.

"Does *this* feel real?" Jack nudged the tickle spot on Finn's waist. "Or here! Or here?" He poked Finn's vulnerable tickle locations.

"Maybe! PINCHUMS! STOP!" Finn squawked and jumped to his feet, snickering.

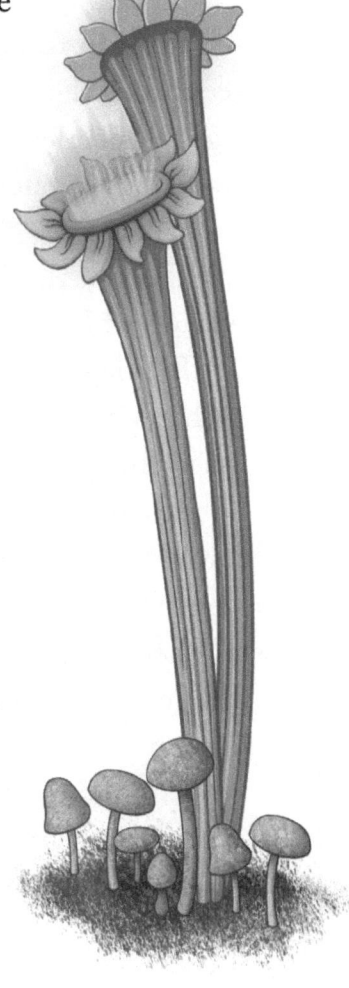

They both took deep breaths while Jack got to his feet. It felt good to laugh – even if he felt guilty for laughing while Jenny was still missing. But now he was going to find her!

Finn grabbed his fallen bag and returned it to his shoulder. He raised an eyebrow and pointed at the trail.

Jenny's footprints were visible in the dust ahead.

"Yup!" Jack said.

The two boys started down the passage. It wound to the right, and then to the left. It led up and down. Sometimes they were rewarded with Jenny's footprints in the dust. Sometimes the trail was more rock than dirt and there were no foot prints at all. But the passage never split so they had to be on the right track.

At the second hard bend in the path Jack jumped back into Finn with surprise.

"Woah!" Jack gasped.

Right in front of them was the biggest bug they'd ever seen! Blue. Four-feet in length with shiny wings and long legs... it perched atop a mushroom and munched on what was left of a much smaller bug.

"What the —" exclaimed Finn (he did not like bugs).

"Do you think it will it attack us if we try to pass it?" whispered Jack.

The bug looked up as if it understood and gave them such a withering glance, that Jack was embarrassed to have asked the question.

Jack and Finn picked up big rocks they could potentially throw at it, and they inched along the opposite wall. They were feeling relieved to have passed it, when they saw another enormous bug! And another! There were so many different types of insects! They all seemed busy about their lives so eventually Jack — and even Finn — began to relax a little around the strange creatures.

The plant life flanking the trail also grew more diverse with colorful mushrooms and strange flora. At times it nearly obstructed the path. Big glowing bugs fluttered above their heads and flitted about the fire-flowers.

At times the tunnel widened and the ceiling lifted into large cavernous spaces, but Jenny's footsteps led them toward where the space dwindled to the size of school corridors.

Once Jack felt accustomed to the giant bugs, he found himself to be more curious than frightened. But the large insects and worms still gave Finn the heebie-jeebies, which emboldened Jack all the more. The always cool Finn was downright jittery!

Finn put on a brave front. "This could be the setting for one of our crazy stories."

"Yeah, all we need now is for A WEREWOLF TO JUMP OUT!" Jack raised his arms in monster attack mode. "ARRRRHH!"

Finn pushed him back with a laugh. "Seriously, don't do that. I'm already creeped out enough as it is." Finn stopped. "It still doesn't seem possible that this is all real. It's too..."

"Weird?" Jack offered.

"Yeah. Giant mushrooms and insects like this don't exist."

Jack looked around. "Okay."

"I'm probably at home in bed drooling on my pillow." Finn mused.

"Or maybe you're in *my* dream!" Jack countered.

Finn pretended to think. "Well if it's your dream —
make some sunflowers!"

"Sunflowers?"

"I like sunflowers," said Finn.

"You're the one who thinks it's a dream!" Jack pointed
out. "You make sunflowers."

Finn stared at the mushroom patch by the wall. He
concentrated and held out his hands like he was doing a
magic trick.

"Abbra-caddabrrrah! Sunflowers!!!"

Nothing happened.

"If this was a dream *I'd* be running around naked,"
confessed Jack. "I'm always naked in my dreams."

"Be my guest," laughed Finn.

"But it's *not* a dream," teased Jack. "And besides the
naked one is *always* the dreamer. You said you're the
dreamer!"

"Well, if that's the case," Finn stopped and posed like
he was a stripper. He grabbed the bottom of his t-shirt like
he was about to pull it off. Then he stopped. "Nope. Maybe
I'm not the dreamer after all. It's you that needs to strip!"
He grabbed Jack from behind.

Squealing, Jack squirmed out of Finn's grasp. Their eyes
met for a weird moment before looking away. But Jack's
heart was pounding with a rush like he'd just been tickled.
Finn looked embarrassed and stepped back, surreptitiously
adjusting his jeans.

They were still catching their breath when they noticed a large fuzzy worm lounging on a really big shelf fungi. Finn gestured. "That's too weird to be real."

The worm looked back indignantly.

Finn heard a quiet step and spun around, "BACK! NO TOUCH!" Finn successfully countered Jack's tickle maneuver. "We probably shouldn't be touching so much!"

Jack cringed. He'd taken it to far. He always took it too far. He was touching Finn *too much*. It was creepy. He didn't want Finn to think he was *like that*.

Jack liked Finn more than he should. He knew Finn liked him – as a best friend – which was not quite the same way that Jack liked Finn. Getting older was complicated.

There was an uncomfortable silence.

Jack felt like his face was glowing bright red. Redder than normal. "We gotta keep going. Jenny."

Finn stared quietly at a strange plant and poked his finger at a green flower that retracted inside itself. "Pirate Jenny's probably looking for her pirate ship."

Jack relaxed with the game change. "A pirate ship? Underground?"

They started walking again.

"The tunnel's gotta come out somewhere."

"And that's where the galleon is going to be! Maybe we'll have to fight pirates to rescue her!"

"We could sneak up in a row boat in the dark of night," Finn offered.

"Dinghy."

"Who ya callin' dinghy?"

Jack swatted him. "The row boat's called a dinghy, Dinghy!"

"Oh!" Finn laughed. "Then we could climb up the anchor rope."

"I can swim too. We don't need a dinghy."

Jack gave Finn the eyebrow.

Finn corrected himself. "Okay, No dinghy needed!"

Jack sighed. "But I'm no good at rope climbing. I'd make a lousy rescuer. You actually have to be good at stuff to rescue someone."

"Well then, I guess we'll just have to leave Jenny with the pirates," Finn acquiesced.

"Guess so," Jack mused. "It's just that little sisters are so hard to come by. We probably should put forward *some* effort."

Finn poked his shoulder. "You're good at lots of things. You can charm these pirates!" suggested Finn.

"Are you saying that I'm charming?" Jack asked softly. "Charm isn't really a skill!"

"Sure it is. We'd have both been grounded for weeks if Mrs. Misener had reported us for sneaking into those caves at their farm last summer. She looooves you!"

Jack shrugged, "Well she is really nice once you get to know her. Did you know that she makes soap? She has lots of interesting hobbies."

"But you wouldn't know any of that if you weren't a charmer!"

"It's not charm. It's just being curious... and interested in folks and what they do." Jack kicked a sparkly rock further down the path. It nearly hit a large red caterpillar, which happened to be crossing the path.

Jack immediately gushed, "Woops, sorry Mr. Caterpillar. I didn't see you there." Jack apologized to random things all the time. He apologized to an actual chair the other day when he accidentally knocked it over. He couldn't help it. Apologizing was part of his DNA.

Finn carefully walked around the caterpillar. "Freaksville. That thing is three-feet long! Where the heck does a three foot long caterpillar come from? Do you think these things bite?"

"They look kind of cuddly to me." Jack looked at its scarlet plushy fur. "We *could* be under the garden I suppose..."

Finn ducked to miss a low flying firefly-like-thing. "Ahhh!" Finn gave Jack the eye. "Drugs! Gots ta be your dad's mushrooms!" He laughed and spun around. He looked at the red caterpillar and got a mischievous expression on his face. "Do you think these things are edible? We are going to need food at some point..."

Jack blanched.

Finn teased, "Don't look at me like that! Have you never read any survival books? At some point we're going to need food! A caterpillar like that might be the key to our survival if we get hungry enough."

"Oh PLEASE!! I know that you've probably got tuna sandwiches in that bag of yours, and who knows what else. You've always got food in there."

Finn lowered his voice dramatically. "Sure, but what if we're still wandering these tunnels in a day or two?"

"I'm not eating caterpillars! That's all I'm sayin'!" Jack crossed his arms. "Nope! Not going to happen, Greenbean."

"AND THAT SSSENTIMENT ISSS GREATLY APPRECSSIATED!" said a voice near their feet.

The boys jumped to see the red caterpillar's head lift above its fuzzy body. It regarded them rather sternly. Under all that fur was a face!

"You can talk?!" said a surprised Finn.

"OH! MYYY! Can I reeee-ally?" responded the strange creature sarcastically in a high fake baby voice. Then its voice deepened, "It isss good of you to sssa-hay ssso!"

"Now, I know we're dreaming for sure," Finn gasped.

" H a p p y dreamsss, I hope?" asked the red mound of fur. At that, the tunnel erupted into giggles. The boys spun around. Caterpillars were everywhere! Sitting atop toadstools and curled around the fire-flower stalks. They came out of every crevice and hidey-spot. And they all were laughing and pointing with whatever tiny hands weren't holding onto their perches.

Finn was stunned. "I'm so sorry, I didn't know you were... uh... whatever you are!"

"Cleee-arly." The little speaker gave an amused sideways glance at the others. "Oh that'sss all ri-hight. We were only just discusssssing eeeating YOU! So I sup-*pose* it ISss only fair."

Finn squirmed. "I'm not quite sure what to say to that."

Jack spoke up. "Of course we'd have NEVER tried to eat you! That's just Finn talking. Sometimes he says stuff without thinking."

A caterpillar on a lavender mushroom then rationalized. "If he doesssn't think, then maybe we *caaaan* eat him after all?"

Finn turned a pale green to match his hair. "I DO TOO THINK! I just didn't think that *you* thought! I would never..."

The first caterpillar interrupted him. "Well the truth of the matter is that *now* that wee've had a conversssssa-ation, I would hope zat weee are off eee-ach other'ss menu? My name isss George. And I am NOT a CATERPILLAR! I. AM. A FUZZY-WIGGLE!" This was said with far more dignity than Jack or Finn would have expected from a caterpillar.

Then with a smile and a sly glance at Jack, George added, "And, jussst sso you know, and NOT that it isss at ALL important, but ye-esss weee ARE quite cuddly."

George rubbed his head against Jack's knee.

Finn changed the subject. "*George* is an interesting name for a cat- uh, fuzzy-wiggle."

"It wass given to me by a human who was much politer than yooou."

"It's a pleasure to meet you, George," Jack said while cautiously stepping back. He didn't want to step on anyone.

"I'm Randy!" said a fleshy worm with hairy tufts. He held out a tiny paw.

"Nice to meet you, Randy." Jack carefully shook the little extended hand.

Finn did not shake the small pink hand.

"This one has nice manners!" A furry pink one fluttered her lashes at Jack.

Jack could see that Finn was really uncomfortable.

George wiggled around Jack's leg with a grin. Jack politely reached down to rub the critter's fuzzy head.

The fur was very soft. George's eyes closed and his smile stretched wide in pure ecstasy.

Suddenly the boys were swarmed by fuzzy-wiggles. They crawled up the boys' legs. The boys fell under an undulating pile of fuzzy-wiggles desperately wanting attention. Every time Jack stopped petting, little mouths opened to reveal startling rows of sharp teeth.

"Ick, Ick! ACK! STOP!" shouted Finn. He quickly extricated himself from the pile feeling more than a little freaked out. "Get away from me! PLEASE!" He added, *"I'm ready to wake up now."*

Jack crawled out of the pile while still cuddling the pink fuzzy-wiggle. The other fuzzy-wiggles were envious.

Jack addressed the group of fuzzy-wiggles as his fingers kneaded her luxuriant fur. "I'm sorry. Please. It *is* really wonderful to meet each of you, but we're looking for my sister. She's lost. Has a little girl come by? A girl wearing a pirate hat?"

Fuzzy-wiggle heads popped up at that.

"Oh. Oh ye-esss," said George. "We liked HER. She'ss the human who gave usss our wonderful namesss!"

"She wasss fabulousss," gushed the fur-less Randy. Jack remembered Randy far too well. It felt really creepy when he'd accidentally touched him in the pile.

"When did you see her?" exclaimed Jack.

"Oh, AGES ago," said an orange and blue striped worm named Beatrice.

"It was just a moment ago," piped up Burt (fashionably yellow and chartreuse).

"We're not very good with time," shared George with an edge of superiority. "But time issn't tha-haat important in the grahnd sschee-heme of thingsss."

"Well time's important to us, and we need to move on. NOW!" said an impatient Finn looking at Jack.

"Yes, we really do," added Jack who knew it was time to go.

"Oh ple-heeaessse stay here with usss! She'll come back eventually." All the fuzzy-wiggles batted their eyelashes. "They all do. Mosstly."

"Unless she getsss eaten," considered Burt.

"There isss that," said George.

Finn started walking. He shouted over his shoulder, "Hasta la vista."

Jack repeated, "What? Eaten by what?"

Burt shrugged. "Just eaten."

Jack hesitated. "Oh, uhm..." Finn was making tracks. "Nice to meet you!" He hurried after Finn.

Jack remembered that he still held the pink fuzzy-wiggle in his arms. He stopped.

"I didn't mean to take you away from your friends." Jack exclaimed.

"But I want you to take me away," replied the furry cuddler. "I *like* you." Her voice was soft and persuasive as she nuzzled into Jack's chest.

"Oh... okay? If you want," whispered the boy. "Maybe you could tell us what to watch out for? So we don't get eaten? I'm Jack, and that's Finn. Do you have a name?"

The pink caterpillar smiled and batted her eyelashes. "Pinkie. The girl named me."

Pinkie had a very nice smile, if you ignored all her sharp teeth.

"No, don't bring her." Finn had been listening in.

"She can be our guide, out Sacagawea!"

"Really?" Finn pointed at her. *"You. Don't eat me!"*

"Not unlesss I get very, very hungry," she winked.

Finn moved a little more quickly down the trail. "Just puttin' this out there, Jack. I'm not comfortable with this."

Jack laughed. "Don't be silly, Pinkie's not going to eat us."

The pink fuzzy-wiggle snickered softly in Jack's arms.

He caught up to Finn who was now standing in front of a giant Fork in the middle of the path.

Finn gave a big exhale. "Jack, I don't think we're under the vegetable garden."

Chapter 7

The Wishermans' Big Wish

Pirate Jenny

Jenny crawled up the long dark tunnel following Mr. Wisherman for what seemed like forever. It was cold. Her bare knees thought that she'd never see light again! She'd bumped her head five times on low bits of ceiling. (She'd had to take off her hat and carry it).

After a bit, there was a slight warm glow beyond her guide's waddling form. He was able to stand up in the tunnel. The glow increased till the tunnel opened into a small cave with a round window in the far wall, revealing a blinding blue sky beyond. The ceiling was still too low for her to stand, but she could sit up. It was quite a cozy underground home.

She brushed off her skinned knees, which were not happy with all the crawling. The light revealed lavender dirt? Her knees and hands were coated with a fine layer of lavender powder. She brushed it off as best she could.

Around her were all the ingredients of a comfortable cottage. Everything was shades of lavender. There was an old stone fireplace that beckoned her to its orange warmth. There was a rough wooden table, with five three-legged stools around it. There were painted pictures on the wall, knickknacks on the mantle, and delicious smells in the air – it reminded Jenny of her mother's soap. Puttering in front of the sink, was a female version of the Wisherman.

Wisherman called out. "Halloo Fuzziboo! We's just passing through." Wisherman turned to Jenny. "This be Mamy uh... oh..." he frowned. "Wisherman."

Mamy Wisherman looked at her husband askance. "What's a human child doin' in me kitchen? And why'd ya done gone and telled her our real name?"

"Ah, BLAST IT! Ah didn't tell her it was our REAL NAME! She thought it be a fake name! Ah were bein' extra clever wi' that switcheroo! Why didja have ta go and tell her it wasn't fake?" he moaned.

Now that Jenny crouched next to them in the light, she could see that neither of the Wishermans would be taller than her waist. Their bodies were big lavender puffballs.

Her guide had a long patchwork jacket that pushed his fluff to the front, while Mamy had a sort of patchwork apron that pushed all her fluff out the back. Their faces, arms, and legs were a pale shade of green. Mamy had a second and smaller lavender powder puff on top of her head flanked by two pointed ears that wobbled as she shook her head at her husband. His head was fluffy too, but it was trimmed down like a flat-top haircut – which made his ears seem even bigger.

Wisherman gave a sigh and a shrug. "Mamy, this be Pirate Jenny."

Mamy gave Jenny a bit of an eye.

Jenny tried to sit up like a fearless, but very polite pirate.

"Has she eaten anythin'?" asked Mamy with a stern look on her face.

"What do ya take me for! Of course not!" answered an absolutely indignant Wisherman.

At that, Jenny realized that she was hungrier than ever (what with all the delicious smells of Mamy's cooking). "I wouldn't mind somethin' to eat, if you could spare it."

There was an awkward silence till Wisherman spoke up, "Well missy... um, the thing of it be, ya can't eat or drink nothin' here, or ya can't go home."

"Oh?" said Jenny as her stomach growled loud enough for the Wishermans to hear. Her initial spirit of adventure had departed. She was a seven-year-old pirate. She was tired. And she was hungry! But, she was NOT going to

THE WISHERMANS' BIG WISH

cry. PIRATES DON'T CRY. Not even when they are *really* hungry. She was more than ready to go home to her family if she just knew how to get there. She curled up on the floor next to the miniature fireplace. She was absolutely not getting teary eyed.

Mamy let out an exasperated sound. "Yar just goin' ta hafta do it!"

"No, Mamy! Ah worked too hard fer 'em!"

"But ya can't be lettin' that girl go be starvin' herself, Papy. She's gotta eat somethin'! Look at her."

Jenny was absolutely not crying.

Papy Wisherman gave a sob of despair, looked at Jenny and took a long slow exhale like he might cry. Papy gazed helplessly at the ground but couldn't speak.

Mamy hugged Papy consolingly. "Now, ya don't hafta give her a lot – she can be clever about it. But, the girl's gotta eat. And she can't eat what we be eatin'."

Papy unstrapped the basket from his back, and stepped closer to Jenny with a serious look on his face. "Jenny, me girl, ya can't be eatin' food here. Ya can't e'en be drinkin' the water. Faerie food would keep ya from goin' home."

"Oh. Faerie food?"

"But, ya can eat and drink the food that *yoou* wish for – as then those vittles is coming from yar head – not here. Ah can spare ya a *few* wishes just to keep ya from starvin'. But... it be *hard*."

Mamy sank down on a stool with teary eyes. "Forgive 'im missy. We don't mean ta be ungen'rous. But, we're sore pressed. We do be needin' as many wishes as we can get."

Their anguished faces distracted Jenny from her tummy growlings. "What for?"

"She took our babies!" Mamy cried. "The Queen's Redduns came inta our home an' they done took our wee ones an' we've gotta get 'em back before they's... used up!"

Papy continued, "At the Wish Market, we can trade these wee wishes fer bigger wishes."

He ran to the open door, looked outside, and then shut it. He turned back to Jenny with a whisper.

"If ah could get us a big 'nough wish, ah could get past the palace magic and make me a door right inta the Blue Queen's closet! Ah'll sneak in and get our babies back!"

"This queen doesn't sound very nice." Jenny asked. "Where am I? It doesn't sound like Washington."

Papy looked at Mamy.

Mamy looked back at Papy, "Well we might as well tell her the rest, as we've done gone this far."

Papy carefully extracted a wish out of his basket and held it out to Jenny in cupped hands. "Ya should make yarself somethin' ta eat. This is goin' ta take a bit of explainin' an' you be hungry. Now, ah can't tell ya what ta wish fer, as then it would be me thinkin' instead of yar thinkin', but ah might be tellin' ya ta be *smart* about yar words – if ya be gettin' me drift. This bein' a magic place and all..." He looked at her knowingly and held her eyes.

Papy carefully deposited the living wish into Jenny's outstretched hands. It looked up at her. Close up, it was shimmering and golden with beautiful veins and patterns in its wings. It didn't seem to be truly solid. Like a dream, it was hard to focus on. It shifted and changed too much. It crawled across her hand and looked up almost friendly-like.

"I don't want to hurt it." Jenny worried.

"Oh, no dearie. They be waiting ta become somethin' else. They sorta exist for the sole purpose o' changin'!"

Jenny had heard her share of faerie tales at bedtime and even more in Jack and Finn's tree-house, so she thought a bit before she whispered her wish. "I wish I had a magic bowl – that I could travel with – that has always got food in it when I'm hungry! *With* a spoon."

There was a tinkling sound. The glowing moth disappeared and was replaced by a beautiful silver bowl with a lid and a silver spoon, which attached to the side when not in use. It seemed to know that she was hungry as it was filled with buttery scrambled eggs.

"I almost forgot to ask for a spoon!" Jenny confessed.

"But ya got it in time! See Papy, she's a smart one. Now she needs one more wish so she's got somethin' ta drink too."

Papy reluctantly offered up a second wish.

Jenny's mouth was still a little full with her second bite of eggs, but she said, "I wish I had a bottle with good stuff to drink whenever I'm thirsty."

Again the glittering wish disappeared from her palm and in its place was a crystal bottle with some sort of liquid in it.

She took a sip. It tasted a little bit like orange juice mixed with something like chocolate, but it was perfect for breakfast. Which was Jenny's favorite meal.

So while Pirate Jenny ate from her endless bowl of scrambled eggs, Papy told her a story. "Ya be in the kingdom o' Frey. It used ta be a peaceable sort of place fer a faerie kingdom, all things bein' considered."

"Frey?" Jenny reflected. "Have my parents have ever been here? My dad goes somewhere every day. He says it's to the office."

"Well, we don't see no big humans here, except fer the one of course, a long time back. He was all right." said Papy. "But, uh, we do see young 'uns come through every once in a while." Papy winced.

Mamy pursed her lips and didn't say anything.

"Are there many faerie places like this?" Jenny asked with a mouthful of breakfast. She figured pirates don't have to be perfectly polite.

"Loads! Er, so ah'm told by the nixies. Ah couldn't reckon how many. Though not all like Frey. Not that ah've ever been t' another. But, ah be thinkin' thar be places hidden all over. Wherever thar be doors that are unused an' places ta make folks curious, all it takes is a *what if* in a dreamy git's mind an' that wee notion starts takin' root like a seed, a wish, an' it can grow inta all sorts o' wondr'-blime things."

"An' awful-ick things too–" added Mamy.

"Yup," Papy sighed. "We gots all sorts of critters here. Purty and ugly, an' useful an' frivol'us. Ya gotta be careful as what ya sees on the outside, be not always what ya get when ya take a closer look!"

Mamy burst in. "Like the Blue Queen! She's –"

Papy humphed at her. "We mostwise get along just fine. We don't get in each other's way. Ah be from a long line of Wishermans an' we've been livin' in this hill for as long as wee wishes ha' been dancin' around in the caverns below. An' that be a mighty long time!"

"But, tell her 'bout the Blue Queen." Mamy interjected.

"Ah'm gettin' thar! We never paid much 'ttention to Kings and Queens. They had their doin's and we had our doin's! But outside that window be a biggish place! Ah s'pose it needs a measure of organizin' and those there royalty folks have some purpose in that respect. But we never paid them no mind. It pro'bly works better in that there human world where yar from, but here no one much cared one wit 'bout how gov'ment works unless you be havin' a gnarly-cross patch wi' yer neighbor. We didn't have much. We just want ta go 'bout our doin's without much bother."

"The Queen!" hissed Mamy.

"Yeah, ah'm gettin' thar! Well, somehow or other this new queen set herself up and surprised all o' us who warn't payin' attention. Suddenly, thar be new laws and new ways ta get inta trouble. Somehow's some folks came ta be more 'mportant than they were, and others got more likely ta get stomped on."

"Not like the old mer'King who were nice 'nuff." sighed Mamy.

"Mer'King?" asked Jenny.

Papy smiled. "He used to be o'er in the Bay of mer'Rin, where all the merfolk lived. If cit'zens had problems they'd go ta him and he'd make decisions that'd be fair 'nuff, and kept most folk happy."

"There are mermaids here?" asked Jenny with a fair amount of excitement.

"Used ta be, but they's all be gone now." sighed Mamy.

"They done disappeared someways and this giant blue lady took charge and everythin' started ta change up. Ah hear she be purty 'nuff. but–" Papy lowered his voice to a whisper. "That don't mean diddly if she don't *act* purty as well."

"Why did she take your babies?" asked Jenny.

Papy growled. "Everybody has ta be 'useful' now. Even babies! She takes *lots* o' babies now! She finds uses fer 'em!"

"What would she do with your babies?"

Mamy burst out in tears and Papy turned red with embarrassment and anger. It looked like he wasn't going to speak, but then he just came out with it.

"Ya may have noticed that we Wishermans be proud Fluffballs. We've a beauteous lavender dust and a lovely smell – if ah don't say so me-self. Each family be a different color, but wi' the Queen bein' blue, she wants our lavender babies fer her hideous cheeks."

"The queen is using your babies as powder puffs?"

"They be small and easy for her ta pick up." Mamy sobbed. "She's giant. Lots bigger than ev'n you be!"

"That's awful!" said a shocked Jenny.

She was exhausted. But Jenny adjusted her pirate hat and looked squarely at the Wishermans. "I'm going to help you get them back, but – I might need to take a nap first."

The Wishermans looked at the little girl who was twice their height.

Papy was skeptical as to how useful she'd be. "Well when ya be ready, we'll go about barterin' fer those two big wishes at the Frey Wish Market. One fer the babies an' one ta take ya home. Maybe then we'll talk 'bout how useful ya might be."

Chapter 8

The Nature
Of Wishes

Jack

"Jack, I don't think we're under the vegetable garden. It's too weird!"

Finn stared at the giant fork in the path. It extended all the way to the ceiling – where glowing bugs fluttered against their reflections. Some of them fluttered about Finn and Jack as well. They seemed to like Jack better.

Finn then noticed the restroom. "Hey! Facilities!! And a drinking fountain! We can't be that far from civilization! It's almost like an underground amusement park."

"Well that's crazy convenient!" Jack set Pinkie down on a wide mushroom, and opened the door. "It's got a bathtub? And it's stocked with toilet paper. We've got to be close to somewhere." Jack saluted. "Ma Nature's calling!" And in his deepest Arnold voice he grunted, "I'll be back!" Jack stepped into the restroom for some much needed rest.

Finn

Finn took a sip of water at the fountain, and noticed Pinkie daintily nibbling on the edge of her mushroom. He took a deeper drink and wiped his mouth with the back of his hand.

"So, where are we, Pinkie? You live here. How do we get back to the surface?" Finn crouched down by the mushroom where she stretched out.

Her eyes tracked the flying gold bugs above him. She purred, "My deliciousss Finn, I've never been anywhere. I've no idea how –" She leaped and snapped at a fluttery bug near Finn's face.

Finn screamed to see those giant teeth near his face. He fell on his butt as she retracted coyly to her mushroom.

Pinkie grinned mischievously. "Sssorry. Girlss gotta eat. Didn't mean to ssstartle you. Wishess are hard to catch. One hasss to be fassst."

"Wishes?" Finn gasped.

A toilet flushed and Jack burst out still buttoning his shorts. "Everything okay? You screamed!"

Jack

Finn glanced up at Jack's worried face. "I'm okay. Little Pinkette just showed me how fast she can move. But we're good." Finn stared at Pinkie. "So why do you call these bugs 'wishes'?" Finn pointed to the fluttering things which had retreated to the ceiling.

Jack didn't understand what they were talking about.

"Becausse that'sss what they are. Thisss tunnel isss full of wishesss." Pinkie gestured at the fork and the bathroom. "How do you *think* these sstrange thingss ended up here?"

"The little golden moths grant wishes?" Finn asked.

"They don't *grant* wishess, they ARE wishess. But mostly only if they like you." Pinkie looked at the wishes again fluttering about Finn's head. "They do sseem to like you." She added flirtatiously. "But they like Jack better."

Jack realized that he had a virtual halo of glowing bugs fluttering around his head.

Finn scoffed. "But, there's no such thing as wishes. That would be like magic or something."

Jack agreed. "Like giant mushrooms and talking caterpillars."

"Fuzzy-wiggles," Finn corrected.

"Absolutely impossible." Jack pointed out.

This was crazy.

Finn smiled. "So I can just wish for anything?" he asked tentatively - his stomach growling.

"Try it." Pinkie watched with curiosity.

"I wish I had a tuna melt sandwich on sourdough - with a pickle on the side." Finn rattled off the top of his head.

"You don't like pickles." Jack observed.

"But, you do." Finn smiled and Jack's heart melted a little bit.

He heard a tinkling sound and one of the fluttering wishes disappeared in a flash. On a nearby mushroom appeared a crispy tuna melt sandwich on sourdough wrapped in wax paper. And it was still hot. With a pickle on the side (which Jack helped himself to).

"Holy crappola!" Finn was stunned. "OH! Did I just kill a wish?"

Pinkie smiled patiently at Finn. "No. Wishess *want* to transsform into sssomething else! They are in sstasiss ... like a flying cocoon perhapsss, just waiting to be sssomething more."

"Even if that something is going to get eaten?" asked Finn looking hungrily at the sandwich.

"And then becomes a part of you. It merges with you. Wishes don't die. They... travel. And what are you Finn, but many, many wishes that have come to be?"

"Magic exists?" Finn rolled the words around in his brain.

Jack tilted his head. "Jenny. A fresh new roll of good toilet paper. That explains that! Jenny's been here. I don't think there's ever been a seven year old so obsessed with good toilet paper. I bet she wished for that restroom to be here!"

Finn interrupted. "Jack, want to split a tuna melt?" Then remembering Pinkie. "We could split thirds?"

"Yes! I'm starved." exclaimed Jack.

Pinkie sniffed. "That's sssweet, but no... that doesn't sssmell like sssomething I would eat."

Finn shrugged. "Your loss!"

Jack took the half-sandwich that Finn offered and asked with his mouth full, "What do you eat then? Other than wishes and theoretically... us."

"Fuzzy-wigglesss live on love and affection – with a ssside of mushrooms, but if we want to get really big, there'sss nothing like a tasssty, fluttering wish."

Finn looked up. "They're all over the place. Is that why you fuzzy-wiggles get so enormous?"

She giggled. "We can get *much* bigger than this! But wishesss are hard to catch from the ground without bait." She batted her eyes at the boys and the fluttering wishes over their heads.

"That's why you wanted to come? We're your bait?" clarified Jack.

"You wound me, Jackie." Pinkie teased. "I *do* like you. I even like you, Finn. Though it's halvsiesss as to whether I want to eat you or look at you." She smiled. "You are rather pretty."

Finn stammered but no words came out.

Jack crossed his arms and looked down at the pink fuzzy-wiggle. "You won't eat tuna, but you'll eat us?"

"Oh, but I wouldn't." Then she added, "You ssmellsss tasssty, but human blood isssn't healthy for usss." She closed her eyes and sighed with delight. "I prefer wiggling golden wishesss."

"Huh." Finn was wondering. "Caterpillars typically build a cocoon and become something else like a butterfly. I know you're not a caterpillar, but..."

"Do you turn into wishes?" burst out Jack.

Grinning ear to ear, Pinkie hopped off the mushroom and started crawling down the trail. "Boys, I'm going to be the biggest wish that anyone ever wished."

The boys looked at each other in surprise.

When Jack started to follow Pinkie, Finn touched his arm, "Wait. My turn for a pit stop while we're here." The door banged shut behind Finn.

Jack took a drink from the fountain and the fuzzy-wiggle waited for them.

Jack was thinking. "If you eat wishes, doesn't that make you a –"

Pinkie shrugged her non-existent shoulders. "I'm sssimply drafting othersss into my... enterprissse."

"And they don't mind?"

"No more than being asssked to dance."

Jack reflected. "Hmmm. If human blood isn't healthy for you, what would happen if you did eat it?"

Her voice quieted, "I'd become a dark wish."

"Dark?"

Pinkie's eyes looked troubled. "Bessst not discusssed."

Jack wasn't sure if he wanted to get close to her with all this talk of human blood. "So, you aren't going to bite me."

"Ask too many questions and you might find out." she growled.

The toilet flushed and Finn was back.

Jack stared at the two tunnels. "So which side of the fork did Jenny take? The path is rock in both directions with no footprints." He then had a second thought. "Pinkie, would one of these wishes get us home?"

Pinkie smiled. "No, these wishes are too small to take you that far." She considered the paths. "Perhaps we should take the tunnel that leads *up*?"

Jack nodded. "Makes sense to me. Greenbean?"

Finn shrugged. "Pinkcheeks, let's find Jenny and figure out how to get home! Our folks have to be wondering where we are."

Finn set off down the trail.

Jack and Pinkie followed behind.

Jack could see that Pinkie still gave Finn the creeps, but he thought she would be useful in this strange place.

"My parents have got to be crazy worried," thought Jack guiltily. "First Jenny. Now it's me who is gone! But we'll find her!"

Chapter 9

Changeling
Times

Mr. & Mrs. Saunders

When Jack did not appear for lunch, Mrs. Sanders went into a panic. She ran frantically around the property calling his name.

Mr. Sanders hurried outside when he heard his wife shouting.

Then they thought to look in the mushroom cellar.

There was Jenny! She was sleeping – curled up among the mushrooms in one of the beds of straw. She was naked and very white. At the other side of the room, in another long bed of Mr. Saunders special mix of sawdust and manure lay the sleeping, unclothed bodies of Jack and Finn. And each child's hair was stark white.

Why were they so white and naked?

Mrs. Sanders checked Jenny's pulse. Though it seemed normal, Jenny did not seem capable of waking up.

Mr. Sanders checked the boys. It made him uncomfortable seeing a naked Finn unconsciously spooning a naked Jack. Both were very pale and skinnier than he remembered. But, of course he didn't actually look at Jack that much. Not really. Mr. Saunders worked a lot of hours at the office and was exhausted when he got home. At home he mostly watched TV because it was relaxing. Jack really needed to watch more television! It would give them more father and son time.

He ran up to the house to get blankets, while Mrs Sanders didn't let the children out of her sight. When he returned, they wrapped each child and carried them up to the house.

They called Finn's parents and then drove the three children to the hospital. Each had a ghastly pallor and wouldn't wake up.

Finn's foster parents arrived at the hospital as soon as they could get there. It had been a crazy day for them. They were fostering nine children and two of the new arrivals had the flu.

The doctors couldn't figure out what was wrong with the kids. The children were very pale (the white hair suggested a great shock), and oddly they no longer had any fingerprints. The tips of their fingers were as smooth as the bottom of a spoon. But they slept peacefully.

Chapter 10

A Journey In Disguise

Pirate Jenny

P irate Jenny slept very well. She'd had the oddest dreams. Her hand touched rock. Jenny raised her head and remembered. They weren't dreams. She was lying in a pile of lavender blankets in front of a small, stone fireplace.

Apparently part of being a Fluffball was to leave a trail of color on everything you touched. It did smell nice though. Even her skin was getting a dusting of lavender.

"Mornin', little lady!" greeted Mamy.

Jenny looked over to the cheerful little woman standing near her feet.

She pulled her blankets around her and sat up. The cave was snug and warm.

The curious couple was just sitting down to breakfast.

Next to Jenny, she found her silver bowl with *Juicy-Squirts* inside – probably her favorite cereal ever. It was berry flavored with a *burst of liquid sweetness in every crunch*. The crystal bottle was filled with something like hot chocolate – again with a fruity hint.

The Wishermans ate plates full of quivering purple balls called scrumble-berries. They smelled delicious, but not so delicious that she wanted to be trapped in Frey for the rest of her life and never see her family again.

"Scrumble-berries be why the Wishermans have such beauteous lavender fluff!" boasted Papy.

"Wi'out scrumble-berries our wee ones won't be makin' the pretty color the queen wants afore long," worried Mamy. "It'll be the color o' whatever they be eatin'!"

After breakfast was cleaned up, Mamy pulled out a bag of clothing. "If ya're to be troopin' 'bout the countryside, ya can't be lookin' like a human girl. Ya'd be cage-snapped in no time and sold to the Queen."

"Why would she want me?"

"'Cuz ya be human!" Papy exclaimed. "Y'are a val'ble comod'ty around here."

"It's fer yer blood." whispered Mamy. "But I'll have ya made up so fine that no one will knows ya from a swamp-witch."

"My blood?" echoed Jenny.

"Yes, dearie. Jes' too terr'ble ta talk about." Mamy wouldn't say another word about it. She pulled out a bowl of pigment and soon Jenny's face and hands were painted a muted lavender. She also gained a hump on her back (to store her pirate hat, magic bowl, and bottle.) Mamy fashioned a course woven cloak out of a patchwork blanket with deep hood to complete the disguise.

Jenny was still processing the idea that the Blue Queen would want her blood as she crawled out the front door after Papy and Mamy who were wearing backpacks. Jenny stood up. It was nice to be able to stand straight again.

That was when she noticed the sad look on their faces.

Jenny spoke quietly. "You're not coming back here."

"Nope." Papy sighed. "Once we get our babies back, we can't never come here ag'in as the guards'll be lookin' here first."

"Maybe we'll head east towards Whisp terr'tory," mused Papy.

"We don't know where we'll be endin' up," said Mamy, sort of determined. "But so long as our family be together, it don't make much never mind. We'll make a happy place somewhere even if it be down in the Bog Lands."

The morning mists were disappearing in the bright sunny morning. Papy locked the door, "just in case things turn out diff'rent than 'spected. Maybe, we might be able ta come back someday."

The front of the Wisherman home was neat and well-loved. Tucked into the side of the hill was their round wooden door (painted lavender) and under the round window was a bed of flowers (lavender, purple, and blue), and behind a small fence were quivering scrumble-berries on wooden lattice-work in a well tended garden.

"A safe journey to ye!" squeaked a voice from the base of a bush. Jenny was surprised to see a foot tall mouse in overalls with his small family behind him. The group gave Jenny curious looks but asked no questions.

Papy gave a rare smile. "Tootles, thanks fer lookin' after things. We may be back or maybe not. Now, ye be careful-like if the Reddunns come thru!"

"We'll be snug-safe. Don't ye be worryin' 'bout us. We be small and easy ta overlook." harrumphed Tootles.

With a wave to the tiny family, Jenny and the Wishermans ambled down the hill.

Mamy sighed, "They be our gardeners, and mighty fine folks. Mice be the best gardeners."

"I've never seen a mouse talk before." Jenny observed.

"Fancy that." Mamy said in surprise. "They be nice 'nough... fer a 'trixer. All animals be talkin' here. And lots of the trees an' plants too!" she sighed. "Hard to know if the quiet ones are thinkin' bein's or not sometimes. I s'pose we're all relatives somehow, ev'n if we don't understand 'em. In yer world, could it be that you jes' don't talk their soul-speak?"

"Dunno." Jenny mused. "Not sure I ever heard of anyone trying to learn squirrel, or dog, or mouse."

The late morning air was crisp. The blue sky above and the gentle winding path below made one think that nothing bad could ever happen in a place so beautiful. The trail led down the hill and wound between flowerbeds full of unusual flowers. Odd gnarled trees stretched mossy limbs over their path creating a tunnel of green.

They passed neighbors sweeping their porches or trimming hedges. Each one came in a variety of shapes and sizes. None were human. The first house was round like a giant egg and filled with what appeared to be a family of large rabbits, who hopped upright like kangaroos and wore jackets and trousers. They reminded Jenny of the Beatrix Potter books.

Mamy didn't much like them *B-Trixers* in general, though she did fine with them individually. (Papy said, "they jes' wandered inta Frey, an' they jes' dinna belong here!"). But Jenny thought that they seemed pleasant enough. There were a lot of Beatrix Potter-like refugees who had built homes along the path they traveled. According to Papy, an island to the south had once been their home, but it had broken up and sank. The inhabitants piled onto any boat they could find and sought refuge on the continent of Frey.

"Not like the old days!" Papy commented while they passed a busy possum family. "There's just too many of 'em *furry-ners*. They keep makin' too many wee ones!"

"They'll be squeezin' us out wit' all their furry ways," complained Mamy.

Sometimes they'd pass strange creatures who looked like no animals that Jenny had ever seen. Some lived in tree houses. She saw tall spindly beings who traveled along the path in woven cocoon-like carriages, which reminded Jenny of gypsy wagons. Or old leathery beings in large hats atop unicycles, who'd wave to shiny striped quadrupeds singing drinking songs and tilling their fields. There was so much to see, smell, and hear that Jenny was in a continual state of surprise.

After they'd traveled a bit and the sights lessened in novelty, Jenny asked again, "Why would the Blue Queen want my blood?"

Papy walked alongside Jenny. "Well, there be two types of wishes if ya don't count big or small in the mix. There be reg'lar wishes, and there be dark wishes."

Mamy shook her head. "Dark wishes jest be trouble."

Papy continued. "Unless ya be a human, reg'lar wishes take a bit of coaxing to work. Ya have to keep 'em 'round ya and talk to 'em. Be friendly like. Once they get ta know ya, they might do ya a good turn. But, humans be diff'rent! They get their wishes right off as wishes take natural kindly to human types. This frustrates some folk no end - and 'parrently no one gets more angered 'bout it than the Blue Queen herself. The story be that she's turned ta dark wishes ta get what she wants. Dark wishes be hatched from fuzzy-wiggles growed on the blood of human children. Those wishes don't 'spect no niceties. They do exactly whatcha ask fer."

"But, they don't always do whatcha want!" Mamy muttered.

Jenny's new violet eyebrows scrunched together under her hood. "If there's no humans here, where does the Queen get children?"

"She's gots little secret doors all over t'place that lead ta your world – like the one ya came through. She catches children, then milks the blood out of 'em ev'ry mornin' like cow-beasts to feed her worms. She prob'bly has her Redduns 'ready off ta find ya and add ya ta her stable."

Jenny stopped and stared at them in horror.

Papy raised his hands to calm her. "But her palace be a bit-ways off. It's above Nor'city and that's a long shot away. It'll take a time for 'em ta get here and track ya. But they's got pow'ful noses."

Jenny's jaw dropped.

Mamy butted in, "Shush, Papy! Ya be scarin' her. Dearie, don't worry. Ya been crawling in fluffball dust since ya met Papy. Thar's nothing better ta make ya downright invisible to trackers. They won't be able t' smell ya at all."

Further down the canyon Jenny noticed the tops of roofs through the trees in the distance. As they got a bit closer she noticed burn marks on the trees, and bushes growing out of the rubble of burnt homes.

"What happened here?" whispered Jenny.

"The Blue Queen's wot happened," mumbled Mamy.

Their trail followed along the cliff base. As they passed around a large outcropping of orange and red striped rock, Jenny saw that the remains of a village lay below in a river valley. The river that they had been following from the east joined up here with a tributary from the north, and this village was nestled at the meeting of the two rivers.

A few homes still stood amid the ruins. Many looked to have been repaired from what remained of their neighbors' homes.

Jenny read a broken sign by the trail. *Welcome to Whippledell!* Like the village beyond, the sign had seen better days.

"The queen came ta power in a confusin' time." Papy said. "No body were right sure of wot happ'n'd ta the merKing, an' the Blue Queen were talkin' lots 'bout makin' Frey safe from furry-ners. She *seem'd* like she might be all right ta be in charge. She started l'arnin' the names o' folk real friendly-like. Next thang we knows, soldiers be attackin' villages and killin' and carryin' folks off! Folks gotta be 'fraid o' her. If'n she knows yer name, she kin kill ya just like that! She's got a great mem'ry fer names! So, folks do wot she says!"

They ambled along the main road of the village. An older white furry creature in a pink apron was sweeping off a ravaged porch. It looked like her home had experienced a fire recently. She gave them a miserable nod.

Papy waved. "Hiya Gertie. We, uh – jest takin' a wee 'venture wi' our friend, who be uh– a swamp witch. Nice sort uh – them swamp witch types."

Gertie was taller than Jenny and was sort of human-like. The longer fur on the top of her head was pink and lavender and swept up into a fancy hair-do that had seen better mornings. She had big eyes in a large head, and her furry body was sort of pear shaped. Gertie seemed weary.

Mamy pushed them all forward. "We gots ta be hurryin' 'long – sick kids ta tend!"

Gertie nodded with resignation, disappointed to not hear more news and returned to her sweeping.

"She be a fae," Mamy said quietly. "Thar be more of 'em in Frey than other sorts. Her nephew Floogle an' his fam'ly were carried off ta the castle wi' the rest. She be ev'r so worried 'bout him. Don't know if they be alive er dead."

Next door an elderly reptilian creature with eyeglasses sat in a rocking chair with a book. He nodded to them as they passed.

As Jenny and the Wishermans walked down the street with their packs, there were greetings and offers of tea and biscuits. Papy and Mamy were not unknown in this village. They politely waved, but kept to their path.

A stone bridge crossed the little river. Beyond the bridge, they passed empty homes and forsaken gardens filled with weeds.

Mamy sighed. "A lot of the folk that used ta live here – nice folk too – are now slavin' at the castle. If they be still alive. And now there be not 'nough hands ta care fer the fields here. It's a tough time fer all folk."

They spent that night curled up comfortable in a cave above the trail, and the next morning the three hiked along hidden paths till noon. They now hid behind bushes whenever they heard anyone coming up the road.

By late afternoon, Papy was leading Jenny and Mamy along a hidden path following the giant walls of OrangeRock

Canyon. The rock baked in the hot wind, so the shade of the foliage around them was welcome. Tall trees sang a rustling song of round silver-green leaves. They shimmered in the breeze like sequins on a Sparkletts' truck. The leaves' pattering sound lulled her worries of getting back home.

Bees with orange and blue stripes buzzed about strange flowers. Large butterflies fluttered about sun-dappled patchwork glades between the trees.

The canyon shifted to the left as they descended the canyon and became greener and lusher with growth. The sun was hot. Jenny appreciated the increasing shade that the higher cliffs provided. The main road below meandered in and out of sight between the trees.

Jenny realized that Papy was speaking.

"– when we get t' the Market, we may ha' some diff'culty gettin' our two big wishes. Hard ta perdict. Fortun'tly, with ya bein' in the tunnel wi' me when I be fishin', ah got an uncommon big haul of wishes. Ya be the best bait fer wishes I e'er had!"

"I was your secret bait?" Jenny laughed.

"Ya sure be. And, so ah's be tryin' to show me apprec'ation by helpin' ya ta get a big wish too. Though it might be tricksy."

Mamy nodded her head, which made the poof on the top of her head and her ears wobble. "The Water Witch is mighty pec'liar and tough to fig'ur out."

"But Mamy, she knows us. Ah've been doin' bus'ness wit' Mordette fer years now. She'll do us right. 'specially with Jenny wit' us."

"Oh, but that's what ah'm worry-shakin' about." Mamy argued. "Can we trust her? Jenny's worth a whole heap ta the Queen, and Mordette loves a profit."

"But Mordette don't like the Queen none."

"Where is the Wish Market?" asked Jenny.

"The island moves, but will be on the coast where the Riddle River pokes out in a few days. It floats about but it's usually thar on Nickelday."

"Nickelday?" asked Jenny.

"Nickelday! What's this? Don't ya know the days of the week? Ya look old enough ta know better!" griped Papy.

Mamy looked embarrassed for Jenny.

"But, we don't have a Nickelday where I come from." asserted Jenny.

"That is ridi'culous! How can ya not know the days of the week. Ev'ry six year old knowed 'em. Thar be eight days in a week. Thar be Nickelday – that's the first day of the week and good fer doin' chores. Then Wompday – named after the anc'ent god Womp – who did lots of Wompin' when *he* was aboot. Yessiree... young-uns just don't womp like we did back in my day..."

"What's Wompin'?" Jenny asked.

"Don't int'rrupt! Now, let me see. Next comes..."

"Shh!" Mamy warned and pulled both Jenny and her husband behind a bush.

There was a hubbub in the canyon below. A muddy dust storm whipped trees out of its path. It was one of the strangest sights that Jenny had ever seen.

The tornado of wet red dust traveled up the road! The tornado was taller than the trees. As it approached, Jenny could see arms and legs and blurs of creatures spinning around in the column of red goop. It zoomed right below their hiding place and on up the canyon leaving gooey trees and bushes in a slimy wake.

"Redduns!" Papy exclaimed. "Them's what the queen has sent after ya. We better be gettin' a move on."

"But, what are they?" Jenny asked.

"They be a dark mix of Red Cap and Fire Lizard – with a dash of Goblin," shuddered Mamy. "They be a wee bit dizzy, but they be persistent."

Papy set off down the trail. "We need ta get ta the Wish Monger and her floating Wish Market."

"Mordette the Water Witch?" Jenny clarified.

"Mordette." said Papy. "And if'n we're lucky, she's goin' to help us get two big wishes."

Mamy shook her head. "Maybe. Like you say, it's goin' ta be a wee tricksy."

Chapter 11

Red Snot Monsters

The Redduns

Even Redduns were not quite sure *what* they were after the dark wish. They were a perfect example of what can happen when a dark wish goes wrong.

Redduns were originally a variation of a Red Cap. Unpleasant faeries who dye their signature caps in their victims' blood. Everyone should have some sort of hobby. Splattering copious amounts of blood was their hobby. A way to pass the day like someone else might play checkers. This particular tribe of Red Caps had a spot of Goblin in their genes, which gave their large noses an obsessive sense of smell; and their scaly scarlet sheen came from a red dragon grand-sire.

The Blue Queen was one of the few who appreciated their enthusiastic skill set and naturally hired them to be part of her royal guard. She found them to be mildly incompetent but useful minions.

The land of Frey encompassed many difficult places to reach. This complicated the duties for a well-meaning tyrant. So, the Queen gave the Reddun tribe one of her treasured dark wishes to help them travel with more speed to these far flung locations.

The leader of the Redduns – Rudolfen by name – held the dark wish in his ruddy fingers and said "Ve vish ve Redduns ta be faster zan fast and ta go vereever ve want in ze blink of un eye!"

Well, that is what he intended to say. But for better or worse, Rudolfen had a terrible cold that morning and instead of saying *blink of un eye*, he sneezed.

And the dark wish obeyed!

From then on, the Redduns traveled in a giant tornado of sneeze. In their wet sneezy form, they could penetrate the smallest of cracks and reach the most impenetrable of places! They were as unimpeded as a sneeze from an uncovered mouth.

But unfortunately from then on, they couldn't help but catch each other's colds! When one travels together in a whirling, mucous-y army and your bodies are half air and half red booger dust for the duration, it goes without saying that it's not terribly sanitary.

Even so, they were as ruthless as a well-traveled virus.

Because they could not get rid of their colds, they began to look at their sickness as a badge of honor. A sign of their strength! They began to brag!

"I'ma so sick zat I coughed up a gunky as big as a Horned Banana Slug! AND ZEN AH ATE IT!" boasted Rolfer.

"Zat be nufink!" jibed Rubette. "I coughed up a gunky ze size of a Gnarled Sea Snail – complete vith shell! AND ze fing crawled away!" She cackled so hard that she snorted out a waterfall of ick.

All the other Redduns were impressed. Rubette was a slick number with curves like a ski slope covered in mucous. She had a slippery reputation for being fast.

The Blue Queen gave matching magical red handkerchiefs to each of the Redduns, which always stayed clean and dry no matter how much you used them. The Redduns were terribly proud of these symbols of favor.

Yet after their transformation, it became problematic to sneak up on anyone. Someone always sneezed at just the wrong moment.

On this particular day, they'd been traveling faster than fast – as usual. *Fast* being a relative term. They were much faster than a turtle, and generally faster than a typical goblin on foot. But sneezes are unpredictable and their combined sneeze rarely took the most direct route to anywhere.

The entry bell had announced the arrival of a child. They loved tracking down children, but it was frustrating that they couldn't have any bloody fun with them. They also needed to check the battery on the portal intake scanner to see if the changeling spores were generating correctly. Rudolfen worried about automation stealing the their jobs.

"Automation!" Rudolfen grumbled as they reached the crack in the rock above their destination.

"Vut?!" screamed Rolfer (at least it might have been Rolfer - it is difficult to tell when they were all disembodied body parts whirling in a gooey tornado)

"Neveryemind!" Rudolfen shouted back (at least he thought that it was his mouth that said this)

The tiny hole in the cliff was hardly big enough for a stinkbug to climb through, but the spinning mass of Redduns slipped right through and down through a series of cracks and fissures! Down to the tunnel deep below the earth! There were children to catch!

No one could escape the Redduns!

Chapter 12

Unexpected Events

Finn

Magic is a real thing? Finn still half doubted what he'd seen and tasted. But it *was* a really good sandwich. Crisply grilled bread, mouthwatering, gooey cheese and fresh tuna.

If magic existed, could he use it for more important things? Bigger things than magical tuna melts?

Finn had a secret that not even Jack knew about. He had a horrible disease that nobody knew about. His legs were covered with ugly lesions. That's why he quit swimming! They weren't exactly painful, but they looked awful.

Finn was afraid to show his foster parents. Mr. and Mrs. Jones regularly reminded him of how much work teenagers were to take care of. They resented that Finn had had never tried hard enough to get adopted. They hadn't intended to raise teenagers! Mrs. Jones liked cute babies. Precious infants! Precocious toddlers! Teenage boys were not interesting to her. His foster parents wouldn't want a kid with skin cancer! Maybe it was something contagious! He'd have to move to a new home! Probably some sort of awful group home. Finn wouldn't be able to see Jack any more.

Losing Jack was not an option.

So Finn hadn't told anyone what was going on.

But maybe this magic could cure him? Probably not. But what if? Since June, Finn had come to accept that he was going to die of something awful while still only a teenager. The white spots got way too obvious when he took a shower with the guys on the swim team. It was easier to say he had a rash from pool chemicals. His foster parents hadn't cared enough to question it. Even Jack believed him. But someday he'd probably be covered head to toe with the ugly white lumps and he'd look like a something out of a horror movie.

He knew he *could* tell Jack about a skin disease, but who wants to be the dying kid? And maybe Jack wouldn't want to hang around anymore if Finn turned all Quasimodo.

Maybe it was a punishment because he didn't pay attention in church. Maybe it was leprosy!

He probably shouldn't even touch Jack. Finn should absolutely avoid any skin to skin contact. But he kept forgetting.

Finn fiddled with the key around his neck. Aside from not dying a slow, excruciating death, he also had another wish... a wish that he'd carried since he was little... a wish that wove through every fiber of his being. Finn wanted to know what had happened to his parents! Were they dead? Were they alive? Why did they leave him at that aquarium?

"I wish I could find my parents," he whispered quietly. A tinkling sounded. Finn was afraid to hope that his wish might be answered. But no parents magically appeared. Maybe they really were dead.

Finn looked back to see Jack still chatting with Pinkie.

"Hey slow pokes! We're never going to get anywhere!" Finn was annoyed that Jack was bonding with that pink fuzzball.

Finn's relationship with Jack was complicated. He'd long figured out Jack's big secret. It scared Finn, but not for the reasons Jack was afraid of. What if these white spots were contagious? What if he was a walking Petri dish of disease? What if he endangered Jack every time they touched?

Finn didn't know how to talk to Jack about it.

Finn's key floated up from his chest and still attached to the cord, it hovered in front of him.

That was weird.

He removed the cord from around his neck and held it out. The loop of leather did not hang down straight. The key hung at an angle. Like a magnet, it pointed down the path.

"Check this out." Finn showed Jack what his key was doing.

"That's strange." Jack mused. "It's not metal. It's some sort of stone, isn't it?"

"I think it's pink jade."

"But it acts like it is pulled like a magnet."

"Like a compass?" Finn put the cord back around his neck, but he could still feel the key directing him forward.

They shrugged at each other.

It's hard to tell time underground. They'd been walking for what felt like forever. The now violet-hued tunnel snaked up and down, and turned this way and that. They didn't seem to be getting anywhere. The tunnel never branched. There were plenty of critters about, mostly disturbingly big insects, but no more Fuzzy-wiggles. And no more fluttering wishes about.

Finally Finn suggested they stop to rest. Finn pulled out his sketchpad and tried drawing the wall-climbing plants and some of the buzzing insects around them. He felt tired and discouraged, and not very talkative. But Jack didn't seem to notice. Jack chatted away with Pinkie like everything was fine.

Above them was a skeleton of a leviathan half embedded in the rock wall. Its teeth were huge. Finn was glad it was dead. He decided to sketch it and envision what it once looked like. Drawing was a form of meditation to him.

When they set off again, Finn was in a better headspace. What would it mean if magic *is* real?

Jack

"I'm beat." Jack plopped down on a wide rock at the side of the tunnel.

"Holy crapola. Me too." Finn plopped down next to him. "We gots to sleep at some point."

The tunnel floor was now mostly rock. They had no way of knowing if Jenny had passed this way or not. They hadn't seen Jenny's footprints since the fork in the road. But it was also really rocky, so they wouldn't necessarily show up.

"Split a PBJ?" Finn pulled a wrapped sandwich out of his incredibly useful bag.

"Sure. How much food do you have in there?" Jack was more freaked out than he wanted to admit.

"Not much." Finn pretended to be calm as he sat there with his half a sandwich. "Maybe Pinkette will be useful after all," he mumbled. "Just kidding!" he intercepted Pinkie's glare.

Jack gave Finn a disapproving look as he scratched Pinkie's head. She coiled about his feet. She was getting a lot bigger. "But, what if we never get out of here?" Jack leaned against Finn.

Finn blushed suddenly and stood up. Jack felt stupid. Finn obviously didn't want to be touched, but he kept doing it.

Finn pulled out their water bottle. "We've got to find more water at some point." He took a swig and passed it to Jack.

They'd filled it earlier from an underground stream, but that was a ways back. The water hadn't killed them yet, so it must be okay to drink?

Jack took a few swallows and passed the almost half full bottle back. "Maybe we should go back to where we were before. We can hit up that stream again, then maybe go back to the Fork?"

Finn didn't say anything right off. "We could," he sat back down. "But I've got to rest for a bit. My feet are killing me."

Neither intended to fall asleep.

It seemed only moments later when Jack woke up and realized his head was resting on Finn's chest. Pinkie's warmth was settled across their feet. Finn's arm wrapped around Jack and it made him feel... safe? Finn's chest rose and fell. He could feel the beat of Finn's heart.

When Jack moved to pull away, the sleeping Finn pulled Jack closer. But Jack needed to move. He was keenly aware of a significant tent erected in his shorts. He needed to extricate himself before Finn woke up.

Jack tried to pull away again, but Finn's hold tightened and his eyes opened. He looked at Jack with a surrendering smile.

"No worries." Finn sighed.

"But–"

"You've been poking my thigh all night."

Jack was mortified.

"It's okay," Finn whispered. "I've got one too."

Jack glanced at Finn's jeans. "Oh. You do." He wasn't exactly sure what to say next, but his heart was thumping madly.

Then Finn started giggling. And Jack started giggling. For a moment he forgot how scary things were.

Finn gave Jack a kiss on the forehead. Jack impulsively kissed Finn back – on the lips. There was a moment of indecision, and Finn returned that kiss.

Time disappeared.

Jack had never kissed anyone before. It was amazing. He hadn't ever considered that tongues were part of kissing. But apparently tongues were indeed part of kissing.

And Lips! He'd not realized that when lips touched lips, they felt like nothing else! Softness and plumpness, instinctually exploring movements entirely new. He definitely wanted to practice this a lot more.

Jack couldn't help but think, *is this weird?* To be kissing Finn? He'd wanted to kiss Finn forever, but he didn't really ever think it would actually happen. But kissing Finn wasn't weird. It felt natural. And Finn was smiling. Jack felt a weight lift off his chest. Their kisses were... life changing.

Afterwards, they just laid there on that rock... oddly comfortable in each other's arms.

Everything was suddenly right in the world. Whatever world this was. It was all... okay.

Jack whispered in Finn's neck. "Wow. That was... wow. I didn't know I was going to do that."

Finn kissed Jack again and closed his eyes. "I shouldn't be kissing you, but I'm glad you did. Didn't mean to fall asleep. Anything coming down the trail could have eaten us."

Finn sat up, pulling Jack with him. And they couldn't stop smiling.

Pinkie rolled over on her back and started snoring.

Then they were giggling. For some reason neither of them could stop laughing even though it wasn't that funny.

"Why shouldn't you kiss me?" Jack asked after sobering up a little. "Church stuff?"

Feeling guilty, Finn exhaled and stood up. Stepping over the fuzzy-wiggle at their feet, he put some distance between them. "I need to talk to you about something."

"Sure."

"Uh, next rest stop."

"Okay." Jack wondered if he screwed up somehow. *But no, he likes me. We're going to figure this thing out. And we're going to find Jenny! We are!*

Finn

Finn felt awful about kissing Jack and staying silent about maybe having an awful disease. Would Jack forgive him if he confessed? Finn hoped that magic was real. Maybe it could heal the white lesions on his legs, or whatever was wrong with him.

But maybe he was paranoid about nothing. Maybe the sores weren't contagious? Kissing was probably safe?

Pinkie still gave Finn the creeps. He didn't like seeing this carnivorous thing wrapped around Jack's neck. Finn wished it was just the two of them. It would be easier to talk... really talk.

Jack threw a pebble at his back.

"Finn, why are you being weird?" Jack hesitated. "Did I have bad breath? Am I a bad kisser? I haven't kissed anyone before. I think I can get better at it. Talk to me! Say something!"

Finn sighed. "No Jack, you were... that was nice." He shrugged quietly. "I haven't kissed anyone before either. I liked kissing you..."

"Then why are you being weird?"

"'Cuz I AM weird!" Finn deflected.

Smiling, Jack poked him. "I like you weird. But what's the flavor of weird today? Unless it's because..." Jack moaned. "Do you feel guilty about us kissing? That we might be... you know..."

"No. Yes. But no." He couldn't talk with *her* there. "I'm just not ready to talk about it yet."

"Okay." Jack's mood began to wilt. "But *something's* bugging you..."

Pinkie snapped up a fluttering wish and belched. "Exscusse me," she mumbled and nodded off to sleep again around Jack's shoulders. She had greatly increased in size and was starting to look like a very thick, pink boa. A very heavy boa.

Jack placed Pinkie on the ground. "You need to walk for awhile. You're getting heavy – no offense." Pinkie stretched as only a worm can stretch and wiggled forward taking no offense at all. She looked pleased that Jack had noticed.

Finn pulled his arm. "Jack, can we speak for a moment? *Without her,*" he whispered.

"Why? Pinkie's one of the team now."

"I wish it was just us." Finn muttered under his breath.

Jack wanted alone time too, but said, "She's going to be useful. I can feel it. Maybe she'll help us find Jenny."

Finn hissed, "She's a frickin' worm! What's she gonna do that's gonna be useful? Weave a frickin' cocoon? *It should just be us!*"

Jack countered. "It didn't bother you when Millie hovered around all the time."

Finn stopped. "What? What's that got to do with anything?"

"Pinkie's not even human!"

Finn blushed. "What? You weren't... that's just... you were jealous of Millie?"

Jack turned bright red. "Maybe."

Finn smiled softly. "Oh. Wow. Hmmm –" Finn stared at Jack like he was crazy, "No... no. No. It's *always* been you, Jack. Always... but... it's complicated."

"Oh?" Jack smiled. "Well I'm pretty smart if you just talk to me."

Finn shrugged, "In a bit. I'm sort of figuring out my own head right now. I just need to think."

Jack

Pinkie waddled behind as they ambled up the path. Jack had never felt such a rush of the adrenaline. Finn liked him! Like REALLY liked him. Jack's heart melted into liquid fire and surged through every vein. He felt surer and stronger and clearer than the old Jack. He nearly felt like he didn't need to apologize for existing anymore. Jack felt more like the Jack he'd always wished that he could be, but feared that he would never be.

Finn liked him! Finn liked kissing him! They might even do it again at some point. Hopefully soon.

Jack had never considered magic to be remotely possible. But here, Jack was surrounded by impossible things. The idea of Finn liking him *like that* had seemed doubly impossible. He sure hoped he wasn't dreaming. Church preached that there was no *happy-ever-after* for people like Jack.

In a sudden wave of guilt, Jack wondered if their kiss would send them to hell?

"Stop. I can read your mind." Finn grabbed Jack and pulled him close. Finn kissed Jack again, right there in the middle of the trail. "Don't feel guilty about this."

Time disappeared.

"Remember. You –" he touched Jack's chest, "You are the only one for me, Jack. I've got some serious stuff that

I've got to talk to you about, but I've no doubts about you and me. I really care about you. I always have."

And they kissed again.

They were still just standing there holding each other, lost in their embrace, when Pinkie tugged on Jack's pants. Pinkie stretched up and flicked her tail. "Carry me please?"

Finn groaned. He did not like bugs, worms, or fuzzy-wiggles. Particularly this one.

Jack was indeed tired of her company, but he disengaged with Finn and picked her up. She was heavy. She promptly went to sleep wrapped around his shoulders. Soon, she'd be too big to carry.

Jack also agreed that a little privacy at some point soon would be a good thing.

They continued walking.

The boys could still see the occasional giant bone embedded in the wall, but no complete skeletons. As they'd descended deeper underground, the light-giving flora increased till nearly everything around them glowed.

The path proceeded upwards for a bit, then it spiraled down and leveled out near a stream.

It began simply as a spring coming out of the rock between some ledges of fungi on their right. The water crossed the path in a wide muddy rivulet, which they hopped over. Other rivulets appeared and they soon became a deep sloshing river along the left side of their trail.

They could hear tumbling water ahead.

The tunnel's violet hues transitioned to a smooth blue-green rock streaked with golden yellow striations, which hinted of sulfur deposits – confirmed with a whiff. Not enough stink to be unbearable, but enough to remind Jack of angry pulpit sermons.

"Whew!" Jack exclaimed. "That's nasty!"

"Fossilized dinosaur farts! That's what sulfur really is. Read it on the Internet! Fossilized dino farts!"

"Ha!" Jack loved Finn's stupid jokes.

Jack noticed Finn's necklace floating up in the air, pointing towards the sound ahead of them.

Finn jogged up the trail with his bag swinging at his side. He turned to look back at Jack, "Can you hear it? Sounds like a waterfall!"

Finn raced around the bend in the tunnel and the sound of pounding water.

Jack sagged under the extra weight of Pinkie across his shoulders. He had to stop for a moment. Crap, she was heavy!

Finn

Finn ran up the trail to see beyond the crest and he found the source of the sound. Their river shot out beyond the cliff in a thundering torrent. The waterfall crashed down to a misty lake, which stretched across a vast cavern beyond.

"Check this out!" Finn hollered back over the sound of the waterfall.

Finn couldn't see Jack due to the jumble of boulders, but Jack's voice reached him. "We should go back! We haven't seen Jenny's foot-prints since the fork. We should go back!"

"Okay, but just a minute!" Finn yelled, "I want to check this out!"

Jack answered something, but Finn couldn't understand. The sound of the fall was deafening.

Pinkie

Pinkie had been feeling funny for awhile now. She was bigger than ever and lazily wrapped around Jack's strong shoulders like a pink stole. She'd been gobbling up every wish that came too close to her greedy jaws. Now she was strangely content and dreamy.

Finn

Finn was absentmindedly fiddling with his key when the cord and all slipped from his fingers and bounced over the edge.

"Damn!"

His Key! Finn plopped down flat on the rock to better see where his key fell. His eyes scanned the drop. The key was there on a rocky ledge! It glinted in some sort of nearby light.

It was some distance down, but if he was careful he could climb down and get it.

Finn heard Jack saying something behind him.

"What?" Finn shouted.

Jack's voice could hardly be heard over the noise of the water. "We should go back!"

Finn hollered over the roar, "I dropped my key! Just a minute! I'll be right back up!"

Finn carefully edged down the rocky outcropping beside the falling water, until he was about fifteen feet below the path above. The key sparkled from light coming from a cave behind the waterfall.

He picked up the key and returned it to his neck.

Looking towards the cave, Finn expected to see another phosphorescent plant, but the color was wrong. This was very pink light. And in the blue-green environment, it stuck out. Finn half slid down a bit of loose rock to better see into the cave's entrance behind the waterfall.

Jack

Up top, Jack laid across the rocky ledge to see what Finn was up to. "What do you see down there?!" He yelled over the roar of the water.

He saw Finn edge his way behind the fall.

Pinkie sprawled out on the rock beside him. She almost looked – well not that he'd ever smoked marijuana himself – Jack didn't do that sort of stuff, but he'd seen kids that were stoned before – and her eyes had that same spacey look.

Then Pinkie's eyes popped wide open and her outcry scared Jack half to death.

"Ssomething's coming!" she screamed. "Too sssoon! And Jacksy, I'm about to change!"

"What?" Jack shouted over the water. He sat up and looked at her.

She cried out, "Oh, Jacksy! I want to do sssomething important when I become a big wisssh. Through you! Remember me!" All at once – her eyes – wide and startled, Pinkie condensed in on herself in a strange kaleidoscope of color with a freakishly bizarre *whoosh!* Then that whoosh expanded and coalesced into an enormous fluttering ball of pure golden light that fluttered right in front of Jack. It was so bright he had to squint.

"Pinkie?" Jack gasped, not sure what just happened.

The golden ball shot straight into his open mouth and down his throat! He couldn't breathe! His gut burned impossibly, then his chest! The fire spread to his limbs and surged in scorching heat throughout his body! Jack had never felt such pain before.

Jack was screaming when the Redduns arrived.

The Redduns

The fearsome Redduns whirled to a stop, dropping the net full of fuzzy-wiggles, which they'd collected further up the tunnel. The Queen could always use more fuzzy-wiggles! The Redduns had been prowling underground for days searching for this kid!

Their stuffy yet accurate noses had successfully led them to this half-conscious, gasping boy near the top of a waterfall.

A fuzzy-wiggle stretched a fuzzy nose out of the net and looked at the writhing boy. It said, "George, I think we know him. But, humansss do look alike."

Another pushed forward to take a look. "Burt, I do think you're right, but he's changed –"

"Shaddup!" shouted the sniffling Rubette who gave them a whack, rolling the net to face the other direction.

OLLY, OLLY, OXEN FREY

The Redduns sniffed about. They only detected one human child. So, they pulled the oddly colored and delirious boy into their snotty embrace, and with a huff and a puff and a great deal of impressive hacking, their snotty storm magically traveled up through a maze of cracks and crannies and reached the surface in a great blubbery sneeze.

It was time to get back to the castle and do laundry.

Chapter 13

Changeling
Their Ways

The Changelings

The hospital sent the kids home on Monday evening. They had opened their eyes on Sunday afternoon. They'd looked around their shared partitioned room rather stupidly, but other than their newly white hair and pallid complexion and having no notion of who they were, they appeared to be in perfect health according to the hospital. The doctors mumbled something about shock, and amnesia, and perhaps an iron deficiency, and limits of insurance. They recommended bed rest and a return to normal surroundings as quickly as possible. They suggested a follow up appointment in a week.

So, the kids returned to their respective homes accompanied by their hospital bills. As a foster kid, Finn's health services were covered by the county. But Jack and Jenny's coverage wracked up some serious co-pays, which left their dad gasping. Even so, Mr. and Mrs. Saunders were happy to have their children home again – even if they did seem little different.

Authorities checked out Mr. Saunders' mushroom operation of course. But it checked out and the entire episode was filed as an unexplainable mystery with a happy ending.

The children seemed to pick up on their identities fairly rapidly after that.

Most folks noticed a distinct shift of personality as each began to navigate the world outside their rooms. For one thing, they now really loved their smart phones. Jack, Jenny, and Finn each previously owned cell phones before this, but the old Jack, Jenny, and Finn rarely spent much time on them. Those three kids were always more inclined to explore the bumps, tumbles, and scratches of the non-digital world.

But the new Jack, Jenny, and Finn took to their phones like ducks to water, mice to cheese, and dogs to mud. They now spoke to their parents in grunts and indecipherable murmurs while staring at their phones, if they spoke at all.

Finn's parents liked the new Finn much better. They understood a boy who liked his smart phone. Mr. and

Mrs. Jones very much appreciated their own smart phones. This new Finn went to Tuesday night bible study with no complaint – though he was glued to his phone throughout the lesson. But, small steps... The new Finn seemed more... normal.

The Saunders had mixed feelings about the change in their children. The new Jack and Jenny were certainly simpler to have around the house. They made no mess. They hardly went outside. After a bit, they were even pretty dependable with their chores with not a word of complaint. Jack didn't see Finn anymore, but they apparently texted regularly, so Mrs. Saunders supposed that was all right. That's what the kids did these days. It all seemed more comfortable in some ways that she didn't want to think about too much.

Millie

Millie was the only one who was suspicious about the new versions of her old friends.

She knew something larger was wrong, but she couldn't quite put her finger on exactly what. Jack didn't look at her like he resented her anymore, which was new. And Jenny took no notice of her – which was strange for a little girl who always hung on her every word. And Finn, well... Finn stared at her in quite a new way when she visited them in the hospital.

Chapter 14

The Nixies of Loot's End

Pirate Jenny

The Wishermans and Jenny traveled down OrangeRock Canyon until it expanded into broad farmland around the Riddle River. Despite regular rest stops, they were all exhausted.

From the top of a low hillock at sunset, Papy pointed to their right, where the river entered a swampy forest before the Riddle River reached the vast sea – which sparkled in the distance.

"Jenny, me girl, we be camping rough here tonight, but by tomorrow night, we'll be right comfortable in that forest." Papy Wisherman said with a big smile on his face.

"Oh Papy, we ain't be goin' and stayin' with the nixies agin! They ain't no proper type fer a young girl ta be hangin' 'round."

"Who're the nixies?" yawned Jenny.

Papy pulled out his pipe and started inspecting the little glen behind them. "Oh, don't ye mind Mamy. The nixies be all right w'me. Ah done 'em some good turns in me time." He took a puff of his pipe and sent out two smoke rings. "We're goin' ta be needin' a few things ta catch our big wishes, and they'll be havin' what we be needin'."

From Mamy's "Harumph!" Jenny deduced there was some disagreement on the creatures, which made her a bit curious. She wrapped herself up in her Swamp Witch cloak and pulled out her silver bowl and spoon. Mamy started organizing their dinner of scrumble-berries, while Papy set out their bedding a few feet away. After dinner the Wishermans went right to sleep. They snored. But Jenny was used to it after two nights in their company.

She wondered if her parents and Jack were missing her. Of course they missed her. School would have started... yesterday? She'd been in Frey for three days. She didn't want to go home till she rescued the Wishermans' children. And maybe all the other children too? That's what all the girls in the books and movies would do.

She'd sort out her parents' questions when she got home.

Kids always went home at the end of those books. She didn't have to worry... she hoped.

Nedderlin Swamp was a tricky place to navigate. The Riddle River pierced its way through the center of the swamp like a needle piercing a gob of phlegm. It was an icky path and lacked purpose.

But Papy knew secret logs and roots to travel by and they made good progress all things considered. By late afternoon, they were near halfway through the swamp and in sight of a strange tree village on the muddy bank of the river. *Welcome to Loot's End* said a crooked sign.

Jenny had never seen such a peculiar collection of trash assembled into a... well, it was colorful, and beautiful in its way. There were rainbows of strings and rope and twine that stretched from tree to tree like laundry lines. From these hung rows and rows of socks! Striped, polka dotted, cartoon covered, plaid, solid... all hung in sweeping rows back and forth throughout the village trees.

She thought, *so, that's where all the missing socks go...* Additionally there were round platforms sticking out from the trees like fungal growths, but they were decorated with bright magic-trick handkerchief awnings and... what looked like doll furniture?

Closer to the ground were boxes piled into towering spirals that wrapped around the tree bases. Each open box contained little apartments, which reminded her of nests – if the nests had been crafted by a toy designer.

She even saw little houseboats that looked like toys. Everywhere she looked there seemed to be human trash that had been cleverly repurposed.

Amid all of it, were small-ish fluttering creatures that moved very fast through both water and air. They were smaller than *Barbies* but bigger than *Brats*.

"Are those nixies?" asked Jenny.

"Yup!" Papy said with a smile. "Watch out, here they come!"

"Hold on to yer val'bles!" Mamy whispered. "They'll steal ya blind."

"We dinna steal!" A squeaky voice popped up near Jenny's shoulder.

"Not much-wise!" dismissed another voice down by her knee.

"Ya gotta hat under yer hump! Do ya really want it?" said a third.

"She not be usin' it. I think it be fair game!" said the first and Jenny suddenly felt her pirate hat inching out from under her cloak.

"Stop that!" yelled Jenny and shook her cloak till it was free of nixies. Then she grabbed her hat off the ground.

"That is MY pirate hat and nobody else's!"

"Many pardons t'be sure!" giggled the one who might have spoken first, but Jenny now had lost track of which one it was, as they moved around her so disconcertingly fast.

"We's just bein' friendly!" explained another.

"Do ya need this bowl and spoon?" asked a green one who started to float off with it.

"Give that BACK!" shouted Jenny as she snatched it out of the small Nixie's grasp, who then went into a bit of a nose dive after letting go of it.

Papy got the nixies' attention by hollering, "Me friends! It be so nice to see each of ya! Please don't take anything from Jenny here, or me Mamy. They don't yet un'erstan' yer ways. But, ah've brought some gifts fer ya that ya can steal o'er and o'er as much as it suits ya!"

At that, Papy opened a bag of small bric brac and the nixies swarmed it like bees.

"I do hope ya understand." piped up a wee voice quite close to Jenny's ear – making her jump. She turned to see a Nixie fluttering there. "We be only takin' from folk we like! That's why it be fun! Birdle takes me stuff all the time!"

Birdle zoomed past with a giggle.

"But, ain't people stealing your stuff kind of irritating after a while?" questioned Jenny.

"But, it tisn't *really* stealin' if folks don't want it. And we share everythin' here, so tis more of a lovin' game fer us! We be the very nature of loviness!" proclaimed the green nixie.

A deep growl behind them surprised them both, "Neddy, I don't think she's goin' ta understand ya ways."

Jenny turned quickly and shrank to see a big creature sitting amid the darkness of the winding tree roots. It was man-like with the head of a goat, and big curling horns on either side of its face. She instinctively recoiled from it... him. It was definitely male. He wore very little clothing beyond the tiny loincloth that left little to the imagination. Its hairy legs bent sort of backwards like those of a goat.

"Ah, shut yer trap ya big phooka!" Neddy shouted at the goat-man with a squeaky laugh and flittered off.

Neddy's rudeness softened Jenny's attitude toward the strange monster, though she was still pretty uncomfortable with how naked the creature was.

She pushed her nervousness aside.

"I'm Pirate Jenny," she stuck out her hand.

The phooka looked startled and stared at her hand with confusion.

"I'm sorry," sputtered Jenny. "I was just going to shake your hand. Like a friend, see?" She reached forward and grasped his large, clawed hand.

The phooka stared at her.

"Jenny! Ya be gettin' away from that thing!" hollered Mamy. "Ya can't never trust a phooka!"

"But, Mamy, what if he's a nice phooka?" Jenny turned and asked.

"Thar be no such thing as a *nice phooka!* It t'ain't in thar nature! Those shapeshifters be more likely ta eat ya."

Jenny still had hold of the phooka's hand and she caught a look in his eye. "Well, I don't think you'd eat me." She gave his hand a firm shake and let go of it. "It's nice to meet you, Mr. Phooka."

"Yar Mamy's prob'bly right. Ya shouldn't trust a phooka." mumbled the phooka as it ashamedly turned to go.

"But, you ain't told me YOUR name yet."

Turning back, the goat brows lifted with curiosity and then a curious goat smile spread across his face. "Ya can call me Footbe."

He stared at her closely for a moment, then he disappeared into a dimly lit cavern within the tree roots.

After a feast (that Jenny couldn't and didn't particularly wish to partake in) the entire village of Loot's End broke out into a wild party. At first she thought this was a celebration of their visit, but she learned from Papy that the partying was a nightly behavior.

She was tired from their travels, but from her high perch on a tree root at the edge of camp, it was fun to watch all the crazy antics that the colorful little nixies got up to. Each nixie would swipe stuff from other nixies, and it was a wild game to see them try to protect their hoards, but add to their hoards at the same time. None of the little creatures seemed to take ownership all that seriously.

Jenny didn't think she could live like that. She liked her stuff. But perhaps she now understood the nixies a little better.

"They be silly wee mites, but it's interestin' to live among 'em for a bit," came a growly voice behind her.

Jenny turned to see the phooka sitting on a root slightly above her. His face was in shadow with only spark-like reflections of the fire in his eyes.

"Hi Footbe!" Jenny hesitated. "They sure don't treat you very nice. Why's that?"

"Ah suppose ah've gotten used to it. Just part of bein' a phooka. We aren't too terr'bly trustworthy."

"But, I imagine you're as trustworthy as you want to be ain't you?"

"'Trustworthy' – 'tis a bit of a gray area – we all do what we gotta do..." He said reflectively while gazing at the fire below.

"I suppose," Jenny murmured. "But you're not evil like the Blue Queen is. She must be horrible."

The Phooka smiled. "Oh, but the Blue Queen can be nice when she wants ta be, an' beautiful in her way."

"But how can she be nice if she's as evil as people say?" Jenny wondered if maybe the phooka worked for the queen.

"Evil can be very nice – when it wants ta be. Most evil folk don't think they're bein' evil at all. It's a gray-ish world. What be evil but selfishness run amuck?"

"I'm selfish sometimes," Jenny confessed. "Does that make me evil?"

"Don't know," he shrugged. "Do ya try an' think o' other folk too?"

"Well, I try but I'm not always good at it."

"Well then, ya might have a little evil in ya," he chuckled. "Ya 'lways have the choice."

The night grew quiet as the nixies started a game of hide and go seek. The swamp was filled with the sound of crickets and the occasional splash of an alligator. Some sort of night bird hooted above them.

Jenny could smell wet tree roots and rich muddy pools of darkness. It didn't smell good but it didn't exactly smell bad either. It smelled like... life? Maybe it smelled like death. Or perhaps, Jenny thought it was a glass half-full or half-empty sort of thing. She decided the swamp smelled like living stuff.

"Mamy said that you're a shape shifter? Can you transform into anything?"

Footbe heaved a sigh. "Phookas can change inta anythin' 'bout their same size." Then he added bitterly under his breath, "And some can do more'n that."

Jenny looked at Footbe with awe. "You can change your shape –"

"Ah can't do nothin' of the kind," he interrupted.

"But–"

"Most phookas can. But, ah can't," He whispered with finality, "My life be a bitter one."

"Oh," said Jenny.

They sat in silence as whoops and hollers erupted from a sudden chase in the nixies' game below them. Mamy and Papy had gone into the little tree-cave nearby where they'd be staying the night. Jenny had been told not to stay out too long.

"There's something I don't understand," Jenny began. "At the nixie feast down there, they served a big roast something."

"And, did you eat any of it?" asked the Phooka.

"No, I can't because... well, I just can't. I have my own food. Um... allergies. But, I thought all the animals in Frey could talk?"

"They do."

Jenny stared at him.

"Then what... er... who were they eating?" gasped Jenny.

"Some sort of gator ah 'spect," answered the phooka.

"Alligators can talk too?"

"If ye're brave enough to in't'ate a conversation, ah s'ppose they do." chuckled the deep voice.

"But doesn't mean that they are a person if they can talk?"

"Do ye consider plants 'persons'?" came the reply.

Jenny laughed, "But plants can't talk. Of course, they're not *persons*!"

"Maybe ye can't understand 'em, but plants talk. I 'ssure ye. Ah've met some very talkative-like shrubs. And trees be lovely ta spend time with. Nicer than a lot o' other folk ah could mention."

Jenny was horrified. "But, what about carrots? And, uhm... Brussels sprouts?"

Footbe mused. "Well, perhaps for yarself, if ye can't understand a critter, it's okay ta eat it?"

Jenny was confused. "That doesn't make sense. I can't understand Spanish or Japanese but my mom wouldn't fry 'em up for Sunday night dinner."

"Maybe. But p'haps on some level that's what we all do," muttered the phooka.

She gave the phooka a questioning look.

He continued, "Eatin' be a part o' life. We get nour'shment from eatin' other livin' things. Everythin' eats somethin'."

"But..."

The phooka stopped her. "Ah've no partic'lar answers for ye. Ah s'pose we all just do what we think be best." Then muttered darkly, "It be a hard world – more bitter than sweet."

Jenny didn't find that answer at all satisfying. "Did you have any of the gator?"

"No," he chuckled. "Too chewy for me likin'."

Jenny lapsed into silence.

The gravely voice purred again from the darkness above. "What are ya? If ya don't mind me askin'?"

"What? Oh..." she stretched, finally feeling her lids to be a bit droopy. "I'm just a girl – uh, swamp witch. I mean a girl swamp witch! As opposed to a BOY swamp witch," she ended lamely.

"Ah see," the phooka said thoughtfully.

Jenny yawned. "Well, I'm thinking that it's time for me to turn in, before Mamy and Papy start worrying. It's been nice to talk with you Mr. Phooka."

"Footbe."

"Yes, okay. Mr. Footbe," she yawned again. "Good night!"

"Good night, Pirate Jenny," murmured the phooka, who sat contemplatively on the root for sometime after that, staring after the little *swamp witch*.

The phooka was remembering something.

Apparently, the nixies hosted various sized guests somewhat regularly, so Jenny and the Wishermans were tucked safe and comfortable within a Fluffball sized tree-root hollow – a smaller version of the phooka's. It was a bit small for Jenny, but it was kind of fun at the same time.

She had made it through the evening without anything disappearing, though the Wishermans did lose a scarf.

"Why's everyone so unfriendly to Footbe?" Jenny asked while she rolled herself up in her cloak on a not entirely soft mattress of leaves and stuff that she didn't want to inspect too closely.

"Footbe? The phooka?" questioned Papy.

"Why don't you like him?"

"Well, phookas in gen'ral are most-wise lookin' only for their own good, an' that part'clar phooka is cursed with a shunnin'. He ain't 'llowed ta live 'round good folks. He gotta brand on his behind given him by the Blue Queen, herself."

"The same Blue Queen that you don't like?"

Mamy growled. "Yeah, but sometimes even she be knowin' what she be doin'. Phookas are no good. They be just born that way."

Jenny watched while Papy pulled out a long stick, some netting, and the Hula Hoop that he'd bargained for with the nixies. He started weaving them together into what looked like large butterfly nets.

"Are those to hold the big wishes?" Jenny asked.

"That's what they be!" Papy answered.

"If nixies go back and forth between Frey and my world, couldn't I just hitch a ride with them when we're done rescuing your kids?"

"Nah. The doors they go through be much too tiny fer ye ta fit!"

Jenny sat up and looked out a round window that was framed by roots. She watched the nixies climb into their socks for the night. They reminded her of little sleeping bags on a clothesline.

Jenny wasn't sure she could ever get used to all the back and forth of possessions, but it seemed to work for the nixies.

She lay back on her lumpy bed.

"Good night," she murmured.

"See ya in the marnin'," mumbled Papy.

Mamy was already sound asleep.

Morning came with a *BOOM!*

Jenny gasped and sat up. Outside their door she could hear screaming.

Papy was at the window hollering, "PIRATES!"

Chapter 15

The Mermaid

Finn

Finn heard nothing of what had happened up top with Jack. With the roar of the water hitting the lake below him, Finn carefully maneuvered his way across the wet and treacherous rocks towards the waterfall. A glowing cavern could be seen behind it.

Obviously, the chamber was not created by Mother Nature. Marble columns flanked the entrance and the floor was a checkerboard of violet marble. In the center of it all, a crystal tube stretched from floor to ceiling. Its base was marble, but sculpted to look like intricate undersea plant

life. The tube gave off the gentle pink glow that he'd seen from outside.

Within the glass – floated a mermaid. Asleep?

Finn couldn't believe his eyes. She was the most beautiful being he'd ever seen.

Her hair was a pale shade of blue – nearly white. It floated around her like she was in some sort of underwater hair commercial. Her tail was a soft shade of lavender with sparkly depths in its scales. And her skin – well it was hard to describe. It was fair and similar in color to Finn's own skin but opalescent like the inside of an oyster shell.

She floated. Thick blue lashes rested on high cheekbones. It was as if Finn had waited all of his life to see her – and she did not disappoint.

Finn loved all the carved undersea flowers and sea flora, and the winding tentacles weaving through the design of the pink marble base. It was beautifully fitting for the creature inside the glass. Worked into the sculpture was a brass steam-punk sort of injection device that seemed designed to treat the water?

And in the center of the base, right in the front, was a round flat surface with a keyhole in the center.

And he knew right then, like it was all tied up with fate. He didn't understand how events conspired for him to be in this place in this moment. But the keyhole was for HIS key. It didn't make any sense. Yet the key had brought him here. The key around his neck with *Finn* carved into the top. The one that he'd had since he was a baby. It matched the carvings around the keyhole.

He looked around the rest of the small cave. There was nothing but the tube. There were no clues as to who she was or what was going on.

Finn couldn't wait to get Jack down here. This was amazing.

He dropped his bag on the floor, took a last glance at the sleeping mermaid and edged his way out from behind the waterfall (getting wet again in the process). He crawled up to where he'd left Jack at the top of the waterfall.

No one was there. No Jack. No Pinkie.

"Jack! JACK!" he called.

Then he saw the red on the ground. Red like blood, but thick like – snot? It was disgusting. But – he didn't think it was blood. Or was it?!

Finn ran down the path following the trail of goo until it disappeared into a crevice in the rock.

He looked about. "Jack! JACK! JACK!"

He could only hear the roar of water.

NO! His heart was beating so hard he couldn't think. Jack! *He couldn't be gone.* Jack wouldn't have left without him! Jack! Finn sank to the path. It was like he'd been punched in the gut. Jack! He almost couldn't breathe.

Finn was alone! Jack was gone! Just like that.

He couldn't believe that Jack was gone! Did Pinkie eat him and escape into the crack? He disliked her, but he didn't think she'd do that. She might've eaten Finn. But not Jack. Damn this place! How was he to know what the rules were here?

If Jack was still alive somewhere... and Jack *had* to still be alive somewhere... he couldn't think otherwise! *Finn had to find him.*

The mermaid. She *looked* nice. Of course, she could be a sociopathic man-eater. He'd read the stories where mermaids were homicidal. But she *looked* nice? Maybe, she would help? He'd try to wake her up.

Finn raced back down the trail and half slid, half skidded down the embankment, nearly falling into the lake far below. Splashing through the edge of the waterfall, he entered the mermaid's chamber again.

His bag was lying where he'd left it. The mermaid was waiting for something.

For Finn?

There was the keyhole. He hoped it did something useful.

He removed the pink jade key from around his neck. Holding his breath, he slid it into the keyhole. It fit perfectly. He turned it gently and heard a faint click beneath the floor.

Bubbles filled the tube, hiding the mermaid!

Finn grabbed his bag and jumped back as the lights sequenced through rainbows of bubbling water.

The tube began retracting into the floor, and as it descended he could see that the top lip of the tube was lower in the front, causing the water inside to pour frontwards. The checkered floor's slight grade (which he hadn't noticed until now) sent the wash of water out towards the lake.

But alarmingly, as the tube descended into the floor, the mermaid who'd been so beautiful – began to shrink and distort! By the time the tube fully descended into its base, the dazed creature in the shallow pool looked like a... a humanoid monkey with a polliwog tail. Like the old cartoon advertisements for *Sea-Chimps* in Finn's vintage comic book collection. (Of course the real *Sea-Chimps* were just brine shrimp that terribly disappointed the kids who ordered them).

But here... right here in front of Finn... was the real deal. Like Gollem with a fishtail and boobs. Long, dangling boobs. And she had straggly white hair. She was about three feet long... high... he wasn't exactly sure how one would go about measuring it.

Her.

She looked at herself in horror and on the verge of hyperventilating.

She screamed at him, "WHAT HAVE YOU DONE!! THIS ISN'T HOW IT'S SUPPOSED TO WORK!!"

Finn had no idea of what to say. He simply stared at the little creature in surprise. He sank to the floor and put his head in his hands. He'd never been so stressed before in his entire life.

He didn't know what to do.

The creature was clearly exasperated. "THE CURE! YOU'RE SUPPOSED TO ADD THE CURE *BEFORE* YOU TURN THE KEY!"

Finn exploded, "How the HELL am I supposed to know about a frickin' cure! Did you leave any instructions! NO! Look around! I am so SICK and TIRED of this ridiculous place!" He plunged his face back into his hands. "THIS DAY CANNOT GET ANY WORSE!!!" He shouted.

The little sea chimp with the boobs gazed at Finn and sighed, "I think I'm your mother."

Chapter 16

Blood Hall

Jack

Jack woke up in a very scary place. His arms were manacled out to either side like in a crucifixion, and he was almost naked!

His head jerked down to see that he was wearing DIAPERS! With a baby blue diaper pin. DIAPERS?!!! He was completely freaked out on so many levels. Someone had taken his clothes off! Someone and had seen him NAKED! Where were his clothes?

He was manacled half way up an enormous stone wall. There was a little outcropping for his butt to sit on. The ground was far below him. His feet rested on a narrow ledge. To either side he could see other diapered kids for at least three rows above him and then another three rows below him. There were a lot of children manacled on this giant wall.

Jack looked down again and his heart beat at the distance between his feet and the floor.

The light was dim. He was in some sort of golden spotlight. Across the room, he could dimly see a stone wall where large cages were stacked, but it was too dark to see what was in the cages. Being almost naked made him feel particularly vulnerable. At least it wasn't cold. The kids around him were pale and of a variety of ages. Mostly his age and younger. None of them seemed very alert... it looked like they'd been drugged.

Jack gradually became aware that the golden light around him was coming from himself! He was GLOWING! That was weird. His skin was golden and radiant like he'd just leveled up in a video game. In a flash, he remembered Pinkie bursting into a giant, golden, fluttering wish and zooming down his throat. He remembered the pain. Then awful red creatures. Then nothing. Finn! Where was Finn! Did they get him too? Could this be what happened to Jenny?

He strained his neck to look for either of them.

Jack didn't see them, but that didn't mean anything – it was a big wall. They could be here somewhere. He didn't know what to do! He wasn't even sixteen! How was he supposed to know how to deal with stuff like this! This is the stuff they should be teaching in school instead of stupid football and baseball. They should teach kids how to escape from manacles and dungeons!

Would his parents ever know what happened to him? To Jenny?

And he was crazy hungry.

He began to be aware of small creatures climbing up and down the grout lines in the wall. They looked a bit like large beetles, but they had little human-like faces. They wore pointed red hats that cantilevered off the back like woodpeckers.

Tubes ran along the grout lines. Red tubes. These tubes ran up to little buckets under the wrists of each child. Hanging under each child's wrist was a little swing situated under two nipples that hung from the veins in each child's wrists.

Little beetle-men sat in the tiny swings and merrily milked the children's blood. They sang as they milked:

> "*Red may be the milk from thee!*
> *More white each morn ye'll prob'bly be.*
> *Thy face be white, thy neck be white,*
> *thy hands be white, thy feet be white!*
> *Yet ye've no need to take much fright —*
> *We take not much, so dream ye free,*
> *While we milk yer blood from thee!*"

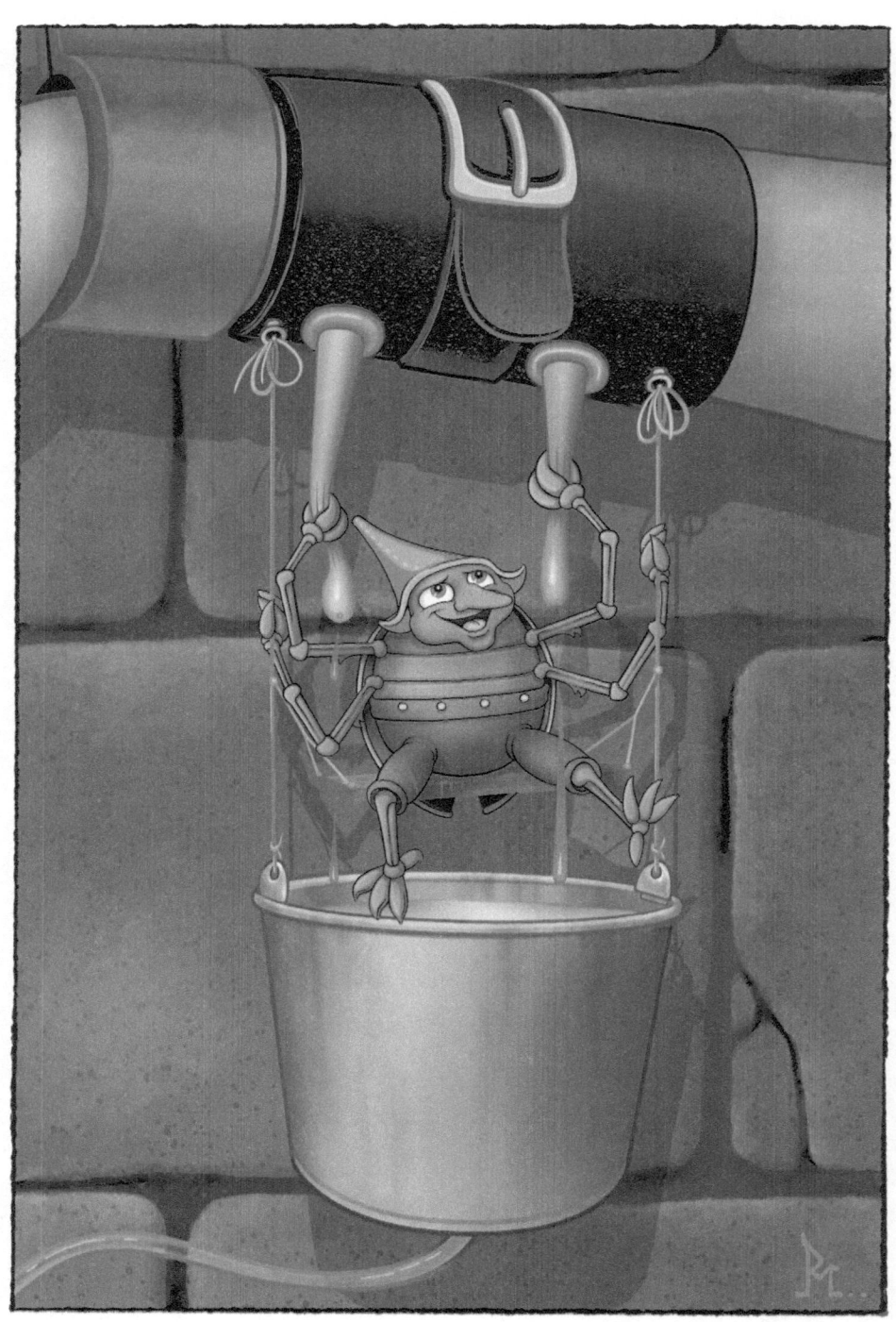

Jack was more freaked out than he'd ever been in his entire life. The children seemed half asleep and unaware of what was happening to them.

Just then came a wee voice. He turned his head to see one of the little creatures step off of the grout-line running behind his head and step onto his forearm.

Ouch!

"So, how ye be doin' this fine morning!" asked the beetle-man with a cheery wave.

Jack felt tiny pin pricks as this bug-like person walked across his skin. He shook his arms and body wildly. "GET OFF OF ME!!" he screamed.

But horrifically, the creature did not come off his arm. The creature had curved little prongs on his feet that hooked into his skin like a mountaineer. The little prongs hurt more than ever after shaking his arms like that.

The creepy beetle-man smiled. "Don't ye be like that with me, me friend! We're goin' ta be havin' a nice time tagether! I'm goin' ta be givin' ye some nice dreams! Won't ye be likin' that? Now, what be yer name?"

"I'm uh, Jack? Where am I! Where's Finn? Where's Jenny?" Jack's panic was increasing so fast he could hardly speak. He could hardly breathe!

"Oh, calm yerself down, me-boy Jack. Yer a guest of the Blue Queen! Now don't ye feel lucky at that! Ye arrived by yerself, but who knows, thar may be Jennys and Finns on the wall here. I ain't learnt all their names as we're each special assigned so we c'n get ta know the right sorta dreams ta make ye most happy. Ain't that thoughtful of the Queen?"

It was a nightmare that Jack couldn't wake up from. All of the events that led up to this moment piled up in Jack's head and he simply broke. He fell apart and started sobbing uncontrollably.

The little man whispered in a panic, "Hey, now don't ye be goin' like that! Uh, me name be Pricker. Don't cry." The little creature looked around rather embarrassed. "I'll be losin' me job if ye dinna pull yerself together. I'ma here ta make ya happy – not sad!"

Jack sobbed harder. His shoulders shook with gasping breaths that he'd lost every bit of will to control.

"Thar, thar... ye know ye be mighty special – what with yer glowin' and all. We're act'ally not quite sure jes' what ye be – all golden-like. Who's ta say what's goin' ta be happenin' ta ye. And the Blue Queen herself is comin' all ta way here ta see ya! Ain't that an honor for ye?"

The little creature with the red pointed hat took another apprising, conspiratorial look at Jack. "Ye seem to be a strong stout lad – perhaps ye'd be likin' dreams of this

Jenny lass ye be mentioning? I could give ye some sweet dreams 'bout her – eh?" He grinned devilishly.

Jack gasped mid sob and gaped at the little man in horror. "She's my little sister!"

"Oh, well, that may be a wee bit irreg'lar, but.... oh." Pricker took another look at Jack and reassessed. "Well how's 'bout dreams of that boy... Finn, he be called? Maybe ye'll be liking those dreams better?" he said with a knowing smile.

Jack screamed with every ounce of his being. "GET AWAY FROM ME! I *WISH* EVERY ONE OF YOU DISGUSTING LITTLE CREATURES WOULD GO AWAY!!"

Pricker's eyes widened at the sound of magical tinkling and then, the startled little man disintegrated into nothing. He was gone. And there was silence. All the merry singing in the vast stone room had ceased.

Jack stretched his neck this way and that. All the awful little creatures were gone. Just like that.

He hardly knew what to think, but when he looked down, he saw that his left leg was no longer glowing.

"Oh," Jack thought.

A moment passed.

"I *wish* these manacles would release me?" he tried.

There was another delicate tinkling sound and both manacles clicked open. He quickly grabbed hold of one and found himself hanging above the floor far below. Two of his fingers were no longer glowing.

"Pinkie... thank you. Thank you," he whispered. He took a big breath and steadied his thoughts.

A thick red tube ran down to the floor to his left. He edged his way over and climbed down it like a rope. He ignored its bloody contents and hoped it was tightly secured at the top.

At the base of the wall, he stood back and looked up at the rows of half conscious children who were unaware of everything.

Jack ran along the base of the wall to see if either Jenny or Finn were among them. No Jenny. No Finn. He counted fifty-seven kids in all.

He didn't know what to do.

Jack looked around the vast room. He didn't see his clothes anywhere. Globular lights were mounted in iron tentacles that sprouted from the walls in a few spots. The ceiling was high. The stone masonry around him was like that of a medieval dungeon but there seemed to be a tentacle theme worked into the rough stonework. Above that, there were rough hewn beams supporting a dark ceiling. To Jack's left was a monstrously large Gothic arch and a large hall beyond.

To his right the wall was a honeycomb of tiny arches and staircases sized to the little red-hatted creatures. Who were now... gone. The miniature stairways seemed all the smaller for a room otherwise proportioned for a giant.

Opposite to the wall with the children was the wall with the stacked cages. Heavy footfalls sounded in the great hall to his left.

He turned to the unconscious children above him on the wall. He didn't know what to do!

Then he did.

"I wish all the locks in this room would unlock and that each of you children wake up in your own homes – healthy and sound!" he called out.

There was a tinkling sound. And they were gone. Every single child. Gone. Hopefully to their homes.

And gone also was the glow from his arms, torso, and right leg. It didn't appear that he was glowing anywhere now.

Whoops.

No more wishes. He ran towards the stack of cages to hide.

"Well. That was impressive," came a thunderingly loud yet surprisingly sweet woman's voice. "Irritating of course. But... impressive."

Jack turned towards the arch and saw the largest woman he'd ever seen. She was taller than the tree that held their tree house. She was blue. She wasn't human... there was something reptilian about her face.

The Blue Queen.

OLLY, OLLY, OXEN FREY

She was beautiful in a peculiar way, though her chin curved up into a horny point, as did her eyebrows and her cheekbones, which swept out into their own points. Her hair – if it was hair, swept back up from her head and gave her another six feet of height as it curled and flared out like shelves of lichen.

And Jack felt helpless. He was in a diaper. His knees were shaking.

He was frickin' terrified.

But then, he sensed that he DID have *one wish* left. He could feel it!

Jack knew that down in his diaper, there was *something* that was still glowing...

Chapter 17

Not Entirely Human

Rip-One

Rip-One was the Redduns' dispatcher and accountant. All organizations have someone who does the bookwork. It is often hard to remember that behind every group responsible for horrible behavior, there is probably someone who tallies those horrors up into hopefully lucrative little columns. What's the point of bad behavior if it's not profitable?

Rip-One was not particularly good at accounting. Nor was he particularly violent by the normal standards of his Redduns family. His name had nothing to do with

performing violent acts, but had everything to do with why he didn't travel in the intimate swirl of goo with the rest.

Rip-One struggled with gas. Not just the mild little toots of your grandma gas, but *foul-and-effusively-flatulent-with-a-tendency-towards-disturbing-wetness* sort of gas. The type of gas that not only clears a room, but burns it down and requires hazmat suits for a good fifty years afterwards sort of gas. And as tolerant as the Redduns were towards other ickiness, they drew the line at gas. Gas is flammable (as many a drunken frat boy has had the painful opportunity to discover). When a swirling tornado of snot is infused with as much gas as Rip-One could produce, the dangers were tangible.

It wasn't fair of course! He deserved to be out adventuring and having nasty fun with the rest of them! But it was not to be. Rip-One was given the job of bookkeeper – because it kept him out of the way.

This morning, he sipped a hot frothy cup of bloody mouse latte and lazily perused the messy stack of reports. Rufus and the gang had returned from their mission. They laughed! They congratulated themselves on their cleverness in the echoing hallway outside his little office. He'd wanted to go on that mission, but they'd turned him down *again*.

He hated them. He wanted to be one of them. He hated every gooey brother and sister he had. But... it was awful to always be alone.

In front of him was a printout from the most recent intake door. He was rather proud of how he'd modernized things. Using a combination of magic and mortal world supplies that he'd cleverly bargained for from the nixies, he'd installed scanners at each of the traps where children fell into Frey. He also had installed alarms around sensitive locations around Frey. When any of these were triggered, he sent out the team.

The child was supposed to have been a seven-year-old girl – which was not what they just brought in with the wiggling bag of fuzzy-wiggles. The old scanners now were rather belatedly showing the arrival of two almost sixteen-year-old boys. He was surprised they got through the door, as sixteen-year-olds were almost too old for the Queen's needs. Obviously one of them was still free – in addition to the seven-year-old. That dodgy battery in the scanner was crazy-making.

The device scanned the bodies sucked through the magic door, and also kept the door shut against adult humans. They also collected the genetic data for the quick grow changeling spores that were released after the children were grabbed. It had clearly malfunctioned from its years of non-use. Maybe the tube was clogged. Something was wrong. He'd have to go out into the field and check it out. Of course, that first changeling seed would probably be defective... sitting at the end of the tube like that and exposed to air. Hard to say. Changelings often don't live long enough to become human. Probably didn't matter. They were just temporary copies. But he did need to check the device to make sure it was working.

That door hadn't picked up any children for years. He'd been ready to submit a *change-in-location* form to the *Acquisitions Department* who handled those things. He was rather fond of a feathered lizard in there who wore the most tantalizing red glasses. Sheela. He still might submit the form as it would give him an excuse to say hello. Sheela had no sense of smell whatever. He found that kind of sexy.

The Queen would like that fresh stock of fuzzy-wiggles.

Rip-One took a second glance at the report. This was interesting. One of the sixteen-year-olds was only *half-human?* It wasn't clear what the other half consisted of. That spore's genetic material would have had to adjust to the missing data. It probably simply extrapolated from the human side.

The boy they caught was golden and glowing. Rip-One suspected that wasn't normal. Perhaps the half-human? Either way, there were still two children on the loose.

He could tell the other Redduns. But perhaps not. Perhaps this was an opportunity to show his quality to the Queen...

Maybe he could discuss it with Sheela? The glorious Sheela. Over a warm frothy mouse whipped into a tender romantic meal? *Maybe he could catch these missing children himself?*

Chapter 18

Pirates!

Pirate Jenny

"Pirates!" came the screams of nixies down by the river. Jenny and the Wishermans grabbed their belongings and raced out the door to find someplace safer.

Jenny felt a strange mix of sheer terror and overwhelming excitement. "Pirates!" She desperately wanted to see what they looked like.

Boom!

Crack!

Jenny screamed.

A blast of something colorful slammed into a tree nearby and left quite a dent. The cannon ball broke into a thousand pieces and showered down on them.

Boom!

Crack!

Another ball slammed into a root right above them. They jumped aside as the ball bounced off the tree and rolled near them without breaking.

"That looks like a Jawbreaker!" Jenny ran up to inspect the smoking ball. "The biggest Jawbreaker I've ever seen!"

It was about eight inches in diameter, but she licked her finger, rubbed it across its rainbow surface and then tasted it.

Sweet.

"Yup. That's a Jawbreaker."

She was now more curious than ever to see what these pirates looked like. Mamy and Papy climbed under a root to hide.

"Hurry quick Jenny, or ye'll be cap-smackled!" Papy whispered as loud as he dared.

Jenny turned to follow, but had to take a quick peek

to see the crazy
h a p p e n i n g s
below them.

"No Jenny!
No! Wait! Stop!"
Mamy hissed!

"I'll be right
there!" Jenny waved
back.

Jenny looked.

Below her was a row of
nixies all tied up along a log and they
seemed to be... giggling?

In front of the nixies were the pirates. They weren't at
all what she expected! They were short. Quite short. She
thought they might be about as tall as Papy... about up to
her waist (Whereas the nixies wouldn't come up to her
knee). The pirates had big furry heads atop small furry
bodies. The pirate costumes were amazing. She loved all
the miniature hats and scarfs and blousy shirts.

"Up there!" hollered a high voice.

"– to catch a captive fair!" shouted another voice.

"Behind the tree!! added the first voice.

"She should DESPAIR!" yelled the second.

"Aye, tremble ye! And say yer prayers!" said a third.

"NO ONE ESCAPES THE BROWN CORSAIRS!"
They all sang in unison and leapt in her direction!

And faster than she could have thought possible, Jenny, Mamy, and Papy were trussed up and carried below by a crowd of diminutive, furry pirates.

It was while sitting on the log alongside the still giggling nixies, that she recognized what they were!

"You're Brownies!"

There was a sudden silence. Even the nixies stopped giggling.

Jenny continued. "You're in one of my books at home!"

The brownie pirates all groaned as one!

"Arh! Those cur-sed, blas-ted books!
Damning us to po-esy hooks!!"

sang three tenor brownies in harmony.

"No curse in hell 'smore fine-ly wrought
than forced to rhyme when we would not!"

-added another three who had particularly deep voices.

Neddy the nixie then piped up, "Ye shouldn't be mentioning those books! Its just ter'ble! Since those books came out, the brownies all be speakin' in verse. They ain't even allowed ta do free-verse!"

"That's why they be such fearsome, but romantic corsairs!" giggled little Birdle.

Mamy gave a great big sigh. "I really wanted ta avoid all this."

"Abs'lutely, their po'try is just awf'l!" complained Papy.

Jenny looked at all the tittering nixies. "Ain't you supposed to be a little more upset about bein' captured by pirates?"

A little green nixie piped up, "No! It be ever so excitin'," she shrugged. "Though 'tis true they don't play the takin' game the same as we do."

"But it *is* fun ta get tied up and all!" cooed a pink one. "I so love me a bit of Cap'n Billy Blind!"

The pink nixie wiggled his brows at an extravagantly dressed brownie who modestly shook his head with a raised hand. He sang out with a rather golden baritone voice:

"No time for pillagn' play today
we're here ta take this child away!
We got the word a girl be seen
that might be temptin' ta the Queen!"

At that, Cap'n Billy Blind (who didn't seem blind at all) gave a genteel smile to the crowd with a florid bow.

And Footbe the phooka stepped out from a shadow.

"Ye'll have ta forgive me and these piratical poets. We all be more than tired of our shunnin's from the Blue Queen. We be hopin' that she might be removin' 'em *if* we paid a visit with *yerself* as an offerin'."

Of course it was hard to tell with a face like a goat, but it seemed to Jenny that he looked a little sheepish.

"I told ye he be no good!" cried Mamy.

Soon a pirate ship pulled up alongside the village. Despite the circumstances, Jenny thought it was the most beautiful miniature pirate ship that she'd ever seen. The entire boat was about the same length as her dad's old VW van.

What it had in charm, it lacked in comforts.

The pirate ship was called *The Palmer.* The wind filled out its green sails as it sailed out of the Riddle River and into a beautiful lagoon. Jenny could see the open ocean beyond the harbor's mouth.

The phooka was seated in the back of the ship – filling up most the poop deck – his spread legs allowed just enough room for a brownie navigator to man the wheel. Jenny wondered if that should be *brownie* the wheel... but then again... perhaps not... especially not on a poop deck.

Jenny, Mamy, and Papy sat up front on the forecastle or bow of the boat. Jenny was proud that she knew the correct terms. They were still tied securely.

Jenny felt horrible for disobeying the Wishermans when they told her to hide.

Papy sighed. "Well Jenny, it prob'bly wouldna done any useful-good anyways as they knew you was there somewheres."

Capn' Blind said that Papy would get back his basket of wishes and the giant net thing, but they had been chained up below for *safe-keeping*. The pirates had even offered (in verse) to drop Papy and Mamy off at the Wish Mongers floating island, if they could time it with the floating island's arrival. Jenny was surprised they were so nice. She wondered if she could talk the brownies into *not* handing her over to the Queen.

A young brownie named Gibbie polished wood near her and he whistled while he worked.

Jenny decided to be friendly. "You're doing a beautiful job with that woodwork."

Gibbie gave her a proud smile.

"The chore with boats 'tis not the sea
but all the woodwork that thar be."

"So," Jenny whispered, "I'm a bit curious. What IS a shunning?"

Gibbie gave her a sad look and to Jenny's complete surprise, he pulled down the back of his britches to expose a brand on his butt that said 'SHUNNED!'.

"When ye be shunned, the case is shut!
Ye get a brand upon yer butt!
Tho' could be worse – instead of butts
it might ha' been upon me –"

"Ya jest stop right there!" shouted Mamy. "Thar be ladies present!"

Which made all the brownies nearby giggle hysterically.

But Jenny was undeterred. "But what happens when you get shunned?"

Gibbie opened his arms expansively and sang,

"If ye be shunned, ye're forced to shirk!
Ye can't be used fer hon'st work!"

Jenny laughed, "But if you're wearing pants, how would they know if you've got a brand or not?"

To Jenny's surprise even the Wishermans looked amused at her question.

Gibbie responded,

"But all folks know to earn a crumb
ye gotta show yer boss yer bum!"

Papy spoke up. "That's why all Wishermans be self-employed! Or at least-wise ah'm only employed by Mamy here!" he laughed. "And she's seen me butt!"

Even Mamy laughed at that.

Jenny blushed and wasn't sure what to say. "I don't think it is like that where I'm from. Sounds kinda too personal."

Papy laughed. "Ah can't say, but ah'm a thinkin' it be like that most wheres."

The brownies burst into another fit of giggles.

As Jenny inspected the horizon, she recollected her father saying something about his old boss *riding his ass.* When she got back home, she'd have some serious questions for her father. The adult world seemed like a confusing place.

The brownies were a festive bunch. They burst into song so often that at times it felt like one of those old musicals that Jack liked. The ship sailed out to sea with so much contagious laughter that the captives almost forgot that they were prisoners.

Except for the being tied up part. That part was annoying.

And the prospect of being handed over to the Queen for her blood. Jenny stopped laughing.

Every once in a while Jenny would get a glimpse of the silent phooka at the back of the ship. His face kept staring at her through all the rigging from the back of the boat. She wondered what he was thinking.

Chapter 19

Changeling Suspicions

Millie

Millie didn't understand what was wrong with Finn, Jack, and Jenny since they came back from the hospital. They were... different.

The white hair could be attributed to whatever sent them to the hospital. But that didn't explain how they could become entirely different people.

Millie followed Finn into the library on the boys' first day back at school. She sat across from him at a study table. Finn completely ignored her.

"Finn!" she whispered in a library voice. "How are you?"

"Hmm." grunted Finn, half looked up from his smart phone. He seemed to be reading Wikipedia.

Millie decided on another tack. She pulled out her smart phone and texted him.

> **MILLIE:** Finn? What's wrong? Why aren't you talking to me?

There was a moment of hesitation where Finn read her message and looked up in surprise like he was seeing her in a new light. His fingers started to type.

> **FINN:** Hi Millie. I wasn't sure how well I knew you. Finn is fine. LOL. Fine Finn. I am fine.
> **MILLIE:** Why aren't you talking to me?
> **FINN:** We are in the Library.

Finn pointed to the sign *"Quiet Zone – No Talking Area"*

> **MILLIE:** Okay... Not something that used to bug you.
> **FINN:** Really? That's interesting. Thanks. You're different from the other kids here. Your skin is dark. I like it. You are pretty.

Finn gave her a smile.

MILLIE: Okay. You're being weird. You don't seem like yourself anymore.

Finn raised his eyebrows.

FINN: Maybe I am not. Not Finn. Not-Finn. I like that.

Millie gave him a quizzical look when he looked up at her.

FINN: But do not tell Not-Jenny. HA! She might kill you.
MILLIE: LOL What?
FINN: I think she went bad. Spoiled a bit. She is not as nice as I am.

Finn gave her a dazzling smile. But, it wasn't Finn's smile.

Chapter 20

Fuzzy-Wiggles Uncaged

The Fuzzy-Wiggles

When Jack had wished for all the locks in the room to unlock, he didn't realize that George and the rest of the fuzzy-wiggles were in the stacked cages on the other side of Blood Hall.

George and Burt watched the giant Blue Queen take a terrified Jack by the hand and lead him off into the corridor. Jack was slightly taller than the queen's knees – which made him look like a young child.

"Well, that's the lasst we'll be sseeing of him, I ssupposse," remarked George.

"Pity," sighed Burt.

"But, it wasss nice of him to unlock our cagess before he left." observed George.

"Oh, yesss, indeed! It wasss." agreed Burt.

"I won't misss those pesssky little beatle-men." came Beatrice's voice from below them.

"All of 'em disssentegrated! Jusst like that!" gasped Cynthia snapping her many fingers.

George reached round the bars and opened the latch on the cage door. "All right folksss! We sshould be getting a move on here. No knowing when sssomething nasty might return."

There was a bit of a racket as all the fuzzy-wiggles opened their cages and climbed down the rather rickety structures to the stone floor. The noise was only increased with Burt's shouts to be quiet. Six arms plus varied protuberances were handy when doing extensive climbing. *It was one of the qualities that made fuzzy-wiggles a superior species, George thought with pride.*

There were fourteen fuzzy-wiggles in all.

"Oooh, it isss a bit cold-ish in here." commented pink skinned Randy who lacked the fur of the others. "Burt, would you sssnuggle clossser to warm me up a bit?"

"Pleeassse Randy. Not! Now!" hissed George, who went on to whisper, "Well my noble fuzziesss! I propossse we try to essscape through that network of sstaircasesss on that far wall." He pointed to one of the larger arches in the Beetle-folk architecture.

"Ass opposssed to the hallway that leadsss to the Blue Queen." observed Beatrice.

"Uh, yesss." confirmed George.

"Oh, I second that! I second that!" shouted Burt who was then interrupted by Lance who wanted to second it also. Which turned into a clamor when all the fuzzies competed to second George's excellent idea.

"Quiet down my noble fuzziesss!" George attempted to bring order. "You can all sssecond it! You don't have to fight about it."

"But, how would that work? We can't all be sssecond." asked Randy.

"Yes, sssomeone would be a third or a fourth – or dare I sssssay it - a thirteenth!" proposed Cynthia.

There was a serious bit of grumbling – as no one wished to be the thirteenth. THAT would be entirely unacceptable!

"AHH, BUT, we *could* all be in agreement as ONE!" suggested Beatrice.

There was a quiet cheer of approval. Being ONE was preferable to even being second!

So with a fresh burst of unity, the party of fuzzy-wiggles waddled as quickly as they could possibly waddle to the little staircases, after which they successfully wiggled their way into the smallish quarters of the beatle-folk – who now only seemed to be dusty bits of memory on the floor of Blood Hall.

Chapter 21

The Island
of Jack

The beetle-men (and beetle-women) did not disintegrate like Jack and the fuzzy-wiggles thought. Jack had just ardently wished for all of them to be *gone,* and as magic is not inherently unkind, and as Jack was also not unkind, the beetle-folk simply disappeared from the castle and remarkably reappeared on a small, unpopulated isle south of the Bog Islands.

Naturally this sudden change was a big surprise to every one of them. But after the shock wore off, the beetle-folk were thrilled. They had been locked into servitude to the Blue Queen for generations (beetle-folk don't live very long). Being inherently industrious, they were not terribly daunted by the prospect of creating their new civilization from scratch. It was a rather nice island.

Eventually Pricker's story got around – of the golden boy *Jack* – who had rescued them all from eternal servitude. The island was named in Jack's honor – *The Island of Jack*. From then on Jack was worshiped as a deity. Every year at Jackmas, all the island's inhabitants wore diapers in honor of Jack, their great golden god, and prayed for the day that he might return to them.

Chapter 22

Long Last Weirdness

Finn

"I think I'm your mother," said the wrinkled little sea chimp with the dangling boobs.

Finn was definitely not looking at his mom's boobs. His alleged mom's boobs. Finn muttered like a mantra while staring at the ground. "No-no-no-no-no – This is *not* how I meet my long lost mom. NO."

"You're older than I expected. You *are* Finn? Aren't you? You had the key –"

Finn cringed. *This was a nightmare.*

Finn nodded hesitantly without meeting her eyes.

He took slow measured breaths so he wouldn't hyperventilate. He'd never been so weirded out in his life.

The creature wouldn't stop talking. "How old are you?" She looked apprehensively at the tall boy.

"Fifteen." he stared at the veins in the marble floor.

"So many years! *Fishfins!* Where to start? My name is Meryth. Meryth of mer'Rinn – *but I think* you can call me Mom."

Finn was not sure what to say to that. So many complicated feelings...

"So much time has passed!" She was quiet a moment. "My dear Finn. This isn't how I wanted this to happen either. Where's your father?"

Finn couldn't look at her.

She sighed. "You have his satchel. I'm sorry. I know this has to be a lot to take in." She paused. "Finn? What's the matter? Oh, my dearest boy... why won't you look at me?"

Finn was very uncomfortable and fumbled for words while keeping his green eyes on the ground.

"Oh my dear Finn. Won't you forgive me? I didn't want to abandon you..." his mother pleaded.

Finn squirmed. "I'm kind of uncomfortable. Your, uh, Boobs –"

"Boobs... What? My... breasts? What do they have to do with –"

"Oh! Yes! My bag!" Finn suddenly remembered. "I've an extra t-shirt in there!" Finn began scouring the contents of his bag.

His mother was at a loss for words. "I'm not sure what –"

"So you can cover up!" Finn held out a blue shirt while looking the other way.

"This is about... what... my BREASTS? I really don't understand." His mother asked incredulously.

Finn took a deep breath. He couldn't believe that he had to explain this. "I shouldn't be seeing my mother's boo-" he stopped. "Breasts. Especially if you're my MOM! Which I'm still not clear on!"

There was a beat of awkward silence.

"What type of twisted world were you brought up in? Are you saying that breasts are always covered up where you were raised?"

"Well, yeah. No. There's actually lots of um, them – in movies, in magazines... just not MOM breasts!"

There was silence.

Finn found the silence excruciating.

His mother felt speechless. "I'm not even sure what to say. I'm NOT going to cover up! You'll just have to get used to it!"

Finn opened his mouth, but nothing came out. He inspected the marble pattern on the far wall.

His mother continued, "Granted, I don't look like I *normally* do." Her voice took on a watery cast. "I've always been proud of my beauty – and my BREASTS," she added rather defiantly.

Finn couldn't imagine having this same conversation with his religious foster-mother. He appreciated his foster-mother in a way that he'd never fully considered before.

"But, you did see my breasts... before... before – " she asked hesitantly.

"Well, yes – and no – " Finn lied.

Of course he saw her breasts. They were hard to miss. But he wasn't going to admit that he was looking at his mom's what's-its! "I was seeing a *MERMAID* for the first time! YES! You're beautiful! You're probably more beautiful than anyone or anything I've ever seen in my entire life!" he turned to her. "But, I didn't really notice your um... breasts in particular. Uh, they were there, but didn't really see 'em. Like to really look at. Maybe it was all that hair? Your HAIR looked GREAT underwater! It was all floaty and everything..."

More awkward silence. Would she think it was weird that he noticed her hair but not her breasts?

"Okay." She took a breath and rolled her eyes. "Moving on, what's going on in Frey? Something must have gone wrong. I don't know what's happened since you hatched and your dad put me to sleep."

"Hatched?" Finn exploded.

"Of course. From your egg!" she laughed. "How else do you think you were born?"

"Uh... okay... let's skip that part for now... my father? I have a father?"

His mother looked at him with some concern.

Finn continued. "Scratch that! That's stupid. Yes, of course I have a father. But WHO IS HE? Is he a mermaid... or a merman or whatever like you?"

"Well, your father can't be a merman or you'd have a tail!" She laughed and it was one of the most musical, yet most exasperating sounds he'd ever heard. "Your father is human. He's from the human world... I'd hoped he'd be here with you," she said wistfully looking about.

Finn was stunned. But who was he? What had happened to his father?

His mother continued. "*I* couldn't keep track of the egg of course. With all the Merfolk getting turned into THIS..." She gestured to herself with disgust. "Your father and I used water magic to create this tube to keep the disease from progressing, and I sent your father to the Southern Islands to look for the cure... something clearly went wrong."

Finn was lost. "Okay..."

"I'm sorry. I know this is confusing for you. I asked your father to hide you till things were safe. Horrible things were happening in Frey. Mermen have an egg pouch in their tummy to keep an egg safe till it hatches. But your father was sadly deficient. So we waited till you hatched.

Your species is awfully confusing. I can't imagine how you hatch eggs if your men don't have pouches!"

She suddenly looked at Finn with curiosity. "You're half human and half merman – do *you* have a pouch?"

"Wha–? Eh no! No pouches!" blurted Finn, immediately feeling his gut for the appearance of a pouch. "Not... that I've noticed." He couldn't help but remember the green scales that had been appearing on his hip for the last few months. Great! A new thing to worry about.

"Pity." His mother gave him a sympathetic look. "But, don't worry, you might develop one yet," she offered encouragingly.

"Great," Finn mumbled.

The little sea chimp with the boobs moved on. "We can talk about your father later. First, what's going on in Frey without the mermaids?"

"I've never heard of a place called Frey," Finn shrugged.

"We're under Frey. Your father built the crystal tube deep beneath our sea-cottage on the Bay of mer'Rin."

It was getting too complicated. Magic. Mermaids. BOOBS! Finn groaned.

"All I know, is that Jack and I fell through a wall, and we've been trying to find his little sister who got pulled through before us. We've been wandering these tunnels and we can't find his sister! And now Jack's missing! And I can only find a trail of disgusting red goo that leads to a crack that I can't get into – AND MAYBE JACK'S DEAD,

BUT HE CAN'T BE DEAD!" All of Finn's feelings poured out in a rush. "And now you and your boobs are here and I don't know *how* I feel about *that!* And I have to find Jack! That's all I can think about right now. I HAVE TO FIND JACK!"

Finn felt more like that puddle of red goo up top than a fifteen year old boy. Mer-boy. Half mer-boy? Whatever he was.

His mother's voice brought him back from total panic. "So you grew up there? In the human world? I'm starting to understand things better." She touched his arm. "If I get back to my real body, I might be able to help you find your friend... Jack? We need to get up to Frey. Red goo sounds like the Redduns. They are servants of the upstart queen who I suspect did this to my people. Your father and I were in hiding after she came to power." His mom's webbed feet slapped on the wet tile as she moved to the front of the chamber dragging her thick polliwog tail behind her. "If the Redduns took your friend, and if she still commands from the northern hills, Jack will be at the old castle that she commandeered. Perhaps she has his sister as well."

"How do we get up to the surface, and this castle?" asked Finn.

"Across the lake is a tunnel to the surface." said the small amphibious creature with the boobs (that Finn wasn't looking at). "Your father used to have a boat stored below."

She stopped and gave him a sideways glance.

"Do you have something to eat? You wouldn't believe how hungry someone can get over fifteen years."

He looked in his bag. He had one more sandwich. Tuna. He sighed. He handed it over to her.

She gave half of it back. "We'll split it! I love tuna sandwiches! Your dad used to make them. I lived near Seattle... in a cabin for a bit. That's where I met your father."

She could see his interest perk up.

She laughed again.

Finn wondered how mermaid laughter could be so inhumanly beautiful and incredibly irritating at the same time.

Or maybe that was a mom thing?

Chapter 23

In The Blue Boudoir

Jack

The Queen's boudoir was blue. Blue as the ice where man has never tread. Blue as the veins in those hospital charts. Blue as death in those horror movies that use too many filters. There was altogether too much blue in the room as far as Jack was concerned.

Jack was sitting in a large blue enameled bird cage hanging from an ornately crafted stand in the corner. Fortunately there was no bird in the cage with him, as he was convinced that it must have been a very large meat-eating bird. He carefully nudged aside the scattered bones, which littered the bottom of the cage. Even so, the fabric of his diaper was not much of a barrier between his butt and the cold dirty floor of the cage.

It was colder in the Blue Queen's boudoir than it was in the hall where the bleeding was done. There was a sort of feeder hooked into the cage bars that appeared to have once functioned as a toilet for prisoners in the past. Jack sat on the other side of the cage due to the smell. Nasty. Maybe the Queen didn't have much sense of smell. He shivered, pulled his knees up to his chest and wrapped his arms around his legs to stay warmer.

After the queen had stepped through a grand arch into what seemed to be her bedchamber, Jack had taken a quick peek into his diaper to confirm that he still had the one wish left. Yup. His boy-parts were glowing with a golden light. That was a weird twist. He knew that he'd have to be smart about spending his last wish.

He was crazy hungry at this point. He hadn't eaten anything since the PBJ with Finn in the tunnels. That was like... a day ago?

On the previous evening when the Blue Queen had first discovered him, Jack didn't know why he hadn't run. He hadn't even thought about running. He'd read about snakes hypnotizing their victims. Or maybe that was just a Disney movie he'd seen. He'd always thought that was pretty stupid. But he just froze up – like a rabbit. Like, she might not see him if he stayed perfectly still. But nope. She'd looked down at him... and she'd smiled.

The Blue Queen was horribly frightening, but not in the way that Jack had expected. He had seen his share of horror films. But it wasn't like that at all. The Queen was a giant, blue-scaled humanoid.

Freaky.

Check.

Jack's height stood slightly above her knee. Below which, her legs bent backwards like a dinosaur's leg would bend. She wore diaphanous robes that flowed about her, and the tail extended behind her, much like a T-Rex.

Also freaky.

Double check.

But oddly, none of these things were what made her so frightening.

Above the narrow waist, she was like a woman. Her arms were long and slender with three clawed fingers and clawed thumb on each hand. Her face was humanoid and narrow, with the lower jaw projecting further forward and her brow slanted back to meet thick fungal-shaped curls, which expanded into tiers of teal growths that curved up and over her forehead. Her chin projected into a thin horn, and delicate horns curved out from her eyebrows, ears and cheekbones.

Again, super freaky.

Triple check.

But as weird as all those things were, none of these pushed the freak meter over the edge.

It was her excruciatingly good manners. Bad people weren't supposed to be so polite – were they? He wasn't sure what to make of how nice she was.

She was downright friendly.

"Well that was impressive," she had said sweetly. "Annoying of course. But... impressive."

Jack had felt terrified. There was a disconnect between her words, and something behind her twitching reptilian pupils.

"I just got the last bit, but I was fascinated to see you sending all those children home."

Jack wasn't sure what to say. So he said nothing. She had beautiful eyes. They seemed to care about him.

"But, naturally those children are going to miss the beautiful dreams that I was giving them. It was quite selfish you know – stealing away all those happy dreams from those poor dears."

Jack thought – yes, it *was* quite selfish of him! He hadn't thought of it like that! He always messed things up. How could he have been so selfish? He should have first asked each child if they *wanted* to be sent home.

"I'm sure your intentions were good – even if you sent *all* those children back to their *unhappy* lives. And now,

I also have to find new servants to care for the rest of my children. I'm not clear just what you did with them, but those poor dears are gone as well. There's no one to feed the rest of my children now."

Jack felt awful about what he did. What could he have been thinking? Wait! What did she mean by *the rest?* Were there more children who were held prisoner here?

She continued. "Of course, I'm curious as to exactly *how* you did it."

Looking into her eyes, Jack wanted to please her. "I did it with a wish your majesty."

"It must have been quite a big wish to send *all* those children home."

"Oh it was!" Jack suddenly remembering Pinkie diving into his mouth and exploding inside of him. Pinkie. He remembered Pinkie. *He remembered Finn. He remembered Jenny.*

"And *where* did you ever find such a big wish?" Her purr was as impatient as a prehistoric feline.

Jack's head cleared a little. He stayed silent and stared at her incredulously.

The Blue Queen was not bothered by his lack of an answer.

"What should I call you? If you are going to be a guest in my home, you should really tell me your name." she said sweetly.

Jack hesitated and blurted out, "Fred?... your majesty." Why did he say Fred? He remembered that his mother used to say, "Never give out your name to strangers." And this lady did qualify as strange.

"Well, Fred? Walk with me, Fred. I'd love to show you my castle!" The Queen's giant hand reached down and took his small hand and drew him along side of her.

Jack was a toddler next to her. He was barefoot and in diapers. He'd never so appreciated the concept of clothes before. Being naked and small made him feel helpless.

The Queen hadn't seemed to notice his lack of apparel. It reminded him of those stupid dreams where you find yourself in your underwear and nobody notices. He couldn't remember what those dreams were supposed to mean. Obviously irrelevant at the moment.

Out in the hall stood a frightened guard at full attention. It stood about eight foot tall on two legs, and was not remotely human. There was a horn coming out of his snout and flared forehead like a triceratops.

"Gornal, I'm rather disappointed with how you've failed in your duties here," said the Blue Queen.

"Yer Maj'sty, Ah were inspectin' ta edder Hall." quavered the guard.

"Oh, that's all right. I'm sure it won't happen again," smiled the Queen.

"Oh thankee yer Maj'sty fer yer un'erstandin'"

"Don't mention it," she smiled wickedly and sweetly whispered, *"Melt. Gornal. Melt."*

Jack screamed when the guard literally melted into a puddle of gray goo.

The giantess cheerfully called down the hallway. "Hello! cleanup in Corridor Five!"

A very big lizard-like creature rushed into view and curtsied. "Yes, yer Majesty."

The Queen reflected a moment. "I've a sudden craving for baby horny-blit soufflé tomorrow night at the palace feast. I think we have some young fresh ones in the dungeon."

The Blue Queen pulled Jack along beside her and they continued their walk. Jack didn't know what a *baby horny-blit soufflé* was. He had been feeling kind of hungry himself, but one glance at the puddle of goo made him lose his appetite.

"As I was saying, I do hope you have a *lovely* visit here. I do so want to make you happy," slithered her echoing voice far above him. She sounded sincere. He had the peculiar sense that she desperately needed to be liked. Jack could feel the need rolling off of her in waves.

As they progressed, Jack began to hear the sound of hundreds of children crying and screaming.

The queen looked rather put out. "Looks like the *rest* of the children have woken up."

They passed by an arch to a room like the one he'd been a prisoner in. Jack was shocked to see another wall of diapered children. They were awake. Screaming. A few minutes later, he saw a second and a third room of captive children manacled in rows on tall walls. Crying and screaming. The echoes rebounded down the vast stone corridors.

He'd not saved all the kids held prisoner in the castle! He'd only saved *one* room of kids.

The Blue Queen gave a big sigh. "Yes, without my beetle-men to put my little guests to sleep with nice dreams, they are quite unhappy – and hungry, till I find new servants. And *it's all your fault* you know. All of that pain those children are experiencing... you were quite selfish you know – destroying their caregivers."

He could still hear echoes of screaming children many corridors away. The beetle-men were gone. The children were awake.

At least, further blood-milking seemed to be halted for now.

The queen was still talking, "... so, you see I only take a little bit every day and I give them very nice dreams. It is a fabulous arrangement all around," she smiled happily and looked at him for agreement.

Jack nodded.

But now it was the next morning. At least it felt like that. He'd spent a chilly night in the cage, leaning against the bars. They left bumpy imprints in his shoulder.

The bedroom suite was as big as the inside of a cathedral, as befitted a queen as tall as a house. She was twenty feet tall? Eighteen? Twenty-five? Jack had never been good with estimating heights.

He thought that his cage was at least twenty feet above the floor. If he got the door open, he didn't have anything to make a rope with. Some of the skinny bones might work for picking the lock. Not that he'd ever picked a lock before. It looked easy in the movies. How hard could it be?

He had one wish and he wanted to be optimistic, but given the size of the wish in his diaper, it did not give him a great deal of confidence that it would take him very far.

Jack drifted to sleep again.

When Jack awoke and found that the Blue Queen was sitting almost below him – in front of the tall, oval vanity mirror.

She looked entirely different from the previous evening. She reminded him of a stone statue weathered by time and wind. Eroded. Ancient. When she looked up at him, something shifted. She was brilliantly blue and young. The exotic beautiful monster he'd first seen.

"Oh, Fred, you are awake! Quick, I need your opinion. Is my blush symmetrical? It almost feels like I might have too much on the right side – and I do hate to be asymmetrical."

Bewildered, Jack hazarded, "Well, it's a little hard to tell from here, but perhaps too much on the right side?"

The Blue Queen looked at herself in the mirror again and tilted her head this way and that. "You might be right." She picked up a puffball and dusted her left cheek.

As she turned back to face him, he was horrified to see that the little puffball that she'd placed in the tray with others like it – was squirming.

They were alive?

"Is this better?" She turned her head in the mirror this way and that with pursed lips to admire her beautiful cheekbones.

"Oh, yes. Much better." Jack responded quickly with as much of a smile as he could give her.

The Queen gazed at him for a moment. She said conspiratorially, "So Fred, I noticed that you were glowing when you made that *wish* yesterday. And I find that – *interesting*. Interesting because it means that you didn't *have* a wish, but that maybe you... *were* the wish. Now, why would that be?"

Jack shrugged. He wasn't sure what to say.

She continued her train of thought, "If you were glowing it suggests that *perhaps* you ATE a wish. Not just any wish, but a very big wish?"

Jack said nothing.

"Or then again, maybe you ate many small wishes?"

Jack continued his silence.

"It'd never occurred to me to eat wishes myself, silly as it might sound. One hates to experiment on oneself, and it is dangerous to experiment with others who might be – irresponsible with their wishes."

She poked a finger inside his cage with a painted purple claw as if to tickle him. "But *you* seem to have come out healthy and sound. Aren't you?"

"Yes! I'm fine!" Jack exclaimed – pushing himself against the back bars.

She smiled and pulled her claw back.

"I'm a little cold though," he whispered.

"You are looking a little bluer than you did yesterday, but it's really rather attractive on you," she giggled. "You match my room and I do so love for things to match."

"If I get sick, you might discover a variety of other colors in this cage," Jack hinted.

"But I won't keep you here *that* long, darling. I'll have you bled white by then. I'm starting to think it would be kinder to bleed children all at once. I'm going to have to reflect on this."

"Are you like a vampire or something?"

"A what, darling?"

"Do you drink blood?"

"What a horrific thought. Of course I don't. The blood is for my worms. The ones who turn into my wishes."

Jack panicked, "But that's murder! What about the happy dreams you say you love to give them?" He tried a new angle. "You must care a little bit?"

"Oh, that's so sweet of you to say. Of course, I love them," she purred.

"But -"

"I love them the same way that you love your bacon."

"But that's not the same at all."

"Oh, but we all eat something. What types of things do you eat? I've read all about your human world in the minds of the children that have visited me. What about the dreams of the pigs or carrots?"

Jack was startled. "Carrots have dreams?"

"Well of course they do, darling."

"But..." Jack muttered. "Children are different from carrots."

"Of course you'd say that. You're not a carrot. I'm not judging you. Cycle of life and all that... and all of you children believe in a heaven of some sort, so I'm just sending you there quicker! To me you're all just – carrots." She smiled innocently.

Jack didn't know what to say to that. He had a sudden fear of her reaching in and pulling off a leg, like he'd grab a grape off a bunch.

But that was evidently not her plan. She started humming to herself and waltzed over to her open wardrobe and thumbed through her dresses.

Jack began to wonder about the extent of her magic. "Did you say you read minds?"

"Of course I do, darling. You are wondering if I am going to eat you."

Jack started, then thought again. He focused his thoughts on... hmmm... he couldn't help it. He thought about Finn. Naked. He couldn't help it. It just popped into his brain.

The Blue Queen saw his expression. "But darling... don't look so startled. I won't eat you today," she laughed.

OMG. She's totally faking it. She can't read minds. She's had lots of kidnapped kids to interview. To study.

Jack tried again. "But why would a powerful queen like you need more magic? You must be more magical than anyone else in the world!"

She looked at him quickly and he feared he'd laid it on too thick.

She cocked her head to one side and looked at him. "I am very good with name magic. If I know someone's name, they will do all sorts of things for me. *Suck your toe, Fred. Suck your toe.*"

Jack was really glad she didn't know his name. Then he suddenly realized he needed to keep up the pretense and stuck his dirty toe in his mouth. He didn't want to think of the germs he might be ingesting.

She stared at him a moment before she turned back to her closet.

"Mmm." Jack wondered how long he'd have to suck his toe.

"Stop sucking your toe, Fred. Stop sucking your toe." She laughed over her shoulder.

Jack hastily pulled his toe out. It was a lucky thing that he was flexible.

She thoughtfully fondled a sparkly turquoise dress. "There is so much good I want to do in the world. Perhaps by upping the bleeding schedule, I can create more good sooner!"

"What type of good things do you want to do?" Jack asked from his cage.

"That's a silly question." She smiled. "Good is good, isn't it?"

"I guess so."

"Well, I simply want a world where everything makes *me* happy."

"What if what makes you happy, makes other people unhappy?"

She laughed. "Then those people are selfish, don't you think?"

As she danced off to her bedchamber with the sparkly gown, her tail knocked over a tall rack of feather boas that billowed in the air.

Jack's hand shot out and grabbed a giant indigo boa that floated just within his reach. The rack itself landed softly on a giant over-stuffed chair.

Asphixia

The Blue Queen was humming a perky tune when she left her chambers. She didn't say goodbye to the little pest in its cage. The boy vexed her. She'd have him bled when she returned. First she had to work out the issue with the missing servants. And deal with Mordette.

Jack

She never returned to see fallen coat rack or the boa that Jack had pulled into the cage. It was so bulky that there'd have been no way to hide it. He wrapped its surprising warmth around him and started picking the lock with a shard of bone.

It was not nearly as easy as mystery novels made it sound. But he had lots of time and no distractions – and many shards of bones to experiment with.

No one could have been more surprised than himself when the lock finally snapped open.

It was a long drop to the floor. Longer than the length of the boa. But the top of the vanity table was not too far away. Jack could see a sort of route once he got there, if he jumped down via the plush stool in front of the vanity.

He pushed the rusty cage door open and tied off the end of the boa to a bar of the cage. Giant feather boas are not very easy to tie knots with, but once accomplished he felt like Tarzan as he climbed down inside the fluffy mass of feathers. He tried not to breathe in the feathery wisps around him.

When Jack reached the height of the tabletop, he began swinging back and forth to span the four-foot distance to the edge. At full swing, he let go of the boa and landed with a thump on the tabletop.

The puffballs in their tray were squeaking, and bouncing up and down in their efforts to get his attention. They were cute little critters. They would probably be about a foot tall

if untied. Now that he was closer, he could see that they were each gagged and hogtied. Their eyes pleaded as they wiggled.

Of course, Jack couldn't leave them. He pulled out the knife-like shard of bone that he'd tucked carefully into a hole he'd made in the side of his diaper, and began cutting through the cords binding their hands and feet. He could see that they were children.

"Shhhh!" Jack whispered. "I don't know how much time we have."

"Thankee mister!" gasped the first one to get the gag out of its mouth.

"Do you have names?" Jack asked while cutting the last one's bonds.

The three seemed identical at first, but up close he saw slight differences.

"Ah'm Bilbe!" said the first one while rubbing his wrists and ankles.

"Ah'm Dilbe," whispered the second one who seemed a bit shy around Jack. She was a girl. He wasn't exactly sure how he knew. Her face was a bit narrower than Bilbe's.

"Lilbe," sighed the third one - who was smaller than the other two. Jack was unsure as to the gender. "The beetle-lady didn't come ta feed us this mornin'. We be crazy hungry."

Jack winced when he thought that he might be responsible for the total genocide of the beetle people.

"Well, I'm pretty hungry, too. Are you ready to get out of here?"

The children nodded vigorously and looked nervously about them.

There was nearly a six-foot drop down to the upholstered stool. But the cushion looked thick. Jack didn't see anything resembling rope on the tabletop, and it might be too scary for these kids to jump. But getting down to the stone floor would be the bigger problem.

Lilbe gave a tug to the side of his diaper to get his attention. He grabbed the diaper quickly, as the only thing holding the diaper up was a diaper pin.

"Mister," Lilbe pointed towards the back of the tabletop. "The beetle-lady's tunnel 'twould be easier."

Bilbe and Dilbe pushed at a wooden panel beside the mirror. It revealed a small tunnel into the wall.

"But the beetle-lady might be in there!" worried Dilbe.

Jack squirmed. "The beetle-folk are... gone."

Bilbe smiled. "Suptastic!"

The dark hole was about two-feet high and two-feet wide. It was going to be a tight fit.

Jack hesitated. "Is it big enough for me all the way through?"

Bilbe ran into the tunnel and in a moment came back. "Ye'll fit, I s'pect!"

The fluffballs ran into the tunnel.

Jack got down on his knees and looked into the blackness.

"Crap. I can barely fit." He gave a sigh and squirmed into the darkness on his stomach. He closed the door behind him with his toe and he was in total darkness. He wiggled forward snake-like and tried to not lose his diaper.

He could hear the kids running far ahead.

It was a long dark tunnel. Jack really hated small spaces.

Chapter 24

The Storm

Pirate Jenny

Afternoon deepened into a rich cloud-filled sunset, painting the turbulent sea around the ship in sparkling yellows and oranges. Jenny and the Wishermans were still lashed along the front rails of the ship.

There was a constant flurry of activity around and above them as small sailors pulled on ropes and climbed the forward mast like kids on the jungle gym at school.

The brownie pirates didn't seem to be evil enough to be doing what they were doing. She'd always thought that awful things were only done by awful people. But maybe awful things were done by ordinary people too? The brownies acted friendly, but they didn't seem to care about the Wishermans' children.

Jenny wondered if she'd ever see her own family again.

Footbe and the pirates were taking Jenny to the Blue Queen's castle where her blood was going to be fed to some kind of evil worms. This was not working out at all how she'd expected.

She'd overheard that the pirate ship was en route north to the mouth of the Great River – which led inland to Nor'city, Frey's capital. Papy said the city spread out like a "festerin' rash" across the plains below the castle of the Blue Queen. He and Mamy were not too big on cities.

The Cap'n said that it should be a seven or eight hour voyage to the mouth of the river, but strong winds argued otherwise.

The ship had tarried a short while at the mouth of the Riddle River waiting for the floating island of the Wish Market, but the island never appeared. The Wish Monger was usually on schedule, but occasionally took forays elsewhere if Mordette saw potential profit.

Jenny had never heard of a floating island before, and despite all the scary things going on she was curious to see it.

After a few hours, the ship set sail. Once underway, Captain Billy Blind pushed through the brownies in the forecastle like he expected applause. He was a handsome brownie with a strong jaw and ice blue eyes. He lifted his feathered hat in an extravagant bow to the Wishermans and sang out in his rich baritone voice:

"The Wishin' Market 'tisn't here
we have n' time ta wait ah fear!
A sack o' blood wi' pretty eyes
must be redeemed ta claim our prize!"

His gaze lingered casually on Jenny – the sack of blood with pretty eyes.

Jenny stared hard at him. "Why're you called Captain Billy Blind if you ain't blind?"

The captain sighed dramatically and sang out:

"I never talk with my livestock –
it complicates me work post hoc.
But, if they call me Billy Blind
It's cuz I'm blind ta FEAR ye'll find!"

Mamy snorted. "Ye're not just blind ta fear, ye're also blind ta right an' wrong! And yer meter's off too – figgers ya wouldna know the stress shoulda be on 'lives' not 'stock'," she added in a mutter.

The captain shrugged with a smile,

"Ye think too small, I be not bad,
Tis just me biz'nuss, don't be mad!
I'll bring the Queen her brand new pet –
for profit's dictums must be met!"

The captain gave another dazzling smile and sauntered back towards the wheel shouting directions to the crew.

"That talking in poetry thing gets really annoying." groused Jenny.

Gibbie sighed quietly:

> *"Ye've no idee the truth ye sow.*
> *We hate it more than ye can know.*
> *But, what be worse is ev'ry bleater's —"*

Gibbie stopped with a mischievous grin.

> *"gots ta finish t'other's meter!"*

— completed an exasperated brownie next to him who stalked off in a huff.

Gibbie laughed, and Jenny couldn't help but laugh with him. But then again she remembered where she was headed.

The Wish Market's next scheduled stop should be at the mouth of the Great River on Nerpday — in another two days. That gave time to deliver Jenny up the river to the queen and return to meet the Water Witch.

Gibbie saw her thoughts and quietly gave Jenny a sad shrug. She wondered if perhaps the brownies weren't as fond of their captain as she'd first thought.

Twilight brought hints of an oncoming storm. The waves grew higher and the valleys between the waves grew deeper. The brownies moved Mamy and Papy and their stuff below decks to keep them dry, but Jenny didn't fit below deck and neither did the phooka at the back of the ship. Now that the sails were all tied up and out of the way of the storm, she could see Footbe easily. He often looked at Jenny with confusion, but she didn't know what to make of it.

Tied up to the front rail, Jenny felt more than a little seasick as the boat sailed up one crest and swept down into its trough. It was a veritable roller-coaster and Jenny was no great lover of roller-coasters. Maybe she was going to drown in a shipwreck and she'd been worried about the wrong thing!

Jenny was soon soaked. Every so often she'd catch a glance of the miserable phooka hanging on tightly at the back of the ship. She'd think, *serves you right!*

Captain Billy Blind seemed to be everywhere at once as the seas became choppier. He shouted directions to the crew and pulled and heaved as hard as any of them. She ultimately did some heaving too – though of a slightly different kind.

Then the rain hit. The rain was warm. Warmer than any rain back home in Washington. Jenny's cloak and hat were down below with Mamy and Papy where it was dry-ish. Jenny was drenched. The rain and the wind lasted for hours. Some of the brownies on deck would have been washed overboard but for the ropes attaching their waists to the nearest rail.

The storm lasted all night. Somehow Jenny fell asleep amid the deluge.

Hours later, she started awake when the ship gave a crash, and she was jolted forward.

The early morning sky was clear, yet everything was crooked. She was still tied to the rail, but her ties were loose enough for her to squirm high enough to peer over the rail into the water below. The ship had grounded on a reef. It was stuck fast. Across an expanse of lagoon she could see a tropical island with three mountains poking up from its center.

Jenny glanced to the back of the ship and noticed that Footbe was gone. Was he washed overboard in the storm?

Chapter 25

Watery
Revelations

Finn

Finn looked at the small creature who was supposed to be his mother. Mom? Meryth? He wasn't sure what he wanted to call her. He wasn't sure how he felt about all of this, but if Jack was still alive this sea chimp might be Finn's only hope of finding him and Jenny.

"Your father's boat used to be hidden in the lower cave – behind the waterfall." She took a big breath. "I can't believe it's been fifteen years," she murmured this last bit half to herself.

"Well then, we should get going." Finn suggested.

She looked up at him. "I wish I knew what happened to your father."

Finn angrily held up his satchel. "I was found inside this bag as a newborn baby at an aquarium in Seattle. I wish I knew what happened to him far more than you do."

"I'm sure he didn't mean to leave you there."

"Of course. Whoops! Misplaced my kid!" Finn rarely lost his temper, but he was on the edge of losing it now. "Nobody ever came looking for me."

"You're naturally upset."

"You think?" Finn calmed his breathing. "Let's go. I need to get this over with so I can find Jack."

"I'll do what I can. I hope you can help us. Your father was supposed to be with you. Things have always depended on you getting back in time."

"I don't understand! I'm only fifteen! What help could I have been before now?"

"You're going to save the Merfolk. Or, at least we hoped you could." His mother looked at him with expectant eyes.

"I'm just a kid. I... I'll do what I can? Do I get some sort of magic sword? Or special bag of magic?"

"No, you have everything you need."

"Uh... okay. But I've also got to save Jack and Jenny."

"I understand. Across the lake there's a tunnel that leads to the surface. " She gestured to her strange body. "I don't have much time like this. In a matter of days I'll devolve into a pool of evolutionary goo. I won't be able to help you much then."

A pool of goo? Finn's head was too full to speak. He nodded and quickly dove into his leather bag. He passed by his dead phone and pulled out his water bottle. He filled it from the edge of the waterfall near the entrance. He pulled a large garbage bag and tape out of his satchel and wrapped it all up. His satchel was waterproofed (he did live in Washington), but he wanted to keep his sketchpads and stuff dry if they were crossing a lake. He placed the key once again around his neck.

"You don't need that key anymore," his mom noted.

"I'm sort of used to it," Finn said. He'd always worn it. The fantasy mother produced by his imagination and the key, felt far more like the mother he wanted than the strange creature in front of him.

He nodded towards the entrance, "Okay."

His mom followed him out of the chamber. They shimmied along the uneven trail behind the waterfall. Slippery fragments of shale made the descent to the water's edge a tricky endeavor.

Finn quickly saw that the sharp rocks were too difficult for his mother to crawl over, so he picked her up and carried her like a toddler (her skin felt weird... cold... a little bit like that of a big salamander... he tried not to think about it).

Speech was difficult with the roaring falls next to them. As they reached the base, she directed him with hand

signals to look beyond the torrent of falling water. Ahead was a dark water-filled cavern. Half buried in the rocky sand was an upside-down rowboat near the water's edge. It was chained to an iron stake impaled in the rock wall.

The steel boat was old, but in good condition considering its age. *The Naughty Lush* was painted on its prow in flaking black paint.

Finn laughed. "This was my dad's?"

"It's the boat he was fishing from when we met. We brought it with us." Her wistful look almost made Finn forget that she was a sea chimp. "Much too small for fishing in the middle of the Sound... but perhaps if he'd had more sense we wouldn't have met."

It took a bit of effort to dig the rowboat out of the sand and turn it over. He needed another set of arms. He wished that Jack were there to help. They were a good team.

He wouldn't believe that Jack could be dead. None of this made sense. Finn still half hoped that this was all some hallucinogenic dream from Jack's dad's mushrooms. He wanted to wake up.

"Finn?" whispered his mother's voice. He realized that she'd been talking.

He looked up to see what she had said.

"You remind me of him. Your father. Always in his head. He wasn't much older than you when I first met him."

Meryth's scrutiny made Finn uncomfortable. He glided the boat half into the water and stood knee deep. "Are you swimming or riding in the boat?"

"Who knows *what* is living in that lake!" She shuddered.

"So you're not swimming," Finn deadpanned.

His mother giggled. "You really are so like your father. He used to make me laugh."

Finn gave her a weak smile. There were long oars wedged under the benches of the boat. He slid them out.

He looked back to where she was waiting on the sand.

She was too small to climb over the edge.

Finn patiently climbed out and braved the "dangerous water" and carried her to the boat. He tossed in his bag. He waded alongside wondering if a tentacle was going to grab his ankle at any moment. How could he know what to expect in a place like this?

Finn pushed *The Naughty Lush* away from the sand bar. He climbed in and sat on the center bench facing his mother at the back. He fit the oars into their oarlocks.

Soon the boat was bobbing on its own in the dark cavern, and he carefully turned the craft around with one of the oars. Avoiding the worst of the waterfall's spray, he glided the craft with steady pulls along the rough water at the far side of the fall, which pushed them out onto the underground lake.

It took a few minutes to get beyond the sound of the falls. His mother sat in the back with her sea chimp smile. Meryth looked proud of him as he pulled steadily across the water.

The lake was big and misty. Three football lengths across perhaps? It was hard to tell with the mist. The sheer sides of the cavern ascended to a ceiling lost in darkness.

Occasionally swamp-like glowing forests of algae encrusted stalagmites punctuated the water around them and reached towards the darkness above. Sometimes stalactites descended from above to almost touch the water. Finn maneuvered *The Naughty Lush* through these bayous of stone till he again reached open water.

"You've decorated your dad's bag?"

"Yup."

"You have his artistic talent. The mermen you tooled into the leather are beautiful, even if they aren't *entirely* accurate."

"What's wrong with them?" huffed out Finn, pulling at the oars.

"Well it's just a bit modest. Oh, you'll see for yourself someday," she smiled to herself in a funny way.

"Okay..." he wasn't sure how to understand her critique.

"Would you like to hear about how your father and I met?"

Finn shrugged with an adolescent assent.

His mother smiled and looked out across the dark water. "It's tough to be a teen whether you're human or Merfolk. I thought my parents didn't understand me. Maybe they didn't. I was sixteen when I met your dad. I wasn't supposed to visit the human world. I was told how dangerous it is."

"Washington?" Finn huffed out. He was breathing hard at this point. Rowing took quite a bit more breath than he expected. "I guess it can be a little bit scary if you are in the middle of the Sound..."

"It's a horribly frightening place. But exciting. The nixies' stories convinced me to go. They planted the idea in my head. The nixies spy on humans and bring back unusual things. Objects so strange that we often never knew what they were, or even what they were made of."

Finn stopped rowing for a moment to catch his breath. "What are nixies?"

"Nixies are fairies. They're small. They have wings." She thought a moment. "They're crazy. They're like badly behaved pixies. Nixies take stuff they think no one wants. My father hates them. Or… hated them…" She hesitated, then continued. "He forbade me to visit the nixies. He didn't consider them a good influence for a princess."

"If they steal stuff, maybe he was right." Finn started up rowing again. "Wait, PRINCESS?"

She laughed and ignored him. "Loot's End wasn't far from my father's palace. I would sneak out at night and sit with the gators at the edge of the river and listen to the nixies' stories."

"Gators? As in alligators?"

"Hmm? Of course. Now where was I?"

"You said something about a palace?" Finn offered with more than a bit of curiosity.

"Yes. The house of mer'Rin," his mother said off-handedly. "Well one night I ran away. I didn't want my parents telling me what to do. I knew there was a portal in the ocean to the south of us. It brought me to the Sound near Whittle-Dedee Island."

"Whidbey Island?"

"It wasn't nearly as much fun as I expected. The water is cold and your fish don't talk! I'd never been so lonely in my life! But I'd also never seen a human before. It's so peculiar to see two legs coming out from where there should be a tail. I swam up to some swimmers near a big city and was never so startled in my life to see that they had legs! I guess I startled them too when they saw I had a tail. When I tried to talk it was terrible! They either screamed and chased me, or screamed and tried to get away from me. Lots of screaming. It was awful. I explored the whole coast. I saw Seattle and all its giant towers. The giant ships. But, it was terribly lonely. When a storm hit, I was so depressed that I decided to go home and face my parents."

She appeared to be lost in memories. He'd found a steady rhythm with the oars and *The Naughty Lush* skimmed across the smooth water.

She continued. "The portal is in the deep water west of – uh, Whid-beby Island. And that's where I saw your father's boat. It had over-turned and he was holding on as best he could. He'd been out fishing and had fallen asleep. It had drifted. The choppy water flipped the boat. He was the prettiest man I'd ever seen – with or without a tail. So, I rescued your father... and his boat, and brought them to the beach.

"James was the first human who didn't completely fall apart when he saw me. He was also sixteen and such a marvelous painter. He had wavy blonde hair that got curly when it was wet. His parents were not very forgiving and your father was head-strong and wild. Your father had been kicked out of his parents' house. He lived in a tiny cabin near the water. His grandparents owned the property. He was rebellious like me. I was fascinated with feet," she laughed. "They are so strange looking.

"My father would've been shocked to know that I slept in a human's bathtub for an entire month. But we had such a great time. He'd paint and I'd sing. James taught me a lot about your world."

"My father's name is James?" Finn paused in his rowing.

His mother smiled. "James. James the Stubborn! James the Thoughtful! But I called him – "

Something very big rubbed along the bottom of the boat and a dark form moved out beyond them towards deeper water.

Finn looked behind him towards their destination and put on a fresh burst of speed with the oars.

"I think, we need to get to shore as quickly as possible." said his mother – stating the obvious.

The rocky shore was yet another twenty feet off.

Finn pulled on the oars as fast as he could, but it wasn't going to be fast enough. Something long and very big was moving under the surface. It was headed straight for them!

They were getting closer to the shore.

Maybe they'd make it!

Something slammed into the boat from below! The boat flipped high in the air and threw Finn, his mother, and his bag within reach of the shore.

They scrambled onto the nearest flat stone. Soaking wet, Finn grabbed his bag and a floating oar while his mom crawled higher up onto the rocks behind him. He raised the oar to fight off whatever might be coming out of the water, but was surprised to see giant jaws close around the capsized metal boat, and drag it down to the depths.

The monster was after the boat? Were there creatures that ate metal down here?

So much for *The Naughty Lush*. He felt unaccountably sad for its loss... a little piece of his father had been pulled into the depths never to be seen again.

Finn whirled around when he heard a cry of dismay from his mother.

"The tunnel! It's gone. It's been covered over!"

Instead of the tunnel opening she expected, there was an outcropping of giant irregular masonry – part of a vast series of steps that had been hidden by the mist.

Each step was as high as his waist and a full four-feet deep. The steps ascended as high as they could see. There was a huge rock city built into the cavern walls as the steps receded into the upper distances.

A giant was descending those stairs.

Chapter 26

Wishes To Go

The Fuzzy-Wiggles

The fuzzy-wiggles squeezed through the small hallways of the beetle-folk's quarters. The tiny furniture was soon demolished by the parade of fuzzy-wiggles squirming through the corridors. But, those halls led to a broad balcony overlooking a wide chamber that flickered with blue light. It was *not* as big as Blood Hall but *much* more intriguing.

The chamber was full of dark wishes! None of the fuzzy-wiggles had ever seen a dark wish before, but they instinctively knew what they were. The blue light cast by the fluttering wishes shifted and mesmerized the fuzzy-wiggles. The dark wishes fluttered teasingly close to the little crowd on the balcony.

"Those look delicious!" cried Randy ready to throw himself into the midst of the forbidden delights.

"WAIT! My fuzzy-wigglesss!" shouted a wavering George. "I know thisss looksss and sssmells all very delectable, but we mussst retain sssome ssself control!"

All fourteen fuzzy-wiggles ogled the bobbing morsels in front of them. None of them had ever tasted human blood or a dark wish before.

"But it issn't like eating the blood ourselvess," countered Randy. "We would sstill have our free will."

"Are you sssure?" asked a dubious George.

Burt was drooling. "My free will isss fading."

"George, they do look lovely." Beatrice couldn't take her eyes off of the fluttering blue lights.

More dark wishes than any of them could count.

They had heard of dark wishes, but there were few opportunities to drink human blood in the tunnels. It was a naughty desire they weren't supposed to have. It was a tale told from one generation to the next – and like a bad Santa Claus or an evil Easter Bunny for humans, no fuzzy-wiggle expected to ever see a dark wish.

But, here they were. Fluttering and flitting with their luscious blue light.

The escaping fuzzy-wiggles had stumbled upon Asphixia's dark wish farm. The reason that the Blue Queen enslaved the beetle-folk was not merely for their small size and flexible morality. It was also for their complete inability to wish for anything. Beetle-folk were incapable of using her wishes. It wasn't for a lack of imagination, but rather because they were content by their very nature. The concept of *wishing* was entirely foreign to them.

So Asphixia entrusted the care and feeding of her dark fuzzy-wiggles to the beetle-folk. They fed the children's blood to her captive fuzzy-wiggles, which on turning made them agreeable to the Blue Queen's whims.

Every single one of the queen's fuzzy-wiggles had metamorphosed into dark wishes over the last few days. This room contained her entire stock. For this very reason, the queen had decided to throw a party for herself on the following evening.

The winged temptations became too strong for the little band of fuzzy-wiggles to resist. Like a fraternity house facing a holiday with too much beer, or dogs accidentally left inside a butcher shop, it was chaos. It was a feeding frenzy.

Randy ate the most. His appetite and voraciousness astounded the others. They'd never seen a fuzzy-wiggle spring to such heights before, snapping eagerly at every dark wish he passed on the way down.

Fourteen fuzzy-wiggles dined very well that evening and not a single fluttering dark wish was left by the time they collapsed on the floor in a *wish-full* haze.

George had enough presence of mind to herd his fuzzy wiggles into a small pantry where they could sleep off their wish binge.

But Randy (from the sheer quantity of wishes that he'd consumed) had grown too big to fit through the small door, so he collapsed in the middle of the dark wish chamber – fuzzy in all the wrong ways and too big to move.

So the bloated fur-less fleshy-colored, fuzzy-wiggle with red spots and black hairy bits, slept alone and vulnerable in the center of the cold stone floor.

Chapter 27

A Real Boy

Millie

The screen door swung open with an unwelcome *screetch*, but Mrs. Saunders looked happy to see Millie. The girl stepped into the cluttered kitchen and gave Jack and Jenny's mom a hug.

"It's so nice to see you Millie!" exclaimed Mrs. Saunders. "It's been a crazy few days!"

Millie fidgeted a bit. She'd never come visiting an adult on her own before. "Mom's down in Tacoma visiting Bryton and Grandma Wilde. Gram's been sick. Today seemed a good day for a bike ride, so I thought I'd pop by. Jack or Jenny around?"

"You just missed them! They went off with Finn just thirty minutes ago."

Millie already knew this. Not-Finn had mentioned that he was meeting up with them. Not-Finn hadn't said where they were going. Millie wanted to talk with Mrs. Sanders while Not-Jack and Not-Jenny were out. She didn't exactly have a plan. She just wanted to know if Jack and Jenny's mom noticed anything different about her kids.

"Can I offer you a cup of tea, Millie?"

"Sure!" Millie responded with a smile. It boosted her confidence to be treated like a real adult. Maybe this visit would be easier than she thought.

Mrs. Saunders checked the electric kettle for water and flipped it on. "I haven't heard Jack or Jenny mention you since they got home from the hospital. You haven't fallen out have you?"

"Oh no, Mrs. Saunders. I don't have any classes with Jack. But Finn and I have some classes together. We talk."

"You always did have an eye for Finn, if you don't mind my noticing." Jack's mom said with a sly smile. She excavated some store-bought cookies out of a cabinet and placed them on a plate.

Millie blushed.

Mrs. Saunders hesitated as she pulled out a canister of tea. "I wish I could say differently, but I think you might be hunting in the wrong forest when it comes to Finn. I wish he didn't spend so much time with Jack." She dropped her voice to a whisper. "Not sure if he's a good influence."

Millie felt a little speechless at that.

"Oh, don't be shocked. It's nothing you don't know, I suppose. Finn's mother and I have talked and prayed about this more times than I can count. Hoping for the best. And I'm starting to wonder if maybe my prayers have been answered... at least with Jack. Since he's been home from the hospital, you know, he's not quite the same boy. Not so – " She searched for the right word, "sensitive?"

Millie wasn't quite sure what to say.

"Herbal all right? I've got *Twisted Berry* and *Exquisite Orange*... where do they get these names..."

"*Exquisite Orange* is good." Millie mumbled – not feeling like an adult at all.

She grabbed two mugs hanging above the sideboard, dropped in a couple tea bags and poured the hot water.

Millie began to think that she didn't like adult conversations any more. This wasn't going at all how she had expected. She wanted to leave, but instead she stirred her tea.

Mrs. Saunders registered Millie's silence. "Don't get me wrong, I'll love Jack however he turns out to be, but it does seem nice to see him turn over a new leaf. I was losing hope." Mrs. Saunders added. "But now, he isn't writing fairy tales with Finn anymore. *That* always seemed odd to me. Now he's playing those shoot-em up video games online like the rest of the boys his age – not that I like those sorts of games – but it is a bit more normal, and I don't know, he doesn't always look at me like he might start a deep uncomfortable conversation. I was always a bit afraid of what he might say. Silly me I suppose... a mother worrying about what her son might say."

Millie herself wasn't sure what to say. "Jack has always been really nice."

Mrs. Saunders took a sip of her tea. "Yes. He's absolutely a nice boy. We are very proud of him. Still, I always did have to drag him to church. But now he's growing up. He even went to bible study on Tuesday night without me forcing him. He likes to talk with Pastor Steve. They seemed to get on real well. It all makes me hopeful."

Millie finished her cookies and her tea, and offered a non-committal nod.

Mrs. Saunders gave her a conspiratorial grin. "Maybe you should be turning your eyes toward Jack? You might have better luck?"

Definitely TMI. Millie tried to smile naturally. She put down her cup. "I need to go Mrs. Saunders. Homework. Thanks for the tea."

"I'm sorry Millie. Don't mind me. I'm sure that if you waited a bit longer you'll see them. I bet Jenny would love to see you."

"Would she? How is she doing by the way? I haven't seen her much since..." Millie rinsed out her cup.

"Oh, Jenny? Well... kids do have their moods as they get older and I think she is getting to a sullen phase. It isn't very attractive but I suppose she'll grow out of it. I'd appreciate it if you spent some time with her. She has always looked up to you."

Millie paused and stared out the kitchen window. She placed her cup on the sideboard and moved towards the door. "Oh, I'll see her before long. I was just riding by and took a chance."

Mrs. Saunders sat at the kitchen table lost in thought. "Jenny lost her pirate hat during all that awfulness too. I do miss that silly hat. It's ridiculous of me, I know. She's lost some of her sense of humor... just growing up I suppose."

"I suppose." Millie shrugged and pushed open the screen door. "Thanks again for the tea, Mrs. Saunders."

As she stepped down into the yard, she could see the Not-kids walking down the driveway from the road. Not-Jenny was in the lead and the boys were following behind.

Not-Jenny's eyes darkened when she saw Millie. "What are *you* doing here!"

Millie felt suddenly exposed. "I stopped by to say hello. I had tea with your mom." She blushed. She wasn't sure why this little kid made her uncomfortable.

Not-Jenny made a smiley-face. "Well hello then," She shrugged. "And bye, bye now." Not-Jenny shoved past Millie and stamped up the stairs. The screen door banged shut behind her.

Inside the house Millie could hear Mrs. Saunders' voice, "That didn't sound very nice, Jenny."

"I don't feel like *being* nice."

Millie could hear another door slam inside the house. Mrs. Saunders apparently followed after, and soon came the sounds of an argument.

Millie didn't want to eavesdrop and moved towards the boys.

"This Millie girl *knows,* doesn't she?" said Not-Jack's voice not caring if Millie could hear him.

Millie stopped in her tracks. "I know what?"

Not-Finn smiled at her. "She's all right. You don't need to worry about Millie."

"Who *are* you?" Millie asked. "Where's the real Finn, Jack, and Jenny?"

Not-Jack didn't look her in the eye. His eyes looked lower and he smiled. She gasped and whacked him.

Not-Finn shoved him away and responded quietly with an eye to the screen door. "We actually don't know. We're trying to figure out who *we* are."

Millie glared at Not-Jack as she responded, "I don't understand."

"Neither do we," shrugged Not-Finn.

"But we have clues." added Not-Jack, rubbing his shoulder where she had punched him. "The three of us are trying to pool what we know, but the little creep keeps losing her temper."

"Are you sure you aren't them? Maybe you were brain-washed or something?"

Not-Jack laughed. "They didn't do a good job washing my brain, it's still really dirty!"

Not-Finn whacked him this time. "We're not them," he said quietly. "We're trying to figure it out. They *might* be coming back... but we don't know. It's... complicated."

Millie didn't know what to think.

"Okay." Millie felt oddly flustered. "Do you need some help?"

"Sure," answered Not-Jack suddenly.

"How can I help?" Millie believed in being helpful.

"We want to become *real* boys." Not-Jack said with a funny smile.

Not-Jenny

Not-Jenny sat up in her bedroom steaming with anger. She'd slammed her bedroom door in her *mom's* face and shoved a chair under the knob.

"Honey? Open this door right now!" came the muffled voice of the annoying lady in the hall.

"Go away!" the little girl screamed.

Not-Jenny kicked her shoes off across the room and they knocked over a stupid pirate lamp. It was so unfair! She didn't know how she knew, but she did know that when the real Jenny came back, Not-Jenny would disappear. All three of them knew this. It was sort of hard-wired into whatever they were.

In a burst of unwelcome tears, she kicked and clawed at her bedding till she was too tired to hit it again. It just wasn't fair!

Coming back to herself she was surprised to find that her sheets and blankets were entirely shredded. She whirled around and looked at herself in the mirror.

Not-Jenny didn't look like Jenny when she was angry. She got a lot bigger and a lot scarier looking. A lot bigger.

"Jenny Saunders! You come right out of that bedroom this instant!" came the voice of the obnoxious lady.

Not-Jenny marveled at the size of her claws. She liked the feeling of power they gave her.

She heard the lady sigh and her footsteps receding.

Not-Jenny smiled as her anger dissipated. She shrunk back to her guise of a seven-year-old girl.

Chapter 28

Dark Appetites

Asphixia

The notion of personally eating dark wishes had never occurred to the Blue Queen. Asphixia had been a notoriously picky eater since she was just out of the egg. She was not remotely adventuresome when it came to trying new foods.

But now that she knew a human boy had eaten a large wish and suffered no ill effects, she was thoroughly intrigued. To have the magic running through one's veins sounded particularly thrilling.

Asphixia had no intrinsic magic of her own. She had been clever enough to acquire the virus, which caused all the mermaids to devolve into progressively weaker semblances of their species. And she had been clever enough to take over the rule of law during the confusion that resulted from the mermaids' sudden absence. There is power in ruthlessness. Most people are too nice. Most people don't want to make a fuss and are thoroughly flustered by bold tactics. The best way to get what you want is to simply take it. Of course it helps if you are quite a bit larger.

Asphixia reflected on this delicious new possibility.

"But *how* should I do it? Does one eat dark wishes raw? Or with a family of roasted rabbits?"

There were so many choices.

The Blue Queen traveled quickly downstairs to her dark wish farm. There were hundreds of dark wishes that were waiting for her.

The dark wish chamber was insulated from the hall with an antechamber, which prevented wishes from fluttering out into the main corridor. Asphixia swung open the inner door and stopped cold.

The Blue Queen screamed.

The room was empty! All of her dark wishes were gone! She was furious! How? HOW!

It was then that she noticed the small, bloated worm curled up in the center of the floor. She nearly stamped on it out of sheer vexation, but hesitated at the last minute. These were the creatures that wishes came from. Maybe, there was a path forward after all.

The Blue Queen decided it was time to speak with Mordette. The Wish Monger was the expert on these things. She slipped the small sleeping worm into her pocket.

Rip-One

The Blue Queen did not have a very good sense of smell. If she did, she would have smelled the dark figure that was watching from the hallway.

Rip-One the gaseous accountant had decided to interrogate the prisoner in her boudoir. It seemed that he was the only one to realize that the golden boy was missing. Rip-One would prove that he deserved to be in the gang.

Actually, he deserved to be the *leader* of the gang!

He was going to impress Sheela in the Acquisitions Department! Rip-One was going to catch that runaway boy himself.

Chapter 29

Jack's Culinary Adventure

Jack

After a lot of slithering and more scrapes and bruises than he cared to count, he'd traversed three dark stairways designed for little feet. The tunnel ended in a stone chamber where Jack found that he could finally stand up. Bilbe, Dilbe, and Lilbe were waiting for him. They sure were small. The siblings came up to his knee.

Jack stood up and stretched, quickly grabbing his diaper to keep it from slipping. He cautiously unpinned it and snugged it tighter and re-clasped his diaper pin. "I've got to find some clothes," he muttered.

The room was smaller than the one they'd left. Hardly wider than his parents' two-car garage. But the ceiling was high and the door... maybe twenty feet tall? There was dim light from a cocked transom over the door. Shelves full of food filled the walls. It seemed to be a pantry. There was also an old trap door in the corner that seemed interesting. Jack crossed to the partially open door and peeked out into a stone corridor. The rich smells and the clanking of pots and pans suggested that they were near the kitchens.

The smell of food reminded him of how hungry he was. Above him on a shelf was a basket of fresh baked bread under a towel. He climbed up a huge bag of flour and pulled a roll out of the basket. Still warm and a foot long!

"Hungry?" he asked the worried kids standing below him. He pulled a flaky chunk off the end as he passed down a second roll to the kids.

"Jack," Lilbe whispered. "Ya might not want ta be-"

Jack took a bite. It was the best tasting bread that he'd ever tasted. It was glorious. The taste burrowed its way into every part of his body and his hunger was quickly appeased as he stuffed more and more of it into his mouth.

After the initial ecstasy subsided, he looked down to the kids again. "You were saying?" He asked with his mouth full.

"Oh... nothing," mumbled Lilbe. "Jest, ya need ta be careful wi' fairy food... bein' a mortal an' all."

The kids looked uncomfortably at each other.

But Bilbe quickly added, "But you can toss some more down to us. It won't hurt us none and it might come in useful."

He threw them a crescent roll as big as themselves before the import of Bilbe's words sunk in. But before he could ask for clarification, guttural muttering and heavy steps sounded out in the hall.

Jack dove behind a bag of flour when the huge door swung open. He hoped the creature wouldn't see him. But the cook's quick eye found his paltry hiding spot.

"Mercy! Mercy! What's a child be doin' in me pantry?" exclaimed a giant long-necked silhouette blocking the light. The shadow suddenly took a sneaky look back down the hall and hushed her voice, "Darlin', y'almost scared the poop outa me!"

"Sorry, for startling you Mam. I... I was hungry." Jack mumbled politely with his still full mouth. He was crazy scared, but he'd learned to show good manners when unsure of what else to do. Out of the corner of his eye, he noticed three fuzzballs disappearing into the tunnel they'd just come out of.

Jack's eyes adjusted to better see his new captor. The cook's ostrich pink neck expanded into a wide teardrop of a stomach, which at present was covered with a blood-stained, but once white apron. She was tall. Twelve feet? Below the apron and closer to Jack were large pink, clawed bird feet. But the face was not exactly bird-like. Her long bulbous nose was also her upper lip and was squeezed between two pumpkin sized rosy cheeks. She had no chin to speak of. Her eyes were as large as dinner plates and above that was a scattering of red plumage escaping beneath a big white chef's hat. Her clawed hands were two fingered with a thumb, and her arms were naked of feathers like flightless wings.

The large cook stepped inside the pantry quickly and shut the door. She whispered, "Oh, darlin'. Ye don't need ta worry none 'bout me! Ya'r the one who be runnin' about and not where yer supposed ta be. I'll not tell." The horrifying creature grinned conspiratorially.

Jack decided to just lay it all out there. "Can you help me escape the castle?"

"Well, yer a bold one, I'll say! First let's fatten ya up a bit. Ye look half starved! Then we'll talk." She eyed the bit of bread in his hand. "Was that tasty?"

"Yes, ma'am. It's the best bread I've ever eaten," Jack replied quite honestly.

"Aren't ya the wee flatt'erer," she laughed.

She gave a funny excited squawk, opened the door and whispered, "Come along! And mind ye don't let no one see ya. Ye can call me Doritte."

She spun rather quickly for a creature so large and waddled down the hallway. "Come along! Don't dawdle," she hissed quietly when Jack didn't move. He hesitated to leave the three little ones behind. He stepped into the corridor hoping they'd find a way to follow.

Jack trailed carefully behind Doritte. She had a large, red, feathery, big-plumed butt on her. It wiggled from side to side as she walked.

As the corridor passed an arch into the kitchens, he snuck a peak before he raced across the opening. The workers were small. Smaller than Jack. And they all looked like woodland animals – rabbits, badgers, frogs, and mice – but wearing clothes and standing up like humans. Even a quick glance told him that they were slaves. There was no Snow White *whistling while you work* here. Beatrix Potter by way of Dickens.

Jack's eyes connected for a moment with the eyes of a two-foot tall chipmunk. They were the saddest eyes that Jack had ever seen. He'd never seen a sad chipmunk before. Dogs – yes. Cats – kind of. Chipmunks? Not so much. It had to be really bad in that kitchen.

Jack surreptitiously followed Doritte through a maze of hallways. He occasionally looked back to see if the fluffballs were following, but he saw no sign of them. Several times he had to duck behind large barrels as palace servants traversed the halls, but after many twists and turns, and down one flight of steps, Jack found himself in a dark stone hallway. Doritte stood at the end of the corridor next to a huge wooden door that she had cracked open.

"Darlin'," she whispered in her husky voice. "In here. I'll hide ya here till it's time."

Jack ran from his hiding spot to the door. Inside looked like a classic dungeon cell from a fairy tale. There was a high barred window in the back wall revealing an overcast sky beyond.

"Darlin', in ya go." she giggled. "Ye'll be safe here. I'll bring ye a spot of tasty food in a bit."

Jack didn't want to go in that room, but she unceremoniously kicked him through the door and slammed it behind him. He heard a key turn in the latch.

"Prob'bly not a good idea fer ye ta be here, but I reckon' it couldna be helped," said a voice to his right.

Jack jumped.

There to his left, sitting on a wooden bench that was built into the wall, was a man. A human! He looked to be about thirty-something years old and dressed in rags. There was a strange metal collar about his neck.

"Ya know she's put ya here so she can fatten ya up. She's gonna eat ya," he sighed. "Doritte's been a wishin' for a taste o' human child for a long time."

Chapter 30

The Isle
of Plants

Pirate Jenny

The storm-tossed pirate ship was tightly wedged into the reef. Sharp rocks had broken through the hull in two small spots. Water was leaking in slowly, but for now the intrusive rocks mostly plugged the holes. Even Papy could see through the rails that if the ship moved too much, the under-decks would be flooded.

Captain Billy Blind assured Papy that they had supplies to repair the holes but they'd need low tide to give the crew time to work. That was still several hours away.

The storm had washed away the purple on Jenny's skin. She heard bits and pieces of what was going on from where she sat. The Captain hadn't seemed too concerned about the disappearance of the phooka. Whether the creature was lost during the storm or had left early to explore the island on his own was of little importance. If the phooka was gone, it just meant greater profits when they delivered the *cargo.*

Jenny had mixed feelings about the phooka. On one hand, he'd betrayed them and was willing to give her to the Blue Queen. But she didn't wish him any harm. But again, because of his duplicity the Wishermans might not be able to rescue their children. And she might die! She shouldn't be worrying about him. But...

The Captain strode on deck and called out to his crew:

"Avast ye dogs! We've stuff ta do!
No time fer'a soft an' lazy crew!

He pointed to five brownies on his right:

Ye five start prep to patch the holes!"

Then gathered eight brownies on his left:

"Let's take a boat across these shoals
with any luck we'll find a vill'ge
which we might then rob and pill'ge!
Luck will change if in them woods
we find ourselves a source for goods!

From their place tied up on the forecastle, Jenny and the Wishermans noticed that the brownie crew seemed unenthusiastic about the looting and pillaging. But they were definitely hankering to go ashore.

After various bits of metered muttering, the miniature long boat was lowered over the side. The shore crew climbed down and took their seats. Captain Billy Blind posed heroically at the prow of the longboat as they rowed towards the beach. Gibbie was left to mind the prisoners.

The morning sun was hot. Jenny wished she was wearing her hat, but her pirate hat was down below with the Wishermans' basket of wishes and other belongings.

Jenny could feel a sunburn on her nose and cheeks. Gibbie finally went below to get her silver bowl and crystal canteen when she explained that she had to have special food. Gibbie also pulled together a meal for the Wishermans – which Mamy admitted was not too bad. Gibbie was not a bad sort at all. He untied the prisoners so that they could eat, and never quite got around to tying them up again.

The morning stretched into afternoon with the sounds of pounding and sawing coming from below. The afternoon stretched into evening. The landing party did not return.

Jenny had never really considered the whole pillaging part of being a pirate. Johnny Depp and *Disney* had made being a pirate sound exciting. But she had to admit that it might not be as much fun at the other end of the pillaging.

She hoped the pirates weren't hurting anyone while they were ashore.

The holes in the boat had been tolerably patched by the time the tide changed in the late afternoon. With high tide and the repaired holes, Gibbie and the five crew members successfully maneuvered the ship away from the dangerous bits of reef. They glided into the more placid lagoon where they dropped anchor.

By the time the stars came out and the moon escaped the clouds, the crew began to worry about the missing shore party. They gathered at the side rail and looked across the water at the dark jungle beyond the beach. Jenny thought they looked like a bunch of sheep. None of them were making a move to do anything about their missing friends.

A cold breeze came up so Papy retrieved Jenny's hat and cloak. She bundled up in its warmth. Jenny was impatient to do something.

"What are we waiting for?" shouted Pirate Jenny. "They might need our help!"

When the brownies looked up, they saw a giant pirate standing above them on the forecastle in the moonlight. What a transformation! With her pirate hat and billowing cloak, Jenny cut a dramatic figure and it took them all by surprise. Even the Wishermans felt a shiver go down their backs.

Four of the brownies looked at her with awe, but Gibbie spoke up:

"The girl be right! It's time to act!
Fer now the boat's no longer cracked!
Drop a boat! We'll trust to fates!
Its time to search and find our mates!

Jenny ran to the side of the ship where the dory was being dropped. "Mamy and Papy, mind the ship while we're gone!"

"But, Jenny-girl, the Cap'n's not our friend!" cried Papy.

But Jenny didn't hear him, or she chose not to hear him.

Not one of the crew said anything about her being a prisoner. Five little sailors jumped into the boat after her.

Once they were all squeezed on the boat, Jenny grabbed the oars and rowed them to the shore.

When they ran aground near the beach, they dragged the dory up near the abandoned long boat. The seven brownies looked up at the girl with the pirate hat and the dashing cloak – she was twice their height. It seemed like they were waiting for something.

"Let's go!" she whispered. Jenny plunged into the jungle with the crew at her heels.

Fortunately it was a bright moonlit night. The footprints of the morning's buccaneers were obvious for a bit, but as the vegetation grew thicker, the trail became less apparent.

As Jenny slowly grew accustomed to the sounds of the jungle – which were pretty creepy – she had the sense that they were not alone. It was peculiar. There was movement around them – but it was invisible.

"Stop!" she whispered. She held up a hand.

Jenny listened.

"Hello?" she asked the darkness. "Is there anyone there?"

Silence.

Pirate Jenny tried again, "Can I help you?"

There was no wind, but vines and branches swayed around them. A moth came fluttering by in a spotlight created by the moon. Jenny watched it flitter past a plant. Then curly fat leaves snapped shut around the moth and literally gulped it down. She could see the lump going down the stem and the plant uttered a loud belch.

The brownies all hugged Jenny's knees at that – and she felt like a mother duck with ducklings to protect.

"Hello?" she tried to push down her fear of the unknown.

"She seems nicer than that other one," came a wispy voice not unlike the wind itself.

"I don't know," came another voice. "She's wearing a similar thing on her head."

"My hat?" Jenny quickly pulled it off. "It's just a hat! See?" She waved it in the air.

"She sways nicely."

"And, she *is* polite. I think we should take her to Mother."

With that, a tangle of vines dropped around the little group and pulled them screaming into the branches above.

Jenny clamped her mouth shut and tried very hard not to panic. She shushed the brownies, "Be brave."

Their small copse of trees began to move inland. The tree roots didn't exactly lift when they walked. More like snakes swimming through mud – even though it wasn't muddy. She counted about eight trees in their group, plus assorted bushes, which ambled around the trees' trunks much like happy hunting dogs dance around the feet of their masters.

The vines were not tight, and once Jenny and her brownies got used to the rolling movement, the pirates relaxed somewhat and waited to see what was in store.

"Are all the trees in the forest alive, like you? Or are you special?" Jenny inquired – curious. She'd never seen trees and bushes moving before.

"All trees are special. And of course all trees are alive. Those trees are only sleeping. We all need our rest, don't we?" whispered a friendly voice to Jenny's right.

"I sometimes take naps," Jenny confessed. "even though I *am* seven."

"Naps are good for you." said the tree.

"Ah love ta take naps!" said Gibbie.

"Ah take naps too!" shared another brownie. Jenny thought his name was Nibs.

Soon there was a general hubbub as all the brownies confessed that they took naps when the captain allowed it.

"Why aren't you all talking in poetry?" Jenny exclaimed.

There was a beat of silence.

"Oh! Ah! I uh, don't know!" gasped Gibbie, pausing to see if another would be forced to add a bit of meter. But there was silence!

"The curse be broken!" shouted Gibbie.

"But how?" asked Jenny.

Gibbie laughed. "Ah canna say, me lovely Jenny. 'Tis a mys'try to be sure. But, 'tis a joy to me heart. To all our hearts!"

The brownies cheered. The six little pirates chattered non-stop after that, with not a bit of poesy about them.

The cheering and friendly chatter didn't bother their captors any. The willowy shapes seemed amused with all the excitement in their branches.

About twenty minutes later, they entered a small valley in which trees stood in neat naturally terraced circles along the hillsides. In the center of the valley, Jenny saw the largest tree that she'd ever seen. The enormous roots spread out in every direction. This created a wide rippling open area about her trunk. Jenny didn't have to be told that this was Mother.

As they got closer, Jenny could see the missing crew imprisoned in a cage of living roots from the mother tree. The brownies all clutched the wooden bars and looked out at Jenny in silent terror.

Jenny quickly counted the prisoners. Everyone was there except for –

"Where's the Captain?" burst out Jenny.

"I ate him," answered the thundering voice of the old tree.

Chapter 31

The Ruins
of Frit

Finn

The giant figure that descended the steps with a fishing pole was like no creature that Finn had ever seen before. The being was tall as a house and seemed like a cross between a T-Rex and an old man. Each step sounded like the thump of a boxed refrigerator falling over on its side. (Finn unfortunately knew what this sounded like, much to his foster parents' consternation.)

Finn and his mother ran to hide near the edge of the steps behind a thicket of luminous mushrooms.

"That's a *frit!*" His mother grabbed his shoulder and pulled him down lower.

Above the waist, it was humanoid. Below the waist were the legs and tail of what reminded Finn of a tyrannosaurus. He wore a sort of toga over one scaled shoulder and across the opposite hip. It seemed more decorative than about modesty... as it wasn't modest at all. Definitely male.

The man's jaw protruded in a reptilian way. He had no real nose. It looked like the nostrils you'd see on a snake. His ears, eyebrows, and cheekbones trailed up into horns that flared out to either side. He was bald and his pate arched out in back to a narrow point.

"Are they friendly?" Finn couldn't keep his eyes off the huge man-parts! Four? The creature had four giant, dangling, blue balls – behind an enormous appendage that dangled like a suspended grandfather clock.

"I don't know much about frits. They lived under the North Mountains. They shouldn't be here in the south," said his mother who didn't seem to notice the humongous naked thing.

"This place is so weird," Finn mumbled.

A roar of laughter roared above them like the sound of a rockslide.

"Ah kin hear ya," rumbled the deep voice of the creature. "Yes! Weird it be. All life be a bit weird ah'm a reckoning. Come out. Ah'll not be hurtin' ya." With that, the giant sat down on a large rock and started prepping the giant hook for his fishing pole. The fishing pole seemed to be made of a long rib bone.

Finn timidly stood up. He was a little taller than the giant's knee. "Hello," he stammered. "You're not going to eat me, are you?"

"Ah, a human, are ya? Well, that settles it. Ah kin't be eatin' ya now," the giant chuckled and the echoes of the laugh filled the vast cavern and bounced about the darkness.

"That makes a difference?" Finn couldn't help but ask.

"Frey above, 'n' Frey below is built o' human whimsy. We can't be 'xistin' without yar notions. No one here should be eat'n parts of ar very selves kin we? Ah hafta' admit, ya smell a wee fishy fer a human. But, mebbe ah'm smellin' ta odder one." The giant cast his line out into the lake.

Finn resisted the urge to look back to where his mother was hidden, but his mother spoke up.

"My name is Meryth. I didn't know the frits came this far south," she said.

He kept forgetting that his mother had a name. Of course, she did. Meryth. Why should he be surprised at that?

The giant casually gazed down at the tiny creature addressing him.

"Yer a tad big-speakin' fer a toodle of fish-bait, but yer right enuf. We traveled southerly some time 'go, 'n' we built us a city here by this'n lake. We follow the stone-fish. But, not many of us be left these times." He tugged a bit on his line and yanked it out of the water and tossed it back in.

"Do you get many humans down here?" asked Finn.

"Nah," the giant waved away the question. "Only one ta my memory. Years back and he be lookin' fer somethin'. He looked a little like you but a bit older. But he dinna find what he wanted. An' no, ah didn't eat 'im," he added with a toothless smile.

"How's the fishing?" asked Finn, changing the subject from eating humans.

"Ah do alright. The fish here eat the metal in the rock and they're always expanding the caverns. Which suits the frit. We like a bit of ore in our food. We get sorta grumpy without it."

Meryth's face looked hopeful. "How long ago did you see this man?"

"Oh, long ago... 'bout the time we started buildin' here in the south. Ah don'na think we reckon time like ya do up top. He were a bit older than this lad with longer hair, but sturdy-like and tiny like him." He thought a moment. "He warn't none too friendly."

Meryth whispered, "James?"

Finn piped up with a hopeful smile, "But, we're friendly? Aren't we?"

"Yer friendly 'nuff. Yer nat'rally fussin' o'er a big one like me, but ya seem okay."

"How do we get up to the surface? The tunnel is blocked." asked Finn – hoping the frit might know something.

"That little hole? Well, seems ta me that thar's another hole four steps up. Ah s'spect 'tis the one you want."

"Thank you." said the surprised sea chimp. "Finn! Let's hurry!"

Finn turned to follow her, then turned back. "You said that the – the *frit* were disappearing. Why?"

For the first time the giant turned and gave Finn his entire focus. "Dunno why it's happenin'. We be slow-like turnin' to stone. It may be that our maker has forgott'n us." He exhaled in a rumble and coughed out a mouthful of dust.

Finn resisted his mother's pull. "Is there anything that can be done about it?"

"Ah don'na think a wee one like ye kin do much 'bout it. But 'tis a nice thought, 'n ah thank ye."

The giant turned back to his fishing.

Finn hesitated a moment. "My name is Finn. Thank you for your help. I do hope things get better for you."

It was strange to see such a wistful smile on a creature so large and alien. "Ah be Frayex, liddle 'un. The frit be my folk and ay be ther king. None know what t'future may bring." He sighed. "Fate be in the rocky veins of time yet ta come. It may be t'other human had somethin' to do wi' all this? Canna say."

Finn nodded, unsure of anything else to say. He turned to see his mother attempting to climb the first step. He picked her up and placed her on the step above, then shouldered his bag and climbed after her.

Ruins of an underground city were visible in the dim recesses of the upper staircase. But they needed only to get to the fourth step and find the tunnel. Maybe he could come back and explore with Jack someday.

Or maybe not. Of course they were going to go home as soon as they could.

That's if he could ever find Jack in this crazy place. Jack. Maybe magic could find him! Jack had to be alive somewhere. Finn couldn't allow himself to think any differently.

The possibility of finding his father was huge! Was he still alive? He sounded like a jerk. He had so many questions. Was that his dad who was here before? What had happened to his father?

Chapter 32

The Mother Tree

Pirate Jenny

J enny gasped at the vast size of the Mother Tree whose branches and roots filled the entire valley. The moonlight revealed large gaping holes for eyes and a jagged abyss of a mouth amid roots which wore a rather self-satisfied smirk.

"You ATE him?" Jenny exclaimed.

"Him?! He was *made* for eating!" dismissed the giant tree with a wave of a crooked branch. She seemed like a crotchety old lady. "That creature wasn't pleasant to talk to at all."

Jenny didn't know what to say to that. It was true. The captain *wasn't* very pleasant to talk to. He wasn't a very good person. But, to be eaten?

The Mother Tree's hollow eyes fixed on her. "So missy, are YOU pleasant to talk to? I can't get much out of these others. All they do is whine and wail. We're just trying to decide if they're guests, or if they're dinner..."

"YES!!" Jenny burst out. "I'm very PLEASANT! And the brownies are too!" (Though the brownies were doing little more than whimpering.)

A thick branch reached over and glided a twig along the root bars of the eight caged brownies. "But *brownies* sound rather delicious..."

The shivering brownies began to cry.

"Oh but they SING! And... they DANCE! They are ever so much fun!" Jenny shouted. "They *SING!*" She elbowed Nibs and Gibbie who were squeezed next to her in their vine prison.

"AYE AYE! We SING!" shouted Gibbie, whispering, "Nibs – er... ah, *De Wanderin' Tree[1]* – remember it?"

In a clear (but shaky) tenor voice, Gibbie sang out:

> *"Ah once met a tree, a comf't'ble TREE*
> *what loved all de birds and de breezes so free!*
> *She had a sweet brook– a wee comfy spot–*

---

1. *The Wanderin' Tree can be read in its entirety in the Appendix*

'twas neither too chilly, nor neither too hot!
Not pixies nor squirr'l poop dinna much rile,
her own sunny spot on her own sunny isle!"

Nibs jumped in with another verse:

"She pulled up her roots an' she started ta walk.
Wi' a boat at de shore, she started ta talk!
De boat said, "Come travel wi' me on ze sea!
Come fly like de wind!! On me ye'll feel free!
She straddled his bow an' she sailed wi' ze tide.
Wit' wind in her leaves!! Her branches stretched wide!"

Gibbie began to sing harmony with the next verse, which followed the adventures of the tree as she traveled the world. Soon all the brownies jumped in!

The brownies in the cage started beating percussion on the roots of their cage, and the melody grew upbeat and bawdy. The cage opened up with the tickling percussion, and all the brownies danced with enthusiasm – for their lives depended on it.

The entire crew danced in a conga line around the nearby trees and along the winding root tops. They then launched into a rousing finale in front of Mother – and even Jenny had figured out the words by then:

*"She has a sweet brook— a wee comfy spot—
'tis neither too chilly, nor neither too hot!
Not pixies nor squirr'l poop never much rile,
her own sunny spot on her own sunny isle!"*

The trees and bushes swayed in time to the brownies' song. Jenny was relieved that things were going so well.

It all was going perfectly until Jenny noticed something moving in the Mother Tree's branches. The phooka!

He was quietly pulling off large swaths of the Mother Tree's moss, which hung in long curling tendrils from her branches like hair. He was stuffing it into a large bag that he carried over his shoulder. Neither the Mother Tree nor her arboreal court had noticed the strange parasite yet, so Jenny decided to distract her.

"Your Majesty!" She waved to catch her attention. "Can I sing a song too?" She racked her brain for a song to sing.

The dark eyes turned their black gaze on Pirate Jenny with some curiosity. "Go ahead, little missy."

"Twinkle, twinkle, little star..."

Jenny watched Footbe's dark figure crawling amid the Mother Tree's twisting branches.

"How I wonder what you are..."

Footbe needed to get out of there before the Mother Tree noticed him and dropped him into her giant mouth!

Jenny kept singing, and when she finished *Twinkle Twinkle Little Star,* she quickly started singing *Rockaby Baby.*

"... *when the bough breaks...*"

The Mother Tree interrupted her there. "Why would the bough break? Is this song about maltreating trees by hanging fat human babies from them?!"

"Oh no, Ma'am! It's just a song – uh, I don't know what it means! I uh –"

"THEN, WHY WOULD YOU SING IT!" demanded the giant tree as branches and roots snaked their way towards the girl.

"'Cuz – it's a pretty song that puts babies to sleep –" Jenny had never really thought about the words before. "Hmmm ma'am, maybe you're right. I never really thought about it before. *'When the bough breaks the cradle will fall...'* At the end of the song I think the baby dies... or is probably hurt really bad. The song doesn't make much sense at all. I can't believe my mom used to sing that to me!" she mumbled somewhat abashed.

The Mother Tree's voice softened. "Little missy, you should *always* think about words. Words might be the most powerful magic in the world. Words can save life and they can kill."

Jenny could no longer see the phooka. "Yes ma'am. Thank you ma'am. I should really go, ma'am. My parents are probably really worried about me and there's some really important things to do before I go home."

The giant tree looked at her for a moment and then said, "You may go."

"Thank you ma'am." Jenny said inching away. The brownies were all waiting for her in a clump at the edge of the clearing.

As she turned, the Mother Tree spoke again, "But don't forget your friend." A thick branch came out of her upper foliage. Wrapped in its coils was the phooka – looking thoroughly frightened. The branch stretched forward and held Footbe upside-down above the grass next to Jenny.

"Little phooka, squirrels and birds belong in my branches. You do not." She said with a gentle shake. "But, I know your tale from the gulls that visit, and I know your purpose. You are late. *I expected you long before this.* You *should* have asked permission, but go with my blessing."

A thoroughly abashed Footbe fumbled for words, but in a higher voice than usual said, "I thank ya yer majesty fer yer understandin' o' the sit'ation." He kept bowing and moving backwards till he reached the edge of the clearing. Then with Jenny following close behind, they traveled as fast as they could towards the beach and their boats.

Jenny and the phooka traveled through the jungle in silence after the initial jubilation of their rescue quieted.

Footbe finally spoke up. "Thank ye for tryin' ta distract her."

"I didn't want you to get eaten." Jenny offered, feeling a lot of complicated thoughts. "But, I'm awfully disappointed about you wanting to sell my blood to the queen!"

"Ah be appreciatin' that," the phooka responded. "An' ya should know, ah never intended fer ya to be given ta the queen perm'nent like."

Jenny wasn't sure what to say.

"Ah jest had ta have a reason ta get close 'nuff ta her ta kill her. She's downright evil."

"She doesn't seem very nice." Jenny observed.

"The Queen took everythin' ah ever loved. She took me memories. She took me hope too."

The phooka didn't elaborate, so Jenny asked, "What's the moss for?"

"It's ta fix somethin' the Queen did a long time ago. Ah'm startin' ta remember things. Important things."

Chapter 33

Mordette, The Wish Monger

Mordette

Mordette hated the Blue Queen. It was not an ordinary hate, like the way someone might hate Brussels sprouts or broccoli. Her hate simmered like pools of lava beneath a sleeping volcano. Like lava, Mordette's hate also wore a thin, cool, hard crust so as to appear dormant to the casual observer. Erupting took a great deal of effort, and Mordette hated expending any sort of effort.

"But, Asphixia," cooed the enormous Mordette from where she sat in the shadows. "Why ever do you need me here? My market has a schedule to keep."

The floating Wish Market had been tethered to the roof of the palace for over five days, and Mordette had been locked in the dungeons ever since. She should have said no to the tea. But Mordette loved a bit of tea after a long trip. It had been her undoing.

"But Mordette," the Blue Queen purred. "As queen, I can no longer risk your precious safety – flying about dangerous territory with a valuable cargo. You might be attacked by pirates!"

"Oh pooh. You know I am perfectly safe. I get on just fine with those little pirates. I have magic traps all over my island. And I've a business to run!"

"My dear, when I arrived in Frey as a young slip of a frit, you took such great care of me. You took me into your home when I was all alone in the world. You must let *me* take care of *you* now."

Mordette looked at the stone walls around her. She cursed the day she first set eyes on that skinny, bedraggled frit. She was glad that she'd always kept her true name to herself, purely out of habit of course. Mordette never liked her birth name. Similarly, Asphixia had never told anyone *her* real name. Asphixia was a persona that the young runaway had created while living with Mordette.

Asphixia sighed sweetly. "Oh, and yes, you should have really warned me about those traps. How can my guards protect your island if my soldiers keep getting turned into small furry insects?"

The Queen's minions had been searching her island for the stock of wishes. Ha! She'd have no luck there! If those soldiers were lucky, their enchantments would last till Mordette could escape with her island and the guards would be free of their evil employer.

Mordette's slug-like bulk inflated with irritation. "I've no need for your protection, Asphixia. You know I have clients waiting for me at all my stops."

Asphixia acted like an idea had just come to her. "Now Mordette, I've had some thoughts about that. It's not good to make wishes available to just anyone. Why, only yesterday a miscreant snuck into the castle and assaulted my children with wishes. The poor children who survived have been screaming for hours! That's what happens when wishes get into the wrong hands!"

Mordette's ears perked up. Not that she had external ears in the way you might expect.

She smiled when she reflected that Asphixia had never been quite clear on what type of creature Mordette was. The Queen would have been surprised to learn that the Wish Monger was a nearly extinct relative of the hairless fuzzy-wiggle family. She was nearly as large as Asphixia. Although she *did* eat wishes like other fuzzy-wiggles, she'd never turned into a wish herself. She'd just gotten bigger. And bigger! Mordette was also capable of magic. She'd been careful to keep Asphixia unaware of her abilities. It was better that way.

Mordette feigned concern, "Why Asphixia, that sounds just awful for you." Though inwardly she was delighted with the news.

"It was awful!" gushed Asphixia, possibly believing that Mordette actually cared. "So, you see, I need to have stricter controls over *all* the wishes in Frey. And... I need *more* wishes to take care of all these problems."

"Oh dear. I was afraid you'd ask that. I don't have any stock of wishes at the moment." In reality, the Wish Monger had a considerable stock of happy fuzzy-wiggles and fluttering wishes hidden safely away in a magic room on her floating island. Ha! "Perhaps, if you'd let me leave I could find some for you –"

"That's just impossible, Mordette!" implored the Blue Queen. "I need your expertise here! You know more about wish magic than anyone!"

Mordette looked at her askance, "What *exactly* do you need to know?"

A crafty look slid across Asphixia's face. "It has come to my attention that a wish may be eaten by the caster. But what would happen if I swallowed... say, a worm who had eaten all of my dark wishes?"

Randy the Fuzzy-Wiggle

It should be said that at this point, Randy – who had till now been asleep in the Queen's pocket in a dark wish drunken stupor – Randy woke up quite completely.

Mordette

"A *worm* is just a *worm* till the transformation. It will do you no good." Mordette cautioned, secretly wondering if there was a way to retrieve her distant relative. "Do you know if this *worm*, theoretically of course, has ever consumed human blood directly?"

Randy the Fuzzy-Wiggle

Inside the pocket, Randy knew he had not.

Mordette

"I think not. I personally oversee the care of my flock of worms, and none of them had looked like this one. Theoretically... blast it! All my worms had already turned. This worm must have come from the new shipment... the one with the annoying little human."

Mordette reflected back on what she knew of the distinction between general magic and wishes. "Well what do we know? Frey is built from the seeds of human imagination. We know a little of the human world, but they know nothing of us. Frey and its magic grew from the seeds of daydreams.

"But wishes are different. They're pure unfiltered human desire. They're not simple imagination. A fuzzy-wiggle pops into existence whenever a human child desperately longs for what they're told is impossible. Fuzzy-wiggles retain their sense of self even after they become wishes. Wishes are pure energy that mutate into nearly anything once bonded with their host."

Mordette frowned. "But dark wishes are the result of fuzzy-wiggles fed with human blood. They don't remember who they are. They have no moral quibbles. Their host can use the energy as they wish. A dark wish always does exactly what you ask for. You'd know that better than I."

"But will a worm that has consumed dark wishes, but not blood – turn into a dark wish? Will it obey my commands?"

"I think if that worm has *never* tasted human blood, that worm will show self-control," reflected the Wish Monger.

"Hmmm... I suppose I'll have to remedy that. Well Mordette, it has been lovely to chat!"

The Blue Queen left a trail of rocky dust on the floor behind her. Despite the illusion of youth, Mordette knew that Asphixia was not aging well. Time was not on the Queen's side and she was becoming more desperate.

Mordette had to escape.

Randy the Fuzzy-Wiggle

As the queen strode down the hallway, Randy shivered uncontrollably inside of the Queen's pocket. What had he gotten himself into?

Chapter 34

The Prisoner

Jack

Jack stared in shock at the prisoner on the other side of the cell. He was human! The older man returned his gaze with a curious excitement. He would have been handsome – if not for the crazy glint in his eyes. The prisoner was dressed in rags – which seemed odd next to the clean-shaven face. The ragged blond hair needed a good washing. There was a glowing blue metal donut locked about his neck. It didn't look very comfortable.

"Welcome ta my humble abode, young 'un."

"You're human." Jack observed.

"Well, I try ta be." said the man. His jaw was limited in its movement by the neck device. His mumbling lips gave a sort of ventriloquist quality to the voice.

Now that he found himself with an adult human, all the horrors of the last week rushed upon Jack. Tears sprang uninvited to his eyes. Jenny's disappearance, losing Finn underground, being kidnapped by horrible creatures and waking up on a wall of half-dead kids! A gigantic, reptilian blue lady! He hadn't a clue as to where he was or how he got here! He'd never felt so alone in his life. But maybe this adult would know what was going on.

"That Doritte creature wants to cook and eat me?!" Jack gasped.

"Yup. That be pretty much the gist o' it. I'm sure she be rustlin' through her cookbooks now, afore she somehow misses d'opp'rtun'ty," giggled the man as he eyed the boy in diapers.

"This whole place is a loony bin." Including this strange guy, Jack thought. He looks crazy. He sank to a bench on the other side of the cell. It seemed best to keep a healthy distance from this creepy man who was staring so intently at him.

It was a large cell – dimly lit through the barred window. Prisoners must come in all sizes judging by the large cot on the back wall below the window. The wall behind Jack was rough rock, but the window wall, door wall, and the wall opposite wall (where the man was sitting) were mortared stonework like the rest of the castle. He wondered if there was a way to escape. Adventure books always had convenient loose bits of mortar and a secret passage.

The man now was examining his long, dirty fingernails as he casually asked, "Does the Queen know you're here?"

Jack sighed. "Not exactly. Hopefully she thinks I'm still in the cage in her bedroom."

"Ah, ya came in by one of de Queen's traps? She got 'em all over the human world ya know - ta get her young 'uns. She switches the kids out wi' changelin's so the parents don't know the kids are missin'!"

Jack reflected. "Changelings? Like in the old fairy stories? My little sister, Jenny went missing about a week ago. Didn't see any changelings of her running around. My buddy, Finn, and I fell through... maybe the day before yesterday? Not sure. We hoped we'd find her, but then we got separated."

"Finn, ya say?" The man was suddenly more intent.

"I've gotta find them – but, I don't even know *how* to start looking for them – if I could even get out of here!" Jack ran his hands through his messy hair.

"I been in this dungeon for more years n' I can count. Don't get yer hopes up. But, Frey's a strange, magic place. If ya *did* find yar way out, thar always be ways ta find folk." The man tapped his nose knowingly and winked at Jack.

"Why are *you* here? Does the Queen bleed you too?"

"Nah, she be 'fraid a' bleedin' me. " The man hesitated. "She's got other notions fer keepin' me."

He giggled.

"What's your name?" Questions tumbled out on top of each other. "And where am I! I don't understand any of this!"

"Whoa now. One query at a time. I – uh, I got many names. You *could* call me James. All my names be long ago and meaningless now. Another life. Once thar be a very imagin'tive young human in yar world who met a mermaid and they travel'd back ta her world. She were a princess of sorts, and her father dinna take ta him none at first – bein' wit'out a tail ya see, but she were an obstinate sort and bit by bit her folks got used ta de notion of a man wit'out a fish tail. After a while, her father – who were the King o' Frey – thought a man who walked 'bout might be useful. A man wi' legs could travel 'round where the Merfolk couldna' go."

"Frey... But, how can merpeople be rulers of land if they can't walk?" interrupted Jack.

"The sea-folk dinna ask ta be the rulers. The land-folk asked 'em fer the very reason of them bein' impartial and not tied up in land squabbles. And the king found it was useful to have a disint'rested footed person ta look inta those squabbles up close." The man giggled again.

The guy really was creepy.

"So, that's what you did? Traveled around for the king?" asked Jack.

"It were too much fer jes' one soul, so a helper was brought on – a bright feller – a phooka who could transform inta any creature like he might need ta be investigatin', he even possessed other magic skills when they be needed. A phooka can never put a lie inta his words - bein' a relative of the faerie folk – and that be useful fer givin' testimony an' such afore the king."

"Where is *Frey?* I still don't understand where this is?" Jack felt impatient. Stories about mermaids were all very interesting, but he was starting to suspect that the man was a couple sandwiches short of a picnic. Clearly the guy was bonkers. Jack had to accept the reality that he was on his own again. This adult would be of no help.

"Frey won't be on no human map – though 'tis o' human construction fer good or ill. Frey's where yer imag'native ideas go when yer not usin' 'em. An' that's how de trouble started. Dere'd never been a human here afore. Creative type humans be especially dangerous here. Ideas grow inta real things like magic beans. James were de one who thought up de frit!"

"*The frit?*"

"Notions here are pow'ful things! The ground and de trees be pure 'mag'nation."

"But what are the frit?" persisted Jack.

"*The Blue Queen be a frit.* But, she dinna used ta exist! See, we traveled 'bout on missions fer de King, and in de ev'nin', James liked ta draw and make up stories – just ta pass de time innocent like. James be partic'lar good at makin' up a good tale. But, one of James' idees took root quicker than anythin' and next thing ya' know we got de frit under de mountains like dey always been der! Tee hee! Not ev'n de frit knew dey be jes' born."

"So, I'm not clear – are you James or not?" interrupted Jack.

"I used ta be James... perhaps. And I might be James now, but my memory be a bit shaky."

"Okay – so back to the frit, what *is* the frit?" Jack was feeling irritated with the strange man's tittering.

"A civil'zation o' blue giants what sudd'nly appear'd under the North Mountains. Most-wise dey dinna bother us none, but one of 'em decided she dinna much like livin' underground!"

"The Blue Queen." Jack said.

"Yessiree, the Blue Queen herself. She'd dabbled in magic and poisoned the waters in the Bay of mer'Rin ta get rid of the Merfolk. But, she daren't get rid o' James as folks here nat'rally know'd their maker. If James were ta die, all the frits might disappear. He's ta only human ta think o' 'em. James can't die without mebbe dyin' herself! Though she been hankerin' ta try James' blood on her worms... see if her creator's blood might be something special powerful. But she's afeared ta. So she keeps James here in her dungeon where she can keep an eye on him. She did her best ta get rid of folks 'twould be close ta him. Ha!"

"Okay..." Jack tried to assimilate all the new information.

"Ohh hoo! But, I'm not him! An' she don't know! Tee hee!" Then he scratched his head. "Or maybe I am and I canna remember! Yoo hoo!"

"What's that blue collar around your neck?" asked Jack. The prisoner pulled at metal ring.

"Annoyin' 's what it is! I can't do no magic with dis 'round me neck! Irr'tatin'! James is good wi' *wishes*! James can do 'mazin' things wi' *wishes. Ooooh hooo! James is magic! Yessiree he is! But can't do no magic with dis here collar!*"

Jack interrupted the wild laugh. The man was clearly crazy. "But, how -"

There was a sound in the corridor and the wild looking man jumped to his feet and ran to put his ear to the door.

He hissed out "Hush! Not 'nother word! 'Tis the Queen. Hide!"

Jack jumped up and after a quick look rolled under the big bed beneath the window and tried to not breathe in the accumulation of dust and ick. It smelled bad. The stone was cold against his bare body. He was amazed that the cloth diaper with its one safety pin had stayed together as well as it had.

It smelled seriously bad under the cot. Boy Scout latrine bad (Jack had once joined the Scouts for a long uncomfortable weekend).

Meanwhile, James – or whoever he was – threw himself back on his bench as the large bronze lock rattled with the sound of a key.

The vast door swung inward and Jack could see the big clawed feet, tail, and gauzy fabric of the Queen's robes.

"My dear James. You're looking well."

Jack could hear the smile in her voice. It was nauseatingly sweet – like the last piece of chocolate after you've eaten the entire box.

"I be honored by yer visit my good Queen," said the man's voice in an unexpected monotone.

"Dear James, it is always our pleasure," wheedled the sibilant voice of the Queen. "We need a little favor from you."

"Whate'er you desire me queen," responded the glazed voice of the prisoner.

Jack heard a sound of a knife being unsheathed, and a moment later the man gasped in pain.

"Oh, don't be such a baby in front of your Queen! We only took a small piece of you," she chided. "It's a special occasion, *Daddy*. We figured it had to be you. We *neeeed* it for an experiment."

The man was making some high moaning sounds while the Queen rustled around in her pocket.

"Come here my fat little worm. We've some nice delicious blood for you. A bit of flesh too!" There was a squeak when she apparently grabbed what she was seeking.

"Come now, We just need you to open up and try a tiny taste. Here comes the little birdie! Right towards your mouth!"

Jack heard the Queen let loose with a hiss and a curse.

"Oh, little wormsie-poo... Don't you want to be part of our glorious changes to the world! You need to become a big wish! WE NEED YOU TO OPEN UP!!"

There was a slight gagging and a sucking sound from a small creature as something was stuffed in its mouth.

"There, that wasn't so bad now was it? We want you to grow up fat and strong, now don't we?" The Blue Queen laughed. A white finger fell on the stone and bounced under the bed and hit Jack on the face. He stifled a scream.

"Wasteful! That finger was a little dirty, but we would've eaten it!" A moment passed and Jack held his breath. "Ten-second-rule says we could... but, shouldn't spoil our appetite. Daddy should eat it! It's his after all." Jack could hear her laugh as if she'd just shared an intimate joke. "Now, we've a most delicious little boy upstairs to help our worm get big and fat. It will be such a treat. And we're going to have the most sumptuous feast in the castle tomorrow night. Too bad you can't attend, James."

Jack was exhausted, freaked out, and numb. The giant feet disappeared and the great door shut tight.

The Queen's voice echoed in the corridor beyond it. "Oh, guardy-poo! We need to get some oil on that door!

Our prisoners shouldn't have to listen to that horrible screeching..." Her voice receded.

Jack inched his way out from under the cot, stood, and tried to brush the dirt off his mostly naked body. At the moment the grungy white diaper was the least of his worries.

On the bench, the man rocked silently back and forth holding his bloody hand to his chest and sobbing in silent heaves.

"We need to get out of here." Jack was trying to keep his wits, but what does one say to a guy who just had his finger chopped off. "Should I get your finger for you? It fell under the bed."

The man still rocked silently. He looked at Jack with the blank expression of a man with no wits left.

Jack got back down on his knees and looked under the bed. Beyond the finger, there was a hole in the rock floor. Not a big hole. Maybe eighteen inches round? And above the hole he realized that there was a corresponding hole in the cot - with a lid. He realized it wasn't a bed. It was a latrine for very big creatures. That's why it smelled so bad under there. It was a good thing he hadn't rolled all the way to the back. He'd have stuck his feet or worse in that hole!

But now a small dark shape climbed out of the pit.

Yick! It was some disgusting creature that lives in the latrine!

"Pssst" it whispered. "Jack!"

"Bilbe?" Jack smiled in relief.

"We're here ta rescue ye," announced Bilbe.

A hushed squeaky voice hissed from down the hole. "Bil! Is that Jack?"

"We found him alright!" He whispered back down the hole. Lil! Stay there! We'll be right down."

"Will I fit?" hesitated Jack.

"Ah, sure ya'll fit. If ya kin stand the smell, ya'll fit. An' it's jest a little ways. There be an air vent a wee bit down."

"But my friend won't fit! He's too big and I can't leave him here." He took a peek back towards the prisoner who was rocking back and forth on his bench and unaware of anything but his pain.

Bilbe or Bil(?) lowered his voice. "This be the only way yer gonna get out o' here. We asked the rodent."

Jack looked back at the prisoner. He decided to not be squeamish. He grabbed the pale finger and placed the detached digit beside the man on the bench.

"Here! Maybe we can fix it? I don't know, but I'll be back for you. I promise!"

With that he ran back to the cot, tightened his diaper pin and crawled underneath. With Bilbe's guidance, he nervously dropped his legs into the slimy hole and squeezed his body into the enveloping stench of the dungeon sewer system.

Chapter 35

Changeling Hearts

Millie

Millie agreed to meet Not-Finn and Not-Jack after school at three o'clock on Friday at Edgewater Park – which was across the river from downtown, Mount Vernon. She wanted someplace public, but a good distance from home. None of them wanted Not-Jenny there.

Seven-year-old Not-Jenny couldn't go far without Mrs. Saunders stepping in. Not-Jenny found this extremely frustrating and for some reason was spending a lot of time by herself in the cellar.

The boys were sitting on the edge of the outdoor stage when Millie got there. There was a metal roof above to keep rain off of performers, but that wasn't a problem today. It was a perfect day with bright blue sky and white puffy clouds. But the boys sat in the shade. She'd noticed that they avoided the sun whenever they could.

"Hi!" Millie was still not clear what the boys wanted from her. When she asked herself what she wanted from them, she tried to convince herself that it was to find out what had happened to her friends. And though that was true, she also was curious about this new Finn. He differed from the Finn she was used to.

"Hey," said Not-Finn.

"Hi!" said Not-Jack. He was looking at her weirdly. "Ready to make us real boys?" He said with a stupid smile.

Millie hesitated thinking perhaps she shouldn't have agreed to meet these boys after all. What was she thinking? They weren't Jack and Finn even if they looked like them! "Uh... you are going to need to define that."

Not-Finn looked a little embarrassed and turned to Not-Jack. "Hey, I'm still not sure it works like that."

Millie had a wave of comprehension. "It most definitely does NOT work like that." She could feel her cheeks turning red.

Jack scoffed. "Fuck. We've seen videos. We've seen how it's done."

Millie exploded. "Jack Saunders! Or, Not-Jack Saunders! Whoever you are. If you want to pass as the real Jack, first off, *we* don't use language like that!"

"Everybody talks like that! What's the big deal?"

"We..." she gestured to encompass Finn as well, "have bigger vocabularies than that! It makes you sound stupid."

"Whatever," Not-Jack scoffed.

"Wh–" Millie felt speechless, then burst, "and *more* importantly, we are only fifteen years old! I don't know what type of videos you've seen, but having sex does not make you a *real* boy."

Not-Finn looked embarrassed, but Not-Jack was ready to argue.

"Of course it does! That's how it works in songs and movies! You're not a *real* man until you've done *it!* We've been online. WE'VE WATCHED TV!" spouted Not-Jack looking a little angry.

"Well if you're thinking that I'm going to have sex with either of you, you're crazy! I'm not going to do that for... for years and years! I'm going to focus on school and – well, I'm just not in a hurry to do that! It's a grownup thing. There's lots of time in the future for *that!*"

"But not for us," murmured Not-Finn.

"Yeah... and *why* would that be?" scoffed Millie.

"We *have* to become *real people*," whispered Not-Finn rather desperately.

Millie stopped and looked at them. "I'm not sure what it means when you say that," answered Millie. "Talk!"

Not-Finn took a breath and then spoke carefully, "We don't have memories from before the hospital. But we learn really fast... how to speak, and act... we've spent hours on the Internet reading everything we can find. We're not sure what we are – but, we don't think we're human."

Not-Jack cut in. "But there *is* stuff we do know! Stuff that doesn't make sense... but we *know* it."

"Like what?" Millie whispered. She was trying to decide how crazy this all was and whether she should make an excuse to get out of there.

Finn looked her straight in the eyes. "We know the other Finn, Jack, and Jenny are all still alive, but they are... in another place. Like in one of those science fiction movies." He held up his hand. "We don't know where. We're just... temporary... placeholders for them. When they come back, we disappear."

"Disappear?" Millie scoffed.

"Poof!" Finn made a disappearing gesture with his hands. "We aren't exactly clear how it works."

Millie took a big breath. "Okaaay. What does that have to do with you 'becoming real'?"

Not-Jack looked more thoughtful. "Well, this big-boy and I figured if we could become not just duplicates – maybe we wouldn't disappear? Like when you rename a file so it doesn't get copied over, when a file with the same name is dropped in the same folder. We have to become people in our own right. Real."

"It's our theory," Not-Finn added.

Millie mused. This was all crazy. "What does Not-Jenny think about this?"

Not-Jack sighed. "She's planning to kill the real Jenny when she shows up."

"But that doesn't sound very nice." Not-Finn quickly added, seeing Millie's wide eyes.

"But it does come down to self-preservation," Not-Jack offered.

"But *we* wouldn't do that." Not-Finn corrected, looking sternly at Not-Jack. "There's *got* to be another way."

Millie took a seat on the edge of the stage with them.

"Well, saying I buy into this trip to crazy-town, and I'm NOT saying I am, but from everything I've ever read – and granted, I'm just a kid – but doing *that* doesn't make you more real! It's probably just going to make your life a lot more complicated. My mom would say it's one of those things that works better when you're older."

"But we might never get older if they come back!" burst out Not-Jack.

Millie reflected on what makes a person, *real*. How do you even define *real?* When had she felt most alive? Because that's what this was all about. Wasn't it? Being alive?

"Now again, I'm not saying I believe any of this, but I *think* the times when *I* feel most alive are when I'm helping other people. When I forget my *self.* Maybe that won't work for you. I don't know. But becoming a real boy... a real man... a real girl or a real woman is not about sex... especially when you are just a kid! I'm pretty sure of that. It has something to do with thinking about someone other than yourself. Not staring at your own navel all the time."

"The doctors never even noticed that we don't have real navels!" laughed Not-Jack. "They are totally fake. At least I think they're fake. Show me yours."

"Are you trying to get me to whack you again!" Millie gave him the evil eye, then returned to her point. "When you focus on others – there is a kind of rush when you know that you've done something good. At least, it makes *me* feel more – *real.* Does that make any sense at all?"

"Like Pinocchio," mused Not-Finn. "wanting to become a real boy – then helping Geppetto."

"What?" Millie stopped. "Oh, yeah... I suppose. Showing that you can care for someone besides yourself."

"I didn't take that story seriously," snarked Not-Jack. "'Cuz my nose don't grow, but I've got something else that does..."

"STOP." Millie put her hands over her ears.

Not-Finn elbowed Not-Jack to shut him up.

"We can give it a try? Can't hurt?" shrugged Not-Finn.

"And we can always use the other option as a back-up." added Not-Jack.

Millie gave him an incredulous look.

"Or not." Not-Jack squirmed feeling very conflicted.

Not-Finn nudged Not-Jack's shoulder with his own.

"Actually, it's kind of a relief," sighed Not-Jack. "I was stressing about this. It looked interesting but kind of uncomfortable at the same time. But maybe I was watching the wrong videos... she was wearing this thing..."

Millie stared at him. He stopped.

Not-Finn spoke up. "What you want us to do?"

Millie raised an eyebrow and thought for a moment. "Well I'm meeting my mom at the homeless shelter in downtown, Mount Vernon at four-thirty. We help out with their Friday dinner every other week. We work in the kitchen and wash dishes – it helps out the shelter a lot. The shelter feeds people who don't have money for food. You could try it tonight? Call your moms and ask if my mom could stand in for them. Maybe they can fax a permission slip or something."

"What's a FAX?" Not-Jack asked.

"My foster parents have one," replied Not-Finn.

Not-Jack followed his lead. "Okay."

Not-Finn smiled at Millie like he was looking forward to the evening.

Millie found she was starting to maybe like Not-Finn more than the real Finn. Of course the real Finn was her friend and she wanted him and the others back. Yet Not-Finn looked at her differently than Finn ever did. But she was *not* going to be doing *that*! She wanted to go to college someday and – she was only fifteen! BOYS!

Boys can be so stupid – whatever flavor they come in, she thought as they walked to where they had left their bikes. The homeless shelter was only across the river.

Chapter 36

Finn Gets
A Surprise

Finn

F inn carefully lifted the small weak body of his mother to the top of the rocky fourth step, it was as high as his waist. The light from the glowing fungi which sprouted from every crack and crevice revealed how pale his mother was getting. Her skin now looked paper thin.

As he pulled himself up onto the step, he now could see a triangular gap between some rocks to his left at the cave wall.

The old giant, Frayex, was humming a peculiar lilting tune while fishing from his rock. The notes were not like anything Finn had ever heard before, but they were peaceful and melancholy. He found himself wondering about frit culture. What had their lives been like before their present troubles?

The oversized steps led up through a haze towards a colossal city, built into vast rock walls far above. It was spectacular and ascended the sides of the cavern in wide terraces. It was hard to believe that all of this was built in the time since Finn was born. Hatched? Whatever. It had been an empty cave then. When Finn had been in the egg, the tunnel to the surface was unobstructed. But since that time, a colossal city had been built, steps had blocked the passage, and now that city was dying for mysterious reasons. He could see unmoving gargantuan shapes in the mist. He wondered if they were statues, or if they were frit who had turned to stone.

"We need to keep moving," came the breathy voice of Meryth – his mother. He was starting to accept that she might really be his mother, as weird as that was.

Finn lifted her fragile body and held her to his chest. He carefully crossed the rock strewn step to the cave mouth. The opening between the two boulders was plenty big once they got close. It was about five feet wide at the base and peaked at about ten feet.

His shirt and jeans were still wet from their dowsing in the lake. Even his boxers under his jeans were wet along with his shoes and socks. It wasn't very comfortable. At least his bag with his sketchpads was dry. Finn wished he had another set of pants and shoes in his bag. There was probably going to be a rash by the end of the day.

He did have a t-shirt in there. The one he had tried to push on his mom. Black and short sleeve from a Celtic fair that he'd gone to with Jack's family. They saw a cool bagpipe band called *The Wicked Tinkers*. He set his mom on a flat rock and stepped behind a rock and stripped. He squeezed his jeans, socks, and boxers out the best he could, and put them back on with the fresh t-shirt. Better than nothing. Meryth looked better from her dunking despite her illness. Maybe she needed to stay wet? He was starting to forget about her exposed boobs. He wasn't sure if that was weird or not.

Finn shouldered his bag and picked up his mom again. The dimly lit tunnel led up. The path's twisted ascent followed the course of the much larger steps outside. At times the wall opened up to let in light and offered a peek at the gigantic city. Phosphorescent fungi provided some light in the tunnel along with an occasional large, phosphorescent insect. None of these bugs spoke to them. He wasn't sure if they were being unfriendly, or if they just didn't talk. Nothing seemed dangerous so far, but Finn kept his eyes open.

Eventually, Finn stumbled and Meryth suggested that they find a spot to sleep. They found a nook near the side of the trail and he was asleep in minutes. It had been a long day. Despite her own exhaustion, Meryth's motherly eyes kept watch.

The next morning they traveled upward faster than either of them expected and they were often surprised to look out on dizzying depths. They wound around the metropolis' empty plazas and crooked towers. Occasionally they would see frits going about their daily business below. He would be as small as a toddler in that giant city.

They'd eaten everything edible in Finn's bag and were getting really hungry. He worried about his mother. She was already weak from whatever was wrong with her. She said that she was tougher than she looked, but he suspected that she was lying.

Huffing and puffing after hours of walking upward, Finn and Meryth looked out from the top of the city. Beyond this point, they would no longer have the city to their right. It was a remarkable view. Goodbye to the city of the frits. He hadn't asked if the city had a name.

Finn placed his mother gently on a bed of tiny mushrooms, then sat down himself. He was breathing heavy. His fresh t-shirt was drenched with sweat, and his damp jeans definitely needed a wash from all the dust and dirt of the tunnel. "How far is it to the surface from here?"

"I don't know. I've never been this way. This tunnel and that chamber were your father's creation. He made it with wishes to hide me while he searched for the cure. He described the tunnel to me many times, but I only came down the one time when he was ready for me, and that was with another wish."

"I tried a wish once! I wished for a tuna melt sandwich on sourdough with a pickle on the side for Jack. He likes pickles. The sandwich was delicious." I wish I had a wish right now, I'd order us something tasty!"

"They're actually hard to find, Finn. You were very lucky." observed his mom.

"I didn't think there was any such thing as magic."

"Neither did your father, but he became very good with wishes. They began calling him the Wish-Master. There'd never been a human in Frey before. He was the first. Wishes have a curious affinity with humans. No one, including my father the king, was quite sure what to make of your father. It was so strange to see a man with legs."

"Why did you come back to Frey with my dad?"

"Well it's hard to be a mermaid in your world for one. But also, none of us *can* stay long in your world. Eventually, Frey sucks us back. I warned James that it would happen. He wanted to come to Frey. To be with me. I warned him that he'd never be able to return to your world, but he said *that I was the best bit of tail he'd ever find.*" She giggled. "He came back with me. He was such a bad boy."

Finn smiled. Her face always lit up when she spoke about his dad.

"My father of course did not approve. Everyone thought him deformed, an aberration, not good enough for me.

But with time, he charmed them all. My father was often asked to settle disagreements between land-folk. They knew that the Merfolk would be impartial. James ended up being really useful to my father. He could go on land and investigate. Frey folk saw him just as impartial as Merfolk. He became a representative of the crown. Land-folk liked him. He couldn't live in my father's underwater palace, so he and I built the Cottage-By-The-Sea where we *could* live together. You'll see it when we get to the surface!"

Finn saw that it was time to be getting on. She was tired. He needed to get her to wherever they were going.

"Next time we stop, I want to hear more about my dad. But for now, we have to keep moving." Finn gathered her up in his arms and stood.

Maybe nakedness was something that one got used to. Finn realized he'd forgotten all about his mom's naked... chest. He wasn't sure if that was okay or not. Maybe he should still be feeling shocked or embarrassed. But there's only so long that someone can blush. At a certain point you just have to get over it.

His mom was a frickin' MERMAID! It was still sinking in. How freaky was that? Would it give him some sort of Aquaman super-power? Like being able to breathe underwater or have super strength? At the moment he was pretty beat. So probably no super-strength.

Eventually, they stopped again to sleep. Finn had no sense of time in these caves. When he awakened later he saw Meryth fast asleep. She did not awaken when he pulled her into his arms and began walking again. They had to keep moving. They had neither food nor water left in his bag.

The next stretch was not as well lit as the lower tunnel, but occasional patches of glowing fungi kept them on the path. Just as Finn felt that he couldn't take another step, Finn saw light ahead. It wasn't bright – but it was brighter than the fungi. Curiosity propelled Finn forward until he reached a cathedral size cavern which opened to the night sky. Finn sank down on a grassy slope just inside the cave mouth. The air was warm. The moon was bright. And big.

There was a pond here. Meryth awoke at the smell of the water and eagerly slipped into the pond's embrace and soon looked much better than she had.

"Look!" she cried. "Mugwort!" Meryth began picking various bunches and stuffing them in her mouth. "Want any?" She looked up to see if Finn was interested.

"Maybe?" Finn reached over and grabbed a stalk of greenery. He sniffed it. "Uhm, it *smells* like sage..."

He pulled a leaf off the stalk and tasted it. Swallowed. He made a face.

Meryth swallowed a mouthful, "You don't like it?"

Finn ate another leaf. "Well, it's not exactly bad. I am hungry..." He tried another taste. "Eh... it's just kind of bitter... there's got to be something else 'round here that's edible."

"It'll give you crazy dreams tonight," she giggled like she was getting high off the stuff.

Finn laughed. No dreams could be weirder than his present reality!

Finn grabbed a flashlight out of his bag and walked down an overgrown path that was flanked by trees. There was a winding creek to his left. He seemed to be in a culvert running down from the hills behind him.

When the path turned to the right, Finn stopped short. Far below in the distance a wide bay led to a moonlit ocean. Was this the Pacific? Or was this an ocean not on any map from home? Dark arms of land stretched out on either side to embrace the bay. In the center of the water he could see the small shape of an island.

So, this was Frey. Finn took a big breath. The air was sweet. Different than the air at home. It smelled of flowers and a spice he couldn't identify. He could smell the far-off ocean and moisture in the air, not unlike on a rain pregnant day at home. It felt like a place where anything might grow.

He wished Jack was here to see this. It was like a moment from one of the tree-house stories they'd make up. Not knowing what had happened to Jack, created a deep hole in his heart. Jack was the writer for Finn's drawings. Jack was the words to Finn's story. He hadn't ever realized how much he depended on Jack. He'd always been there. And now he wasn't.

Finn scouted for berries or nuts. Kids in adventure books always found berries and nuts to survive on. Didn't they? How did that work? How do you know that a berry isn't going to kill you? He'd been afraid to try the mushroom in the tunnel.

Well even with a flashlight, he couldn't find a damn thing in the dark that looked remotely edible.

Finn trudged back to their spot. He found some redwood sorrel by the side of the trail – which is a little bit like a tart salad-green. After the Redwood Sorrel he coughed down more of the mugwort because he was hungry, but it hadn't improved in flavor.

His mother was nestled on the pond bank among the rushes. She was tired. What would it be like to be trapped inside a sick body? It would be awful. And frightening. He was still nervous about the lesions all over his legs. He was starting to fear it was not a normal disease and that it might be something else far scarier.

But the air was soothing and comfortable. Finn imagined that Hawaii would be like this. He knew he shouldn't fall asleep, as there could be danger. He leaned back against the rock of the cavern entrance to keep watch... he wasn't *that* sleepy...

Finn's dreams were strange. The images kept shifting. Jenny was trapped in a deep hole and he couldn't reach her.

Then the hole was a cave and his foster parents were calling him in to dinner, but Jack wasn't invited and Finn decided he'd rather eat with Jack – and his parents hugged each other and melted into one creature. A Sea Chimp! It was Meryth – who kept trying to hug Finn. But Finn thought she was disgusting and pushed her back till she became a gooey bloody pool with gooey arms that stretched out to grab Jack. She pulled Jack into her bloody depths, and Finn couldn't reach Jack's hand. Jack's hand disappeared into the blood! Because of Finn.

Finn dove headfirst into the pool of blood but he couldn't see Jack, he couldn't see anything but blood. He couldn't find the surface and didn't know which way was up or down. Finn couldn't breathe! He was drowning! And then he wasn't! It was no longer blood around him – but water! Good clear water that enfolded his body and swirled around it, and he could breathe! And he could swim! He was naked! He was gloriously free! He was a merman!

Finn woke up. He was in the pond. UNDERWATER.

"AHHHHHH!" Finn's head broke the surface of the pond as he screamed.

Finn looked down. Not only was he naked, each of his legs had turned into long green fishy frog-legs! Iridescent scales started on his thighs just below his hip and ended in horrible fin-feet.

"AHHHHH!" he started screaming again and scooted out of the water. There was a hint of dawn in the eastern sky. But the moon was still bright.

Finn had to be dreaming.

"What's wrong?!" Meryth rolled over – still half asleep despite his outbursts.

"I'm a... uh... MY LEGS! They're AAAAH!" Mid-scream, he suddenly realized that he was naked! "Ohh!" Finn jumped back into the privacy of waist-deep water.

"OH!" yawned Meryth. "Wonderful. Your heritage is finally showing."

"What! NO!! This is NOT wonderful! It's FREAKSVILLE! My legs! THEY'RE MONSTER LEGS!"

"Oh pooh. It's a little weird that you have two tails instead of one, but that's just your human bits confusing things. You should be able to walk around still. You don't need to be *quite* so dramatic about it." Meryth rolled over to go back to sleep.

"But WHY?" shouted Finn.

She sat up again and considered. "Well it *might* have been the mugwort. I did tell you it would give you unusual dreams, and you *are* in Frey now. Frey is made of dreams."

"Do you mean every dream, every nightmare will become real when I wake up?"

"No, no, no. Not *every* dream. Mugwort *sometimes* unlocks things..."

Finn's jaw dropped. "You knew!" Finn accused her. "YOU KNEW!"

Meryth thrust her little jaw in the air and sniffed. "Of course I didn't know... I thought *maybe* of course. But I didn't *know.*"

"Oh my god! I can't believe this! I'm a FREAK now!" A sudden thought occurred to Finn. "Wait! Can I un-dream this?"

"I don't think so," giggled his mother. It WAS an irritating sound. "This is who you are! You just never believed it was possible when you grew up, so your body didn't develop... like it *should* have. You're half mer! The dreams simply let you become yourself. Didn't you ever suspect that you might be different?"

"I might have wondered if I was gay! But I never thought I would turn into a FROG!"

"You're not a frog! Frogs wear bow-ties and inappropriate hats. Most of them at least. You have Merfolk blood in you. That's a great honor!"

An honor? It was a complete disaster.

Finn was silent. The scales that had been showing up on his hips and thighs... they were why he'd stopped swimming at the Y. Crap! What would his foster parents think when he got home? They hated anything unusual.

Meryth stifled another yawn. "I'm going back to sleep. Wake me when it's light."

Finn looked over at his mother. She seemed to be asleep again. He had to try walking – but he didn't want to flash her when he stepped out of the water.

He climbed up the bank and stood up. His legs did seem to be legs – they bent at the knee like they used to, and his feet – though enormous – still worked like feet are supposed to. Though it was hard to get used to their size. He'd never fit into his favorite *Nikes* again. He had *Creature From The Black Lagoon* feet. They'd never let him on a swim team now. He'd get stuck in a government lab if he ever went home again.

Jack will freak out when he sees this! Assuming they could find Jack. Of course they would! He couldn't think differently. But Jack might be totally creeped out by monster feet!

Maybe, he could get an overcoat? He could hide it!

The light was increasing with the coming dawn. Fortunately it wasn't cold. But with the sun Finn could see that his skin was even whiter than before! Crap! Looked like he'd never get a tan now. So much for that fantasy!

He tried to see his reflection in the pool but that was pretty hopeless. He felt his face with his fingers and it still felt the same, but there was something like closed gills along the side of his neck.

Finn checked out his guy-parts. They still looked normal. No additional balls or fins down there. His butt had the beginnings of the white scales that grew dominant and bluer on his thighs. His butt still felt like his butt.

But then the true weirdness began, his legs were like two fish tails... if fish tails had knees. He had long fins on the back of his thighs and his calves. What were they called? dorsal fins? He wasn't paying attention that day in biology. He never thought it would be important! HA!

The scales were more teal than the green they appeared under the pond water. They sparkled like the inside of an oyster shell and that coloring continued all the way to his feet – though it did get a bit deeper in tone. It *was* kind of beautiful in a freaky, I-can't-believe-I'm-a-monster sort of way.

Clothes! Where were they?

Finn ran up the bank to where he'd fallen asleep. His t-shirt was crumpled up next to a bush. It was disgustingly dirty from dirt and sweat. The green pullover was dry but stiff from the murky water of that cavern. His shoes were there, but useless with his monster feet. As were the socks. His muddy jeans were completely split open, and his thoroughly ripped Hawaiian print boxers were strewn across a branch near the water.

He grabbed his boxers and pulled them on but they were too ripped to stay up. He grabbed his ripped muddy jeans and quickly realized that they wouldn't fit over his dorsal fins.

"Those aren't going to fit," commented his mother.

Finn whirled around and clutched himself for modesty.

Meryth laughed. "You'll be more comfortable going without all that. No one here cares much."

"Well, I care!" Heat flooded his entire being.

Ultimately he had to settle for just rethinking the Hawaiian print boxers. They had little hula dancers and palm trees on them. He wrapped his belt around his waist and pulled the fabric under and over it to create a Tarzan like loincloth – with little hula dancers.

As the sun rose, Finn folded up the rest of his clothes and stashed them inside his bag just in case they might be useful at some point. He hoped.

Feeling a little bit like an albino ape-man from a horror flick, Finn held his head high and said, "Let's get going!"

He gently picked up his mother and started down the path from the night before. His new feet were actually pretty sturdy. He didn't have to tiptoe carefully lest he step on a rock. They were tough. He didn't understand why the Creature From The Black Lagoon always staggered around like he was constipated. The new feet worked fine.

But, it was really strange to be walking around mostly naked.

They were halfway down the slope when Meryth cried out.

"There! At the bottom of the hill!"

Finn stopped. "What?" He saw a sort of forested hillock at the side of a river.

"The Cottage-By-The-Sea! That's the cottage your father and I built," she said excitedly. "We're almost there!"

Chapter 37

The Island of Lost Merfolk

Pirate Jenny

There was a celebration when Jenny, Footbe, and the crew climbed aboard the pirate ship. The Wishermans were quite relieved. They'd been convinced that something terrible had happened. Jenny had become like one of their own children – even though she was twice their height.

"Three cheers fer Jenny!" shouted Gibbie. He was still flabbergasted that they hadn't been eaten by the giant tree. "Ya saved us from bein' a tree's dinner!"

"I never were be thinkin' that good manners was more pow'ful than a sharp sword, but she done it!" cheered Nibs.

"CAPT'N JENNY! Jenny de PLEASANT!" shouted a pirate in the back.

"Jenny de POLITE!" came another voice in back.

And of course that got a big laugh.

"Cap'n Blind jest called de tree names and shouted *'Unhand me ye damn tree!* De stupid git!" laughed another.

'Unhanded right inta dat giant maw." guffawed Nibs.

It was strange. No one missed Captain Billy Blind.

No one missed having to speak in verse either. Apparently the curse had been connected to the Captain and his past behavior.

Jenny raised her hand to get permission to speak.

There was sudden quiet.

"Okay," Jenny stammered. "I guess, I *could* be your captain for a bit. But I will have to go home at some point."

She knew *Jenny the Pleasant* wouldn't strike terror in the heart of battle. But then again, she was revising her notion of what pirates should be about. Even the skull on the Jolly Roger that rippled from the top mast could look a lot friendlier. She put it on her "to do" list.

After much celebrating, everyone collapsed in their beds as the sun rose on the horizon. It had been a long and stressful night.

By mid-afternoon, Pirate Jenny stood on the quarterdeck in her cloak and her big pirate hat. She looked down on her assembled crew, the Wishermans, and Footbe in the back. "My hearties! Uhm, thanks for making me your CAPTAIN! I thought I knew all about pirates, but I now know I don't know much at all about being a pirate – especially about being a pirate captain! But I do have to say that pillaging doesn't seem very nice – now that I've been up close."

"Y'ar right, Jenny!" shouted Gibbie. "Taint nice at'all."

The pirates laughed and mumbled in agreement with that core assessment.

"The only FUN place ta pillage is Loot's End, 'cuz the Nixies *lets* us do it!" offered Nibs. "Little Birdle loves gettin' pillaged!"

There were catcalls and shouts of "Aye, she do!"

Jenny was not exactly sure what they were talking about, but it was clear that she needed to take control of the meeting before she heard adult things she didn't want to hear.

"Attention!" she shouted. "ATTENTION!"

But the pirates didn't pay any attention and were as noisy as ever.

"SILENCE!" roared Footbe the phooka.

And there was silence.

Footbe growled, "Pay respect ta y'ar capt'n! She's wot saved all our lousy bums from gettin' eaten by a tree! Ah don't know 'bout you, but *ah'm* a curious 'bout wot yer pirate queen has ta say."

Every eye turned to the seven-year-old girl who nervously stood above them on the quarterdeck.

"Thanks Footbe." Jenny started quietly, but then gained confidence with all the friendly faces in front of her. "Well I was thinking, *maybe* we could be nice pirates? WHY DO ALL PIRATES HAVE TO BE BAD AND MEAN? We could do fun stuff instead! Like... every night we could have a tea party before dinner?"

The brownies cheered. Tea parties were good. No one ever got stabbed at a tea party.

With the brownies still smiling below her, Jenny felt it was safe to continue.

"And well, I'll have to go home to my parents eventually, as they must be getting awful worried about me. But before that, I've gotta help Papy and Mamy Wisherman get their kids back. They were taken by the Blue Queen."

All the brownies shuddered.

"It will probably be really dangerous but seein' as you're all brave pirates you won't be afraid to help?"

The brownies silently looked anywhere but at their captain. They liked the tea party idea *much* better.

The phooka spoke up, "Ah'll help ya Jenny! With yer stock o' wishes, and yer natural 'ffin'ty wi' 'em, those l'il ones be good as rescued!"

He glared at the brownie crew. "An' if we stop at a cert'n island on the way, I can get 'nother secret bit o' magic ta fight the Queen."

At that, the crowd burst into smiles! A stock of wishes! A secret weapon! Well that made all the difference in the world! The brownies all cheered! They'd be happy to help!

Jenny could see that the Wishermans' opinion of the phooka had improved a great deal with Footbe's offer to help rescue their children, but they still were a bit suspicious.

"We can't be fergettin' that he's a phooka! They're deceptive critters!" cautioned Mamy when she and Papy were alone with Jenny on the forecastle.

"Phookas have a chang'ble nature – inside and out. They can look and act like whatever suits 'em! He still might be an agent o' the Queen." warned Papy.

Jenny was inclined to defend him. "Well, Footbe said he can't change into nothing else."

Papy shook his head. "Well then he be lyin'! That just makes no gosh darn sense. All phookas be shapeshifters! Some of 'em even got other surprisin' magic! Yer haf ta be careful wi' this 'un."

With that, Mamy and Papy went down below to help prepare the tea party, for as Mamy put it, "Brownies ain't never part o' no tea party that ah's ever hear'd of!"

The ship was still anchored in the harbor. The sky was blue with gentle breezes, which gave no hint of the storm that had driven them to that coast just a day and a half earlier.

Jenny could hear that the tea party was a hit with the brownies. Mamy was mighty surprised at how easily the pirates took to good manners and pleasant table conversation. Except for when the brownies started talking about the size of their *shunnin's* and began dropping their pants to compare butt brands and, surprisingly, they did vary in size quite a bit.

Jenny had to laugh from where she was sitting up on the deck.

Captain Billy Blind hadn't allowed tea parties, as he feared it might make his pirate crew soft. But of course sitting down and enjoying a hot cup of tea with good friends should never be mistaken for weakness.

Jenny couldn't fit down below so they brought her tea up top deck and she had it with Footbe. She looked longingly at the warmth and good cheer she could see through the hatch into the galley. It made her own home and family seem that much further away.

Jenny sat near the poop deck where Footbe was seated. They sipped hot tea and laughed at the sounds of frolicking brownies downstairs mixed with Mamy's hollering and Papy's guffaws.

Footbe (being the size of a full grown man) was so big and heavy that he couldn't move much aboard the tiny ship. He tried to sit square in the middle-back as best he could with all the rigging running here and there around him, and his legs to each side of the wheel-master. His weight tended to make the front of the boat lift up a little bit.

Footbe alternately sipped his tea, and puffed on an ornate pipe that he carried around in the bulging pouch on the belt of his loincloth. The pipe was carved to look like an octopus, which shot out smoke instead of ink.

Jenny sipped her tea. "Where's this island you want to go to, and why d' ya want to stop there?"

Footbe blew out a series of smoke rings that dissipated in the light wind around the boat. "Ah've been rememberin' things. Surprisin' things." He paused and looked off into nowhere. "Till now, ah ain't been 'memberin much from the time afore the Queen branded me butt. Ah've been wanderin' place ta place... gettin' run off from most. Most folks don't like phookas. The nixies seemed ta be the only ones that dinna mind me hangin' 'bout."

"But now you remember something?" Jenny asked.

"Ah do. An' it all be YER doin'! You bein' human. Ah remember 'specially bein' 'round humans afore this. An' mermaids! Ah think ah was 'round humans and Merfolk quite a bit afore me shunnin'."

"You've met MERMAIDS! I've ALWAYS wanted to meet a mermaid! I bet they're beautiful! My friend Finn –

back home – he loves mermaids too! He draws 'em great! I wish he was here."

"Finn? Finn..." Footbe's eyes looked off towards the horizon.

"I don't expect you've met. Finn's back home in my world. He's best friends with my brother Jack. But tell me about mermaids! The Wishermans said they were all gone." Jenny was curious to know more.

"Well ah can't remember all dat much yet. But der be two things ah do remember. First, de Merfolk were bein' sick somehow and ah was sent ta get moss from de Mudder Tree ta help 'em. But after de shunnin', ah fergot ev'rythin'! She took me mem'ries! Ah don't know if de Merfolk still be livin' or not. But if dey are... somethin' 'bout de island here triggered me thinkin' 'bout de moss. So when ah woke up dat mornin', ah went off ta find it ."

Jenny reflected, "And the Mother Tree knew about your mission! I didn't know birds and trees talked! This is such a crazy world. Can I see it? The moss?"

The phooka pulled open the large burlap bag beside him and it glittered with lumpy sparkling moss. There was quite a bit.

"It's beautiful. So now what do you do with it?" Jenny loved how it shimmered in the late afternoon sun.

"Ah need ta take it ta de Island o' Merfolk. It' be in de Bay o' mer'Rin.

"Do you think they're still alive?"

Footbe blew another smoke ring. "Mebbe. We'll see."

"Do you think they'll help us?"

"Dey bear no love fer de Queen wot made 'em all sick in de first place."

Jenny thought about how long the Wisherman kids had been held by the Queen. Did they have time to save Merfolk too? And the human kids! She'd almost forgotten about them! She was never going to get home!

Jenny scrunched her eyes. "You said you remembered *two* things."

Footbe got a far off look in his eye. "Thar be magic we can use near de Island o' Merfolk. Merfolk magic. Magic dat might help us get ta de Blue Queen real quick-like. It's all a bit fuzzy in me memory ya see... but ah'll know it when ah see it."

The Bay of mer'Rin was on the map. There was also an island next to the *Island of Merfolk* called the *Isle of Judgment*. Nibs, the navigator, took readings with a sextant and reported that the bay was to the northeast. With good winds they'd be there in a day or so.

It was the first time that Jenny had seen a map of Frey and its surrounding territories. She could also see an island in the southwest, which was newly marked as *The Isle of Plants*. Far to the northeast on the other side of the continent was a mountainous coast marked *Whisps,* and along the southern coast was an area marked *Bogfolk,* the northern mountains belonged to the *Frit,* but the bulk of the continent was marked *Frey.* She could trace her route down the *OrangeRock Canyon* with the Wishermans, the *Riddle River,* and the location of *Loot's End.* It was interesting to see it all laid out on the map. Jenny had traveled quite a distance since she arrived in Frey.

Jenny slept another night on the prow of the ship with a big pillow under a pile of cloaks and blankets that Gibbie pulled together. It was a warm night but not unpleasant. Jenny sitting up front with the crew's quarters below her helped to balance out the weight of the phooka in the back.

Jenny had never been an early riser at home, but the next morning her eyes opened with the sun. She might see a real mermaid today! The air was crisp. The layers of warmth dissuaded her from actually rising, until a shout pealed out from the crow's nest.

"Land ahoy!" squeaked the little brownie.

Jenny sat up and looked over the edge of the boat's rail. A distant shoreline opened into a bay.

But she only saw one island in the bay instead of two.

She jumped up and maneuvered her way to the back of the boat. (of course the front of the tiny galleon lifted a bit as she moved towards Footbe.)

"Footbe! There's only one island!" shouted Jenny.

"No, thar be two." he said lazily.

"I see only one! Where's the other?"

"'Tis an Island o' Merfolk."

"Yeah..."

"That island be underwater o' course where Merfolk be more comf'table."

"Oh."

The small Palmer and its rippling Jolly Roger sailed up to a small island that was little more than a large rock. It wasn't very impressive. Jenny figured the rock was about as wide as their house at home. The Isle of Judgment. Just a big irregular rock.

In the waters nearby, they could see the shape of a submerged island. They'd avoided sailing directly over it as it came quite close to the surface in places. There were mysterious shapes below the surface, but it wasn't clear what they were.

The long boat brought Jenny, Gibbs, and Wishermans to the rock's edge where there was a granite slab for a landing. Footbe swam the distance - he was too big to fit in the small boat with the others.

Jenny wondered how a creature with hoofs could swim. But he swam well enough.

He pulled his wet body out of the water. His dripping goat face and furry body reminded Jenny of a dog who'd just had a bath. He smelled a bit like a wet dog as he shook himself and sent water drops in every direction.

Everybody complained as they tried not to get wet.

Jenny couldn't see the point of visiting this giant hunk of rock. That's all that there was. It was just a big collection of granite boulders, which towered around her.

"There's nothin' here!" whispered an exasperated Papy. "Ah told ya he was up ta no good!"

Footbe ignored him. After a moment of reflection, he found a gap between two rocks, which revealed a well worn path. He entered without looking back. Jenny and Gibbs followed and the Wishermans trailed behind. Their path spiraled down till it reached an elaborately carved stone portal around a dark cave opening.

"Jenny, don't ya be goin' in thar with that creature!" warned Mamy.

Jenny followed Footbe.

Six feet inside the cave the trail stopped at a solid wall of rock.

Footbe looked back at her with a goat-faced smile. He then turned back to inspect the wall in front of him. He closed his eyes and thought for a moment.

Jenny was uncomfortable. It wasn't clear what Footbe was doing.

Footbe raised one hairy hand to the wall and after a moment of feeling about he pressed a finger into an indent.

"Ah had ta keep 'em safe, so ah locked the Merfolk up ta hide 'em from the Queen."

There was a rumble under their feet, the sound of rushing water, and in a moment the wall rumbled to one side revealing steps descending into blackness. Footbe stepped down. A dim light began to glow above a grid of sculpted seaweed patterns in the ceiling. Carved sea life swam through the rock with such great ingenuity it nearly felt alive. Marvelous coral patterns formed arches over their heads. Even the Wishermans couldn't restrain their gasps. It was beautiful.

"When the Merfolk were asked to arb'trate 'tween the fightin' o' the landfolk," Footbe paused momentarily to see if they were following. "There needed ta be a special-like place where the two folks could meet."

"The Isle of Judgment." whispered Papy. "Ah'd always hear'd of it, but ah never thought the outside would just look like a rock. It was supposed ta be fancy lookin' up top too."

"It be under a spell, Mr. Wisherman. I had ta keep the Blue Queen's soldiers from findin' ther way in."

The staircase was wide as if created for large groups of people. Everything was wet, but it was now dry enough for them to descend. It reminded Jenny of a fancy subway staircase that she'd seen once in a picture. At the base of the steps was a wide frieze across the wall, which depicted strange land creatures meeting with even stranger sea creatures. A hole in the ceiling illuminated the chamber with natural sunlight and sparkled off the likeness of a silver leafed muscular merman. Metallic rays emanated from his scepter. The mer'King.

It was spectacular. It was exciting!

Below the frieze, wide steps split to the left and right and descended deeper into the rock till they both met up again in a chamber patterned with stone sea flora stretching far over their heads. The floor was a checkerboard of blue stone, and before them was a window looking into the depths of the blue lagoon.

And there it was! Jenny could see overgrown towers and twisting shapes of the underwater Island of Merfolk. It was an extraordinarily alien underwater city designed for mermaids and mermen. There were no steps or bridges. She thought it looked like a city where everyone could fly. And they would have been able to fly... in a way... through the water.

But it was overgrown. The towers sparkled like ground bones glittering in underwater light. Seaweed and coral strangled empty doorways. The city was dead.

But, another sight upstaged the underwater city. At both ends of the chamber in which they stood, were rows and rows of tall crystal tubes sprouting like bulbs from a garden of marble flora. Some were empty except for black goo pooled at their bottoms... but most of the tubes held sparkling fluid and unusual sleeping creatures.

"What are those?" Jenny asked.

"Merfolk an' assort'd mer-critters." answered Footbe.

"Where's the mermaids?" cried a disappointed Jenny. Those strange fishy creatures were *not* what she'd expected at all!

Chapter 38

Practical Book-Keeping

Rip-One

Rip-One noticed the sensor go off immediately. It was probably just a seagull or something, but it warranted investigation and it would get the rest of the team out of the palace.

He wanted more freedom to be able to track the missing boy, and he didn't want Rudolfen or that disease-ridden Rubette to swoop in and steal his moment. Rubette was a reason in herself to not go whirling around the country in a mucous-filled mass of infections. Who knew *what* she was carrying?

She could never compete with the glorious and incomparable Sheela of the blue scales. That fan-headed-goddess-of-paperwork! Rip-One would show Sheela that he was worthy of her notice! He would make an impression that Sheela could not ignore!

He yanked on the red rope, which rang a bell in the Redduns' quarters below his office. He spoke into the tube.

"We've an intruder on the isle in the Bay of mer'Rin. Might be jest a seagull trippin' the wires, but ye should check it out. Mebbe some critter's found an entry inta that place."

And just for the fun of it, he farted into the tube resulting in a crescendo of screams back from below.

Rip-One was all powerful.

Chapter 39

Escape Gets More Complicated

Jack

Jack shimmied down the stone hole that was slimed with years and years of poop. He seriously didn't want to lose his grip and fall into the stinky darkness below him. His eyes adjusted to the phosphorescent lichen, which apparently lived on smelly stuff. It dimly revealed disgusting streaks of brown and green yuck on the walls and in the gaps in the stonework that Jack used to climb downwards. Every handhold was slippery and disgusting beyond any measure of pure ick he'd ever conceived of in almost sixteen years of life.

About ten feet down, Jack found a dark hole in the side of the chute. His nose was still overwhelmed, but it *seemed* less smelly in that direction.

"Jackbe! In here!" called out a voice deep within.

"Lilbe?" He pulled himself into the narrow opening and crawled forward. Bilbe followed. The smell did seem to be improving, but he realized he was now wearing much of what he was smelling.

"Lilbe! Is there anywhere I can wash all this crap off? This smell is nasty. Guards will be able to smell me a mile away!"

"Dilbe scouted a spot up 'head where we heard water! There be a quick-water that runs under the palace, and hot pools there."

"Okay –" He gasped. "My nose is dyin'." Jack wiggled his way forward, snake-like, as fast as he could towards a dim glow ahead.

Lilbe ran on before him with a giggle. "Yer *mighty* smell-some, Jackbe!" She waved her hand in front of her nose.

Ten more minutes of tight squirming brought Jack to the end of the tunnel. He looked out on a small cavern filled with the sound of running water, and conveniently lit by glowing orange fungi. The uneven rocky ground was about eight feet down. A series of steaming pools and smooth, orange rock filled the area below him. Beyond that, he could see an underground river that tumbled around a bend to his right.

Jack could see Lilbe climbing down the rock wall below him. Dilbe was dipping their toes in one of the pools.

Bilbe was behind him shouting, "Jack, don't stop! It smells real bad and ye be blockin' all the sweet air!"

Jack wasn't sure how to get down without breaking his neck, as he was crawling out of a tight hole head first. There were quite a few pipes that indicated the castle above used this cavern as a hot and cold water source. He looked up.

There was a pipe going into the rock overhead. It crossed over to his left and ran down the wall.

He rolled over on his back and reached up and touched the pipe with the end of his fingers. It was warm but not too hot to touch. He skootched out a bit further till he could fully grab it. Hanging from the pipe he slowly pulled his crap-smeared body out of the hole till his feet swung free.

And that's when it happened. The diaper that had heroically held together for so long, slipped down to his ankles and dropped to the ground far below. He hung from the pipe clothed in poop, but otherwise – Jack was stark naked.

"He's got a glowin pecker," observed Dilbe.

"Wowee!" said Lilbe.

"Hmmm. That's interestin'," noted Bilbe, forgetting his rush to get out of the tunnel.

Jack felt his dirty face flush beet red. He hung there helpless for a second and then hand over hand he carefully reached the vertical pipe on the wall. He clung to it and the privacy it afforded. Using the pipe he climbed and slid down till his feet touched the floor of the cavern. He immediately jumped into the closest steaming pool.

"AHHHH!" Jack screamed at the hot water and climbed out as quick as he could. "That's boiling!"

"'Tis not really *boiling*." noted Dilbe. "But 'tis pretty hot. That one o'er thar, be a bit cooler for ye." Dilbe pointed to a really large one that was a few pools over.

Jack saw where Dilbe was pointing. He ran over and jumped in. He felt uncomfortable when the three puffballs jumped in as well. They were soon splashing and having fun, climbing out and jumping and he realized that they were naked too. Apparently they didn't even wear clothes. With the fluffy round exterior, it hadn't occurred to him. And yes, they had parts as well, even if they were not quite recognizable under their wet fluff. They were definitely a different species. He tried not to look.

Jack ducked his head under the surface and ran his hands through his hair to clean the crap out of it. He scrubbed his body as best he could with his hands. There was a good bit of current that flowed past and poured into the river below. After a bit, the pond cleared of all the crap that he'd washed off. But, they all moved to a cleaner pool anyway. Dilbe knew which ones were okay to climb into.

He ducked under water again and back up and it was nice to be clean again. "Thanks for rescuing me," he took a deep breath and exhaled. The heat of the water was comforting and enveloping like a warm comfortable blanket.

"No worries!" shouted Bilbe just before he dropped like a cannonball right next to Lilbe.

Around them, the cavern was filled with different varieties of mushrooms and strange fungi. Lots of them were gigantic and species he'd never seen before, but here and there Jack noticed mushrooms he had seen before. Oyster mushrooms which he knew were edible, and Reishi mushrooms which made people sleepy. They were a lot bigger than the ones in his dad's cellar, but he recognized their distinctive reddish-orange crescent shapes growing among the rest.

It was weird to be sitting naked in a pool with other people. Oddly enough, he had to admit that it was the first time he'd felt safe in days. As if Jack had been holding his breath for a long time. A really long time. Even before this whole adventure started, he was always trying to be someone else. Even pretending a little bit with Jenny and Finn. He was always filtering without even being conscious of it. Showing people what he thought they wanted to see. Maybe he'd never really been naked around anyone else before. Not really naked... like his inner self naked. He didn't know what people would think of him if folks knew the real, unfiltered Jack.

He'd tried talking about stuff with his parents a few times, but it was complicated. They always got uncomfortable. He didn't even liked to think about his secrets even to himself. Jack was always clothed with the Jack he thought that the world wanted to see. Always. Holding his breath.

But here he was. Naked in a warm pool with three strange creatures who didn't even remotely care that he was naked. It was surreal. And they liked him. Being naked was surprisingly freeing. It was just Jack in all his imperfection with no apology. Not that he wanted to stay naked. He needed clothes! But for the moment he was more comfortable without clothes than he would have expected.

"Why's yer nubby-parts glowin' gold?" asked Dilbe – startling him out of his thoughts.

Nubby-parts? Jack moved to cover himself, but then he realized that none of the others were even slightly self-conscious about it. He looked down and there it was – slightly obscured, but glowing under the water.

"That ain't reg'lar fer humans... is it?" queried Bilbe, staring into the water analytically.

"Uh, no – a giant wish dove down my throat before I was captured. I was glowing all over, but I used up most of the wish when I sent a roomful of kids home to their parents."

"So that be what stuck in the Blue Queen's craw when she brought ye in! We dinna quite know wot she was talkin' 'bout before." cried Lilbe. "Just think, ye could haf saved yerself, but instead ye saved all those kids."

"I didn't really think about it."

"Yer a hero, Jackbe!" gushed Dilbe.

"There're three more rooms of kids I didn't know about. I screwed up! And if I'd thought about it more, maybe I'd have used it to find Finn and Jenny. They might be in those other rooms!"

"Who'r they?" asked Lilbe.

"Jenny's my little sister. She fell in one of the Queen's traps a week ago. She might be in one of those other rooms. Or maybe those red monsters didn't catch her and she's somewhere else. I just don't know. I'm not even sure how to find her. And Finn's my... my best friend. He was with me in the tunnels when I got caught. He could be in one of those other rooms too. I have to find out if they're there. They *all* need to be rescued."

"And the b'Trixers," sighed Bilbe.

"Who're they?" Jack asked.

"Did ya see the workers in the kitchen?"

"There was a chipmunk and a few others."

"The Blue Queen uses 'em as slaves in her kitchen, and the rodent said they're now also carin' fer those kids 'cuz the beetle-folk are gone."

"Who's this rodent?" asked Jack

"Ah, we met him when we was lookin' fer you. He's a b'Trixer," replied Bilbe. "He makes Doritte's lunch e'ry day 'for her *noonie nap.*"

"Who are these *b'Trixers?*" asked Jack.

"They been 'migratin' from some place that was dyin'. Folk here don't like 'em much. But *we* like 'em fine," said Bilbe.

"We got neighbors that'r b'Trixers. We play wi' thar kids," offered Lilbe.

"Our mum don't like 'em much," added Dilbe.

"She ain't used to 'em. She'll come 'round," reflected Bilbe.

"She likes Tootles. The mouse family what watches the garden." pointed out Lilbe.

"B'Trixers need ta get out o' here too. The Blue Queen eats a couple of 'em a day." said Dilbe.

"What! She eats talking animals?" gasped Jack. "Animals that can think and... be like people?"

Lilbe was surprised. "But, Jack. All animals in Frey are people. They all talk. Even plants oft'n talk. We be part plant ourselves!"

"So... " Jack thought a moment. "Wait... then, what do *you* eat?"

"We be eatin' mostly fruit, but meat-eaters usu'lly eat critters they dinna like."

Jack looked at them with his mouth open.

"'Ye wouldn't want to eat someone ye *liked*, would ya?" observed Lilbe.

"No, I suppose you wouldn't." Jack was still not understanding this. "So no one cares that the Queen eats her slaves?"

"Not much. They be 'migrants. Furry-ners. 'Trixers. They're from someplace else." reflected Lilbe.

Bilbe raised his hands. "But we care. We need to rescue 'em all 'fore we go."

Dilbe poked Jack in the shoulder. "She's havin' a feast tonight fer all her butt-lickers and what-all. Doritte's gonna start cookin' a whole bunch up later today."

"Why don't they run away?" asked Jack.

"She has big horny-blit guards, and well, thar's nowhere ta go. The townsfolk below the castle would jest turn 'em in if they caught 'em. Or maybe even eat 'em. These are hard times fer most folk."

"So, that's what a horny-blit is..." mumbled Jack.

"The b'Trixers be kinda beaten down, an' hopeless." reflected Bilbe.

Jack thought a moment. "Does the Queen normally eat horny-blits?"

"Whatcha talkin' 'bout, Jack?" asked Lilbe.

"When I was caught, the Queen said she was in the mood for a *baby horny-blit soufflé.*"

"Don't think the horny-blits would like that, the Blue Queen got thar families in the dungeon. She talks when she fiddles wi' makeup. She keeps hold o' the families o' all her servants. Keeps 'em in line –"

Jack felt hopeless. "So, we've got two rooms of kids – where Jenny and Finn might be, and a whole bunch of animals that need rescuing."

"Yup!" the three kids chorused.

"What can we do?" murmured Jack.

"Ye could help 'em wi' yer magic!"

Jack squirmed. "What? I don't think I have enough magic for something like that."

Bilbe squinted into the water. "Yeah, it does look kinda small."

"It's bigger than yers!" noted Lilbe.

Jack's face was back to a bright red.

"Hey– yer face be turnin' color! Is it magic too?!"

"STOP!" yelled Jack, who immediately swam to the other side of the pool to get some space.

The three wet puffball kids sat on the other side of the pool and stared at Jack. He reflected. What choice was there? Could he do something about it? The idea of being cooked and eaten was awful. And he couldn't leave without being sure about Finn and Jenny. And, of course all those kids...

"We need a plan." Jack said quietly. "A plan that doesn't require magic."

The three kids stared silently back at him with expectant smiles. He clearly wasn't going to get a plan from them.

"Okay. We got two or three walls of human kids hanging in the blood milking rooms, where I also might find Finn and Jenny. We've got your animal friends scattered throughout the castle if they are slaves – but, the ones getting cooked are probably in a holding pen near the kitchen? And hopefully still alive? There's also that prisoner that was in the cell with me. The Queen chopped his finger off right in front of me!"

The three kids cringed.

"We need a plan." Jack repeated.

The three kids nodded, waiting for his brilliant plan.

"I DON'T KNOW! I'M ONLY FIFTEEN! I'M NAKED! I DON'T UNDERSTAND ANY OF THIS!" Jack pulled himself out of the hot water and sat red-skinned and cross-legged on the side, completely forgetting his nakedness.

"Sorry, Jackbe." Lilbe murmured.

"Why do you call me *Jackbe* sometimes?" He looked up. "And sometimes you call each other *Dil*, *Lil*, and *Bil*, but at other times you–"

Lil's voice responded simply, "We adds the *be* on the end ta be friendly." Her siblings smiled at him.

Jack smiled back. "Oh, it's a term of affection."

"I think once upon a time it was supposed ta remind friends ta... *be*. In the moment like. E'en when it's crazy. But now we run it all together fast." reflected Dilbe.

The kids nodded.

Minutes passed. The sound of the flowing river filled the cavern. The sound was peaceful. Jack noticed the Reishi mushrooms again. They made folks sleepy...

Jack looked over towards the bend in the river. "Where does that river go?"

Dilbe raised their hand and waved it urgently.

"Uh, yes, Dilbe?" Jack asked.

Dilbe stood up. "That goes outside to a waterfall. We be on a mountain – far 'bove Nor'city. There be a path here that goes 'longside the river 'til you get to the fall."

"And then?" asked Jack. "Does the path go any further?"

"Yeah, but ah'm not sure where it be headin'. Once outside, the trail be goin' back inta another cave." explained Dilbe.

Jack thought another moment. "Can we get up to the kitchen from here? Do the Queen's folk ever come down here?"

Bilbe proudly raised his hand.

"Yes, Bilbe?"

"Jackbe, the way down here be too small fer the Queen and her big folk. She might ha' servants that can fit. Someone's gotta work on the plumbin'."

"Jack, they're all goin' ta get eat'n!" said Lilbe.

"I get it. Can you get a message and some mushrooms to the rodent? And another message to the horny-blit guard about his kids? I *think* I have a plan." Jack took a deep breath.

The three puffballs cheered.

"But do you know where I can get some clothes?"

Chapter 40

Randy's Dilemma

Randy the Fuzzy-Wiggle

Fuzzy-wiggles have an old caution passed from generation to generation: *Dark deeds come from dark tastes.* Randy's gluttony had gotten him into this! *He couldn't see how he'd get himself out of this mess.* Randy curled up tightly in the shadowy folds of the Blue Queen's pocket. His trim peachy figure was now bloated beyond recognition. He'd always been rather proud of his figure. It had somehow made up for his lack of fuzz. He might not be fuzzy, but he could wiggle with the best of them.

Now Randy wasn't sure if he could even wiggle. He could jiggle. That wasn't the same thing at all. All fuzzy-wiggles wanted to get big, but not like this. Or maybe this was normal? He wasn't sure. He'd eaten far more dark wishes than any of the others. So much so that he couldn't fit into their hiding place. He'd never really been one of *them* to begin with. He was alone.

He didn't have to prove anything to anyone! Especially them. They had never been nice to him.

The human girl – Jenny – she was the first being who'd ever been kind to him. *She* said he was beautiful. Weird no-hair Randy – beautiful. Ha! Of course that was when he was thin. She might not think he was beautiful now.

The Queen also said that he was beautiful. She just wanted his magic. She would eat him as soon as he transformed. He didn't want to be part of a creature like her.

But Randy wouldn't have a choice! He'd tasted human blood! He had always been curious. Blood was supposed to be delicious. Randy hadn't quite cared for it.

The prospect of losing his free will was disturbing.

Wishing should involve *teamwork*. It should not involve bossy-pants behavior by the host. Was he changed forever now that he'd drunk human blood?

Most of the weight gain had come from eating all those dark wishes – *they* were delicious. But that wasn't the same thing as drinking human blood. At least, he didn't think so from what he'd overheard from his pocket. The bloody finger had been disgusting. He couldn't imagine that ever being *delectable*.

Randy's knowledge of humans and their blood consisted of rumors and piddly-squat. There hadn't been many humans in Frey other than the kids who wandered in.

The life cycle of fuzzy-wiggles, is a simple one, though not well understood by non-fuzzy-wiggles. Fuzzy-wiggles hatch from eggs. The eggs are typically found among phosphorescent fungi clusters – as these supply glowing nutrients for the baby worms. The fuzzy-wiggles grow over time and eventually burst into a wish. This is where their life cycle gets a little... *fuzzy*.

Some wishes are eaten by growing fuzzy-wiggles. This accelerates the consuming fuzzy-wiggle's growth and results in that fuzzy-wiggle becoming a much larger wish than those raised purely on fungi. Wishes often seek to be caught, perhaps in the same way that parasites seek to be consumed by a host. A wish desires connection with a wisher, much in the same way that a human desires physical connection to other humans. When connection is achieved and a wish is fulfilled there is a powerful and invisible blast of joy. The wisher fertilizes the wish with imagination and the resulting explosion of possibilities produces eggs for more wishes. The bigger the wish, the bigger the blast. These wish eggs appear near fungi (among the *wild-wish* eggs produced by the longings of human children) where the cycle starts again.

Like dandelions, wishes strive to make more wishes.

All fuzzy-wiggles dream of big blasts.

Of course, dark wishes – exacting wishes that hurt others – create a different sort of egg... a different sort of creature that Randy didn't like to think about. No one knew where dark eggs appeared after a blast.

He had to admit that getting bigger was a rush! He was longer than the queen's hand at this point. He'd always prided himself on his trim no-nonsense figure, but maybe his extra girth was not bad! Maybe it meant more possibilities! But possibilities for what? He had no allegiance to the fuzzy-wiggles who had always teased him.

What did Randy want?

Randy wanted to be a big blast of a wish. Maybe the Blue Queen's wish would be Randy's way of making the biggest blast ever... Maybe the Queen's wish wouldn't be as dark as all that...

He could see through the sheer fabric of her pocket to some degree. On the way to the prison cells, the Queen had passed through two large chambers with children chained to walls. Afterwards, she passed through the kitchen and gave directions to the cook, Doritte.

Randy noticed a room with a large number of small weeping creatures. They were unpleasantly loud. He couldn't think very well with all that racket. Fortunately the Queen didn't stay long there.

"Just cook all of them! But is that all you have? They aren't very big. I'm inviting everyone in the palace to the feast. I've a special announcement!"

Doritte bowed most humbly. "Ah'll send out fer more! Ah kin promise yah a grand feast!"

Randy didn't pay much attention to what the Queen said. It was much nicer when they finally left the dungeon. He couldn't think with all that wailing.

After traversing many corridors and staircases filled with creatures who stopped to bow as the Queen passed, the Queen entered her private blue chamber.

She screamed.

"Damn that precious runt of a boy! He's gone!" The Blue Queen snatched Randy out of her pocket.

He could see an empty cage hanging from the ceiling. "I was going to drain him for you my sweet, so you could get even bigger and fatter." She sighed. "But he won't get far," she stepped into the corridor. "Floogle!"

Randy could see the small furry fae quivering at attention below. "Yes, yer maj'sty?" The creature was shaking.

"There was a child in my room. He escaped. Have you seen him?"

"No, yer maj'sty. He's not been in this corridor. I'd have seen 'im." Floogle clearly expected to be turned into goo at any moment.

"I'm sure you would have." She smiled sweetly. "Find him. He'll be here somewhere."

"Yes, yer maj'sty?" He ran off like his life depended on it.

She gazed after Floogle... musing. "He's too frightened to have helped the boy, but maybe I'll make an object lesson of him anyway for the other servants. Incompetence is never acceptable."

Asphixia stepped back into her bedroom and held Randy up to her lips and kissed him. "Now, where were we?"

Randy was happy that the Blue Queen seemed to like him.

"Now what shall we *do* with you my little worm while we wait for you to transform. Maybe I should start draining all those children in the Blood Halls to give you another snack."

Randy foggily reflected that he didn't quite like the taste of blood. "I'm not all that hungry, yer Highness," he slurred still feeling a bit woozy from his earlier banquet.

She raised a pointed eyebrow in displeasure as she looked down at him.

"Maybe later?" He mumbled.

The Queen stared at the engorged pink worm in her hand and smiled a disturbing smile. "Then, I'll just have to think of what I'll do with you in the meantime..."

Chapter 41

Changeling Minds

Not-Finn

Over the summer, Millie and the real Finn had signed up for Saturday morning art classes in downtown, Mount Vernon. This was in addition to their art electives at school. Not-Finn found this art filled schedule extremely intimidating.

He didn't know how to draw!

Not-Finn struggled with the whole concept of creativity. The real Finn was crazy talented and Not-Finn wasn't remotely artistic. He feared that his lack of ability would out him as an impostor.

And he didn't understand why Millie didn't seem more upset about her missing friends, as she obviously cared about them.

Every night before bed, Not-Finn explored the Internet to better understand the nature of creativity. But the creative process completely baffled him. He had absolutely no opinion as to whether something should be yellow or purple. And the idea of drawing something was pointless if you could just take a photo with your phone. Maybe he wasn't wired to be creative? Not-Finn was good at logic. He was good at math and any subject where the answer was clear cut and obvious.

When they arrived at their first Saturday morning class, Millie forced Not-Finn to sit at a table up front.

The art class drew kids from local schools around Mount Vernon, as well as attracting home-school kids who'd signed up in hopes of meeting kids who didn't go to church. (Not that they were looking to do anything wrong... they were just curious to meet a heathen – as everybody in their world was church-going.)

Ruby the Artist

Ruby was a painter and she ran the craft studio. She hosted the classes to supplement her living as an artist. It was challenging to sell enough paintings to afford rent, food, and new tattoos.

Today, Ruby stood in front of the class wearing a fitted red skirt, a tight, black t-shirt, red-framed, bottle-thick-lensed, cat-eyed glasses (chosen to match her red lipstick), and carefully coiffed, crayon-red hair. And very black eyebrows.

"Attention class! Attention! Today I want all of you to make believe that you're homeless! *Yes! Even you Cynthia!*" She directed that comment to a pink haired home schooler who had taken a previous class. Cynthia had been giggling with her friends and looking at young Finn (who seriously needed some sun).

"What would your grocery cart look like? How would you decorate it? What would you put inside it? Sketches first, then next week I'll have real carts that you can decorate! Bring what you think you will need next Saturday, so you can put it all together. We'll show them off that Saturday evening at the *Hopin' With The Homeless* gallery show to benefit the shelter down the street. Each of your carts will have your own box for visitors to put donations in. We'll see whose box gets the most donations for the shelter!"

"My cart is going to have a stereo for sure!" shouted a boy at the back.

"Can I paint my cart pink? I love pink! I want to do mine all in PINK!" implored Cynthia. She smirked her challenge at Millie from the other side of the room.

This was going to be a long morning. Ruby looked at Cynthia. "You can't paint the carts. I have to return them to Piggleton's Market, who is very kindly loaning them to us." She considered Millie's raised hand with a sense of dread. "Yes, Millie?"

Millie took a breath. "Should we make some rules about *exactly* what a homeless person could *feasibly* do? Most of those people don't have the luxury of "designing" their carts."

Cynthia snorted. "Don't be such a spoil sport, Millie. They have oodles of time and if I were homeless, I'd have a fabulous cart," she bragged. "My cart would be so amazing and high tech that I'd be offered a job! It would happen so fast I wouldn't even be homeless anymore!"

Ruby the teacher took a big breath and gave her best yoga smile. "If you're not sure what to do, Millie, meditate on what it means to be homeless." Ruby meditated on this subject every month when it came time to pay her bills. It was why she was teaching this class instead of creating art.

"Can I spaz it up with lights and a battery? I bet I could do something spastic with chasing LED lights," speculated Jimmy who hardly ever spoke up – but when he did, he always managed to conjugate "spastic" into a wide variety of sentences. Ruby didn't think he actually knew what the word meant.

Not-Finn

After class Millie and Not-Finn rode their bikes toward home. Millie had been quiet for most of the ride.

"Millie! What's up?" asked Not-Finn for the third time. "Are... are you worried about Finn and the others?"

Millie thought a minute and glanced over at Not-Finn. "Of course. But for some reason I trust you when you say that Finn is okay. I don't understand it. But I... I sort of trust you."

"Maybe you shouldn't. I'm not human."

Millie coasted along beside him. "You seem more human every day."

Not-Finn thought a minute. "I know Finn's alive. But I don't know anything else. Jack and Jenny are alive too. We're all connected. Somehow. It totally freaks Not-Jenny out." Not used to so much exercise, Not-Finn wiped the sweat dripping into his eyes. "But something else *is* bothering you."

Millie sighed. "Oh, nothing, I guess. This class assignment just seems weird."

"Weird?"

"Wrong."

"How's it wrong?" asked Not-Finn feeling mystified.

"Well. I don't know," she reflected. "If it makes money for the homeless shelter, I guess that's good. But none of these kids really get what it means to be homeless. They've no idea. Homeless folks are more worried about where they're going to sleep next, or where their kids are going to get their next meal. How will their kids stay warm on a cold night? Rigging up a grocery cart with LED lights isn't a priority for them and would probably just get them arrested or mugged."

"Homeless people aren't very creative then?"

"No, I mean, well... I guess they're like anyone else... some are creative and some aren't..."

"But, you're angry..." Not-Finn was confused.

Millie let out a scream of frustration. "It just seems like a really shallow concept for a project about the homeless. I don't know what to do without it looking like it was created by a clueless rich kid."

"Hmmm. Well I don't think that you're clueless. It probably doesn't make sense to me, 'cause I'm not *really* human. I do have an idea for the project, but it's probably not very good. It's not colorful or anything."

Millie slowed her pedaling. "What?"

He slowed his pedaling to match hers. "Just do what you said."

"What's that?" Millie stopped her bike in the shadow of an old tree at the end of their street. She looked at him.

"Well I could get a lot of old blankets, pillows, and a baby doll from our basement. We've tons of old stuff with all the foster kids that go through the house. I could fill my grocery cart so that it looks like a safe place for a baby to sleep. Maybe store some baby toys around the outside. I could call it... hmmm... *Baby Hopes?*"

Millie was quiet.

Not-Finn stopped next to her. "It's probably a stupid idea. It won't be cool looking with flashing lights and stereo. I don't know about design. But maybe you're thinking too much about it. Making it too complicated. Maybe the point is to show what people without homes need? Shouldn't the purpose of art be more important than fancy colors and lights?"

Millie stood and stared at him with an open mouth.

"You ARE creative after all! You're right! I was getting all crazy about Cynthia, but I was doing the same thing as she was! I was competing with her. Trying to be more sensitive to the homeless than she was, I..." Millie gasped. "Wow, I need to totally rethink what's possible here." She jumped on the bike pedals and shot off down the street with Not-Finn following behind.

He wasn't sure what just happened. He shouted after her. "I'm not creative! I was just being logical!"

But, maybe creativity wasn't all gut instinct and designer colors... maybe it was problem solving? His brain was reeling. Maybe creativity was also about caring. With each day, he was increasingly starting to care more about someone other than himself.

Millie was waiting for him at the next corner.

Not-Jack

When Not-Jack walked into the breakfast room on Saturday morning, he was surprised to see his *parents* already at the table.

Usually he was down first. Then Not-Jenny. They were the early risers in the house. Then these adults who were supposed to be their parents.

But today – no Not-Jenny.

Instead, here were the adults that he generally tried to avoid. Not-Jack was suddenly afraid that his *parents* were going to ask something that he couldn't answer.

Maybe they'd figured him out!

Impersonating Jack was tough.

As far as Not-Jack could figure, the real Jack had different personalities around different friends. Each group of friends expected Jack to be just like them. One group liked sports, another group hated sports. One group talked about nothing but video games, but Not-Jack found a journal entry where Jack had written *"I hate video games!"*

Jack actually kept notes about what each of his friends liked! Those notes had been really helpful to Not-Jack. There was a version of Jack who talked golf and football with his *dad,* and a Jack that seemed to like cooking. There was a Jack who had hidden old Playboy magazines in a chest in the tree-house to pull out for Bryton and Finn. But at the bottom of that same chest – beneath a board, he found a stash of stories Jack had written about guys-falling-in-love-with-other-guys. Nobody knew about *that* stash. Maybe Finn knew about it. But Not-Jack didn't think so.

Not-Jack studied the stories that the real Jack had written. In each story Jack became someone new. He couldn't figure out who this Jack kid was. It was bewildering to try and become him.

Maybe over time, Not-Jack could become his own person. He could cut his hair differently and dye his hair. Maybe he could run away and leave the other Jack behind? If Not-Jack was no longer trying to be the real Jack – if he became someone new – would he still disappear when the real Jack returned? If he was no longer just a miserable copy?

So, much that he didn't know!

Not-Jack spent most of his time with Not-Jenny (who was always angry), and Not-Finn (who always talked about Millie).

But Not-Jack had survived a whole week!

His *mother* coughed.

"Jack, could you sit with us for a moment?" asked his *Mother*.

Not-Jack slipped quietly into a seat at the end of the table. His mushroom heart was beating hard. Was this it? "Where's Jenny?" he asked.

His *Father* uncomfortably cleared his throat and said with a bit of surprise, "Uh, your sister is misting the mushrooms. She seems to like it down there. It gives us a chance to talk... with you."

"Okay."

His *Mother* took a deep breath. "Jack, your father and I have been talking... we know this is a really hard thing to discuss, but if you ever need to talk to us about... um, sex type things, we want you to feel... uhm... comfortable bringing uh, those types of things up." She looked incredibly uncomfortable. She looked pointedly at his *Father* – clearly indicating it was his turn to talk.

"Uh, yes," said his *Father*. "Uhm, well... you know you can always talk to me about anything. About sex, uhm things. I'm always here for you." His *Father* looked like he wished he could be anywhere else other than sitting at that kitchen table.

Not-Jack felt relieved. He'd read a blog post about this. How to comfort parents who don't want to talk about sex, but feel like they have to. "Oh. Thanks Mom and Dad. I, uh, think that I'm good. The Internet and all... uh, I think I've got that stuff figured out."

His *Mother* got a worried look. "You're not watching porn, are you? You know that Pastor Steve warned –"

"Stop! Of course, I don't watch porn." (Though of course he did. How else was a fifteen-year-old going to learn about sex in a house that doesn't talk about sex.) "I visited that church site that explains it all."

His *Father* looked doubtful, but looked too relieved to question Not-Jack's truthfulness. His *Mother* clearly wanted to believe.

His *Father* pushed back from the table, but his *Mother* yanked him back down to his seat.

She paused. "Are you... do you ever have sexual feelings about other boys?" asked his *Mother.*

Not-Jack felt a giant virtual spot light shine down on him. He wasn't sure what to say. He'd not really figured it out. He was barely a week old.

"Do I have to make a decision now?" he asked.

"No, of course not!" His *mom* blurted out. "You know, we don't really understand it, but we uh... love you no matter what," she whispered. "But, maybe you'd like to talk to Pastor Steve about it?"

Pastor Steve was the youth pastor who visited Not-Jack in the hospital. He was at the bible study earlier in the week. The young pastor was tall, blonde, muscular, and kind of hot. But, of course that didn't mean anything.

"I'd love to see Pastor Steve."

Not-Jack met Not-Jenny in the mushroom cellar a little bit later. Her face held a look of absolute hate.

She asked him, "Can you *feel* them sometimes?"

"Sometimes." Not-Jack whispered.

"It's creepy!" she hissed.

"It *is* kind of weird." Jack agreed.

Not-Jenny snapped an Oyster mushroom out of its cluster and started picking off pieces like she was picking apart the real Jenny. She looked angry. She looked frightened.

"It's like a little tug behind my tummy," she muttered. "I see 'em in my dreams. They're going to come back." She yanked up a new mushroom and twisted its head off. "Then *we're* dead."

"You scared?" asked Not-Jack, watching the mushroom bits pile up on the planting medium. She'd picked apart quite a few before this one.

"Of course I'm scared! And I don't like that Millie either. She knows too much."

Not-Jack squirmed. "Millie's okay. She just wants to help."

Not-Jenny gave him a look of disgust.

"They're going to come back! We have to be ready! It's either them or us. Time for you to pick a side, buster. Time for you to get angry!"

Not-Jenny transformed right in front of him.

Not-Jack didn't feel angry at all. He felt terrified.

Chapter 42

The Cottage
By The Sea

Finn

F inn didn't see any cottage down in the river valley. It was quite a distance away yet. He did see a sort of mound. There was a lot of foliage, which made it a little difficult to make out. It would be a hike. He was still getting used to walking with his new feet. It was like wearing swim flippers. Though perhaps easier – as the fins were part of him and could flex, and contract, and grip the path.

The morning air was cooler as they got closer to the ocean, but it wasn't uncomfortable on his bare skin. There was a light fog in the lower valleys. He gently carried his mother down the rough path. The hidden sun still lurked behind the hills behind them. Which meant they walked westwards. The hour was still early.

Below, lacy trees with lavender flowers poked out of the mist. Sleepy wildflowers of every description surrounded the path – small closed blooms waiting for the day to wake them up.

It was dreamlike.

The nearby tree trunks were gnarled and made Finn think of ancient beings guarding the valley. The trees twisted in tandem with the others across the hillside as if dancing in slow motion to the wind's music. He itched to draw them. The trees seemed to watch as he and his mother passed beneath their branches.

The fog dissipated somewhat by the time they reached the river valley.

It was windier as they got closer to the ocean. He couldn't see the ocean from here, but he could smell it. The salt breeze was brisk but not bothersome. His mother's hair whipped about her face. Finn was glad his hair was short enough to stay out of his eyes. Seeing was good. He was carrying fragile cargo.

She dozed in and out and wasn't looking great. Her light blue skin had become flaky and almost pure white in areas. Did he even know enough to keep her alive once they got there?

The switchback reached the bottom of the hillside, and then it expanded into an open path, which followed the bank of the river to his left. On the right, the land ascended in tangled vines and dancing trees.

The level path allowed him to increase his pace. Finn worried. Meryth reminded him of a pet salamander he once had. It had died. There was so much he didn't know about keeping things alive.

He crossed a stone bridge, which arched over a subsidiary creek babbling out from a wild mess of undergrowth. To his left the river was about fifteen feet wide and very deep. He felt a crazy desire to dive in.

"Oh! We passed it!" Her quiet voice surprised him. He'd thought she was asleep. She pointed back behind them.

"Where?" Finn looked around. All he could see was the wild mound of... it looked like rose vines. They seemed to encompass the entire side of the hill there.

"Back there – up that creek," his mother whispered.

He crossed back over the arched stone bridge. An overgrown path led deep into the tangle of vines.

"Okay," he answered. The thorns looked sharp.

"It's there..." she said weakly.

Finn looked down. She'd passed out.

He inspected the long unused path. He shifted his mother's small form and with one hand he carefully lifted an overhanging branch. The way was rocky. Finn proceeded about twenty feet, till the way was barred by sharp vines.

Clearly, no one had come this way in years.

He wasn't sure what to do. It was hard to even turn around, as the thorns seemed closer than they were a moment earlier.

"Mom?" he whispered to her still form. "I'm not sure what to do here."

"What d'ya want?" burst out a tiny gruff voice.

Finn looked up but he didn't see anyone. Just vines, thorns, and rosebuds. Yellow rosebuds. Vivid yellow petals.

"Bud! Ya gonna answer me?" came the voice again.

Finn whirled around to find the source of the voice and gashed his arm on a thorn in the process.

"Ouch! Where are you?" he asked impatiently.

"I's right in front of ya! What are ya, blind?" barked the little voice.

Bleeding, he turned more carefully this time and saw a rose's petals moving like little lips and gesturing with nearby leaves. The rosebud shouted, "Well?"

"I *think* we's got what we need!" came a voice near Finn's elbow.

He glanced to his elbow and instead of seeing red blood he saw his blood was white and opalescent! That explained why his skin was now so... alabaster. He wondered again how permanent all these changes to his body were. He couldn't go home to his foster parents like this!

Finn squirmed when he saw the yellow rosebud near his elbow eagerly licking around the thorn that had drawn his blood.

The little authoritative voice in front of him continued, "None can enter without de blood of der majesties Meryth or James in der veins.

"Buddy! He's yummy! He's a little of each! Hey! Can I gets me anudda' taste?" begged the little voice below him.

At once and from all directions many small voices began begging for a taste of Finn. It'd never occurred to him before how bloodthirsty roses were.

"Nope! All o' you'se back off now!" the first rose hollered over the rest. "Young Majesty, Yer Rose Buds welcome ya! It's been a long time since we had royal blood in dese here walls. Who's de dead fish?"

Finn held her more tightly to his chest.

"The Princess Meryth," Finn responded with hesitation. "My mother."

At once all the rose vines retreated with a gasp to reveal a round, wooden door, which had once been green. Whispering among themselves with surprise and excitement, the vines continued their retreat. He soon found himself on the front step of a cottage built into the side of the hill. Beside the covered porch, the cottage wall arched over the creek that was now more visible due to the retreat of the vines. The water was deeper than he had realized and it apparently traveled right through the cottage's interior.

Yellow rosebuds clustered and whispered about the roof-line and the round-mullioned windows. Their vines wound about the rough timbers, which criss-crossed the aged plaster. For some reason the feisty rosebuds reminded him of affectionate guard dogs who impatiently longed for attention.

"Thank you," he said to them with as much graciousness as he could muster.

"If dat's Princess Meryth, de medicine cabinet will help ya," whispered a helpful bud near the door.

"Uh, thanks. I really appreciate that," Finn answered.

He asked himself (even when he found it) how the heck he was supposed to know what type of medicine she'd need?

Finn turned the handle with his free hand and pushed. The door swung open with a groan – like it hadn't been opened in many, many years.

One by one, round globes of warm light flickered into brightness. They revealed an entry hall with a stone floor and exposed woodwork, which twisted in and out of the amber plaster. Finn thought the lights must be magic. There was quite a bit of dust, but there was a cozy feel that was welcoming after a long journey. The deep creek babbled along one side of the hall.

"That's cool. A creek inside the house," he thought.

As he proceeded down the hall, he could hear a variety of squeaks and beeps like a machine long dead was coming to life again.

The corridor ended at an arch with double doors. The dark wood had been carved into an beautiful, open lattice-work of fish and plants, through, which he could see lights appearing in the room beyond. Still holding his mother tenderly to his chest, he used his free hand to push open one of the swinging doors.

The room took his breath away. It was irregular in shape but more or less round. The curving shapes made him think of Art Nouveau. The ceiling was high and domed with stained glass in the center. A great yellow rose filled the center of the skylight. The yellow of that rose shimmered and somehow contained every color in the rainbow. It was the cheeriest yellow that he'd ever seen.

To his left, the creek spilled out of a teal colored pool with inlets that wove throughout the room. They reached under little bridges and beside round platforms. The predominant colors seemed to be yellow, orange, and lavender with splashes of red and green. The furniture tended to be overstuffed, comfortable looking, and low to the ground – clearly situated to facilitate interaction with the water areas. This was the home of a human and a mermaid.

Around the room were arches that clearly led to other parts of the dwelling. The waterways led to those rooms as well. As it was a home inside of a hill, the roots of trees came down from the ceiling and had been groomed to become part of the living space.

It was dusty.

He dropped his bag on a couch and stepped into a nearby pool with his mother. He gently laid her on what appeared to be an underwater couch near the surface. He wasn't sure if her head should be above water or below and finally settled on letting it slip below the surface. She still looked peaceful so he supposed it was okay. He then had second thoughts and pulled her head up and rested it on a spongy cushion growing on the underwater couch.

The whirling and whistling continued. The home seemed to be coming to life. He wondered where the medicine cabinet would be and what it might look like. All the shapes he could see were organic looking – like every piece of furniture was grown rather than built.

He was debating whether to leave her while he explored the house, when a sound behind him made him jump.

Finn spun around to see a strange creature stepping out of an alcove. It stretched like it was just waking up.

It was willowy and tall as a grandfather clock. Well, it was a grandfather clock in the sense that its chest consisted of a clock face (it showed nine-thirty-five), and a long, but solid white beard extending down from the kindly features above. The beard was carved to conveniently part to either side of the clock face. The creature had four legs like a pit-bull, a feather duster tail, and long green arms, which tapered into graceful fingers.

The green face froze when its big eyes noticed Finn. It bent over to get a closer look.

"Why, hello there?" It adjusted the lenses over its rust colored eyes to better focus on the boy with the fishy legs.

"Hi, I'm Finn."

The creature's manner blossomed from cautious to ecstatic. "Oh delightful! You're finally here! It has been such a long wait! Oh, master Finn! I am so excited to see you!" it gushed.

Finn couldn't help but take a step back. "Who exactly are you?"

"Oh goodness gracious, pardon my manners!" the green face cried out. "I'm the butler here! The major-domo! I'm the one who gets things done and supervises the staff!"

Finn didn't know what to make of the fluttery creature. "Oh. Great." He wasn't sure how to proceed. "Do you have a name?"

"A name? Oh my word. No, it never occurred to me that I needed a name. Your father never gave me one. He just called me *Butler*."

"Why would my dad give you a name?"

"But young master, he didn't give me a name."

"But, why would he be the one to name you?"

"He's my creator! He made all of us that work here."

"All of you?" Finn spun around to see that they were not alone! All sorts of creatures had crept out of nooks and crannies and adjacent rooms. Each one was unique and obviously curious about their new visitor.

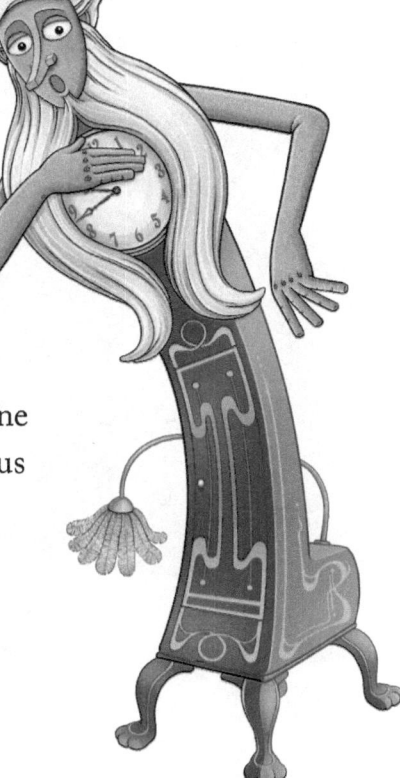

"We're all here to serve you!" piped up a cheerful, round creature that he'd mistaken for an ottoman.

"Do any of you know where the medicine cabinet is?" he begged the small crowd.

All the creatures began clamoring in a surge of excited voices, till a small wooden cabinet ran up on four little legs and skidded to a halt in front of him with the sound of rattling glass.

The wee cabinet was round at the sides, with two doors in front. They sprang open to display rows of little glass vials – each jumped up and down and waved little glass arms to get Finn's attention.

"Pick me!" pleaded each of the vials, anxious to please.

At the top of the stout cabinet was an arched backboard with two proud eyes.

Finn led it to the edge of the pool where his mother still slept.

"Can you help her?" Finn jumped into the pool beside her. "My mother, the Princess Meryth?"

The tall butler craned over the top

of the crowd at the edge of the pool. "Dear me, dear me! This is terrible!"

"But can you do anything?" Finn cried out.

"She needs to be in the laboratory!" answered the butler urgently.

Finn lifted her carefully and stepped out of the pool. Doors opened by themselves at the far side of the room and the crowd of creatures split to guide his path. Finn almost didn't notice the little mop creatures that followed after him to wipe up his watery footprints.

The lab was wide and seemed to stretch about a third of the way around the perimeter of the central room. A number of tall glass cylinders around the far side reminded Finn of the tube where he had initially found his mother.

There was a pool in this room as well and he later noticed that it connected via an underwater tunnel to the main pool.

Finn stood with his mother in his arms and looked expectantly at the butler who rubbed his hands together nervously in the center of the room. In front of the butler, was a control panel and an oval platform with a pool in its center. There were so many jewels set into the control panel that it looked like one of his foster mother's craft projects.

"What do I need to do?" Finn asked impatiently.

"Goodness gracious, I... I'm not an expert at this sort of thing! I know how to run a household, but... this... I... well..." The butler looked panicked.

Finn gasped out impatiently, "She's going to die if we don't do something."

The butler drummed his green fingers on the jeweled panel. "But I did watch your father! And he did provide me with a most excellent memory."

The entire room watched the tall hesitant creature.

The old creature continued. "Well... if you could place her in this small pool."

Finn placed his mother gently in the water. He stepped back.

"Then your father would press..." The butler (with some anxiety) pressed a large ruby on the left side of the panel.

There was a whirring and a tube of glass began to rise around the small pool. But it wasn't glass! It ascended to a height of about ten feet and it sort of crystallized. But it wasn't ice.

At that point the butler (who looked more assured now) pushed a sapphire on the right, and the tube began to fill up with water. His mother floated up with the rising fluid till she hovered somewhere in the center as the tube filled to the brim.

There she floated unconscious and helpless. Finn realized how attached he'd become to this strange little creature. His mother. She really was his mother.

"Is she going to drown under water like that?" Finn asked.

"Of course not. She's a mermaid," replied the butler.

"What do we do now?" worried Finn.

The old clock-man sighed nervously. "Now we need to talk to the medicine cabinet and see if they remember who helped out before," he turned to the little cabinet who ran jingling up to where they stood. Its doors popped open.

"Well? Do any of you remember?" asked the butler sternly.

At once there was a flurry of excited discussion between the little vials. Some of the whispering appeared heated, but ultimately five fragile looking vials stepped forward. Each held up its tiny arms to Finn to be lifted over to the platform, where they gathered in a little crowd.

"You're all sure about this?" quizzed the butler rather sternly of the wee glass beings.

"We got this," said a perky vial filled with a bright purple liquid.

They marched over to a small hole near the tube, uncorked themselves, and then took turns lifting their companions up and dumping their colorful contents into the hole. Miraculously, as each vial stood upright again, they magically refilled with fluid. Three of the group had to be emptied multiple times. But soon they each re-corked themselves and gave the butler a thumbs up.

Finn carried each back to the cabinet.

The tall grandfather-clock-butler sighed. "Yes, so here we go!" He inserted a pump-like device into the hole and pulled a fluid filled cylinder up, now full of colored liquids. A nebula of colored fluids writhing in a tube.

He now pushed the cylinder back down and the liquid was pushed into the crystal tube with his mother. It spread quickly and soon the water emitted a soft pink light that cast a rosy glow throughout the room.

"Is that it?" asked Finn excitedly. "Will she be cured now?"

"No, but that should stabilize her until we have the cure. This is what James did when she first fell ill. Before he hid her underground."

"What happened to my dad? Did he find the stuff for the cure?"

"We've been asleep since the day you and he left us. You hatched right after he left your mother in the cave. We've all been waiting for you to return!"

Finn felt rather crestfallen at this. "Waiting for me? What can I do?" He was about to ask more when his stomach growled. He realized that he was crazy hungry.

"Do you have anything to eat? And drink? I'm starving!"

There was a babble of squeaks in the crowd of creatures around him and a sudden rush towards him! Finn hollered when was lifted by many tiny hands and carried back to the main room, where they dropped him in front of a low table.

"Don't do that! Ever! I can walk!" His heart was still thumping wildly.

The butler rushed up apologetically. "Oh dear Sir! I am so terribly sorry. I'm afraid the staff here is terribly literal, and we thought you were starving and couldn't get here on your own."

"Oh," Finn said and looked at the host of abashed creatures who were weeping to think that they'd made him unhappy. "Uh, thanks? I appreciate your concern?"

A collective happy sigh tittered throughout the room as the little creatures sniffed back their tears and stood smiling at him.

"Food?" he hinted.

Again! A whirlwind of activity and hardly a moment had passed before a feast filled the table in front of him.

"Wow, that was... fast."

There was another happy sigh throughout the room.

Finn quickly saw that he'd have to be careful what he said. Words meant a lot here.

He didn't recognize all the food on the table, but it all smelled good and he quickly made a plate-full. It had to be magical food, as there'd not been enough time to prepare it. But, it smelled real.

Now that he was seated and his hunger was increasingly satiated, Finn inspected the creatures who happily watched him with adoring eyes.

Some were tall and skinny, some were short and stout. They all seemed to have eyes but not all of them had mouths. They all looked like they had been carved from clay and then animated. They were in a variety of bold colors. They each seemed to be designed for a purpose. Some seemed to be sentient furniture. Some seemed designed to do housework.

Already he could see adorable beaver-like creatures with wide tongues who busily licked up the accumulated dust in the room. The dust came out the other end of the creatures in neat crisp cylinder shapes, which were then picked up by the ottoman creature who had its top open like a lid. It carefully placed each cylinder of dust inside.

"Mr. Butler, what do you do with all the dust you collect?" Finn said with his mouth still full of something unknown but delicious.

"The dust? Why that is precious! Dust is the building block of Life! It's what we're all made of!" responded the incredulous butler.

Finn had never thought of dust like that. *Dust to dust* had never struck him as house dust. The stuff his foster mom was always fretting about. He'd have to tell her about this when he got back – but no. He didn't know if he would be *able* to go back with fish legs. He wondered if his foster-mom would miss him. He wasn't sure that she would. The thought left him feeling a little hollow.

A small mop waddled over to his knee and gave his lower leg a hug. It was sweet. Apparently it sensed how he felt. He gave a gentle ruffle to the top of its round head.

"Thank you little Moppette," he smiled. Finn looked up at the butler. "Mr. Butler? Can I call you something different? Something friendlier?"

The tall grandfather clock-like creature looked a little doubtful. "If your Majesty wishes?"

"How about Bromley? Bromley the Butler." Finn had always liked the name Bromley since he'd heard it in an animated film.

"Oh," the butler hesitated. "Bromley? Bromley. I don't know. I've never had a name before. I'm just a butler. Would it be appropriate?"

Finn laughed. "Of course! You're a person! You need a name. You're not *just* a butler."

"But I'm not a person. I'm a servant."

"Of course you're
a person!" Finn
started to

wonder what his father must be like to let his servants think that they weren't real people. "Names mean that you are... special. That you are unique."

"Bromley the Butler," Bromley looked at Finn a little queerly. "Well thank you, Master Finn, I think. It is peculiar and will take some getting used to." He rolled the word around on his tongue a bit. "Bromley... Bromley..."

"All of you should have names!" Finn announced to the room. All movement ceased and he felt lots of eyes suddenly looking at him. But first he had to find Jack! And Jenny!

"But I can't name you right now – I should get to know you first! And first we need to save my mother. When I come back from finding the missing ingredient? Or perhaps you want to pick your own names?" Finn explained.

They all shook their heads. They apparently wanted to wait for Finn to name them.

Bromley sighed, "I may be too old to adapt to having a name."

Finn turned to the butler, "How old are you?"

Bromley cocked his head to the side and thought. "Well, I was the first servant your father made after they finished the cottage and that horrible phooka left him. After that, James knew he'd need servants that would be loyal. So that's when he made us. How old are you, Master Finn?"

"Fifteen. Sixteen in a couple months – in November. I don't really know which day specifically. I always celebrate it on the eighteenth with Jack's birthday."

Bromley gave a pleased smile, "As to that, you hatched on the second day of Windermas, the day before your father took your mother to the chamber underground. He entrusted you to me! It was such an honor. Then James returned, put you in his bag, he locked up the cottage, and we've been asleep ever since! So, if I add almost sixteen years to..." the eyes closed as he did some internal math. I am sixty-four years old!"

"But, that's impossible. That would make my father really old!" Finn exclaimed.

"Your father is about eight-five, I believe," stated Bromley proudly.

"But, that means he was like seventy when I was born!"

"Is that unusual?"

"Yes."

Bromley smiled. "Well, Humans don't get old very quickly here. Time is less... strict in Frey, as I understand it. James tried to explain it to me but I never quite understood."

Finn wondered if he would ever stop being surprised at anything in Frey. Eighty-five! His dad was born in the 1930s?

The room around him was quickly transforming into a cleaner version of itself. The table was cleared of the feast.

Bromley clapped and each creature disappeared into its cubbyhole.

Moppette was the last to leave. She had been stationed by his webbed foot and lovingly caressed his scaly shin and lower dorsal till Bromley kindly but firmly shooed her away.

Finn waved at her before she disappeared into her nook.

Finn shook his head. "I have so much to do. I need to find my friend Jack and his little sister, Jenny. But I don't know where to begin! And we need to save my mother."

"To save your mother, we need the ingredients for the cure," said Bromley. She will know how to find your friends."

"What do we need to get for the cure? I can't wait for my father to get those ingredients. He's missing."

Bromley smiled broadly, "There are only two hard to find ingredients. And now that *you're* here, at least we have *one* of them."

"Oh? What's that?" Finn was mystified.

Bromley gave Finn a happy grin. *"Your blood!"*

Chapter 43

Mer-Magic

Pirate Jenny

P irate Jenny stared at the hundreds of strange creatures floating in the crystal tanks. They didn't look like mermaids to her. They were strange, misshapen, and small. She'd always thought merpeople would be pretty... and well... bigger.

Footbe noticed her expression. "Jenny, this ain't what they really be lookin' like. They's cursed."

"They don't look like monkeys with fishtails?"

"Nope, they be real purty," chimed in Mamy.

"If'n ya like fish," added Papy. "They be a wee bit annoyin' act'ally. Too much gigglin'. E'en the men."

Jenny had forgotten that the Wishermans were standing behind her.

Papy approached Footbe. "But, can ya fix 'em? With that magic moss ya brought?"

Footbe fidgeted as Jenny, the Wishermans, Gibbie and Nibs stared at him expectantly for his answer.

Footbe stared into space like he was remembering something important.

He turned his goat-eyed gaze to the rest. "Ah well, ah can't jest now." replied Footbe. "Thar be one more thing we'd be needin' ta restore 'em, an' ah'm not yet quite sure how ta get it."

"What? Why are we here then?" exploded Pirate Jenny. "There's kids that need saving while we dawdle around here!"

"Ah know, ah know. We be here as ah DO know where the MER-MAGIC be kept. King Posei be workin' on something special-like when he be cursed."

The Wishermans looked skeptical.

The phooka's padded hoofs clacked up to the wall at the back of the chamber between the two staircases. Carved sea animals and swirling shapes dazzled in the stone. The phooka walked along the wall dragging his hand lightly along the uneven surface till he reached a point where he discovered a spot in the center of the curling tail of a stone seahorse.

Nothing happened for a moment, but then there was a grinding groan, followed by a sound that reminded Jenny of wind chimes. Spirals of stone began to turn and recede, and rather theatrically, the wall opened to reveal a wide oval portal with a glowing room beyond. It looked to Jenny like a mad scientist's laboratory.

"This be the magic-makin' room." Footbe looked back at them with a smirk of triumph.

Jenny scoffed. "But, how would they be able to work in here? There's no water for them to swim in!"

Footbe pointed to the wall of glass, which looked out on the lagoon floor. "That be just water held in place by magic. 'This be full of water when they work here."

Jenny tried to envision it all underwater.

Footbe entered the lab like he knew exactly where he was going. He passed below giant globes of glass connected with clear tubing, and rows of what appeared to be file cabinets of documentation, which stood open as if abandoned quickly. The documents appeared to be on metal discs- like giant bronze CDs with carved data.

Footbe passed all of that and opened a case in the wall. He grabbed a... Jenny didn't know how to describe it other than to say it looked like a huge spatula that you'd ice a giant cake with.

Jenny whispered, "You came here for a spatula?"

It was a blueish green metal engraved with gold and was about two feet long. The paddle at the end flared out to about six inches wide.

Footbe grinned.

"What is it?" asked Jenny.

Footbe smiled. "It's a *water-whittler!*"

"And what would ya be doin' with it?" asked Mamy.

"Whittle water, o' course! Now, hurry, we needs be goin' 'fore the waters come in. It be on a timer and it prob'bly past time ta be goin'!"

It was a good thing they high-tailed it when they did. Footbe took a brief moment to seal up the lab, but by the time they were halfway to the surface, the water was ascending the steps behind them.

They hurried up the trail, and soon they could see their ship moored in the water nearby.

Gibbie started down to the dinghy.

"Gibbie, wait!" Footbe called out.

They all waited.

The tall phooka stood on a wide rock by himself and held the *water-whittler* out towards the ship. He made a long elegant downward arc with the big spatula like he was drawing a line under the boat. It reminded Jenny of something that you'd see a ballet dancer do. They were all surprised to see that whole section of water lift a little beneath the ship.

Footbe then did another quick gesture with the *water-whittler* that caused both the ship and the bit of water beneath to turn and face them and he performed the slow downward arc again. Jenny could see he was actually slicing through the water. He kept up turning the mass and whittling away at the water beneath the ship, till it broke free of the water below and became a floating bowl of water above the lagoon. She thought she could even see curious fish swimming about inside. The ship's anchor swung free beneath the bowl of water.

Not one of them had a thing to say. They were all downright flabbergasted. She couldn't imagine what the brownies on board were thinking to suddenly be flying in their own aerial pond.

With a small gesture, Footbe brought the ship closer to the island. Then Footbe carved out another much smaller bowl of water beneath the long boat and drew it closer to where they stood. Except for Footbe, they climbed aboard the long boat (getting more than a little wet), while Footbe brought the large ship close enough for him to dive off the rock into the suspended water that surrounded the ship. He swam through the magical hovering water till he reached the ship's ladder and climbed to the deck.

Jenny thought it sure looked peculiar to see a body of water hovering a good twenty feet above the lagoon.

Gibbie grabbed the oars for lack of a better plan and began rowing towards the ship and (for some reason that made no sense) the rowboat and its water moved forward. They traveled through the air a good ten feet over the surface of the ship's water till they came to the side of the Palmer where they jumped down to the deck. They got a little wet in the process as they went through the long boat floating pond to do so. Gibbie brought the tie line with him and tied the smaller boat to the back of the ship where it floated.

The brownie crew were all delighted by the new airborne possibilities. The water and the ship moved as one unit when the sails were dropped. The up and down movement of the entirety was governed by the strange *water-whittler*.

"It be a bit of mer-magic that King Posei was working on ta get a wee bit more mobile across his domains. Somethin' Mordette be helpin' him with. Now we should be able to get ta the Blue Queen's palace a great bit more quickly, dinna ya think?"

The Wishermans felt a glimmer of hope and the pirates haloo'd.

But Footbe interrupted the cheering. "But we be needin' one more quick stop. Right close here 'cross the water. Thar be a horr'ble weapon tha' will be useful."

Chapter 44

Food Flight

Jack

Jack peeked out from behind the same pantry door again. After a healthy nap in the caves and a delicious raid on the food in the pantry, Jack and the Wisherman kids picked a basket full of Reishi mushrooms and the big rescue was set for the lull after breakfast.

The three kids had led Jack up a small tunnel, which came out at the same trap door that they'd seen earlier in the corner of the pantry.

The Rodent ended up being the chipmunk kitchen assistant that Jack had seen earlier. They met with him and the critter had been apprehensive, but he agreed to add the mushrooms to Doritte's lunch. Jack and the kids went to hide in the cavern till it was time.

Till now.

The kitchen corridor stretched out before Jack – with no sign of the chipmunk, or the cook. She *should* be in her office taking her "noonie nap". But the Rodent should have been there to meet them.

Bilbe was scouting the holding pen where the b'Trixers were kept before butchering. Jack worried that he'd be caught, but tiny Bilbe reasoned that he stood a better chance than Jack of not being seen in the kitchen corridors.

Jack was feeling uncomfortably exposed at the moment. Dilbe had found him an apron from the laundry hamper.

"Ah dinna see what yer problem is, Jack. None of 'em workin' in the kitchen wears pants." Dilbe whispered.

The chipmunk size apron was about as long as a miniskirt on Jack and did *not even cover his butt*.

"I'm not a chipmunk! I'm not comfortable with my butt sticking out!" He hissed.

Lilbe looked confused. "Ya don't need ta be embarrassed 'cuz it 'ain't fuzzy. We like ya anyways, Jack."

"Shhh!" muttered Dilbe.

A very large creature just stepped out from the kitchen archway. It reminded Jack of the guard that he'd seen gooified by the queen. Sort of a rhino crossed with a triceratops that walked upright and had pointed buckteeth.

"That's the horny-blit?" asked Jack.

"Yup, one o' two guards fer the kitchen accordin' ta the Rodent. They keep the b'Trixers in line." said Lilbe. "I told 'em 'bout the l'il horny-blits on the menu, an' they were real upset, but still awful scared o' Doritte! They're not sure they can lick her. She's bigger and meaner than they are."

The thing was like eight feet tall and three feet wide and seemed pretty big to Jack. It looked up and down the corridor, and then belched loudly and winked in their direction. It disappeared back into the kitchen.

"That's the sign!" said Dilbe. "Doritte's in her room."

Jack exhaled. The plan was simple enough. While Doritte slept, they were going to release the doomed b'Trixers, and rush them down to the caves below – along with any other b'Trixer they could find. Maybe some of them could free the prisoners in the dungeon if the guards all joined in. And then they were going to see where that tunnel at the end of the river would take them. Hopefully someplace safe. The big horny-blits wouldn't fit down the hole to the cavern, but if they had their kids, they could escape out through the kitchen yard.

And in the commotion, Jack was going to sneak up to find Jenny and Finn... if they were there. And maybe the other kids? He didn't know what was going to be possible. And they'd meet up with the escaped critters in the cavern – or maybe leave another way?

There were a lot of shaky bits in their plan.

Bilbe's head appeared at the far end of the corridor, and moments later he zipped towards the pantry.

"Ah saw 'em! They's still alive," he said in a rush. "Not too far. Jes' 'round the corner ta the right, and then a quick left. Thar be 'bout forty of 'em. Two young horny-blits are in there too. They be mighty scared, Jack. Can't see Doritte anywheres."

"She's in her room!" Jack whispered. "Who's got the key to the holding pens?"

"Doritte o' course." answered Bilbe.

"Naturally," groaned Jack.

"You can steal it from her while she's sleepin'!" said Lilbe.

"Get 'er wi' yer magic pecker, Jack!" Dilbe excitedly pointed.

Lilbe stepped under him to take another excited look.

"Hey," Jack exclaimed, clutching his apron closer around his privates. "Uh, no, I think we better hold that in reserve for emergencies."

The kids all looked disappointed.

"Ya got the holdin' bit down." observed Bilbe.

"That be 'cause he gotta keep it a secret!" noted Lilbe trying to get another peek. "I love secrets!"

"Hm. Then how'r ya gonna sneak inta her room, Jack?" murmured Bilbe.

"Quietly?" offered Jack.

Lilbe smiled. "The guards'll help us if we get the fam'lies out of the dungeon too."

"This is getting way too complicated," sighed Jack.

The sound of knives pierced the corridor. Doritte appeared at the end of it. She was sharpening two knives as she walked and humming a lilting air as she ambled towards the pantry door. A ring of keys hung from her apron.

"She's not sleeping!" Jack uttered in a panic. "Hide!"

Doritte looked at the pantry door and with ruffled feathers she charged towards the pantry. She swung open the door and stopped short.

"Dearie me! Aren't ya the slippery one. I be wonderin' where ya be hidin'! I just be lookin' fer ya."

The kids had scurried back into the hole to the Queen's boudoir, but Jack couldn't get to it in time so he spun around to meet her.

"Hi ma'am." Jack said with a half smile.

"Aren't ya the bold one, ta be stayin' fresh in me own pantry like a bit o' poultry." The giant eyes and beak-like nose stared down at him. "Well nothin' ta be done 'bout it I suppose. I might as well fix ya up now as later. My lunch were ter'ble. Mushrooms! I hate mushrooms. Yer jes' the rem'dy fer that! Come 'long. I'm feelin' a bit peckish."

Her clawed hands clutched his head and dragged him along aside her. He felt like a small puppet next to her. She pulled him into the kitchen and before he knew it he was tummy down on a wooden cutting board with his feet and hands hogtied together behind him.

Jack could see the nervous horny-blit guard on the other side of the room pretending not to watch. Jack could also see assorted uncomfortable b'Trixers around them quietly going about their kitchen duties.

She began spraying Jack with something oily that smelled like butter. It dripped into uncomfortable places.

Doritte laughed. "Don't ya worry, it only smells like butter, an' tho' it be pretty close ta the real thing it be much healthier! Er, so they say."

Jack began coughing and sneezing when she sprinkled herbs and pepper over him.

"If'n I say 'bless ya' now, does that count as grace 'fore I eat ya? I hear bits and pieces from the kids from time ta time – an' it be all so hard ta keep track. I do so want ta be cult'rally sens'tive."

He screamed in pain when she lifted him up by his feet and hands and onto a metal cooking sheet nearby. He could feel the fake butter still dripping off the sides of his body, between butt cheeks and his legs and he could hear it pitter-pat on the metal sheet around him.

She surrounded him with colorful chopped vegetables, "Veggies are good fer ya! They'll make ya nice 'an tasty! But no mushrooms, mind ya, I hate mushrooms! Icky things nearly ruined my lunch today."

Doritte turned to the oven behind her and swung open the massive door. It was the biggest oven he'd ever seen and a blast of heat nearly singed the entire room.

Jack was terrified as he stared into that blaze. And something smelled AWFUL!

"I be doin' a new thing of late," she explained, bending over and looking Jack in the eye. "I be noticing that if I cook at high heat fer a shorter time it be a bit crisper on the outside but more tender inside. It also cuts down on the screamin' time. Ain't I a sweet one?" Her eyes suddenly opened wide. "AHHHHH!"

Doritte was screaming and jumping up and down. The something that smelled awful was now even worse! Her large, feathery, big-plumed butt was on fire! She was waving at it like a dog chasing its tail, but she couldn't reach to put it out!

Dilbe and Lilbe were suddenly beside Jack on the wooden counter and sawing away with kitchen knives at the ropes that hogtied him.

"Oh my god, please get me out of here! Where's Bilbe?" shouted Jack.

"He be playin' wi' fire!" huffed Dilbe.

Amid her screaming, Doritte suddenly saw the kids sawing at the cords binding Jack.

"NOOO!" Doritte screamed and lunged towards them.

But to the surprise of everyone, the giant horny-blit guard grabbed Doritte by the neck and threw her into the gaping oven and slammed and locked the door as her scream rang out behind the door.

"I can't believe I just done that!" muttered the horny-blit as he hyper-ventilated in front of the oven.

"But what about the keys to the dungeon!" shouted Jack over the screaming inside the oven.

"Ah dinna think we should be openin' it now," cautioned Lilbe.

Bilbe climbed up top the counter by way of a stool.

"No worries." Bilbe smiled and held up a ring of keys. "It be rescuin' time."

The kitchen workers were too stunned and terrified to cheer. But a furry fae named Floogle, who'd been standing aghast in the hallway ran into the kitchen and offered to help.

Bilbe took the holding room keys and sped off to release the b'Trixers who had been on the menu. The horny-blit guards – Brendall and Broosen – thundered down the hall after him. They ran from door to door unlocking and calling the prisoners out. The horny-blit parents soon had seven little horny critters in their arms. It is funny how knowing the horny-blits' names completely changed Jack's perception of them. They were no longer monsters, but parents trying to rescue their children.

Meanwhile, Lilbe and Dilbe helped push the frightened kitchen workers towards the pantry and escape hole. Doritte's screams had finally stopped. The kitchen started to smell like a turkey dinner was underway.

Floogle knew the castle and with the dungeon keys, he grabbed the still quite buttery and herb covered Jack and pulled him towards the oversize steps to the dungeon.

At the bottom of the steps, the dungeon guards tried to stop them, but Floogle explained what was happening better than Jack ever could. The guards joined them. Jack had a growing army behind his uncomfortably bare butt. He wanted to go up to find Finn and Jenny – but here he was. He'd just have to hurry.

There were a lot of prisoners! The keys were divvied off between the rescuers. They unlocked doors as fast as they could get them open. Floogle found his wife and kids and herded them up the big steps along with the joyful crowd of freed creatures.

Floogle's family joined the horny-blit family and the other big prisoners as they ran through a back kitchen door, which led through a mud room and to freedom outside.

Meanwhile, Jack ran towards the last two dungeon cells. Jack fumbled with the key in the giant lock so far above him that it was hard to reach. It finally clicked and the massive door swung outward with a screech.

"James?" Jack called out to the man on the bench.

"You came back for me? But you shouldn't," said the surprised, feeble voice.

"I promised I would," said Jack.

The man lunged towards Jack, weeping loudly.

"No time for that! Go!" Jack pulled the man out the door.

A voice called from the neighboring cell.

"Just a moment!" Jack tried to find the right key. They were so big and each had a number on them.

"Thank you," came a muffled feminine voice.

James the prisoner shouted, "No time! Leave her!"

Jack wrestled with the lock and pulled the broad door open. He panicked to see a gargantuan worm in a dark cloak filling the back of the cell. She was as big as the queen! Something like Jabba the Hutt in drag, and a bit like the caterpillar in *Alice in Wonderland* in the way she raised up the front half of her body and gazed down at him. All she needed was a pipe.

"I'm ssso happy to sssee you sssweetie." Mordette gave Jack an appraising look. "You're young for a hero but you are doing ni-sssely."

"Thanks, ma'am – we don't have much time –" but Jack didn't want to be impolite. "I'm Jack."

"Mordette."

"Mordette – " He gestured frantically down the hall.

"Yes, of course. There's *much* to do! I need to rescue those fuzzies and get to my island on the roof."

Jack stopped and turned back to her at that. "Your island on the – "

"My floating island. It's tethered to the roof of the palace."

"Could it carry a lot of woodland creatures and kids?"

"It could," she looked at Jack a bit more carefully. "They'd have to get past the Queen..."

"If I can get them up there?"

"All the merrier. Perhaps I'll see you on the roof then?" she smiled.

Jack knew it would be crazy luck to find Finn and Jenny, free the kids, and get the all other critters up to the roof. "We've gotta go!"

Mordette didn't move for a moment and she gave Jack a careful evaluation.

He wasn't sure how fast a slug could move and thought he was never going to get out of here. "Ma'am, do you need some assistance?"

"Sonny, I just need you to get out of that door! Momma's got some business to attend to!"

"Okay."

Jack pressed himself and his old cell mate against the corridor wall as the giant slug sped past. He didn't expect that thing to move so fast! It was gone in seconds!

Jack grabbed the prisoner's good hand and ran after her – half dragging the bewildered man behind him.

When Jack and his charge reached the kitchen, there was no sign of the giant slug. But the three fuzzball kids were running from the pantry.

"Come on, Jack!" shouted Lilbe. "All the b'Trixers are below! Are ya comin'?"

Jack responded in a panic, "And the big prisoners?"

"They be out that far door ta the outside!" yelled Bilbe. "They be makin' thar own way!"

"BOOM!"

From the direction of that door came the sound of an explosion. Jack's nose smelled something awful. The stench came flooding in from outside as pear-shaped red creature stepped into the kitchen.

"Surrender knaves! Ah took care of all those runaway scalawags out thar, and ah kin cert'nly take care o' young 'uns like you!"

Anger swept through Jack. "Did you hurt them!"

"Ha! No, they jest be o'erwhelmed by me SECRET WEAPON! They jest be passed out in the yard" scoffed Rip-One. "They'll all be back ta work by mornin'! But yer de one I be lookin' for! Say yer prayers!"

The tall red creature swung his bulbous red butt towards them and bent over!

The steps were a lot closer than the pantry.

"UP!" cried Jack as the red creature took a big breath and squinted.

Jack grabbed the three fuzzballs in his arms. Up they ran! The rescued prisoner hopped along after them.

Behind them blasted the loudest fart that Jack had ever heard, but it had hardly subsided when an even louder explosion shook the castle.

"Ovens!" shouted Bilbe.

"Ya really shouldna' mix gas and fire!" observed Lilbe when Jack stopped to catch his breath several floors up.

(Note: Sheela in Acquisitions was indeed impressed, as Acquisitions is located directly over the kitchen. Sheela and her colleagues unfortunately were indelibly impressed into the department ceiling.)

As the small group climbed the oversize steps, alarmed guards rushed past them towards the explosion. They didn't pay any attention to the kids.

When they reached the top of the last set of steps, they stood on an open colonnade. They looked out on Atraugh City below and the country beyond.

"Frey," the prisoner looked at the expanse with a certain sadness, as he fondled a kitchen knife.

It was the first glimpse that Jack had seen of the Frey countryside. The kaleidoscope of color at early sunset was overwhelmingly lovely after the darkness of the castle.

"It's beautiful!" sighed Jack stepping next to him.

"Yes, it is." The rescued prisoner quickly pulled Jack close and thrust a knife against the teen's throat. "Ah'm ver' sorry 'bout this, but we jest can't 'fford ta haf more humans in Frey!"

Chapter 45
The Queen
is Distracted

Asphixia

Unaware of the uprising about to start in the kitchen, the Blue Queen had been uncharacteristically daydreaming in her boudoir on the fourth floor. There were so many possibilities with wishes and she wanted to be ready when the time came.

"So little worm, how long am I going to have to wait? It's been fun, but I'm impatient to start our *big* adventure together," Asphixia lightly drew a clawed finger along the side of the swollen fuzzy-wiggle.

It tickled and terrified him at the same time. Randy squirmed from the overwhelming sensations.

Randy in his bloated state had found that hours of playfulness in the Queen's company had been more than a little distressing, but he was surprisingly relieved that she had not yet acted on her notion of bleeding dry all the children downstairs. He was quite full, thank-you very much.

He was uncomfortably full and not really feeling like himself. Perhaps that's what human blood did to fuzzy-wiggles? Maybe this is what losing his sense of self felt like?

With no one to see but Randy, the Blue Queen had let her glamour drop. She was old. The translucent blue scales of youth became hard and white and rough like old stone. The lavender eyes were bloodshot, and her lichen-like curls looked diseased and worm eaten.

"With you, I'll have true power. Power to adjust the world to my liking. And you're just the beginning. I'll dine regularly on dark wishes with my new diet plan!"

Her finger flipped him on his back and she ran her claw back and forth along Randy's tummy, which made him shiver uncomfortably.

"You know wormie, when I ran away from home and discovered the surface world, I was such a pretty young thing. You wouldn't know it now." She fretted. "Mordette took me in. She takes in homeless stragglers. A ridiculous habit, but it served me well. It was through Mordette that I became acquainted with wishes. Nobody had heard of dark wishes yet. There were no humans in Frey. Then James arrived. Lovely James. It was James who discovered dark wishes... not that *he* needed them. Just an accident. But, he experimented and discovered that if he fed his own blood to worms it helped his assistant to use them. Phookas are not naturally good with wishes. They don't think big enough." Asphixia sighed. "When I dallied with the phooka during one of his deliveries to Mordette, the phooka gave me a dark wish as a token of his affection."

Randy only half followed her monologue. He was feeling a little light-headed.

Asphixia was deep in her memories. "I was rather clever with that first dark wish. I really hated those Merfolk. Always so disgusting with all their giggly ways... near-eternal youth and not a thought in their heads. One has to be clever with wishes. And I was a very clever girl. One wish couldn't make all of those sappy creatures disappear, but one wittle wish can easily make an itty bitty disease. I wished for a disease to wipe them out. It wasn't difficult at all," she laughed.

Randy groaned.

Asphixia looked proud.

"Yes, it was rather smart wasn't it? My dear little wormie, one just has to know what one wants. I'm still not sure *what* I want to wish for *first* after I eat you. There are so many choices!" She disregarded his pain and rolled over on her big round bed. She pulled her lichen curls away from her eyes and gazed across the room at the mirror. "Of course, I want to be young again. But, I also want absolute obedience and respect from all my subjects. I'd also like everything to be shades of blue. It would look so much more soothing."

She lifted Randy up in the palm of her hand.

"Blue is a peaceful color don't you think? No one would ever revolt in a peaceful blue world."

Randy was not paying attention to her. He was thinking of how much he wanted a new owner – then it happened!

He gasped and exploded into a ball of lavender light.

Asphixia didn't hesitate for a moment! She sucked that ball of light right into her mouth. Her veins surged with power. She blissfully hovered over the bed as blue power crackled around her.

This was indescribable! It was a rush! She looked into her mirror. She was glowing a luminous blue. She looked ancient but formidable! She was a GODDESS!

At that moment, a series of explosions rocked the castle.

Chapter 46
A Very Fuzzy Rescue

Mordette

It could be said that Mordette's greatest skill was in tracing the whereabouts of fuzzy-wiggles. She could track their scent from significant distances. She could smell them somewhere in the castle above her.

Their scent wafted down from the upper stories. She waddled up the wide steps and took pride in her ability to go unnoticed. Despite her size, she was capable of chameleon-like color changes, and her robes were similarly designed.

She noiselessly passed through a crowd of gossiping reptiles who worked the upper floors.

414

In minutes the scent led her to a large unguarded door at the end of a long, dark corridor. After a brief sniff, she lifted the latch and lithely waddled through an antechamber and into a room that smelled like dark wishes.

The dim, stone chamber was empty. Mordette waved a hand in a circular gesture and a wobbly light-filled ball of water appeared, and it floated like a circus balloon towards the high ceiling. Its cool glow illuminated the high ceilinged prison cell. She noticed a miniature balcony to her right. She could see little rooms beyond – the home of small creatures not present. A winding staircase led from the balcony down to the floor of the open room.

The *dark wishes* who had once fluttered in that space had a sweet scent like poisonous flowers. If she were a smaller creature it would have made her dizzy.

She focused and her nose led her to a small door below the balcony.

She knocked.

"Knock, knock?" she whispered.

"Who'sss there?" came a fear-stained voice.

"Mordette. Friend to all fuzzy-wiggles," she whispered.

The door opened cautiously. George peeked out. When he saw Mordette his smile brightened.

"Thank goodness it's the Water Witch!" He announced to those behind him. "Fuzziesss, we are sssaved!"

George's fuzzy red form ambled out, followed by Beatrice's orange and blue striped fur, and then Burt and

Teddy and Lance and Cynthia... soon all fourteen fuzzy-wiggles huddled excitedly in front of Mordette. It was quite a group. They'd had to squeeze out the door one at a time as they'd grown considerably.

No more the svelte, young, three-foot long creatures that they used to be. They'd all grown stouter and nearly doubled their lengths from their mad dining frenzy. Each felt a trifle worse for their gluttony. But even so, they were still tiny compared to the enormous Wish Monger.

"My dears! You must be the contingent from the caves. I've heard rumors of you, but I've never had the pleasure."

George (admittedly still tipsy) was enormously flattered! "Graciousss me! To think that THE Water Witch hasss acssstually heard of usss!"

There was a great deal of tittering and stifled giggles.

Mordette silenced them. "Quickly. You are all nearing your time. You must come with me at once!"

"But, how?" moaned Burt. "I'm not sssure I could crawl 'cross the floor."

She opened her cloak. The interior was lined with horizontal pockets... enough for each of the fuzzy-wiggles.

"Sleepin' quarters? Transsspo'tation out o' here! This is lovely!" slurred Burt.

Mordette gestured for speed. "Button up. It will be a bumpy ride."

Beatrice was the last to find her pocket. She sighed, "We were watching the children next door. And the animals. It was ever so interesting."

George nodded. "Yes, sssad you know. Too bad we can't do anything."

Mordette's eyes narrowed. "Do tell."

"Right next door. We had a little window so we could spy right into the Hall," offered Beatrice. "I suppose there's enough time to peek in."

Mordette drew her living cloak around her and cautiously undulated into the corridor. The cloak rippled with fuzzy-wiggle lumps like a down jacket. She glided silently till she came to the large arch into Blood Hall. She stopped short at what she saw.

Sitting across the Hall floor were a great many children wrapped in blankets and a number of b'trixers attending to them.

A small rabbit in a rough dress froze in terror when she saw Mordette in the doorway.

"Oh there now. None of that." shushed Mordette quickly as she hurried into the room. "What's going on here?"

The nervous rabbit whispered, "We were asked ta feed 'em. But look at 'em! They was all locked up on the walls! We found keys and blankets and moved 'em all inta here. But, we don't know what ta do!"

"You are going to get them all up to the roof – that's what you're going to do! My floating island is tethered there. We're going to get you all out of here!"

The small animals and unwashed children looked up at her with surprise.

"Hurry! Quietly! To the roof!" Mordette urged them.

They jumped up as one. The rabbit ran to a small door at the far side of the room. "This way – it goes ta the stairwell!"

Children and b'trixers soon crowded around the small exit. Larger ones helped the smaller ones.

Mordette heard some grumbling from George under her cape, but she hushed him. She stood guard till the last of the little ones slipped through the door.

"And *WHAT* do we have here!" screamed a voice behind them.

Mordette whirled to see the newly empowered Asphixia. She'd clearly eaten that wish.

The Blue Queen had grown to ominous proportions and stood in a halo of crackling blue light. Her haggard features snarled with outrage!

"AFTER ALL MY HOSPITALITY, YOU DO THIS!!" shrieked the giantess.

"You're a terrible host, Asphixia. And you aren't looking too good." Mordette waved her hand and was immediately surrounded in a halo of golden light. It was just in time as Asphixia shot out a bolt of blue lightning from her fingers.

The bolt crashed into the golden halo protecting Mordette and dissipated into a cloud of green gas that hovered between them.

Mordette admired the clever choice. Wishes are notoriously bad in battle (too slow), but wishing for a specific skill at the outset probably did little to deplete the wish.

The Blue Queen continued to bombard Mordette. She unfortunately had no offensive skills whatsoever, and her halo of defense was weakening under the vicious onslaught.

Jack

Meanwhile on another floor another attack was taking place.

The mad ex-prisoner had his knife against Jack's throat. He was hissing, "Humans be a menace ta all that be good in Frey! Everythin' be yer fault! The Frit be yer fault! Dark wishes be yer fault! ME LOST FINGER BE YER FAULT!"

"But, you're human! How can you say that!" choked out Jack.

"Ha -" the man's response turned into a scream.

The three Wisherman kids had attacked the man. Bilbe bit his injured finger – while Dilbe and Lilbe lunged at the back of his knees. Thrown off balance, the group tumbled to the floor and Jack wrested the knife from the man and spun around.

But the man's head had hit the stone floor and he was not moving.

Jack was frozen for a moment. "Is he dead?"

"I canna say, but *that* were disgustin'," said Bilbe spitting and wiping his mouth.

"We gotta go. Now!" said Dilbe.

Lilbe tugged at Jack's hand. Jack woke up to their danger.

They fled down the hallway.

They blindly raced down cavernous corridors looking for another stairwell till they found one and ran up those steps as fast as they could. They could hear the sound of running feet in the stairwell above them, as well as strange explosions and the smell of sulfur! At the next floor Jack looked through an arch to the room beyond and saw the battle between Asphixia and Mordette.

The Blue Queen was terrifying. Her angry screams and shrieks deafened Jack's ears as blasts of blue lightning crackled and exploded around Mordette's shrinking shield of golden light.

Then came a blast more powerful than any of the previous and Mordette imploded into pure golden energy and sent a shock wave through the room. It shook the walls and knocked Jack on his butt.

Even Asphixia fell to the floor, surprised with shock until her eyes fell on Jack.

"Ah! You! Freddy-Boy?" she screeched. She saw his dirty apron. "Ha! Are you joining my kitchen staff?!" She cackled like a mad woman.

She sent a blast of lightning that hit the floor right next to Jack.

She laughed hysterically, "Oh, I'm not going to hit you! I'm going to catch you and drain you of all your blood!"

She fired another bolt of blue fire, but it was intercepted by the golden ball of light that had once been Mordette. The glowing orb, absorbed the bolt, grew larger and engulfed the terrified Jack!

It scooped the teen and the Wisherman kids into its glowing mass and flew up the steps. Flying out of the door at the top of the steps, it dumped them into the twilight of flat rooftop gardens. The shadowy courtyard was filled with topiary creatures, which seemed nearly real in the fading light of day.

The giant ball of light flew over their heads till it disappeared into one of the most unusual sights that Jack had ever seen. A floating island was tethered to the roof.

Mordette had called it a floating island earlier, but his imagination had not been prepared for the sight of the floating green mountain in the early twilight.

It was big. Maybe not big for an island but when Jack compared it to their property at home he figured it could be an acre. The last warm rays of the setting sun burnished the tops of a central mountain with a strange structure built into its side. Lush forest welcomed the eyes. Against all reason, water encircled the island and hung suspended in the air far over their heads, while the bottom of the island poked out below in a tangle of tree roots and packed dirt.

The whole mass hung above the castle wall so the surface of the water was maybe fifteen feet above Jack's head. A long staircase suddenly dropped out of the roots as if to welcome the crowd of children and animals below it.

There had to have been over a hundred and fifty children. It was going to take time to get them all aboard.

"The Blue Queen's never going to fit up that small stairway." He thought. "That might give us a few extra moments. But all those kids and animals are never going to make it!"

Yet, the golden ball of light had not forgotten them. It swept into view and literally scooped up all the children and b'Trixers and carried them up the steps and into the island.

Jack, Bilbe, Dilbe, and Lilbe were sprinting towards the steps when a thunderous explosion of rocks burst out of the center of the courtyard. Plants, statues, and stonework flew in all directions.

The glowing Blue Queen floated out of the dark hole and cackled.

Chapter 47

The Text

Millie

Saturday evening, after a fun day of scrounging with Not-Finn in thrift shops and the Jones' basement for their art project, Millie received a text.

> **FINN:** Millie, meet me tomorrow night at 6PM in the Saunders' mushroom cellar! Important. Life or Death.

Millie tried calling him but he didn't answer. Not-Finn and his foster family had driven up to Bellingham on a family visit. They wouldn't be back till late Sunday afternoon.

Millie figured that she was just going to have to wait.

Chapter 48

Footbe
Unmarked

Pirate Jenny

The Water-Whittler took a little longer to get the hang of than initially hoped. Getting in and out of the dinghy without getting soaked was difficult when there was such a wide ring of water surrounding it.

Footbe initially tried trimming water off on one side of the longboat to allow clear space for exiting, but the boat kept naturally centering itself within the water. This led to the swath of water being too narrow to keep the small boat up in the air and it fell with a great splash and would have sunk if Gibbie hadn't tied it to the ship. But soon Footbe was trying again with the small boat and a new patch of water.

"Tis a good thing we be pract'cin' with the long boat an' no' the ship!" Gibbie remarked dryly. The ship fortunately survived its magical enhancements more by chance than skill.

Nibs ended up crafting a sort of outrigger sort of set up with a couple barrels and an old plank they weren't using anymore (due to the recent retirement of the Captain). The solution wasn't perfect, but it made a sort of bridge out to the edge of the water on either side that folks could use to get in and out of the boat.

The pirate ship moored above the lagoon and Footbe, Jenny, and the Wishermans flew the long boat a short distance over the forest to a spot Footbe chose above the river. Here they descended and moored the boat to a little bridge over a small tributary.

Footbe being the last to debark (and the heaviest) still got a little wet in getting down to the trail, but they all agreed it worked in principle.

"Ah'll be needin' ya to hang back a bit here on the trail while ah be openin' things up." Footbe waved them back and he trudged up the overgrown trail that got thicker the deeper he went into the thicket of vines.

A small authoritative voice rang out from its depths, "None can enter without de blood of der majesties Meryth or James in der veins."

Finn

Finn was soaking in the main pool. The mosaics throughout the pools were extraordinary. As he could now breathe underwater, he explored the extensive underwater halls. The colorful depictions of magical creatures and plants lit up his imagination.

Finn was still light-headed from donating blood. Bellamy had started preparing for the eventual treatment of his mother. After the initial shock, Finn was relieved to hear that the cure did not require *all* his blood. Just a little bit. Something about human immunity mixed with Merfolk genetics. Science was never Finn's strong suit.

Finn wanted to leave right away for the castle to find Jack and Jenny, but Bellamy assured him that the castle was a great distance away and he would need help to have any chance of success. Finn grudgingly acquiesced.

He first needed to procure some sort of moss from a rare tree – hopefully he could find it quickly. It was the final ingredient of his mom's cure. He was hoping to leave as soon as Bellamy found some maps in his father's office.

For the moment, his mother was stable. He'd eaten, he had a safe place to sleep tonight, and he had to confess that he was exhausted. He was surprised to find relief in just floating in the water and letting it enfold him. Maybe it was Merfolk genetics waking up within him. He was really tired. He'd abandoned the tattered boxer loincloth – the cottage creatures certainly didn't care about that sort of thing. The freedom of the moment was more blissful than he expected.

If he wasn't so worried about Jack, Jenny, and his mermaid mom, and maybe his foster parents, he would be in a state of perfect bliss.

He was nearly asleep – floating in the water, when a commotion across the room brought him to his senses. A horrible creature burst through the double doors. Finn instinctively leapt from the pool and stood in a defensive posture as others followed behind the hairy creature.

"Finn?!" came the sound of Jenny's voice.

The sequence of emotions that zipped through Finn's brain were too stricken to grasp, but he leapt back into the pool and stood modestly against the water's edge while blushing[1] profusely (which is a bit of a mystery for one whose blood is pure white).

"Jenny?" Finn gasped.

"Finn?" said the hairy goat-man-creature.

Finn now recognized the creature as a phooka – like he'd seen in storybooks.

Jenny was more than surprised. "What happened to you? And how are you here? Is Jack here too?" Jenny shot the questions out in rapid fire.

---

1 Merfolk have a specific gland that allows them to blush. Yup. Strange but true.

"Finn," repeated the unbelieving phooka.

"Jack's here in Frey, I think, I don't know. We got separated a while back. I don't know where he is – I'm trying to find him –"

"Jack's here?" Jenny murmured.

"I lost him underground, and my mom's going to help me find him –"

"Jack's here?" Jenny was still wrapping her head around the idea. "Wait! You're kidding! Mrs. Jones? She's here too?"

"Not my foster mom – my real mom. She's a mermaid! I – uh, know it sounds crazy." Finn was bright red now. "I – uh got these yesterday." He carefully lifted one leg above the side of the pool to show his scaled leg and big webbed foot.

Jenny silently looked at him for a moment, then she shrugged and said. "Cool."

Finn was caught off guard by her chill response. "Cool?"

"Yeah, you have no idea all the freaky things I've seen. Is Jack different now too? A second head or something?"

"Not... not that I know of..." stuttered Finn.

"Oh," she looked kind of disappointed.

"Finn – " said the phooka.

The boy looked suspiciously at the goat-headed man. "Who are you?"

At that moment a shout came from the door to the laboratory. "YOU! How dare you come in here – you – youuu, AWFUL PHOOKA!!" hollered Bellamy.

Finn had no idea that Bellamy had that sort of rage within him. The slender butler was truly a little terrifying.

"WAIT!" entreated the phooka. "I'm not who you think I am! It's me. It's Footbe! I'M JAMES!"

"What type of second rate creation do you take me for, Pytharus! I know exactly who you are!" shouted Bellamy. "You stole James' secrets!"

"STOP!" hollered Finn over the top of the crowd of voices that were erupting. "EXPLAIN! Who are you?"

The tired looking phooka took a big breath and began. "Ah know ah look like Pytharus de Phooka – my helper from years back. Ah left here usin' a wish to hide Meryth in the cavern ah made. You'd just been hatched, but ah was goin' ta take ya on my quest fer de moss – as you bein' too little ta leave ya. Ah still looked like myself then. Ah didn't know that Pytharus was hunting me using dark wishes from the Blue Queen.

"After I locked up the cottage and set the Rose Buds to guard the place, I set off towards the bay where a boat was hidden. Finn, you were warm in me bag when Pytharus caught me. He were lyin' in wait. Ah only had one wish wi' me and no time ta think – ah had ta send ya somewhere's safe." Footbe stopped and looked at Finn. "Where did ah send ya?"

Finn was still looking incredulously at the goat-headed man, but after a moment he realized a response was wanted.

"They found me in a leather satchel in front of the otter exhibit at the Seattle Aquarium."

"They's got an aquarium now? Good fer 'em. Ah jest love otters. Weren't many of 'em when ah lived there in the forties. But ah guess part o' me thought you'd be safe w' the otters in Seattle."

"Yeah..." Finn scratched his head. "Not sure how that would've worked out. But I was found where some tourists found me, so I *guess* your wish kept me safe."

"Oh." Footbe sighed a bit. "Ah really didn't know where ah sent ya. But ah loved otters since ah was a wee one. Wishes are funny critters. Sometimes they listen mo' ta yer heart than yer sense."

Finn wasn't yet quite sure what to say. He couldn't wrap his head around this creature being his father. He supposed he shouldn't have expected a normal dad after all he'd learned from his mother.

The phooka sighed. "Pytharus knocked me unconscious after he caught me, and after a bit he brought me to the impostor Queen. But he decided to be clever about it. Few but I knew that Pytharus was not only a shape-shifter. He could also cast his shape on others and steal their appearance. He'd not been a faithful to that ugly Frit. He feared retribution when his usefulness were over. And though that evil bitch hated the mermaids (sorry fer my

French, Jenny) she was indebted ta me. I was the one who accidentally created the Frit people. If she hurt me, she might be destroyin' herself. In theory, my blood is sacred and powerful to the Frits. If the phooka looked like me, he'd be safe.

"But from what I hear, it didn't work out too well for him. He's been locked in a dungeon cell. And I got his shunnin' for bein' unfaithful. Asphixia wiped my memories. I couldn't remember nothin' till I met little Jenny in the nixie village. She kinda woke me up gradual-like. I'm even larnin', excuse me – learning how to talk like myself again."

Bellamy stared thoughtfully at the phooka. "But how do we know that any of this is true? Pytharus is a liar."

"It be truesy, boss!" shouted a rose bud from a cluster of buds that crowded around the window. "We tasted his blood. He be James!"

Jenny interjected. "But why do you call yourself Footbe?"

He smiled. "It was the only thing about myself that I could remember. It was what Meryth used ta call me," he laughed, "She were – was fascinated with my feet. It's going to take awhile to remember to speak correctly again. It's been so long.

"So yer my Finn, all grow'd up," burst out Footbe joyously moving towards his long lost son.

Finn had no idea what to say to this hairy goat-man. The experience with his mom had forced him to think outside his expectations – but this frightening creature with the furry man-body who was wearing far too small of a loincloth – the thing was coming at Finn like he wanted a hug!

Footbe kneeled down next to the pool and held his arms out to embrace his son who was pressed up against the side of the waist deep pool.

"Can't. I'm naked just at the moment."

"Ah son, nobody be carin' 'bout that here in Frey. Why yer mom and me – "

"Stop." Finn said quickly before goat-guy shared too much information. "*I* still care about that sort of thing."

"Well – suit yourself! Ha! So ta speak!" Footbe ruffled Finn's hair and stood up. "You take yer time to get used to me. I know I must look pretty frightenin' to you. But fer my part I'm surely happy to be seein' you."

Footbe stood. "We be a'goin' ta de castle. There be childr'n there ta rescue and I promised Jenny that I'd help. But we need ta get ta yer mother as soon as possible. I got the moss. Finn, I kin draw ya a map on how ta find her. Better yet! I can tell ya how ta wish yerself there. Ya can't wait. I'll be back right soon. We need ta be rescuin' her now that we got the cure stuff together."

"I already found her. She's in there." Finn pointed towards the lab.

"She's here?" Footbe gasped with the most wistful look on his face.

"You have that moss stuff?" asked Finn hopefully.

"Yup!" answered Jenny, as Footbe rushed into the lab. She smiled. "He doesn't leave it anywhere. He always keeps it with him in that bag over his shoulder."

"I can't believe he's my dad. Or I believe it but... I don't."

"So Jack's here? " Jenny crouched down by the pool.

"Yeah – Jack. I've got to find him," Finn's heart ached. "If he's still alive," he added.

"Where did you last see him?" Jenny felt like a seven-year-old shouldn't be leading this conversation.

"In the tunnels by a waterfall. I crawled down the side of a cliff to check out the cave that my mom was hidden in. I left Jack up top with Pinkie. She's a fuzzy-wiggle. When I got back up, they were gone – there was just red goo on the trail leading up to a crack in the wall."

"The Redduns got 'im." asserted Papy.

"The who?" asked Finn in a panic. "And you are?"

Jenny jumped up. "Oh, sorry Finn. This is Papy and Mamy Wisherman. I've been traveling around with them. I'm going to help rescue their kids from the castle."

"Oh," Finn looked surprised at the little girl. "Kind of dangerous for a seven-year-old. Don't you think?"

Jenny looked Finn straight in the eye. "Nope."

"If'n the Redduns took 'im, this Jack'll be at the castle too. The Redduns work fer the Queen. She takes kids fer ta use der blood," explained Mamy. When Finn looked alarmed she added, "She dinna take all a kid's blood right off. Jest a wee bit ev'ry day. Yer boy still might be okay."

"I'm going with you – " said Finn. "How are you getting there? How soon can we leave?"

Within an hour they left on their rescue mission.

They'd left Bellamy to prepare the cure for Meryth.

Footbe was disconcerted to learn that Finn had given the butler a name. He feared it would lead to issues like salary and vacation days... *but what was done was done,* he sighed.

Footbe grabbed the weapon, which had brought them to the cottage in the first place. It was a sawed-off shotgun!

When Finn looked at it with surprise, Footbe just smiled and said it was his own creation and that it had been specially *modified.*

Most the small party traveled via the flying longboat back to the pirate ship, but as Finn and Footbe could not both fit in the boat, Finn reassembled his loincloth to retain some modesty and swam via the river. He found traveling by water to be more comfortable anyway.

The pirate ship's green sails looked almost orange as its small bulk soared through the sunset's brilliant clouds over the Riddle River Valley. Finn again chose to swim alongside the ship, and he noticed a peculiar red blur on the ground below them. He poked his head out of the bottom of the aerial bowl of water to get a better look.

Footbe

Mamy glanced over the side of the ship.

"Redduns!" she cried to everyone on deck.

The red tornado seemed to see them as well for it immediately began to follow the ship. A flying ship headed towards the castle was much more important than investigating a triggered alarm. And it didn't take a genius (fortunately) to suspect that the two things might be connected!

"Well the Redduns can't fly," muttered Footbe grasping the back rail with a clawed grip. "And I think we'll be getting to the castle first."

"It's a' gonna be a race," warned Gibbie.

Chapter 49

The Lost Phone

Not-Finn

W hen Not-Finn got back from Bellingham with his *family* late Sunday afternoon, he ran over to the Saunders' place to see Not-Jack. Not-Finn was even starting to think of Mr. and Mrs. Jones as his family. He didn't have much to compare them to, but they were nice enough and seemed to care in their own uninvolved way. They were okay.

Not-Finn pushed open Not-Jack's bedroom door.

Not-Jack was splayed out across his bed with joystick in hand and staring intently at his game monitor.

"Hey Jackie – have you seen my phone?" Not-Finn plopped down on the bed next to him. "I haven't seen it since we hung out yesterday. I think I left it here."

"Can't say I've seen it, Finney-Boy" Not-Jack didn't lift his eyes from the game screen. He was playing a new one: *Big-Boobed Banshee Babes vs the Bar Room Brawlers*, where drunken Irish pub-goers tried to down as many shots as they could – all the while not getting hit by acid squirting out of banshee boobs.

"Hmm, can't think where I left it then." Not-Finn mused getting up to leave. "Maybe I left my phone at Millie's."

"Hey!" Not-Jack hurriedly grabbed Not-Finn's sleeve (totally screwing up and allowing his brawler to be caught by his wife and removed from the game). "Uh, no, um... I'm sure you had it while you were here. And you didn't go back to Millie's before you left for Bellingham did you?"

"No." Not-Finn sat down again. "We left when I got home."

"Don't worry, it'll turn up. Play with me! I've another controller here." Not-Jack scrambled to find the second controller.

"Big-Boobed Banshees? I can't believe that your parents let you get this!" Not-Finn looked at the game box, which left nothing to the imagination.

Not-Jack laughed. "Ha! They bought it for me! They said no at first, but all I had to do was mention liking boys and suddenly they decided to support my interest in boobs!"

"Are you interested in girls?"

"I don't know. It just looked like a fun game – and I like yanking their chain. This game's crazy!" Not-Jack shouted with success as his new brawler pushed an opponent into the path of an acid stream.

Not-Finn watched the game play. "I hate losing my phone."

Not-Jack ignored him.

"You seem on edge." Not-Finn looked at him. "What's up?"

"Ah, nothin'," Not-Jack lied. "I'm good."

He handed Not-Finn the second controller. "Take over Harry McDangle – his character has a stash of milk to help him hold his liquor better. He doesn't fall down as much as the others. The hardest brawlers are the ones who have to pee all the time as they're standing ducks for the banshees."

Not-Finn joined in. Acid shooting boobs were awesome.

Chapter 50

Out Of Body Discoveries

Mordette & Co.

Mordette was as surprised as anyone when she finally transformed into a wish. Maybe it was the impact of Asphixia's bolt of magic that did it.

And to transform in mass with fourteen fuzzy-wiggles surrounding her made the experience even more bizarre. They all burst into wishes as well. She could hear all fourteen shouting and arguing inside of her golden being. They were just as confused as she was. Somehow, they had fused into one creature.

One giant wish. The biggest wish that she'd ever heard of.

It immediately became apparent that they had to work together or they just wobbled back and forth in the twilight like too many fuzzy-wiggles in a giant floating amoeba costume.

But they'd all seen the danger to the brave boy. Asphixia was about to blast him. The fuzzy-wiggles remembered the boy. They liked him. Without discussion they unanimously swooped in and carried him to the roof.

After more tedious argument, they also agreed to fly up into the island, and let down the staircase for the children and animals. When the queen appeared, they carried the children and animals up the steps to temporary safety.

But Mordette had been extremely frustrated with the process since then. She'd had no idea how challenging it was to be a wish. It was not efficient to discuss every single action before it was acted upon. She wasn't even counting the multitude of whispering voices from the wishes that each had consumed over the course of their lives.

She now understood why wishes were better at fulfilling desire, than initiating desire. There were too many voices! She felt helpless as the horrible battle played out below her.

Chapter 51

Convergence

Jack

The floating island and its staircase beckoned with an offer of safety. It was magical to see it suspended over the castle ramparts in the luminous twilight. Jack and the fluffball kids raced towards its sanctuary.

Bolts of blue energy slammed into the stonework around them.

The steps to the island exploded in blue flames. The blast blew Jack against a low parapet, which surrounded the ruins of the rooftop gardens. Bilbe, Dilbe, and Lilbe scurried behind a pile of rubble in the other direction. It was a sheer drop beyond the low wall.

"Fred, Fred, Fred!" The Blue Queen sweetly stepped closer to him. "You've been problematic since the day you arrived."

There was nowhere for Jack to go.

She smiled and pointed at him. "It's time for you to die, Fred." Her voice shifted, *"Die! Fred, Die!"*

But Jack didn't die.

She shook her hand like there was something wrong with it. She looked quite annoyed. "Your name isn't Fred, is it?"

"No."

"I'M SO TIRED OF CREATURES WHO LIE TO ME!" she screamed. She fired a blast at the island above and clods of dirt tumbled down on him.

Jack noticed that only her upper body glowed now. From their conversation, he suspected that she'd eaten a wish – but she *was* a big girl. Maybe that wish wouldn't last very long with her? Between the lightning bolts, increasing her size, and smashing through the castle roof without injury... maybe soon she'd lose her new powers! But he knew that even without the extra magic that she'd be an scary adversary.

He felt like a mouse trapped by a cat. She was enjoying this. She sent a blast to the right of him, then a blast to the left. She enjoyed that he was terrified.

The giantess began to playfully walk away then she turned to fire a paralyzing bolt!

But the boy wasn't there!

One of the vast tangle of roots from the underside of the island had snaked down, wrapped around Jack and yanked him up into its root mass. Jack looked down and gaped. The canyon floor was hundreds of feet below him. It was a precarious position within the upside down jungle of dirt and roots.

"Thanks?" he whispered to the root as it released him – not sure where to focus in a world where anything could be sentient. Where does a root do its decision-making? The roots just looked like normal roots.

Crash! Jack grabbed the closest root and hung on while his feet scrambled for a better foothold among the flailing roots.

A bolt from the Blue Queen hit the island with blinding blue light and everything rocked.

Then from another direction:

BOOM!

Something hit the ground near the queen and exploded.

Jack looked to where the sound originated. What fresh hell was this?[1]

At that moment a small pirate ship complete with its own bit of ocean rose above the battlements at the far side of the castle. It was flying!

---

1. *Yes, Jack Saunders was a fan of Dorothy Parker.*

Jack couldn't believe it!

The Blue Queen was shocked as well! The tiny ship's cannons sent a rain of cannon balls at the giantess. She sent an electrical storm of bolts right back at them, which set some of the sails alight.

A small longboat skimmed out of view from the blackness on the other side of the castle as the ship cannons fired their loads. The boat sped across the courtyard while the Queen was distracted and a tall figure jumped to the ground. It landed with a clumsy roll, but it jumped up with something in its arms.

A flying rowboat? Another person was still in it and was pulling at the oars as fast as he could row. It was flying in Jack's direction.

The root that Jack stood on dropped as if someone else had placed weight on it. He twisted around and narrowly missed a wild knife slash. It was his old cellmate!

"What the hell is your issue?!" Jack shouted. "I rescued you! Get away from me!"

The crazed man lunged toward him again with the sharp blade. Jack tried to escape to adjoining roots. Balancing was tough on the bouncing branches.

"I got up here quick with the wee ones! I've been waiting for you!" The man swung at him again.

Jack didn't swing back far enough and the blade gashed his forearm. "Ow!"

"Nasty human!" screamed the phooka in human guise.

Jack apron's ties kept catching on knobby outgrowths. It was a long way down if he slipped.

The man forced his way closer to Jack. He pushed the boy towards the end of a root with nowhere to go.

"Humans are responsible for everything evil in Frey!" screamed the man.

Jack couldn't step back any farther without letting go of the branch above him.

"Jack! Jump!" came a voice. Finn's voice.

Jack pivoted to one side but before he could even look to see where Finn was, the man madly lunged with the knife and lost his footing.

Time seemed to stop as Jack's eyes met those of the mad man who twisted and grabbed at air. Screeching he fell off the swaying root that they'd been balancing on.

The man plunged towards the small boat, which floated in the air below. But, instead of landing in it he hit the jury-rigged plank that hung over the sides of the boat – flipping the entirety out of the floating pond, sending both the ex-prisoner and Finn into the abyss.

Jack screamed, "NO!"

Finn was a falling speck below. Jack reached out! The wish that he'd been holding onto burst through his veins and out through his hand and Finn stopped suddenly in mid-air above the rocks below. And like a powerful magnet that only attracted merboys, Finn was yanked up at heart-stopping speed to Jack's perch in the roots, and gently into Jack's embrace.

"Finn!" Jack cried.

"Jack!" Finn gasped. Finn couldn't believe that he'd finally found him. He couldn't believe what just happened.

They held each other like they'd never let go.

Footbe

Meanwhile, Footbe jumped to the roof while the sticky cannon balls distracted the Queen. He pulled up his shotgun and fired at the giantess.

This shotgun was his own invention. Instead of cartridges filled with standard shot, the cartridges were filled with small balls that exploded into incredibly sticky webs. One little web wouldn't go far on the giantess, but hundreds of remarkably sticky nets were quite effective.

He shot cartridge after cartridge.

She tried to pull them off but the more she tried, the more stuck to herself she got. She toppled with a crash and lay near the edge of the hole in the roof.

The giant lizard-woman lay there panting. She glared at the phooka with venom. "Pytharus, how I hate you!" she hissed. "I loved you once! But no more!" she screamed with narrowed eyes.

Though incapacitated, the Blue Queen could still utter her wish through clenched teeth. "DIE PYTHARUS! DIE!"

The phooka laughed and tilted his head. "I'm not Pytharus."

With her words, the real Pytharus conveniently died before he hit the floor of the canyon and the magic-nullifying collar about his neck broke open. The phooka in front of the Queen faded and a human form appeared.

"James?" whispered the shocked Queen.

Footbe shot her in the mouth so many times she could not utter another word.

"If you kill me, you and the frits will die."

But Asphixia was past caring. And she was still glowing. And *sometimes* thoughts *are* as powerful as spoken words.

She didn't care if James was the one who had created the frit. She'd left them long ago.

Footbe gasped and sank to the ground unconscious.

Pirate Jenny

Gibbie had directed the cannonball barrage from the forecastle. But the Wishermans had been practically hanging off the ship's rail looking for any sign of their kids, and Jenny had been trying to keep them from falling overboard.

"Ah sees 'em! Mamy, ah sees 'em," shouted Papy.

"Where? Where be ma babies?!" wailed Mamy.

"'hind that thar rubble!" Papy shouted.

Before Jenny could stop him, and while Footbe was still firing off shots at the Blue Queen and avoiding her blasts, Papy jumped into the water around the ship and Mamy jumped after him. They dog-paddled to the edge of the water, which hung suspended over the castle roof courtyard. The two wet fluffballs jumped down to the roof and ran to where their children were hiding. They gathered them up in unending hugs despite the battle going on with the Queen.

Bilbe, Dilbe, and Lilbe were so happy to see their parents that they didn't complain of wet parental embraces.

Jenny impulsively jumped after the Wishermans and crouched beside the reunited family. She cheered when Footbe regained his human form, but Jenny ran to him when he collapsed.

It was in this instant that the whirling tornado of Redduns appeared as a swirling blur of wicked teeth and sharp weapons.

Mordette & Co.

Hovering above all of this was the giant golden wish that was once Mordette and fourteen fuzzy-wiggles.

She watched the violence below with dismay and frustration, as she couldn't do anything about it! Actions had to be unanimous. She had briefly succeeded in getting the team to animate a tree root to rescue the boy. But the fuzzy-wiggles insisted on discussing every proposed action and could rarely find agreement.

George's voice chiding, "Oh, they'll work it all out. It'sss not reeally our affair. Weee did our bit."

Somewhere Beatrice was whispering about how none of this was quite what she'd expected.

Burt was speculating as to whether wishes needed or even used bathrooms. "What do you mean it's not an important question! Seems important considering how many of us are in here!"

Mordette was ready to scream – till they all felt a pull.

"Somebody just used a wish!" noted an excited Trisha.

"Amazing how you can feel it – even up here!" said Burt.

"It's that boy. The one we like," mumbled Teddy.

"He just used it to rescue that other boy," said Lance.

George reflected. "He'sss the one who rescued usss from our cagesss."

"He isss nisscsse," agreed Beatrice.

For once they were all in perfect agreement on what they wanted to do.

Jack

Finn pulled back to see Jack better – but he didn't let go. "I was afraid I'd never see you again. Ha! Pinkcheeks! Why are you almost naked!?" Finn laughed, reached around the apron and spanked Jack on the butt.

Jack turned red. He pulled Finn deeper into the roots where they'd be out of sight from the queen below. "That's what I get for saving your life? Mr funky loincloth?" Jack suddenly noticed Finn's pale skin. "Your skin – WHAT HAPPENED TO YOUR LEGS?"

Finn cringed. "My real mom's a mermaid..."

"Really? That's – uh – incredible!" Jack was speechless for a moment, but saw Finn's wide eyes and pulled him close. "That's amazing! And we've found each other! We can find Jenny and go home. Our parents have got to be crazy worried by now."

"Jenny's here! I left her on the boat!" He pointed to the pirate ship.

That's when they both saw the small figure running across the ruined rooftop gardens toward the queen.

"Is that Jenny?" Jack cried, "She'll get killed! Who is she with? That's the psycho prisoner who – how did he get back up there? JENNY! Get away from him!!" He shouted.

Finn looked to see what Jack was pointing at. "Oh! No – that's – wow –that's what my dad looks like! No – not my foster dad! My real dad! Jack, I can't explain now! Trust me – that's not who you think it is!"

That's when the red tornado of snot and terrible pointed weapons appeared, and also when a giant golden cloud fluttered between the boys and the action below.

If wishes were capable of speech perhaps the wish would have explained what its intention was. But wishes are not capable of speech and Jack had no warning.

"Hey!" Jack pleaded with the enormous wish blocking their view. "Get out of the way! I can't see what's going o–!"

The giant golden mass burst into little stars and funneled itself into Jack's surprised open mouth *and filled him.* The massive golden wish saturated every molecule of his being while Jack choked in terror, and Finn screamed with horror.

This was nothing compared to the experience with Pinkie. Light Burst through Jack's pores and pushed Finn back with a blast. Fortunately he caught a loop of roots before he fell from the tangled nest. He held on tight and tried to understand what was happening to Jack.

This time Jack didn't pass out! It was like he'd just drank twenty cups of coffee! Or a million cups of coffee! The root branches had marvelous textures he hadn't noticed before. A boy nearby was barely hanging on to one of the roots below and he ordered another root to snake over and give more support and pull him to safety. He thought the boy's name was Finn.

Yes, it was Finn.

"I think I know you," he said to the boy.

Finn was speechless.

God-Jack turned his eyes to the scene below on the castle roof where everything had stopped.

Redduns, Jenny, the Wishermans, the pirate ship and even the Blue Queen looked up with the sound of the blast and the scream, and all of them shrank back when they saw the golden being who floated above with no visible means of support. The being was so bright it hurt their eyes. It impassively looked down at the scene below.

In total silence the strange being hovered over their heads. Jenny had no idea it was Jack.

Not even Jack knew he was Jack.

The Redduns were the first to act. They screamed obscenities and began throwing a remarkably large assortment of long pointy things at the glowing being above their heads. All of which became sunflowers as they neared their target. Then they arranged themselves into a bouquet. The bouquet flew up to the pretty boy hiding in the roots beneath the island. He remembered that the boy liked sunflowers.

Finn

Finn hung on to the roots around him and instinctively clasped the sunflowers to his chest like he wanted to hold on to the boy that was torn from him. What had happened to Jack?

Jack

God-Jack hovered above the gooey tribe of redduns below until they ran out of things to throw, after which they jumped up and down angrily sneezing and coughing in fury.

"Cub od dowd, n' fight uss!" shouted Rudolfen.

At that, God-Jack seemed to arrive at a decision. He looked over to the floating pool of water, which had once carried the small longboat. The pool began to bubble and turn golden.

It smelled like chicken soup.

With a gesture, God-Jack sent streams of what was now a hearty, anti-biotic infused chicken soup through the air and down into the mouths of each of the hollering redduns.

But here God-Jack's good intentions went awry. The redduns had been embracing their sickness for so long that there was nothing left of them, but the sickness. The magical anti-biotic meal worked all too well. Once the viruses and bacteria were destroyed – there was nothing left of the redduns but a virus-free red powdery smudge on the stones.

"Hey golden person! Help!" cried out a sobbing Jenny. "Can you help my friend?" She was cradling the dying man's head in her small lap.

God-Jack stared at the girl and the man. They looked familiar.

God-Jack didn't notice the silent glare of the Blue Queen as she decided upon her terrible wish. She would create a virus that would wipe out all life in Frey!

Randy the Wish

Randy's existence as a wish was not remotely satisfactory. He hated everything that this horrible giantess wanted. He saw the world through her eyes but he chose not to look half the time. Just too awful. He did his best to mitigate the worst of her wishes. He spoiled her aim. He made all of her wishes as energy hungry as possible so her power would drain quickly. When she tried to kill that familiar looking human, he softened the blow. He was surprised he could do that.

Odd. This man had all of his fingers.

But what made Randy look again was the little girl. Jenny. That was her name. He remembered her. He'd *liked* her.

When the blue queen's thoughts wished Randy to destroy the little girl and everyone else with a virus, Randy hesitated. He'd decided to grant her earlier wish even though it wasn't spoken... as she'd really wanted it, and he wasn't sure if he *could* say no. He knew that wasn't really how it was *supposed* to work, if he was a dark wish.

Of course he knew he'd have to do it, but *he didn't have to do it right now, did he?* He could do it tomorrow. Or maybe next week? There was no pressing need to do it right this instant...

It was then that he realized that he wasn't a *dark* wish after all! Maybe that *wasn't* human blood that he'd been forced to drink! Maybe he'd never been a *dark wish?* Which meant he could do what he *wanted* to do with her wishes.

He could see the big ugly desire for a virus that would wipe out all of Frey. He could make it. He could. Not all that difficult really. The thought sat there in front of him. Fat and pulsing and stinking like a wet turd with a beating heart.

But what other desires were in here?

Randy looked deeper. The challenge within Asphixia's mind was the lack of space. Everything was so immovable. It was crowded with crumbling boulders of insecurity.

If he was going to be stuck here, he'd have to start redecorating. That was for sure. One structure in particular was far too big for the space – a clawing, grasping longing that overwhelmed everything else.

Randy saw an interesting opportunity here.

Jack

God-Jack crouched next to a softly breathing Footbe and poured energy into the man. The apron had burned away to nothing during the transformation. But he was so bright that no one – not even God-Jack thought about how naked he was. He was hard to look at.

The man was regaining consciousness.

"WHOOSH!"

The muted gasp behind them startled all of them.

They turned to see the Blue Queen rapidly dwindling in size. It was over in moments. There in the midst of gauzy robes was a screaming infant Frit.

The Blue Queen was no longer old. She was no longer glowing. But in answer to her deepest wish, she was *really, really young.*

Chapter 52

Life Is Harsh Sometimes

Not-Jack

The knock on the bedroom door caused Not-Jack to lose focus and die in a stream of boob acid. Life is harsh sometimes.

"Yeah?" Not-Jack hollered over the sound of Darbie O'Thrill's anguished screams.

The door pushed open and Not-Jenny's expressionless face poked in. "Hey, Finn-The-Wannabe-Human, I need your help in the cellar for a minute."

Not-Finn looked up doubtfully. "Uh, sure. Okay."

Both boys started to get up.

"Not you, Jack-Off," she turned with disgust and walked towards the top of the stairs.

Not-Finn rolled his eyes and stretched. "Sometimes she scares me."

Not-Finn's brawler, Harry McDangle, downed two shots of whiskey when Not-Jack silently took over the other's brawler. He listened to Not-Finn follow the scary little bitch down the steps.

Not-Jack was feeling uncomfortably guilty.

Mr. Saunders

Downstairs, Mr. Saunders was watching the first game of the football season, but noticed the two kids pass behind the couch and head into the kitchen. Soon he heard the banging of the screen door.

At commercial break he looked over at Mrs. Saunders, "Since when is Jenny hanging out with Finn – without Jack?"

Mrs. Saunders was decorating a purple baseball cap with pink rhinestones. It was hard to get the hot glue gun to do just tiny little beads without all the stringy threads of glue making a mess of things.

"Oh, Finn's okay." She paused in her work. "At some point we should probably talk some more about Jack. How we want to handle his... liking boys." Mrs. Saunders looked at her husband. He was glued to a commercial about new blue-cheese flavored chips.

"What? Did you say something?" Mr. Saunders looked up briefly when the commercial ended.

"Oh, noth –"

He stopped her. "Wait – game's on!" Mr. Saunders happily immersed himself in football statistics.

Not-Finn

It was only about five o'clock, but the barn was already dark with shadows. The open trapdoor to the cellar was a yawning pit of blackness.

Not-Finn followed Not-Jenny down the dark steps. Mr. Saunders had never gotten around to installing a switch for the cellar lights at the top of the steps.

"What's this about?" he asked, fumbling for the light switch on the post at the base of the steps. He didn't expect the short wooden club that she'd crafted during her hours in the barn until it slammed into the back of his head.

And then Not-Finn knew nothing at all.

Chapter 53

Together Again?

Jack

The baby frit – who moments earlier had been a foul-tempered giantess – was now sitting wide-eyed and silent amid piles of blue and lavender chiffon. The sticky netting had disappeared with her ancient skin during the transformation. Though an infant, she was still taller than Jenny.

In this moment – in the midst of their collective, stupefied silence – Jack remembered himself. He remembered it all. He remembered Jenny. He realized what he looked like. Faster than thought appeared a glamour of the old Jack

– in shorts and t-shirt. He turned and smiled at his little sister.

"Hi Jenny!"

She gasped.

"Jack? What happened to you?!"

Jack reached out and hugged her. "More than you could believe! I was afraid I'd never find you." He had tears in his eyes.

Jenny clutched him hard and burst into tears. "I didn't know you were here all this time! Then we found Finn!" She sniffed back sobs. She'd missed Jack.

"I've got so many crazy stories to tell you!" Jack laughed.

Jenny choked back tears and didn't know where to start with her stories. "I'll believe most anything! I'm a captain of a pirate ship! *(sniff)* And I've met Nixies, *(sniff)* and trees that talk!" Jenny was exploding with all her adventures. "And there are mermaids! MERMAIDS! But they don't look like mermaids! They –"

"Jenny," Jack hugged her again and spoke into her ear, "I want to hear about everything, but... it's going to have to wait." Jack looked over at the baby frit, and at the man below them who was regaining consciousness.

At first Jack only saw the man who'd just recently held a knife to his throat. But quickly it became clear that this man was not the same person at all. There was something different in the eyes. And he wasn't wearing as many clothes as the other guy.

Pirate Jenny

Jenny swallowed her tears and nodded. "There's stuff to do."

She looked at Footbe. It was strange to see him without the goat face and fur. She'd gotten used to him looking like that. But the eyes were still his... and the new face was nice too.

"How are you, sir?" Jack asked.

Footbe lay between them. "Ah'm okay ah think." He lifted his human hand and looked at it with relief. "Better than okay. Thank ya ver' much!" Footbe sat up slowly and gathered together the loincloth that was now too big for him, giving the tie at the waist a tighter cinch so it would stay up.

The Wisherman family stood in front of the baby frit, who had once been a monster. They appraised the creature and shook their heads. The baby was enormous.

"Wot ya think, Mamy?" said Papy. "Think she remembers any o' it?"

"Hard ta say, Papy." Mamy crossed her arms quizzically and stared at the giant baby who was now giggling and watching them in return. The frit suddenly grabbed Papy up like he was a fluffy pet.

"Get 'way fro' me ya foul baby!" Papy squeezed himself out of her arms and ran to a healthy distance. Mamy and the kids ran too as she crawled after them.

Footbe sighed. Battling the ache in his muscles, he stood up. "Excuse me, Ah – *I* think *I'm* the only one big enough to deal with her."

Footbe ran across the flagstones and grabbed the infant's tail and pulled her back from the Wishermans – who were cowering behind a mangled topiary bush.

"Did you do this?" Footbe turned to Jack and gestured at the frit.

Jack looked sideways at the giant baby. "I don't *think* that was me. It's a bit of a blur though."

The teen stretched out his hand. "I'm Jack. Jenny's brother."

Jenny smiled proudly at Jack.

"Footbe, er... James. Finn's dad." They shook hands.

"You're Finn's real dad! Wow."

Footbe nodded happily. Then he sighed and stared at the frit. "But now, just what're we goin' ta do wit' you?"

She was about four foot tall, but he swaddled the baby up in some of the fabric. She went to sleep without much preamble. It had been a long eventful day, and babies do better with naps.

"Jack!" sounded the voice of Finn.

Jack looked up towards the island to see Finn waving. "Jenny, I'll be back. I gotta talk to Finn." He gave her a smile, and then he casually jumped into the air like Peter Pan and flew to where Finn waited in the roots of the floating island.

Jenny was agog.

"I wanna fly..."

Jack & Finn

"Finn!"

"Jack!"

"You look like yourself again! You found some clothes!"

"Not really." Jack in a burst of boldness dropped the glamour. He stood arms out, naked, golden and glowing in front of Finn. He dimmed the glow so Finn didn't need to shield his eyes. "It's just an illusion. Didn't want to flash Jenny."

Finn was blushing. "No, don't want to do that," awkwardly remembering that he briefly flashed her back at the cottage.

Seeing Jack naked – right smack in front of him nearly took Finn's breath away. "Damn." Finn realized his tropical boxers were tenting but it was okay as Jack was also exhibiting a similar bit of enthusiasm.

Jack felt vulnerable and crazy stupid, but he didn't care one bit. Their feelings were obviously mutual.

Though now wasn't the time for – whatever it was that they both wanted to explore. There was stuff to do.

It was a mutual decision to change the subject of their thoughts.

"What's next?" Jack reclined on a root that he'd mentally sculpted into a comfortable chair. He had to confess it was kind of fantastic to just sit there naked with Finn – like it was no big deal. Like he was some sort of forest god. A character in a book. The old Jack could have never been this free.

Jack waved his hand and a root reached out and wove itself into a beautiful seat for Finn as well.

Finn was a little awed at the easy display of magic. He took a seat. Seeing Jack naked was incredibly distracting.

"*That* was a nifty trick." Finn inspected the swirls and beauty of the root-craft chair that he was sitting in. He took a deep breath and thought about his step-parents. Perfect weenie-shrinker. He exhaled. His blood was moving back towards his brain once again. "We should create a to-do list," Finn offered.

A roll of parchment sparkled into existence and floated beside them in the air. Next to it appeared an old fashioned pen with an red ostrich feather.

"Show off much?" Finn remarked.

Jack grinned conspiratorially. "Why the heck not? We're going to have a happy ending! Sparkles and parchment are how I'll write the book of our adventures! You'll illustrate it! We need to get Jenny and get home, but – " Jack paused. "Before that there's stuff that's got to be figured out."

The feather bobbed as the pen scribbled on the parchment. Magic didn't help Jack's penmanship at all (magic can't solve everything).

Finn squirmed as he watched the pen write *Home*. His two monster feet whispered, *Can't wait to be locked up in a government science lab!*

But ignoring those voices, he helped Jack make a to-do list:

1. Figure out what to do with the baby Frit.
    deliver to the frits underground?
2. Go back to cottage to see Finn's mom
3. Rescue mermaids?
4. Send rescued children back home?
5. What to do about b'Trixers?
6. Go home (somehow)

Finn had to ask the obvious. "What *happened* to you?! What's up with all this?" he gestured to the glow coming off of Jack. "Is it permanent?"

Jack shrugged. "I ate a really big wish. Twice. I don't know if the magic will last. It went away last time. But this time it... feels different. Still figuring it out." Jack giggled.

Finn wondered, "Can you take the powers with you when you go back home?"

"I've no frickin' idea! They didn't come with a manual!" He looked up at Finn with a start. "When WE go back home."

Finn gestured to his scaled legs and flipper feet. "Jack, I can't go back! Look at me."

"Maybe you can..." Jack cocked his head and waved his hand – and just like that – Finn looked like his old self!

Finn's feet looked the same size as his old feet and wearing his old green tennis shoes! But when he touched them, he realized that it was just an illusion. A glamour.

"But this isn't real. Will it last if you lose your powers?" Finn hesitated. "I'd end up in a government lab."

"I don't know? But you have to try!" Jack felt helpless. "Don't you want to go home again?" Jack asked. "Our parents have to be really worried about us!"

"Maybe your parents. But... *my* real parents are *here*."

"So that's all for sure true about the mermaid? And that man down there?"

Finn nodded.

Jack let the reality of it wash over him. "Wow, Finn. That's great... You found your parents after all this time."

The glamour over Finn faded like a watercolor left out in the rain, and he was back to his fishy self.

Jack's clothes reappeared as well. Yet he somehow felt more naked than he had been a moment earlier.

This wasn't how it was supposed to go.

Jack

By the wee hours of morning, they were ready to leave the castle. Brendall and his partner Broosen decided to take temporary charge of the castle. The horny-blits promised to see about getting all the staff back to the homes that they never thought they'd see again. Fortunately they had all recovered from Rip-One's gas attack. Even the Rodent was found in Doritte's room where she'd smacked him senseless after finding mushrooms in her lunch.

A couple teams of pirates combed through the castle from top to bottom looking for both unpleasant creatures and frightened b'Trixers. And of course treasure. They were pirates after all.

Bilbe, Dilbe, and Lilbe (along with their parents) climbed down to the caverns below the kitchen and led the terrified animals who had hidden there out onto the dark east lawn, where they joined the rest of the b'Trixers, as well as the children who had hidden on the floating island. Jack fixed the staircase that dropped out of the island's roots.

Jack (in his clothed human glamour) asked if the kids wanted to be sent home to their families, but was interrupted by Papy Wisherman who hadn't been aware of Jack's intentions.

"They canna go back, Jack." Papy said.

Jack stared at him. "What do you mean? I already sent a bunch of kids home."

"But they ar'na' gonna stay thar! They're goin'ta get pulled back 'fore long. They be eaten Frey food. Ya kin try

– but they'll be poppin' back ta Frey 'fore ya know it who knows where or when!"

This was all new information to Jack. He'd eaten things in Frey. He'd eaten bread, and pure magic – twice!

"Jenny!" he turned in a panic to find her.

Mamy touched his arm. "Dinna ya worry 'bout Jenny. We warned her an' she only be eatin' safe things."

Jack turned to Mamy and Papy. "You don't understand. I have to go back! My parents! They've got to be completely freaking out that we've been gone so long! My dad has a bad heart! This could kill him! I have to go home!"

Papy and Mamy looked at him.

Papy sighed, "I don't know wot ta say, boy. Maybe wi' yer magic, ya kin change yerself back ta how ya were 'afore? I jest can't tell ya."

Jack could see the first rays of gold hitting the clouds in the east. There was a whisper of dawn at the far reaches of the ocean. Jack was distraught.

Footbe had been listening. "Jack, the mer'King *might* be able ta help ya. Can't promise nothin'. We'll be talkin' ta him later today, if all goes right."

The crowd of children had been listening to their conversation.

When Jack again asked the group of children if anyone wanted to go home, he was surprised to learn that over a third of the children didn't want to leave once Jack told them the date back home. Many been away for decades

TOGETHER AGAIN?

in human time and there wasn't a home to return to. Jack decided to bring all of them – children and b'Trixers alike onto the floating island. Together they would travel to see the mermaids (assuming they could be revived).

The baby Frit and Footbe came aboard the island as well. Footbe said that he'd take her down to the frit caverns via the tunnel near the cottage. He figured it was his responsibility. Finn said he'd go with his father and see the frits again. Jack was twisted up inside about leaving Finn behind in Frey.

Jack was not sure how to move the island at first. It didn't have any sails like the pirate ship (not that *that* had really made one bit of sense).

All the kids and critters spread out eagerly to explore the island. The children and the b'Trixers who had been hiding on the island had mentioned seeing giant spider-like creatures throwing stones down on the queen during the battle, but no spider-like creatures were found. The island carried mysteries, but apparently friendly mysteries.

On one side of the island's mountain was a strange structure. To Jack and Finn it seemed a cross between the tree-house in the old Swiss Family Robinson movie, and Willy Wonka's toy factory.

The b'Trixers found Mordette's larders. Soon a group of matronly rabbits laid an assortment of breakfast foods on a long table for the famished kids and other animals. But nothing resembling a flight deck from Star Trek was found (which was what Jack and Finn had been secretly hoping for).

In desperation Jack finally just willed the island to move. And it moved!

Pirate Jenny

Mamy and Papy stayed on the pirate ship as Mamy was running the kitchen there, so Jenny joined them. Bilbe, Dilbe, and Lilbe insisted on the island despite Mamy's protestations. The kids pointed out how rare an opportunity it was to travel on a floating island, and that land was probably safer than being in a boat. Mamy waved her hands in defeat.

From her perch on the forecastle Jenny dreamily watched the floating island (complete with its donut of water and white beaches) as the curious flying saucer glided across a sea of puffy clouds.

Jack

Once the island was on its way, Jack looked around for Finn. Jack stood on a beach that he now considered the *front* of the island. Beyond the ring of water, which extended some twenty feet out in all directions from the beaches, he could see a mountainous cloudscape that reached towards the cerulean horizon. From Footbe, he had a general sense of which direction they should be headed. Jack hoped the clouds would clear up a bit so they could see the ground soon.

He discovered a stone well on this beach that was perhaps eight feet in diameter. Instead of water at the bottom of the well, it was a wide-open hole and allowed one to see what lay directly beneath the island.

Jack walked down the beach for some distance before he caught sight of Finn and his father sitting on a log near the water. Footbe had his arm around Finn's shoulder. Jack couldn't imagine his own father doing that. No touching in the Saunders' home.

It looked like Finn was finally getting a chance to get to know his real father.

Jack was happy for him. He really was.

Honestly... but feelings are complicated things.

They arrived at the Bay of mer'Rinn by mid-morning. The pirate ship settled on the clear waters of the lagoon, and the island hovered above the beach near the river that led to the Cottage-by-the-Sea.

Jack asked the b'Trixers to watch the children while the two boys, Jenny, Footbe, and the Wishermans hiked up the trail to the Cottage.

This time the Guard Buds immediately recognized Footbe and Finn and the open stone path was lined with rows of rose buds who happily greeted their masters with a song.

> *"Welcome back oh tasty bosses!*
> *No one's blood is quite so sweet—*
> *Royals with a touch o' fish*
> *have the blood we love to eat!"*

The roses all waved their vines in a sort of football stadium wave.

Jack hesitated to walk past on hearing the bloodthirsty lyrics. "Are they safe?"

Footbe grinned. "Are any roses truly safe? All roses are wee bit vampiric. Haven't you ever noticed?"

Jack always lost some blood around roses.

Finn laughed, "Guard buds, you are the best! Thank you for watching the cottage!" He reached to turn the knob, but the door swung wide before he could grab it.

"Bromley!"

The butler greeted the tired party with an energetic smile. "You're just in time, sirs! Follow me!"

Bromley led the group through a side arch in the entry into a laboratory. Jack tagged along in the rear of the group. The cottage was beautiful!

"Master James! It is most excellent to see you look like yourself again!" observed the wooden-whiskered butler as Footbe hurried toward the tall tube in the center of the laboratory.

There was a strange creature with a fish tail inside it.

Finn got a wistful smile on his face. "I didn't expect to love her so much."

"That's your mom?" asked Jack in surprise.

"Well she doesn't really look like that," Finn explained. "She's beautiful. But – she's kind of cute this way too."

Jack could see the worry on Finn's face.

"Is she asleep?" asked Jack – wondering what she'd look like when she recovered from the virus.

"I think so."

Jack was astounded by the whole underground home. The picturesque cottage in the side of a hill covered with vampiric guard roses, the steam-punk laboratory, the strange organic robots that peeked out from every cubbyhole... everywhere he looked was a wonder for the eyes. He couldn't help but wonder how many things he'd never see if he went home right away.

Bromley waddled over to a small beatnik robot that stood on a broad counter. It was jiving up and down as if it heard music in its mechanical soul. About the size of a large coffee pot, it stood on two silver legs with bent knees. It did the twist. It did a sort of punk bopping to a rocking beat. Little hands snapped fingers to a silent beat. Jack could distinguish no head. Its body consisted of a metal cylinder, which tapered at the base to a small tap. It gyrated its hips back and forth till a little head with a beret burst out of the top. It squeaked, "I'm ready!"

Footbe laughed. "My martini mixer!"

Bromley rushed over and held a small tube under its tap. "He's been shaking the serum for six hours and twenty-two minutes."

He poured a some bright green fluid into a vial for Meryth. "There should be enough for all the Merfolk. Thank goodness it doesn't require very much. It took ages to pulp the moss into juice."

Nearby, there was a tired looking robot that reminded Jack of a peppercorn grinder – it sat on a clear but dirty globe full of juiced moss.

Bromley wobbled back over to the giant tube that held Meryth of mer'Rinn. Then Bromley hesitated. "Master James, would you like to do it?"

Footbe looked at his sleeping wife tenderly. "I would."

He stepped forward apprehensively. He carefully accepted the small vial of antidote. He pulled up the injection tube and poured the green fluid into it. With a thrust he pushed the mechanism into the console and a sparkling, greenish tinge squirted into the bottom of the tube and spread rapidly. It swirled around the small sleeping form.

Jack couldn't quite describe what he was seeing. There was a sparkling and a stretching. The shape morphed into a larger creature – which made no sense to Jack when he remembered his Intro to Physics class. But somehow the small mass became a big mass, which then became – a mermaid. She was still sleeping.

Jenny gasped. "She's beautiful."

She was.

Her pale blue hair floated around her in a wavy mass of soft curls. Her tail was a soft shade of lavender with sparkly depths in its scales. And her skin was fair and opalescent like the inside of an oyster shell.

Jack couldn't help but notice that Finn was staring at the mermaid's breasts.

Finn blushed when he noticed Jack was staring at him. "What? They *are* nice breasts. Not that I'm looking at my mom's breasts. Just something she and I were talking about. I don't think I'm as uptight about naked body parts any more. It's just a body. Is that... weird?" Finn whispered.

Jack shrugged. "I'm not sure what weird is anymore." They weren't even sixteen yet. Seeing naked breasts outside of a magazine was... not normal. He had difficulty meeting his friend's eyes for fear of nervous giggling. Jack thought it was strange how he could feel totally mature one moment, and still be only seconds away from turning into an idiot.

He hoped he grew out of that.

Jack was glad that Jenny wasn't paying any attention to them. She was staring at Meryth. She was in awe.

Footbe knocked on the glass.

Meryth's eyes opened. She looked confused until they settled on her husband on the other side of the glass. She looked down at her body with relief. She smiled. She said something they couldn't understand.

Footbe turned a jeweled knob on the console and the entire tube of water gently swirled down into a pool and Footbe reached into it and lifted her out and into his arms.

"Footbe!" she cried.

"Finbe!" he sighed.

"Finbe?" muttered Finn.

James and Meryth kissed so passionately it was embarrassing for the rest of the room – except for Bromley who gazed on happily. The Wishermans stepped outside.

But Meryth noticed Finn standing awkwardly nearby.

"Finn!" she cried. "You did it!"

Footbe smiled. "And the false queen is no longer in power. We've so many stories to tell you. To tell each other! There's so much that I don't know myself!"

Footbe reached over and pulled Finn into a three-way nearly naked embrace. Finn looked initially uncomfortable, but then relaxed. It felt good to be hugged by one's parents.

Jack was a little envious.

He lingered near the doorway thinking he should leave. Jack felt hollow to see all the love there. The Saunders didn't hug. He didn't belong to a family of *huggers*, but Jack so greatly longed for a hug in that moment.

Jenny still stood transfixed at seeing a mermaid for the first time.

Releasing Finn, Footbe carried Meryth over to a pool and descended the steps into the water and let her slip into the water's soothing embrace. Yet she didn't stay apart from him for long. In moments, Footbe had settled into a comfortable pool seat with Meryth sitting in his lap.

"You must be Jack! And you must be Jenny!" laughed Meryth, beckoning them to come closer.

"I've never met a mermaid before!" said Jenny eagerly. "When I saw the others I was so disappointed! I knew merpeople weren't supposed to look like that!"

"You saw my people?" asked Meryth.

Footbe was kissing Meryth's ear. He could hardly keep his hands off his wife. "We were there yesterday. I'm hoping that you might help us with restoring them, in an hour or so."

"An hour?" asked Meryth.

"Or so," smiled Footbe.

Meryth giggled at whatever Footbe whispered in her ear, but then her eyes fell on Jack near the door. She removed herself quickly from her husband's lap, which had clearly missed her. "Jack! Come here. Finn has told me so much about you." She and Footbe moved up to the water's edge to inspect Jack.

Jack didn't know what to say. If Finn's newly discovered parents knew just *how much* he liked Finn, they would think Jack was disgusting. He might lose Finn. He was going to lose Finn whatever he did!

Jack felt naked – and suddenly he really was. His glamour was gone in a burst of golden light. Every eye in the lab turned away from the glare that poured out from him.

He was a freak! He couldn't even control himself!

Jack panicked. He flew out of the lab and out of the cottage till he hovered over the river.

He wouldn't get to spend his life with Finn! He would have to say goodbye to Finn *forever*. Jack was a horrible person to wish that Finn would give up his lost parents just to go back with him. Jack was awful and selfish! If Finn couldn't see it, his parents would surely see it!

A large oak stretched its branches over the water. Jack drifted down onto one of its branches and collapsed in the tree's embrace. His golden tears poured out in rivers of their own. His sobs came from depths that he hadn't known even existed.

Meryth

Finn raced out of the lab in pursuit.

"I thought Jack was human?" asked a startled Meryth.

"Well, he... he used to be," ventured a confused Pirate Jenny.

Footbe sighed. "Jack seems to have consumed a great deal of magic somewhere in his travels."

"To what effect?" asked Meryth.

"Not sure," Footbe reflected. "He's frightened. He wants to go home to his parents. In fact, we've a whole island full of human children who've eaten Frey food, but who want to go home."

"But, now Frey won't let them go," Meryth finished the thought. "If my father can be restored, he may know what to do."

Chapter 54
Merfolk

Jack & Finn

Finn's head bobbed up out of a swirl of water under the branch where Jack sobbed golden tears. Jack's glowing foot dangled in the slow moving current. Golden light danced in the ripples where the foot touched the water.

Finn tugged on the golden foot. "Hey."

Jack looked down at Finn and sniffed, "Hey."

Minutes passed with no sound other than the water's passage around them and Jack's muffled sobs.

"I'll never see you again if I go home," Jack choked out in a tangle of tears.

"You don't know that," Finn played with Jack's golden toes where they met the water.

Jack closed his eyes as Finn touched his feet. "I hate having to choose between – you and my parents! And Jenny! I know it's not your fault. You want to stay in your parents' world. I get it. You're not really human anymore. It just sucks."

Finn agreed. "It does suck. And not in a good way."

Jack didn't laugh.

The river flowed slowly around them. Finn floated on his back below Jack, lazily kicking his big webbed feet to stay in place.

"We'll figure something out. There's got to be a way." Finn urged.

"Yeah?" Jack looked down.

Finn shrugged. "We'll ask the Merfolk to help us."

Jack's thoughts were somewhere else. "Do your parents hate me? What – I am? What we are?"

"Extremely adorable?"

Jack couldn't answer. He was thinking about how Finn's parents must think he's disgusting. How they must be sick to their stomach to think of their son with another boy.

"Hey – you're talking about two people who fell in love with someone outside their own *species*. They are extremely open-minded. They just want me to be happy. *And you, Jack, make me happy.*"

Finn pulled hard on the foot he was holding. A startled Jack hollered as he tumbled into the water.

Finn wrapped his arms around Jack. They surfaced further downstream. They floated together on their backs.

"Somebody isn't wearing a Hawaiian print loincloth anymore." Jack noted.

"Lost it." Finn smiled. He pulled Jack closer and gave him a kiss.

Jack kissed him back.

They drifted for a bit in the current.

Soon, they thought they might explore the riverbank to see if there was something that they might discover together.

Jack

A little while later, an expedition set out for the Isle of Judgment. Jack left the island floating low above the beach. The Wishermans stayed to supervise the kids. It was possibly the best place ever for playing *Hide and Seek*. Asphixia was in the tree house taking a magically assisted nap.

The pirate ship sailed out near the Isle and dropped anchor. Meryth and Finn swum alongside. Footbe and Jenny rode aboard ship.

Jack flew ... because he could.

Jack couldn't get his mind off of wondering whether the Merfolk could help him return to his parents. Part of him wished that they'd say it was impossible and save him the choice.

Footbe and Jenny would stay on the ship, while Meryth and Finn planned to dive to the underwater laboratory. They asked Jack if he'd like to join them.

"Can I do that?" Jack hovered golden above the water. With all the magic that he'd been doing, he was still just as golden as ever.

"Try it," suggested Meryth.

Finn nodded encouragingly, so Jack tried creating a picture of what he wanted to be in his mind. Instantly, Jack transformed into a merboy with a golden tail and dropped with a splash between Finn and his mom.

Jack inspected his new tail with interest and quickly split it into two so that it matched Finn's fish legs.

Meryth and Finn were laughing so hard at his transformation that they couldn't swim. Waves playfully buffeted them about for a bit.

Jack knew that Jenny was feeling left behind, when the three slipped below the surface with the canister of antidote.

Jack's head popped back up. He called out to Jenny, "Do you want to come too?"

Jenny shouted, "Yes!"

She jumped over the rail before Jack was ready, but before she hit the water she sported a beautiful pink fish tail.

She bobbed back up to the surface and looked for Jack. He was there beside her.

"Jack? Pink! Really? Can't I have a black tail?"

"Black! Are you going Goth on me!" He laughed, "You don't like pink?"

"Pink is nice... but I'm a pirate!"

"Of course," Jack gave a mischievous grin.

Jenny suddenly wore a red bandanna around her hair in an *Argh-swab-the-decks-ye-lubbers* sort of way. It looked great with her existing red and white striped t-shirt, and glittering black tail. She didn't even notice the jolly roger imprinted on her butt.

Pirate Jenny

Jenny could now breathe under water! She swam three somersaults just to see if she could. She could, but it made her rather dizzy.

She was giddy with excitement. She and Jack dove down to join the others who waited some distance below.

Swimming through a twisting maze of coral and colorful plants, the four finally came upon the derelict mermaid city.

Jenny thought it was even more spectacular close up.

Even in disrepair the towers, arches, and statuary were glorious. Beyond the city she could see what looked like a giant cave in the side of a vast cliff.

As they approached, Jenny recognized it as the same Hall of Judgment that she'd been in before. But this time there was no glass. The four swam right in. Jenny could now see that the room was designed for water. Plants that had been shapeless floppy things when surrounded by air, reached up with life, movement, and vibrant hues.

Jenny and Meryth swam towards the wall that opened to the lab.

Jack

Jack and Finn swam to inspect the tubes at one end of the chamber. They held a wide assortment of odd creatures. Some did not look like they would turn into Merfolk – more like mer-animals. The shrunken sleeping creatures came in all shapes.

Finn carried the capsule with the antidote. He nodded towards the lab, which was now open. "I'm going to join my mom."

Jack was startled to hear words underwater. The words had a warbled quality but were understandable.

Jack nodded. "Okey doke!" came out his watery reply.

Finn swam off.

Jack continued to swim above the rows of glass tubes. One of these might be Finn's grandfather, the mer'King. Crossing to the other end of the chamber he inspected the tubes there. Finally on a sculpted dais of marble, he saw a unique tube. It was a bit bigger than the others and was protected on three sides.

Inside the tube slept a shriveled little sea chimp with a straggly beard, which resembled kelp roots pulled from the sea floor.

"What do I want from you?" thought Jack. "Do I want the rest of my life to be decided by an old man who doesn't even know me? He might not even like me! He might not *want* to help me."

Jack floated in the water as he stared at the king.

To all appearances Jack was now a golden half-merboy with two undulating tails. But inside... what was he? Was he an immature fifteen-year-old boy – not capable of choosing his own life?

What did Jack want? Did Jack want to spend his life (if he was lucky) writing stories of extraordinary adventure in an ordinary world? Or did he want to actually live those extraordinary adventures?

What would his parents want for him?

They would want him to be safe. With them. They'd say he was too young to be on his own. After seeing what his parents went through when Jenny disappeared, he could not do that to them again. Even if they weren't parents who hugged their kids, they were still his parents.

He lost track of how long he'd floated there, but jumped when the king's eyes popped open.

A sparkling green solution had entered the king's tube. Around him he could see it swirling through all the other tubes.

Movement. Change. Colors. More change! Bubbles everywhere! Within moments curious water creatures spilled out of their tanks as their tubes dissipated into the water around. He spun around to look. All about him – creatures that boggled his imagination. Giant sea horses and sea pigs! Small aqua-dragons and human bodies with fish heads. And lots of mermaids and mermen! They were so beautiful that Jack now understood why Finn was so handsome. He had faerie DNA. The water was bubbling with happy celebration in languages he could not understand.

Jack felt a stillness behind him. He spun again to see the king. The king had transformed as well. The scrawny creature had expanded with vitality and muscles. His silver beard had grown in fullness across a broad chest. Muscles on top of muscles, and a long, sinewy tail that glittered with purples and lavenders.

The king gazed at Jack with surprise. He clearly wanted to know about this golden merboy with two tails.

Jack realized he should probably bow or something, but his enthusiastic bow turned into a somersault and he unintentionally slapped the king in the face with webbed feet.

Jack was mortified, but the king broke into hearty laughter. Big bubbling rolls of laughter that filled the room with its contagion. The whole room was suddenly laughing at him.

Jack's face had turned orange with blushing.

"I'm so sorry sir!" He blurted out. "I didn't mean to do that! I'm Jack. I'm here with your daughter and your grandson!"

Jack quickly learned that Merfolk love to laugh. Apparently laughter was such an art among sea people that they'd cataloged a total of five-hundred and fifty two distinctly different laughs – each with quite unique meanings. As laughter is a virtual language among the Merfolk, one has to be careful with exactly *how* one laughs. A simple giggle done wrong might commit you to a roll in the seaweed beds.

The Wisherman kids had mentioned that Merfolk could be rather peculiar. Jack could see that if one didn't understand their culture it could appear quite silly. But it did have an order of its own. And Finn's mom was right when she'd said that Merfolk were not particularly modest. He had wondered before in an abstract sort of way where mermen kept their you-know-whats. Now he knew. Not shy at all.

But Jack liked the mer'King right off. King Posei. He was a jolly sort who giggled quite a lot for such a big muscular man.

Jack had asked if *Posei* was short for *Poseidon*, but the king had just laughed and laughed instead of answering. Jack didn't repeat his question. The name was pretty much pronounced like the name of the flower – if you had a mouth full of marbles.

The reunion between father and daughter was touching, as was the meeting between Finn and his grandfather. King Posei looked quite serious when Meryth formally introduced Jack as Finn's consort. Jack blushed again. The king giggled.

It was downright awkward.

Meryth and King Posei sat comfortably at the water's edge. Footbe had swum over to sit by Meryth. The king greeted Footbe warmly. Everyone had grown used to calling James, *Footbe*. So Footbe it was.

The rest of the Merfolk population were impatient to see their old homes and swam off to begin the long task of cleaning the underwater city and making it habitable again.

Sitting at the water's edge, King Posei listened soberly as Jack and Finn asked for his advice.

"Is there any way for kids to go home again if they've eaten Frey food?" Jack had asked.

King Posei sighed with his impossibly deep voice, "There be a cost, my boy." The mer'King was quiet as if unsure how to explain.

"What type of cost?" whispered Jack.

"Frey be woven from the strands of fancy. Everything here be infused with imagination. If ye'd no imagination, ye wouldn't have ever been able to cross over to begin with – no matter what traps the impostor queen had set."

"So –" Jack reflected.

"So, my boy." The mer'King continued, "Merfolk only do water-magic. But water-magic could be enough. Humans are mostly water ye see. I could adjust the children's minds and remove their imagination. With no imagination, they'd be back home immediately. If they don't believe in Frey, the Frey food won't be pulling them back. But they can't *ever* come back. And I can't speak to their happiness without a creative spark in their soul."

Jack sighed. "That's not a good option, is it? So, we can't go home again?" His gut was twisting at all the complicated feelings he felt.

The King held a finger up. "That be for the other young ones. You're a different matter all together. You've become a creature of the air. When the wishes' power entered you, it changed you. Magic now rests in every bit of your being. No one like you has ever existed in Frey – but I'm thinking that you can turn yourself back to your human state once you're on the other side. But your magic and imagination would be gone. I don't think you'd be able to come back."

Jack looked at the King's concerned face, as well as the other faces. Finn's. Jenny's.

"The impostor queen might have put changelings in your place. Standard faerie practice to confuse the mortals. The changelings may not take kindly to your return – if they survive it. Depends on whether they've had time enough to settle in."

"What's a changeling?" asked Jenny.

Footbe scoffed. "Jest a replacement sort of person, walking fungi if you ask me... usually selfish sorts that don't last long anyway. You won't need to worry about them!"

Jack had so many questions, but no words came. He only could murmur, "Thank you your Majesty."

King Posei nodded back at him thoughtfully.

The next couple of days were spent unwinding from all their adventures. Jack and Finn spent as much time together as they could. Jack found he wasn't in a rush to make a decision. It was too hard.

When the situation had been explained, every child chose to stay in Frey, though not without a few tears. Some of the older ones had been missing from their families for many years, but had not grown appreciably older. So it would have been odd if they did return.

The Wishermans suggested that the b'Trixers without homes and the children could live in Whippledell. There were lots of empty homes and a friendly community in the village to welcome them. Mamy and Papy's attitudes about the b'Trixers in general had changed with more familiarity, so they offered to escort them all and introduce them to the village. Mamy was bustling about the island's kitchen putting together food for the journey. Even Bromley brought over bundles of blue carrots for the hundred and forty-five kids to snack on while they waited to leave. The children were running all over the island's beaches, playing and laughing like they'd never been through the horrors at the castle. Jack wondered how the influx of humans would impact Frey. But what else could they do?

Jack wondered about the kids he sent back before. Were they each going to be pulled back to Frey? Where would they appear? Would they be safe? Frey was a big place.

Footbe packed for the journey down into the caverns of Frit. He was not only delivering the baby frit, but also hoping to do some healing and repair work while he was there. He had the basket of wishes that Papy generously offered him.

Finn planned to go with his dad.

Jack had settled the floating island softly into the embrace of the lagoon's waters, making a third island in the bay. Finn was going to make his home on the island when he returned. It wouldn't fly again without Jack to lift and steer it, unless they figured out how Mordette did it.

The pirates were moored near the beach and Jenny was crying and saying goodbye to Gibbie and Nibs and her crew of pirates. The brownies crowded around her and assured her that they'd never forget her.

Jack created a portal at the island's cliff edge. He hadn't known he could do that. But Meryth again had suggested that he give it a try. It is amazing what is possible when one tries impossible things. He felt like Dorothy when Glinda the Good said she'd always had the power to go home. Of course that was not quite true, but the words still stuck in his head.

Bilbe, Lilbe, and Dilbe were hugging Jack's shins. He squatted down and gave each one a hug. He looked the same as when he arrived. The glamour of clothes and normal coloring was easy to hold on to now.

A crowd of familiar faces crowded around Jack, as Jenny returned from the beach followed by her pirates.

Jack and Finn had said their goodbyes more times than they could count. They had no words or goodbyes left, or perhaps too many words that could not even be formed.

Jenny took a big breath. In her pirate hat and red galoshes, her striped shirt and shorts – she stepped through the portal and disappeared.

Jack took a last glance at the company. He took a last look at Finn, embedding the vision of Finn's tear stained face in his memory.

Finn rushed forward for a last embrace. Then Jack tore himself away, stepped through the portal and disappeared.

Jack was gone.

Finn suddenly shouted, "Jack, WAIT!"

Chapter 55

Changeling
The Ending

Millie

At six o'clock, Millie stepped into the silence of the barn. Outside it was not yet twilight but the world was quiet with the expectation of night. The barn was dark except for a square of light emanating from the open trap door to the cellar.

"Finn?" Millie whispered. It was curious. Even though she knew he was not the real Finn, he'd become real to her. She worried about him. Finn wouldn't have asked her to meet him unless it was important.

Millie crossed to the open trap and cautiously descended the creaking steps.

"Finn, are you here?"

The bare bulb at the base of the steps pushed the rest of the cellar into blackness.

"Don't you mean *Not*-Finn?" mocked a voice out of the shadows. Not-Jenny's voice. "You do know he isn't the *real* Finn."

Millie stopped two steps from the bottom and tried to locate where the voice was coming from. "He's real enough... to me."

Now Millie could see her. Her eyes were adjusting to the gloom. Not-Jenny's shadowy form stood a few feet from the bottom of the steps.

"Where's Finn?" Millie continued down the steps. "He's going to meet me here."

"Yes – about that," said the small form in the darkness. "The changeling that was known as Finn isn't really able to talk with you right now."

"Why?" Millie stomach lurched. "What did you do? Where is he?" she demanded.

The cellar rang with a manic, seven-year-old laugh. "You're wasting your time thinking that he's real. He's just a changeling. He didn't have the strength to become anything really REAL."

Millie's eyes were processing more now. She edged away from the wild-eyed child. The back of her foot hit something and she looked down. Not-Finn's foot.

Not-Finn was sprawled awkwardly under the steps. He seemed to be unconscious.

"What did you do to Finn!" She stepped towards the body.

"He was going to die anyway," Not-Jenny scoffed as she watched Millie kneel down. He was still alive, but there was an ugly gash across the back of his head.

She caressed his forehead. "Finn –" she whispered, then to Not-Jenny, "How could you do this? He'd never hurt you. He's kind!"

"He wasn't going to let me do what I need to do!" Not-Jenny's voice deepened and became harsher. "I think the only way to become real is to consume REAL THINGS! And you know too much anyway." she laughed.

Not-Jenny's dark form expanded in the darkness. Millie was not sure what she was seeing – it was like something out of a monster movie.

"What are you doing?" she uttered in horror at the giant albino creature with drooling jaws.

"I'm going to eat you," it said.

Not-Jack

Upstairs in the house, Not-Jack lost another brawler to streams of green acid. He couldn't keep his mind on the game.

He didn't know exactly what Not-Jenny had planned in the cellar, but he suspected that it wasn't going to be very nice. She'd scared him into stealing Not-Finn's phone. No one but Not-Jack had seen the creature that she became when she swelled with anger. He liked Not-Finn. He liked Millie. But he was terrified of Not-Jenny. He couldn't disobey her. Those teeth!

Yet now every time a big-boobed-banshee dissolved another brawler, he couldn't help but worry about what was happening down in the mushroom cellar.

He jumped up. He raced out the door of his bedroom and took the steps downstairs two at a time.

Mr. and Mrs. Saunders looked up at the footsteps thumping down the staircase.

Not-Jack hollered, "Something bad is happening in the mushroom cellar —"

Not-Jack tore through the kitchen and left the screen door banging behind him.

Mr. and Mrs. Saunders exchanged looks and chased after him. The Sunday evening sports played to an empty couch for once.

OLLY, OLLY, OXEN FREY

Millie

The white creature grasped Millie by the throat and its fangs were inches from her soft skin when the pounding boards above them culminated in something leaping on the creature's back from the stairs above.

Not-Jack was screaming and shouting, "NO! Stop!" With one arm around the creature's neck and the other underneath its jaw, he tried to keep its fangs from connecting with Millie.

The slathering nightmare shook itself wildly and dislodged the boy who'd been attached to his back. With one back-handed *whack,* Not-Jack flew into a crumpled heap at the base of the steps.

"Coward!' hissed the creature at the still form of the boy.

A scream came from Mrs. Saunders who was stumbling down the stairs. She bravely pushed past the monster and rushed to Not-Jack's side.

"Jack!" she cried and cradled him into her chest protectively as she cringed in horror at the thing in front of her.

Mr. Saunders who was following on her heels, stopped short halfway down the steps in dumb dismay at what he saw.

The creature was easily eight feet tall. Its skin was hairless and white to the point of transparency. A smattering of sparse hair was a mockery of Jenny's hair. There was nothing to be seen of the little girl that it had once mimicked.

Mr. Saunders took a breath and dived at the beast intending to take it down in a tackle.

Dropping Millie, the beast sneered at the middle aged man and with frighteningly long arms it smacked him roughly to land in a dazed huddle with his wife and his boy.

The beast whirled around to find Millie scooting back against the unconscious Not-Finn under the steps. An arm shot out and yanked a screaming Millie by her ankle towards its dripping jaws.

Millie kicked at air and tried twisting her face away from its foul breath.

The teeth were enormous.

Then – the creature froze.

The horrible creature gave a sudden look of surprise and its eyes glazed white. No pupils. No Iris. White and hollow. Like an empty dried out husk. As did its entire body. And the monster crumbled into the misshapen flakes of a bad dream.

Millie tumbled to the floor gasping.

"I'm back!" shouted a happy voice from the far corner of the cellar.

Pirate Jenny in her pirate hat and galoshes rushed out of the darkness and stopped short at what she saw. Millie coughing and holding her throat like she'd been almost suffocated. Her parents huddled with a boy on the floor looking frightened.

When she saw her parents, she raced into her father's embrace. "I missed you!" she cried. As she reached for her mom she stopped short at the strange white-haired Jack in her mother's arms. "Who're you?" she gasped.

Not-Jack's face held sheer panic. He looked quickly around for the original Jack. This was it.

Mrs. Saunders looked at Jenny with surprise. "It's Jack of course. Are you okay Jenny? Did that thing have you?"

Jenny looked around and then stared again at the frightened eyes of Not-Jack. "Thing? But, you're not –" Jenny remembered. "Are you a changeling?"

It was then that a golden burst of light permeated the entire cellar. Everyone stopped to shield their eyes from the brightness.

Jack

Jack – wearing his human glamour – had stepped through the portal a moment after Jenny, but stopped when he saw another Jack in his mother's arms. A Jack with white hair. He saw the other Jack's terrified eyes as Jenny ran towards them.

Under the stairway, Millie crawled over to an even whiter haired version of Finn. She stroked his forehead and whispered to him.

Jack didn't understand what he was seeing, till he remembered the warning of the merKing. These were changelings.

Something big had just happened. Jack saw terror in all their eyes.

A hand grabbed Jack from behind and he jumped. Finn was there in the cellar with him. The real Finn – with Merfolk legs and monster feet.

"Jack," Finn whispered. "I'm coming with you. I might get pulled back into Frey, or abducted by a government lab, but I'm coming too. But... you might need to fix my legs –" Finn caught sight of his double. "Jeez–"

Across the room and below the steps, Not-Finn opened his eyes to discover Millie looking down at him.

Jack's parents were holding this other Jack in a way they'd never held the real Jack. His parents were HUGGING the other Jack.

His no-hugging parents were hugging this other boy that was not Jack.

Maybe the real Jack was untouchable.

Then Jack felt Finn's arms wrap around him.

Time stopped.

Jack turned to look at Finn. He made a decision.

"Shield your eyes," he whispered quietly.

Jack transformed into a being of golden light.

Everyone in the cellar covered their eyes.

"Jenny," Jack stepped towards the group. His mom pulled Jenny and the other Jack protectively towards her chest, and his dad moved protectively in front of his wife. Jack's heart ached. "I can't stay. *I love you.*"

"But –" Jenny started.

Jack held up a glowing hand. "Trust me."

He looked towards his doppelganger and their eyes met. Was this changeling just a *selfish walking fungi?* Both changelings were clearly frightened. But they were loved. More loved then the real Jack was at any rate. "Take good care of them?"

Not-Jack nodded with wide eyes, as did Not-Finn.

Jack turned to Millie. "Look after Jenny? I'm glad you finally found a Finn of your own," He tried to smile.

Finn stepped up beside Jack where Millie and the other Finn could see him. He nodded to her, and Millie and Not-Finn nodded back.

Jack's glow dimmed as he turned to Finn. They disappeared.

Mount Vernon

Not-Finn healed with time and he appreciated Millie checking in on him regularly. Mr. and Mrs. Jones were of course alarmed by the injuries but even the Saunders had agreed to say that he'd fallen down the cellar steps, as they didn't know how else to describe the events in a way that anyone would believe.

Ever afterwards, Mrs. Saunders was convinced that she'd seen an angel. That an angel – perhaps two of them –had rescued them all from a real live demon.

Of course this propelled Mrs. Saunders towards her church even more, and even Mr. Saunders joined her from time to time now. But even more significantly, the Saunders had become a family of huggers. Having once lost them, Mr. and Mrs. Saunders now could not get enough of their kids. TV took a back seat to doing things as a family.

Jenny and Millie agreed that they had indeed seen angels, and the two changeling boys couldn't disagree.

Everyone noticed that the boys were profoundly changed after that. The boys weren't exactly sure why they weren't piles of white dust, but it seemed a safe guess that Not-Jenny's notion of becoming real through anger and consumption was incorrect. What seemed to have saved the boys was learning to care about someone else. Millie's guess had been right. They'd become their own unique person.

Everyone also noticed that both boys were losing their unhealthy pallor. They were gaining color. Though their hair remained white.

Not-Finn now wanted to be called Finnegan. Millie's and his shopping carts for the *Hopin' With The Homeless* art show were a big success and raised $41.53 more than any of the other kids. They decided it would be fun to create more art together.

Not-Jack suspected that he'd had a close shave in the selfish behavior department. He decided to go by Jack's middle name – which was Neo (Mr. and Mrs. Saunders' first date involved a certain movie). Not-Jack had read that Neo suggested new beginnings.

But Jenny was not the same. A sadness always hovered beneath her efforts to be cheerful around her parents. She tried to tell them about her adventures, but they didn't take her seriously. Their memories blurred the nightmare in the barn till it truly disappeared.

In time Jenny grew used to Neo and Finnegan, though it was painful to see almost identical copies of Jack and Finn. But at least Millie and the boys believed her stories.

Jenny loved her parents – but she missed Jack and Finn a great deal. She missed Footbe and seeing Merfolk. She missed the Wishermans who had become like second parents to her. She missed Gibbie and Nibs and her pirates.

Jenny missed Frey.

Chapter 56

The Floating Island

Jack & Finn

Jack and Finn were sprawled out on the beach of their floating island. It was hovering somewhere east of Loot's End. Time was a little curious in Frey, but the boys guessed that it had been about four weeks since they'd returned.

Of course Finn's parents had been overjoyed to see them back in Frey. Jack was so surprised to be pulled into the family embrace along with Finn, that he found his eyes wet with tears.

Meryth helped her father with restorations to the city of Tryon on the underwater island. There was a lot to be done.

Weeds and red algae had spread through all the filtration systems and would make the city unpleasant to live in till it could be eradicated. But many hands made light work and the freshly awakened populace was enthusiastic.

Word had traveled quickly that the Blue Queen was gone and that King Posei was back. The various communities of Frey traveled to the Bay of mer'Rin to welcome the return of the Merfolk. They naturally brought with them hosts of problems, which had arisen under the long years of the wicked giantess's reign.

Jack and Finn joined Footbe on his journey to the Frit's underground city, which they learned was called Grix. They delivered the baby Asphixia to be raised there. They considered renaming her lest she remember her former life, but King Frayex said Asphyxia hadn't been her birth name. She'd be called the name that she'd had as a child. He assured her that she'd be raised more carefully this time. With the return of Footbe's memory the city was coming to life again. Frits who had turned to stone, found themselves alive once again.

Frayex remembered Finn and remembered Footbe – though Footbe had never called on the frit socially. It seemed that the phooka in Footbe's guise had often tried to find the cave where Meryth had been hidden. If he could have delivered the princess to the envious queen it would have helped him at court. But despite all his unsuccessful attempts at entering the cottage and the Isle of Judgment, the conniving phooka still ended up in her dungeon.

Frayex assured them that if they stayed, they would be honored with a feast of the tastiest rocks in the kingdom. But they had politely declined and returned to the surface.

Under the flag of King Posei, the pirates had commenced a mission of exploration around the southern end of the continent. There were many peoples that were still unknown. There were rumors of a colony of satyrs in the wilderness to the southeast, and Jack and Finn hoped to find them by air with the island.

All the servants at the Cottage-By-The-Sea had names now. Footbe resisted the change and what it meant. And Footbe was right. As soon as they had names, they wanted vacation time as well. He consoled himself that at least they hadn't asked for wages yet.

Finn was disappointed to realize over time that his dad could sometimes be a self-involved dick, but then again he also could be surprisingly generous as well. He knew most folks are a complicated mix of good and bad. He'd rather have a *real* father than a *fantasy* father. Finn held out for some growth over time.

Jack and Finn received a letter via a stork-like creature that the Wisherman family had reached their home safely. Tootles the gardener had kept the scrumble-berries quivering happily on their vines. A healthy diet of scrumble-berries brought back the saturation in their lavender fluff, which had faded during their adventures. The boys sent a note with the same stork creature that promised to visit the Wishermans and Whippledell before long.

The rescued children and the castle b'Trixers were settling into Whippledell, and the villagers were mostly overjoyed to have the young enthusiastic neighbors. Floogle and his family settled back into their old house – which his aunt Gertie had kept up. The old lizard who liked to read on his porch would occasionally yell at the kids when they made too much noise in front of his house. But even he was happy to see the changes in the sleepy village and the influx of energy and ideas. Creative children were of course a danger to all of Frey, but the villagers were committed to warning them of the dangers.

The situation with the b'Trixers was complex. The average Frey citizen confessed to liking individual furry-ners just fine. But collectively there was a stigma that followed the b'Trixers – and a wishing that they'd just go back to their own land (which no longer existed). Jack hoped that at some point the larger Frey population could see the cute critters as friends and neighbors rather than as a threat. The b-Trixers had useful skills. If they were welcomed into the community, who knew what wonderful ideas they might bring to all of Frey.

The night previous to this lazy afternoon on the beach, Jack had overheard a conversation when he'd flown down to the nixie village. (The nixies had offered to bring Jack all of his books and writings from his tree-house in Mount Vernon. They'd also left a letter for Jenny).

"We don't need their cutesy ways here," an alligator had grumbled to a nixie sitting nearby. They'd just finished eating a lost rabbit who had been traveling through the swamp. They were sitting near a campfire at the village's edge and swapping stories about the day.

"But, he was delicious with tomatoes on the side," reflected the nixie moments before she was eaten for the alligator's dessert.

Frey needed sources of food, which were not sentient. It was disturbing to not be sure whether a carrot might start chatting about the weather just when you were intending to make a salad with it.

The boys had become Frey celebrities after all the crazy events at the castle. News traveled fast. Everyone was excited when the floating island with the two strange boys came to visit.

Finn was drowsing in the sand next to him. They had the island to themselves. They'd stopped worrying about clothes some time back. It was remarkable how quickly clothing became a pointless notion, unless it was cold of course. Naturally when the weather turned, clothes would be very useful. But he reflected that they could also just move the island when the weather turned chilly.

Today the weather was beautiful.

Jack trickled grains of sand along Finn's back. He was curious how much sand he could put there before Finn would wake up.

"What are you doing?" Finn murmured.

"I'm burying you a few grains of sand at a time," Jack responded.

"Okay. I'll drown you after you're done," sighed Finn as he went back to sleep.

Jack rolled his golden naked body back into the warm sand and spread out his arms and legs to the sun. It was glorious to just be lazy like this and not be afraid of burning. His old pale skin would have never been able to do this. Finn had happily discovered that Merfolk skin didn't burn.

There was a rustling sound behind them in the tree line. Jack sat up. He only saw the shimmering birch trees that bordered the beach. He saw two misshapen tree stumps that he hadn't noticed before. But he'd hardly taken an inventory of the island's trees.

Jack settled back into the sand and nestled into its warmth. Finn's hand silently crawled across the sand like a spider. It leaped along with the rest of Finn.

"Gotcha!" Finn landed on top of Jack.

They giggled and rolled in the sand.

They were home. Their own floating island.

One tree stump nudged the other with a root.

"What d'ya think?"

"I like 'em," said the other stump with a knotty smile.

The first tree stump (whose name was Burl) wasn't sure. "They might work out. We'll see. There's lots ta do."

"The gold one ain't figg'red the limits o' magic yet... we should prob'bly let'm know," mused Brin. "before he does somethin' he shouldn't."

Burl gave a sigh. "Prob'bly. No hurry. Let's get back ta the cave – an' the map. We need to 'stablish where those dark wishes were droppin' ther eggs..."

The two tree stumps quietly pulled up their roots and crawled off through the woods like giant spiders, leaving behind the two boys on the beach – who were discovering the merits of wrestling punctuated with kisses.

Fippleday, the 21st of Gordiunish (we think)
Jack and Finn's Floating Island

Dear Jenny,

How are you? We miss you! I asked the nixies to leave
this letter for you in the tree house. I hope you find it!

(he means visit us!)
If you __ever__ want to visit Frey again, put the enclosed
golden postcard in any mailbox and it will get to me!
I put a spell on it! Mordette has a magical library and
I am learning crazy cool stuff! Lot to learn of course...
only found it a week ago. Can hardly wait to show you!

I'll pick you up in the tree house two mornings after you
drop the postcard in a box. Write any special instructions
on the card back.

I hope mom and dad are okay? Say Hi to Millie.

Hope the new kids are working out?

We found
more ~~worms~~ fuzzy wiggles   Jack (& Finn)
I'm still getting used to them!

Paul Manchester is a writer, illustrator, and generally creative sort based in Southern California. ThePurpleFantastic.com

Thanks for joining me on this adventure to Frey! This has been a journey. I started off trying to capture the stories that I dreamed up as a teenager, but then the characters started making choices and saying things I didn't expect. It is a curious dance to listen to the characters, yet try not to forget the well intended outline which always needs to bow to the will of the characters.

Frey is suggesting a three book arc at the moment. Frey is a big place and there are a lot of curious places and peoples to explore, and there are still a number of unanswered questions! Jack and his parents have some issues to work out. And I'm really curious about the changeling Neo's future, as well as Millie's cousin, Bryton Wilde, who lives down in Tacoma. Bryton has been helping care for Grandma Wilde who has been battling cancer. There are strange adventures ahead for Bryton in the fantastical land of Frey.

Many thanks to the friends who read an early version of this. I very much appreciated their time and their thoughts.

Paul's books at present include:
Olly, Olly Oxen Frey – An illustrated young adult adventure novel. *Steam Rating 2 out of 5.*

The Alabaster Hedgehog – A new adult fantasy adventure. *Steam Rating 3 out of 5.*

Pursuits of Whimsey – A book of humorous stories in verse. *Steam Rating 0 out of 5.*

If you enjoyed this book, please take the opportunity to post a review on Amazon and Goodreads, or anywhere else you post reviews. Your recommendations are a BIG help to independent authors like me!

Life is always filled with possibilities for the curious and persistent. The world can be a better place and it starts with how you interact with the people in your life. Everything boils down to kindness and respect – for others and for yourself. Outside of that, all doctrine is meaningless.

The Purple Fantastic Steam Rating System

0 ... There is no reference to sex in any significant way.

1 ... There is some acknowledgment that sex and/or body parts exist.

2 ... There is some non-sexual nakedness, and some characters may be aware that sex exists. If there is any sexual activity, it vaguely happens off the page.

3 ... There is some nakedness and there may be some sexual interaction between characters, but always in conjunction with plot.

4 ... There is nakedness and sex that is vividly described, but is still connected to plot.

5 ... There's a plot in this book?

The Alabaster Hedgehog

When 18 year old Thadeus is kicked out of the house for being gay, he takes refuge with a strange elderly relative. He discovers a world of faeries, dangerous beings, and sexy possibilities. He may even find someone to date, if he doesn't end up dead first. *An imaginative and funny read!*

Steam Rating 3 out of 5.

You might enjoy
Pursuits of Whimsey
by Paul Manchester

Life is wonderfully ridiculous at times

... and we each bring our own special brand of crazy into the mix. Whether you are a curious kid, or an adult who hasn't entirely admitted to growing up, this book is just for **you**.

If you are growing sentient fungi in your shower, looking for the perfect spot to bake in the sun, or sometimes doubt you are the amazing person you know you could be, **Pursuits of Whimsey** will provoke and amuse you. Join Mildred the Miserable Mermaid, Blair (with the incredible flair), Betsy Duff, and a host of others in some playful word-play that is entertaining, poignant and worth the visit.

"THIS IS FANTASTIC!"

"DELIGHTFUL!!!! WHAT A TREAT!"

"A BRIGHT LIGHT ON A CLOUDY DAY!"

OUTLAW THE SOAPY SCOURGE

Wil Whimsey
Publishing Co.
wilwhimsey.com

Blair
& His Incredible Flair

by Paul Manchester
(One story from Pursuits of Whimsey)

There was no doubt about it,
despite their despair.
His parents could see
their boy liked to do hair.

Yet he was very good.
No one could deny
that this eight year old boy
could tease hair three feet high…
with ringlets and feathers,
with pigtails and curls,
with strings of brown leather,
whole birds nests and pearls.
All this amid tresses
swirled smartly aloft.
Few parents had seen such singular coifs.

It started when Blair,
(yes, that was his name)
on Sunday at two
called on his Grand Dame
at the Sunny Brooks Home
for the old and infirm.
She bitterly complained
that she needed a perm.

"The nurses are lazy!
The doctors don't care!
And I haven't enough money
to fix up my hair!"
But Blair answered quick,
without missing a beat,
"I'll do your hair Grandma,
I'll fix it up neat!"

He went straight to work
with scissors and combs,
with pill bottles for curlers
and some pencils from home.
He sprayed and he teased
and he scrup'lessly lifted –
pre-dying it to look
hirsuto-roufusly gifted.

And when he was done,
Grandma was such a sight…
that the neighbors all gaped…
and then started to fight
over who would be next
for remedial bliss!
Then the nurses came over
to see what was amiss.
'Ere long, Blair was snipping
and coloring them all!
Nurses and Doctors!
He did wigs for the bald!
The senile! The sick!
With such gentle finesse,
Sunny Brooks soon glowed bright
with the light of his genius.

When Blair's Parents got home,
they were not amused.
A boy should do boy stuff,
and not play with mousse.
A boy should play baseball!
(or tennis at least)
Boys should make slingshots,
or catch little beasts!
What future is there
for a boy who does hair?
They shuddered to think
the possibilities there.

But, that's what Blair did,
for he did it quite well.
And his parents adjusted
to his experiments with gel.

Before long, they allowed him
to do their hair too –
and their fear turned to pride
in their son's derring-do.

For becoming a man
has much less to do
with some skills with a football
or to get black and blue.
The skills of the heart
are what make the man
and using your gifts
the best that you can.
Blair's crafting of hairdos
may not seem worth while.
But the world is more beautiful
when somebody smiles…
And smile? The world did
when it saw his creations!
(And much worse could be said
for some other vocations.)

OLLY, OLLY, OXEN FREY

The Wanderin' Tree

An Olde Frey Drinking Song

Ah once met a tree, a comf't'ble Tree,
what loved all de birds an' de breezes so free!
She had a sweet brook – a wee comfy spot –
'twas neit'er too chilly, nor neit'er too hot!
Not pixies nor squirr'l poop dinna much rile,
her own sunny spot on her own sunny isle.

A bird came one day! A bird o' red hue.
"Your life is so dull! What is there ta do?
Go see de big world!! It's wondrous! It's grand!
That wee creek is nothin', 'tis nothin' but bland!
Oh, come see ta sea! 'Tis seasoned wit' salt!
If ye wilt o' boredom, tis only yer fault!"

D e birdie flew off,
an' her happiness waned.
Her li'l brook shrank
an' her spot was now stained
wit' longin' for somethin' dat she'd neve' seen –
she thought o' de places de wind might ha' been.
De notions were pretty, her trunk wore a smile
an' soon she decided ta leave her small isle.

She pulled up her roots
an' she started ta walk.
Wit' a boat at de shore, she started ta talk!
De boat said, *"Come travel wit' me on de sea!*
Come fly like de wind!! On me ye'll feel free!"
She straddled his bow an' she sailed wit' de tide.
Wit' wind in her leaves!! Her branches stretched wide!

A' first it was splendid!
Her leaves all a twirl!
Yet salty life soon made her roots start ta curl.
Ta dance in da waves is a glor'ous thing –
yet oh how de birds in her branches once sing'd
each mornin' at home – now gulls only screeched!
When she complained – de boat left her beached.

De beach was too sandy,
and much, much too gritty,
but trav'lin' a ways – she soon found a city.
De city was lit up wit' sparklin' lights!
She soon found a spot in a park in de heights.
De view was excitin' – de bushes quite strange,
de trees quite assured her it was a great change!

Till one day a bloke wit' a helmet appeared
wit' ribbons, and tractors,
an' chainsaws all geared
ta chop down de trees – ta clear out de brush!
Ta put up a rest'rant fer folks in a rush.
She pull'd up her roots as her friends was chopp'd down.
Wit' smells o' plants screamin',
she quickly left town.

O h where ta go next?
    She trudged all alone!
Through deserts and jungles,
'cross mountains o' stone!
She met lotsa critters an' listen'd ta all,
she heard lotsa stories some true an' some tall.
She dream'd o' her island, yet nowhere was aught
but mem'ries that sang o' her wee comfy spot.

She wandered de land –
wit' ogre and gnome.
She frolick'd wit' dryads,
yet still missed her home.

Her sweet liddle brook – dat wee comfy spot –
'twas neit'er too chilly, nor neit'er too hot!
Where pixies nor squirr'l poop never much rile,
her own sunny spot on her own sunny isle.

Den one day she got
ta de top o' de world,
dat place where de ice
and de windy ghosts whirl'd.
She never intended ta let her heart freeze –
but hearts aren't quite made ta be free like the breeze.
Most hearts need a home lest dey chill to a funk,
and soon her heart froze wit'in her cold trunk.

535

OLLY, OLLY, OXEN FREY

Encased in a berg of blue ice did she float.
She traveled and slept in dis cold crystal boat.
She drifted half dead for a month and a day.
She melted while dolphins and manta rays played.
Till chance washed her up ashore on a beach.
It was her own isle – she learned wit' a screech!

I t was de red bird! *"Oh where ha' ya been?*
I dinna expect ya ta hold ta my din!
Fer, I was jes' joshin'! I dinna mean naught!
An' now der's a saplin' dat's growed in yer spot!"
De Tree coughed and sputtered from days in de brine,
"My home is no longer? Tis no longer mine?!"
"When home is no longer,
where do I call home?
Oh am I condemned now forever ta roam?"
Still one day, she settled, fer that's what trees do –
a spot wit' no brook, an' no cozy view.
A spot with no pixies, nor squirr'ls what poop'd –
Just her, by herself. She was tired. She droop'd.

W hen birds came ta visit,
dey ask'd where she'd been.
She told dem all stories o' places she'd seen.
De squirr'ls and pixies follow'd soon after
and stayed up late gigglin' in ripples o' laughter,
an' sometimes dey'd cry when dey heard de sad tales
o' young trees chopp'd down, or de songs o' old whales.

Wit' time, a small creek thunk to swing by and list'n
an' slept by her roots – all sparklin' and glistenin'
wit' pixies an' magic an' stories o' gnomes!
All types o' strange critters soon crafted their homes
around her, an' in her – till one day she thought
dat *"tho' I left home – I made my own spot!"*

S o, she's still a tree – a comf't'ble Tree
what loves all de birds and de breezes so free!
She has a sweet brook – a wee comfy spot –
'tis neit'er too chilly, nor neit'er too hot!
Not pixies nor squirr'l poop dinna much rile,
her own sunny spot on her own sunny isle.

Ode to My True Love's Nose

By Papy Wisherman

I love yer big nose!
 Tis glor'ously ample
 'an' hugely enormous!
Yes such a sample
ta rarely be seen!
Its breadth is unequaled!
'T would ne'r be worn
by the timid
and weak-willed!

Yer Nose is a sign
of cour'ge an' strength.
(Yer neck mus' be strong
fer a snoz o' that length!)
Protub'rance mos' noble,
so beaut'ous so large!
Were it a boat,
it would be a barge!

I love yer big nose!
'Tis glor'ous an' fine.
I'm lucky ta have ya,
oh dear wife o' mine.

Dear Carrot

A poem by Jack Saunders

Dear Carrot, please tell me if you have a soul.
Should I feel guilt when you're diced in a bowl?

Do you feel good when you reach for the light?
Do you feel bad when small bugs start to bite?
Do you mind other plants if they don't sit too close?
When thirsty and tired, do you get morose?

Your roots must feel joy when they're snug in the dirt
and taste all the minerals like I taste dessert.
On a moist April day with a sun in the sky,
do you feel so at peace that you don't fear to die?

Will St. Peter welcome you at Heaven's gate?
Will there be a line where you might have to wait?
Are most carrots good? I've seen some go bad.
With sub-standard care, can a carrot go mad?

Wolves will eat rabbits, and rabbits eat you.
And I'll eat you both if you're cooked in a stew.
Yet sometimes I ponder. I look in my bowl,
dear Carrot, I wonder if you have a soul.

Olly, Olly, Oxen Free!

by Paul Manchester

Twist open the doorknobs
you've clung to so tight!
Come out, Come out!
Where'er you be!
Out from the hidey holes
into the light!
Olly, Olly, Oxen Free!

No need to hide kindness!
No need to hide strength!
Come out to your fears,
where'er you be!
No need to hide questions
you've pondered at length!
Olly, Olly, Oxen Free!

Those hidden what-if's
have something to say!
Come out new ideas,
where'er you be!
Start to ask questions!
Craft a new day!
Olly, Olly, Oxen Free!